THE
GIRL'S GOT
SECRETS

The Forbidden Men Series - Book 7

LINDA KAGE

The Girl's Got Secrets

Contact Information : linda@lindakage.com

Publishing History
Linda Kage, November 2015
Print ISBN: 1519115377
Print ISBN-13: 978-1519115379

Credits
Cover Artist: Ada Frost
Editor: Stephanie Parent
Proofreader: Shelley at 2 Book Lovers Reviews
Proofreader: Autumn at The Autumn Review
Spanish Translator : Eli Castro

Printed in the United States of America

DEDICATION

For Eli Castro

(Yes, The Original Elisa)

I can't thank you enough, chica, for all the time and effort you put into helping me with this story and with, well, everything you've done. You're a one-of-a-kind amazing!

AUTHOR'S NOTE

I decided not to italicize all the Spanish terms in this story because there were so many of them. And in some cases, my Spanish translator's suggestions contradicted my English editor's marks (like the capitalization of proper nouns!) so not everything uses perfect Spanish grammar in difference to this being an English-told story, sorry.

For anyone not familiar with a Spanish phrase you may encounter, I have an English translation chart at the end of the story if you'd like to know what each word/phrase means!

PROLOGUE
Asher Hart

I opened my bleary eyes, half-awake from postcoital bliss as the naked woman on top of me shifted, the soft, smooth warmth of her flesh caressing my own. She slid off the bed and presented me with a spectacular view of the most perfect ass ever, and my smile grew eager...until she pulled on a pair of panties and then reached for her bra.

Wait, no, *that* wasn't supposed to happen. Blinking myself back into better consciousness, I tried to sit up and found it damn near impossible. "What're you doing? What's wrong?"

She didn't answer, which wasn't surprising. I hadn't been able to pull more than a dozen words from her since we'd met, and nothing she'd said so far had been in English. But in the lyrics of Jason Derulo, her booty hadn't needed explaining. Not then, anyway.

Apparently, it did now since she'd gone and hidden hers under a silky piece of black lace. And damn, she looked really good in those silky black panties, especially from the back, where I could see two tanned cheeks peeking out the bottom of all that swirling lace.

"You're not leaving, are you?" I tried to sit up again. Still wasn't happening. I frowned at the fur-covered handcuffs constraining me to my headboard and spent a few seconds muttering until I could twist into a somewhat upright position.

Across the room, she pulled on her stretchy black yoga pants I'd taken off last night with my teeth.

I guess it was time to pull out my high school Spanish. This was going to get ugly, but I didn't care.

"Sentarse." Shit, no. That was *sit*, not *stay*, wasn't it?

"Quedarse," I tried again, finally remembering the correct word for *stay*.

The waistband of her pants indignantly snapped into place on her hips as she spun around to send me a lethal glare; not that I blamed her. I *had* just given her dog commands.

I winced and repeated, "Quedarse," then added a pathetic little, "por favor."

She sighed and rolled her eyes before jerking on her top and reaching for her purse.

"No! Don't go. Please, don't go. I'm sorry. I don't know what I did wrong, but I'm sorry. Shit, what's sorry in Spanish?"

"Lo siento," she said, her voice a quiet, sexy hum that was damn near a whisper.

No idea what *lo siento* meant, but it sounded stimulating as hell coming from her lips. My body responded, and I had to bend a leg to try to cover my exposed hard-on, so she wouldn't see how aroused I was while she was trying to ditch out on me.

"Elisa!" I cried, my voice cracking with desperation. I even banged my cuffs against the metal rails of my bed's headboard to get her attention.

When she paused at the doorway, her back to me, I held my breath. Such a crucial moment. Whatever I said now could be the deciding factor for her to stay or go. But all I could think to say was, "I'm sorry." And I didn't even know what the hell I was sorry for. I just knew I'd done something wrong, and it was making her leave.

It couldn't have been the sex. Last night *and* this morning had totally rocked my casbah. It had hers too; the minx definitely wasn't quiet when she came. So, what—

She turned back slowly. My heart stuttered in my chest when I saw the tears streaming down her face. "Elisa?" I whispered, worried as hell.

What in God's name had I done wrong?

"En serio lo siento tanto," she choked out, her face red as she began to sob into her hands. "Tengo que hacer esto."

I shook my head. Derulo was freaking whack. This definitely needed explaining.

But as I opened my mouth to spit out more broken Spanish, begging her not to go, Elisa whirled back to the exit and raced up the stairs until I could hear the door at the top slam shut.

"Hey!" I yelled, my frustration morphing from the worried kind into the pissed kind. "What the hell? Elisa! You can't just start crying and then run off like that. Get your ass back here and uncuff me from this fucking bed! Tell me what I did wrong. Please! *ELISA!*"

She didn't return. And I couldn't chase after her.

I spent the first thirty seconds of my solitary confinement throwing a major tantrum, thrashing on the mattress and trying to dislocate my wrists by failing at pulling them free of the handcuffs. The damn things were no longer fun...or kinky.

The next thirty seconds, I filled the air with a profanity I'd never used before, blatant and blaring. But nothing I screamed freed me from this bed.

After that, the panic set in. With bruised wrists and a sore throat, I wondered how long I was going to be trapped buck-ass naked to my own bed. People would worry about me eventually...after a few days maybe. The guys in the band. Pick. They'd come around to check on me.

But what if I dehydrated to death before then, or the building caught fire and burned down around me? Or...

Fuck. Now I had to take a piss.

Hadn't Stephen King written a horror book about someone left handcuffed alone in a bed? I hated horror movies. I didn't want to star in one of my own.

I jerked on my bonds a few more times to relieve some of my anger and rising fear, but I only succeeded in injuring myself further.

How the hell could she have just left me here like this? It wasn't as if I didn't know where she worked. I could find her. And, oh...would I be finding her. She would not be getting away with this without repercussions.

And what had those tears been about? It freaking

messed with my head. I wanted to be nothing but pissed, except I was worried too. But I tried to focus on the rage.

"Wrong fucking move, princess," I told the empty room, grinning bitterly as I plotted my revenge. Wonder how she'd feel if I handcuffed *her* to a bed and forced her to tell me every mysterious thought in that pretty head of hers with torture tools like feathers...and chocolate syrup?

And damn it, there went my stupid dick again, hardening at the thought of her in handcuffs and drizzled in something that needed to be licked off. Didn't the little fucker realize I was in dire straits here? So not the time to be thinking about sex.

Even if last night had been the crème de la crème of marvelous encounters.

On my nightstand, my phone rang. I whipped my attention that way and gaped at it sitting so close and yet so far away.

It rang again, and I could make out the name "Sticks" on the screen. Perfect. If I could confide in anyone on earth during a situation like this, it would be him. I knew I could count on Sticks for discretion, loyalty and hopefully some freaking help.

Now, I just had to finagle a way to answer his call.

I swung my leg over and used my big toe to try to slide the *answer* button on. Took two tries, but by God, I did it.

With another tap of the trusty toe, I turned it to speakerphone. "Hey, man," I panted out, impressed by how casual I was able to sound while handcuffed buck-ass naked to my bed. "What's up?"

"Not much." His voice filled my apartment and was like music to my ears. "I was starving and thought pizza sounded good for lunch. Want to come with?"

"Sure," I said; I even shrugged a bare shoulder to keep it all laid-back and casual-like. Yep, I was just chilling here without a care in the world.

"Cool. I'll swing by and pick you up in a bit, then."

"Sounds good. But, uh, quick question first."

When I didn't ask anything within five seconds, he said, "O...kay. Shoot."

I bit my lip, debating whether I really had it in me to confess what had happened. The embarrassment would kill me. And though he'd be the kindest about it, I doubt even

Sticks would let me live this down.

But then I thought about the whole Stephen King thing, and my bladder gave another lurch, reminding me how full it was. So I clenched my teeth and sucked up my pride.

"You don't happen to have...handcuff keys, do you?"

CHAPTER 1

Remy Curran

ONE MONTH EARLIER

ROCKING MY ZEBRA-STRIPED Chuck Taylors, ripped fishnet hose, blue jean miniskirt, silver-studded belt and a skintight tee featuring the band The Pretty Reckless, I readjusted my wig full of spiky blonde hair.

My toes tapped to the rhythm of the muffled music hammering through the closed door, and I let it pour through me, plugging me into the mood...until the drummer on the other side of the wall missed a beat.

Feeling the sympathy, I winced even as my heart accelerated with anticipation.

"So long, sucka." The guy next to me chuckled as the guitars and bass inside the studio lurched to a stop, cutting the song short.

I glanced sideways at my bench companion, and he smirked my way, lifting his fist for a congratulatory bump. Since he was decked out in metal and tattoos, I figured he was competition, but ...oh well. I complied, knocking my knuckles against his as a small grin twitched across my lips.

There went one less drummer out of our way.

Picturing the ass-chewing the dude inside the auditioning room must be getting, I began a countdown, wondering there weren't. Besides, I wanted to be in *Non-Castrato*. Their music was my kind of music. Plus they needed a drummer, and I happened to be the best damn drummer I knew. *And* I wanted to show Fisher *my* band could out-rock his sucky, limp-dick excuse of a band any day of the week.

Joining Non-Castrato was the perfect solution for everyone.

The *only* solution.

If only these fools would open their stupid, sexist, pig headed minds to see that.

"Okay, fine," Galloway said with a self-righteous, holier-than-thou grin. "Name me one mixed-gender band that hit it big, and maybe we'll give you a shot."

I smirked. Game on.

"Black Eyed Peas."

"Fuck," he muttered, not impressed as he sniffed derisively. "Those are all singers. They don't play instruments, princess. They're not a *band*."

"All right then." I blew out a breath to flutter the spiky white-blonde wig bangs out of my eyes and began to rattle off a new list. "Fleetwood Mac, Blondie, Jefferson Airplane, The—"

Galloway gave another snort, cutting me off. "Yeah, and the only things the chicks in those bands did was sing. We got Hart; we don't need another fucking singer."

"*Talking Heads*," I lifted my voice to speak over him. "Of which the chick was the *bass* guitarist, I believe." I spiked a derogatory glance to the bass guitar strapped over his shoulder. "And so was the bassist in The Smashing Pumpkins and—"

"None of which were *drummers*." Galloway held up a hand when I opened my mouth to argue. "The fact of the matter is, we don't *want* a female. And it's our band. Our decision. So bye-bye now, sweetie. When I need a groupie to go down on me in the bathroom after a gig, I'll give you a call."

I narrowed my eyes at him only to turn toward the other silent members. "Are you two lemmings just going to stand there and let this douche make all your decisions for you? Is he, like, your *dict*ator or something?" *Heavy on the dick.*

"Look, I'd listen to you," Asher Hart finally spoke up. Dark green, penetrating eyes lifted to coast over my outfit before settling back on my face. When I only narrowed my eyes, he lifted his hands self-defensively. "Honest. But we're picking our drummer by a unanimous vote, and you already don't have that." He glanced at Galloway with an irritated scowl. "Doesn't look like you're going to get it, either, whether he hears you play or not."

"Nope," Galloway said, popping the *p*-sound as he sent me a smug wink.

Tears threatened, but I swallowed them down as I licked my lips. With Galloway, I'd only been pissed by his foul-mouthed rejection. But for some reason, Hart's sympathetic explanation split me in half and left me bleeding.

After a deep breath, I tried one last time. "Fine, then, *Billy*." I focused all my attention on him since *apparently* he was the only guy I had to sway. "All I'm asking for is *one* shot. If you don't like my work after that, you can tell me to kiss your ass."

Galloway snickered. "I'd rather you kiss my dick. And maybe deep throat it a little. Hell, honey, I'm willing to give you a taste now, if you're thirsty." He reached for his fly but Hart sharply told him to cut it out.

Clenching my teeth to hold back my retort, I glared at Galloway, envisioning all the ways I could murder him. None of them were pretty. Or fast.

"Which brings up another reason we shouldn't have a girl in the group," Holden finally put in his two cents worth, his voice soft as he winced. "With Gally around, you'd be suing us within five minutes for sexual harassment."

I rolled my eyes. "Trust me, I can handle the little goat fucker talking smack." I glanced at Galloway with disinterest. "As long as he keeps his hands to himself, I don't give a shit what he says."

Wiggling his fingers, Galloway grinned. "Oh, but these hands like to roam, baby. Especially over a landscape like yours."

Oh, brother.

"Galloway," Asher bit out, his voice a warning. Then he turned to me and shook his head. "I'm sorry; this just isn't the right place for you. I'm sure you have an amazing talent, but we need to get back to our auditions now. We kind of have a time crunch."

My throat went dry and I once again experienced the overwhelming need to sob. But I held it in. Gritting my teeth, I glanced at all three members, who gazed back with three different expressions on each of their faces, waiting for my response.

"So you all would rather be just another rock band *cliché*?" I asked. "With your leather pants—" I pointed toward Galloway with a disgusted wrinkle of my nose before targeting Holden. "—tattoos and piercings, and hot lead singer *man-whore*." With a scathing glance at Hart, I set my hands on my hips. "Good luck getting anywhere with that."

Sniffing my derision, I spun around and marched toward the exit, only to pause at the door and glance back. "Oh, and maybe you should Google Karen Carpenter, Moe Tucker and Honey Lantree. All were female drummers for *big time* mixed-gender bands. Certainly bigger than you losers will ever be. Chinguen a su madre."

I didn't slam the door as the drummer who'd tried out before me had. But it obviously only took one look at my face for all the others waiting in the hall to know just how badly I had failed.

Tucking my pink drumsticks back into my hip pocket with all the dignity I could muster, I lifted my head proudly and swallowed down the pain.

My so-called pal next in line smirked. "Didn't want a chick, did they?" The gleam in his eyes told me he'd known I wouldn't make it all along.

I didn't honor him with a response. Notching my chin higher, I strolled regally down the hall, out of the studio and into the dismal, cloudy day. I didn't burst into tears until I'd gotten into my car and was pulling out of the studio's parking lot, the defeat making me drippier and even more pissed that I had to own ovaries and so many freaking emotions.

CHAPTER 2

Remy Cussan

THIRTY MINUTES AFTER the ruin my life had become, I turned down the volume of "I Love It" by Icona Pop on the radio and parked a block away from Castañeda's Méxican restaurant.

Face wiped free of the thick black eyeliner and lipstick I'd worn to the audition from hell, I checked my reflection to ensure my eyes were no longer red and puffy. When I saw myself, though, I snorted. Proof of my tear-fest might be gone, but I looked hideous anyway—as virginal and Christianly as a Sunday-school teacher. And yet I knew my uncle still wouldn't approve. The tyrant preferred me in turtlenecks and cardigans over drab, ankle-length skirts made of sackcloth. But I had compromised as best I could with jeans—the denim ripped out in the knees—and a loose black sweater that liked to dip off one shoulder and revealed the strap of my purple tank top—to match the purple highlights in my hair.

My punk-rocker wig gone, I finger combed my dark mane one last time and then grabbed my purse.

I bypassed the main entrance of Castañeda's and ducked

down the alley beside it, calling a greeting to Mick, the homeless guy who camped out there and waited for stray scraps.

After unlocking the back door of the restaurant, I slipped inside and hung my jacket on a hook. Behind me, the radio played a familiar Latino tune while a humid heat crawled up the back of my sweater.

"If you keep coming in late, mi padre's going to take a strap to you, prima."

I yelped and spun around to find my cousin Big T, short for Tomás, mixing dough. Half a dozen raw, already stuffed and sealed empanadas sat on a cookie sheet ready to go into the oven. A hairnet covered his dark head of thick black hair and flour powdered his heavy arms up to his elbows.

"Cállate," I muttered as I stashed my purse and found my own hairnet to slip on.

He belly laughed. "What's this? I abandon my post at the stoves to take over your oven job for you and all I get is a shut up? In Español, no less. My sweet prima offends me."

Realizing I *had* been bitchy to one of my favorite people on earth, I let out an apologetic sigh. "Plus a great big gracias and kiss on the cheek for my wonderful Big T." I wrapped my arms around his wide barrel chest from behind and leaned over his shoulder to stamp a big, wet, sloppy one right to his cheek.

He flushed but grinned his appreciation as he shrugged me off and continued to mix the dough with his beefy hands. "Shoo. Enough of that. Tell me how your audition went. You must've done well if you stayed this late. Made the first cut, ¿sí?"

My smile dropped. "The audition? It was...bien." I nudged him aside with my hip and took over where he'd left off, since the baking was technically my job. I put all my attention into pounding my palm into the dough that suddenly worked as a nice stress ball. Fold, pound. Flour. Fold, pound. Forget all auditions, sexy lead singers, and the tears it had brought. Flour. Fold, pound—

Tomás grasped my elbow. "Hijo de puta, it's dead already. Stop torturing the poor dough."

I scowled at him but obeyed, yanking up the rolling pin and flattening it into a disc. Crossing his arms over his chest, my perceptive cousin leaned his back against the table beside me as he studied my face.

"They're not the only band around, you know."

I ground my teeth, trying to ignore him as I snagged a knife, then a nearby plate to use as a stencil and cut the dough into perfect circles. "But they're the *best* band."

He snorted. "Matter of opinion."

A die-hard Los Horóscopos de Durango fan, he didn't get my fascination with all things pop, rock, or punk.

"Hey, wipe the glum off your face. Abuela's here tonight, working the cash register. Seeing her is always reason to smile. Plus, she'll know as soon as she gets a look at you that something's wrong. You don't want to upset our fragile, aging grandmother, do you?"

After he arched a censorious eyebrow at me, I sighed and let my shoulders deflate. "No. You're right. I'll stop being a drama queen."

"Bien. Because it makes you a total pain in the ass to be around." Then he picked up a handful of flour and flicked it at me...as if that would help cheer me up or something.

"Tomás Emmanuel Fernando Castañeda!" I screeched in outrage and tore off my hairnet, frantically brushing flour from my locks. "How could you? Pendejo."

"Elisa!" The sharp crack of my uncle's voice instantly had me snapping to attention and lifting my shoulders until my back was military straight.

Fuck. Even though I felt like I was at home in this building where I'd spent most of my childhood, I never failed to flinch at that voice. But I hated getting caught spouting expletives in front of Tío Alonso. It reminded me too much of when I was little and he'd smack my knuckles with a spatula every time he heard me curse.

He no longer verbally censored my language or took a spatula after me, but he sure as hell sent me the ultimate scowl of disapproval as he plowed into the room.

Drawing in a short, bracing breath before turning around, I looked up at him and said, "¿Sí?"

"Llegas tarde."

I shifted my weight uneasily from one foot to the other as I stared at the patriarch of my family. Though I had lived with and been raised by my grandmother, Tío Alonso—my grandmother's oldest son as well as Big T's dad—had been the only father figure in my life since I was two. So, despite the fact I didn't care for his autocratic attitude, he still knew how to make me behave...and rebel.

After lifting my chin, I gave him a tight nod. "Yeah, I know I'm late. I'm sorry, but I..." I paused, trying to come up with a plausible reason for my tardiness that wouldn't get me an overly long lecture—since he abhorred my love for his least-favorite kind of music—but he obviously didn't want to hear excuses today.

"Carmen didn't come in tonight. We need you up front, pronto."

I bit back an immediate curse. But...damn it. I hated waitressing more than anything. Fingering the hem of my sweater, I said, "I'm not dressed to work out front."

"Solo hazlo," he muttered his command.

"Sí, tío querido." My answer made him scowl, because it reminded him how much of a tyrant I'd repeatedly told him he was. He hated it when I called him *uncle dearest* in my sweet angelic voice, like some kind of meek servant—since he knew I was anything but meek or sweet—about as much as I hated how he refused to call me by my first name.

Tío Alonso was the only person on earth who addressed me as Elisa, my middle name, because he thought Remy was much too masculine and not nearly Latin enough for his taste.

"And Elisa?" he grumbled, his accent thickening with his irritation.

I sighed, wondering what he was going to pick on now. "¿Sí?"

"Limpia tu camisa." He waved his pointer finger at my sweater.

I glanced down to see flour spotting the cloth. Muttering under my breath, I beat at it, to clean it off as best I could while Tío Alonso pushed his way back through the doorway and left us.

Behind me, Big T chuckled softly at my scolding.

"Idiota," I hissed at him, using the much more kosher word this time, just in case Tío Alonso could still hear us. "Look what you did to me."

He only smirked harder. "Hey, I didn't know you were going to be forced to waitress tonight."

"How about *you* wait tables then, and I'll finish up these empanadas," I begged, fluttering my lashes at him. But I must've tried that trick one too many times; he totally wasn't swayed.

"Not on your life, prima. Get out there."

"Asshole." I flipped him off before hurrying my way through the doorway and finding myself behind the front counter facing the dining area where dozens of tables were already full. Ugh! I so did not have the disposition to be a good server tonight, and since it was a Monday, more of the family scene would be present, including obnoxious bratty kids and irritable fed-up parents.

The joy.

Wherever the hell Carmen was, I hoped her absence from here was worth it, because I was going to kill her for making me go through this today of all days. If I hadn't been forced to work right now, I'd be at home, slaughtering Nazis or zombies on my Call of Duty game...because I was in the perfect mood to draw some virtual blood.

I was fishing a spare waitressing apron out from under the counter along with an extra order pad when a soft voice called my name from the cash register. I glanced over and caught sight of my tiny, gray-headed grandmother perched on a stool watching me.

I'd totally forgotten Big T had said she was here tonight...if that didn't tell you how scattered my brain was after my auditions.

"Abuela." I hurried to her to give her the dutiful grand-daughterly hug. "Te extrañé."

Abuela had been my legal guardian since I was nine, when enough drugs had fried my mother's brain to the point she'd been put away in a mental institution. But since Abuela had lived with Tío Alonso ever since they'd come to the US on work visas two years before I was born, I'd been raised pretty much under his roof...and his rule. And even though my grandmother could be sassy when you crossed her, she was still the sweetest soul and usually compliant to her eldest son's authority.

"Mi linda nieta," she murmured, cupping my face and looking into my eyes. "Te ves triste."

I forced a smile and shook my head. "I'm not sad," I tried to reassure her in Spanish, all the while biting the inside of my lip and hating that she could always see so much in me. I couldn't tell her about my failed audition either; she loathed my kind of music just as much as Tío Alonso did. "Just...upset about having to wait tables."

Shaking her head, she swatted me away, telling me to get to work before commanding me to stop by more often to visit her. With a quick kiss to her cheek, I was off and catching a table of waiting customers that my younger cousin Luis didn't seem to have gotten to yet, since he looked busy trying to clean up a drink spill across the room at another table.

"Hola. Buenas noches," I greeted with a smile to the family of three I approached. "Have you guys gotten your drinks ordered yet?"

Castañeda's boasted authentic Méxican food, despite the fact that the crunchy tacos here were nothing like a true taco back in México, where my family had migrated from. Tío Alonso called the tacos we served the locals chingaderas, aka pieces of shit, but they were one of our most popular orders, so we continued to supply them.

Other than that, everything else we served was a true Latino dish. And everyone who worked here was of true Latino descent. I was nearly the exception, since my blood was diluted. My father had been American with German-Irish ancestors, and he'd stuck around long enough to marry my mom and get me the Curran surname before he'd taken off to parts unknown. But I looked Méxican enough and my mother had been a Castañeda, so I guess that gave me my "in" to work at the family restaurant.

And gave me the enjoyment of having the kid at the table in front of me spray my pant leg with queso-gooped snot as he sneezed on me.

Nice.

I smiled through clenched teeth at his parents as if everything was bien, even though I wanted to strangle their brat who was currently singing about Bob the Builder at the top of his lungs and tossing his tortilla chips onto his seat so he could march them into crumbs as they studied their menus, oblivious. Gritting back my irritation, I took their order and escaped before I unloaded my frustrations of the day onto them.

Six hours later, I trudged into my apartment and flopped onto the couch, where I moaned out my misery and slapped my hands over my face.

This—*this*—was my life. And it looked as if it was going to remain my pathetic existence for the next long while. No drumming position. No new band membership. Nothing but serving asshole customers who wrote *LOL* on my tip line instead of providing a single penny of gratuity after my damn fine waitressing, if I did say so myself, despite how much I wanted to curl into a ball on my sofa and cry while killing things on video games...and maybe stuffing my face with chocolate and ice cream. And piña coladas. God, and drowning myself with *so many* piña coladas! And maybe singing really sappy, sad love songs like "My Heart Will Go On" as I envisioned all the zombies I slaughtered were Fisher...or that bassist for Non-Castrato and the way-too-hot lead singer, Asher Hart.

Work had somewhat helped distract me from my melancholy all evening, but now, not even the half a dozen smelly grease stains on my clothes or my sore feet could keep my mind off those stupid auditions and that bastard group of band members who'd laughed in my face. Actually, my greasy smell and sore feet only helped *highlight* how awful it all was.

I was never going to be accepted into any band. I don't know what I'd been thinking to audition today. Not even dating the lead singer of Fish 'N' Dicks had gotten me into *their* band. Why had I been so certain someone else would accept me? I was the biggest failure I knew. I'd never gotten anything I'd truly tried for or dreamed of obtaining in my entire life.

A father who stuck around and a sane mother who loved me? Denied.

Finishing college and showing my uncle I wasn't worthless? Nope.

Marrying Braden Fisher—who was supposed to be the great love of my life—and creating the best band ever with him and his crew? Hells to the no.

Finding *any* man to love me? Nada.

Becoming a drummer in whatever band took me in and playing in front of a live audience? Not even a freaking audition.

Hating how miserable and sad and dejected it made me, I focused on the rage. I balled my hands into fists of fury and muttered to the room at large. "I'm never listening to your stupid music again, Non-Castrato."

I really didn't expect the room to respond. So when it said, "I had a bad feeling you didn't get it," I yelped out a startled scream.

Whirling toward the doorway of the kitchen, I scowled at my roommate for scaring the crap out of me. She'd piled her flaming red hair into a mop on top of her head and sported a green cami and shorts that barely covered her crotch—her usual around-the-house gear, regardless of whether it was summer or the middle of winter...though it happened to be November.

Cradling a steamy mug that smelled like cappuccino with both hands, she carried it into the front room and curled onto the couch beside me to give me the ultimate sympathetic sigh. "You would've called hours ago, screaming and ecstatic, if there'd been good news."

My lower lip trembled. I never could handle pity well. "Fuckers wouldn't even let me audition."

"I'm sorry, puta." I have no idea why Jodi always used the Spanish word for whore as a term of affection for me, but ever since I'd taught her the translation, that's what she'd affectionately called me. Today, it only made me cry harder though, because it reminded me how much she loved me, and I really-really needed some love right now.

Damn ovaries.

"Was it because you're a girl?" she asked.

"Yes." I wiped at my eyes, only to pause and give her a sharp glance. "Wait, how did you know that?"

She shrugged. "Because their name is Non-Castrato and castrato means—"

"I know what the fuck castrato means," I snapped, feeling a mite bit testy...and pathetic...and fairly worthless. But music was my life; I'd majored in it in college for a good three semesters before I'd dropped out at Fisher's insistence that he needed me on hand for his band stuff. I'd even written a paper about how young boys in the 1700s had been castrated before puberty so their voices would remain high, leading to the very term, castrato. I wasn't a complete idiot—just maybe half an idiot. Fine, three-quarters. Whatever. Still. I did know what castrato meant.

"Of course you do," Jodi cooed, patting my leg. "But what I can't figure out is why you're sitting here, letting those pricks make you cry."

Leave it to my roommate. She was quick to sympathize, but just as quick to give me the kick in the ass I needed to end my pity party.

I blinked and wiped my face. "Because I've dreamed my whole damn life for exactly this kind of opportunity. I have practiced, and sweated, and *bled* to be the best goddamn drummer there is. And they wouldn't even fucking *listen* to me!"

"Exactly," Jodi said. "You have worked at this for *years*. Why are you giving up now? Non-Castrato isn't the only band. I'm sure you can— "

"But they're the one I *wanted* to join! They were good and going places. And I want to be a part of that. It's just...something about them *felt* right." Until they'd treated me like crap and told me to *git*.

"Then make yourself a part of it, damn it."

"Whatever. I don't want anything to do with the scumbags now. What I'd really like to do is force them to listen to my talent and then laugh in their faces and deny *them* when they beg me to join their sucky band."

"Ooh, yes. I like that idea." Jodi pointed at me before taking a sip. "Do that."

"As if I could." Defeated, I tossed my hands into the air. "Bastards won't listen to a girl drummer, remember?"

"Then don't be a girl drummer," Jodi rolled her eyes and muttered, "Gah."

I froze, staring at her. "Wait. What? Do you mean, like..." I flashed my eyes open wide as I flew off the couch to grip my head in both hands. "Oh, my God. You're a genius. Do you think you could do it? Do you think you could make me a man? Like...just for an hour?"

Jodi shook her head, obviously not following my train of thought. "Huh?"

"This is exactly what you're going to college for. To make special effects for movies. That includes masks and such, right? Could you make me a guy? You know, like they made Robin Williams into a woman in *Mrs. Doubtfire*?"

"Um..." Trilling out a nervous laugh as if she wanted to believe I was joking but feared I wasn't, Jodi shook her head. "I don't think you realize how much time and work would go into making something like that. And it'd be even harder to make it in any way realistic."

Desperate, I grabbed her hand, my gaze beseeching. "It only has to be believable long enough to get me through *one* audition. After that, when they hear how great I am, then

I'll rip the mask off and tell them, *ha*, a girl can be good, so go fuck yourselves."

When leery temptation loomed in my roommate's eyes, I knew I had her. I just needed one more good solid beg to break through her resistance. "Jodi, please, I *need* this. I'm counting on you and your amazing talent to help me find a little justice in the world...for *all* women."

And... Jodi melted. I held my pleading stare as her internal conflict crumbled to dust. "Oh, all right. But if tomorrow is the last day they're holding auditions, we need to get started, like, *right fucking now*."

CHAPTER 3
Asher Hart

STRANGE FACT ABOUT ME: I totally dug strange and unusual facts.

I knew the term for killing your uncle was avunculicide. Your sister: sororicide. Your wife: uxoricide. Slaughtering everyone in the hopes of wiping out humankind in general: omnicide. But I did not know what it was called when you wanted to murder your fellow bandmates, and I really thought I should become familiar with that term since I was seriously considering employing it.

They were driving me out of my fucking mind.

We'd made a deal before hiring the next drummer that everyone had to agree one hundred percent on someone and vote with a unanimous thumbs-up before we let the next guy in. I hadn't been too keen on the last drummer we'd had from the beginning. There'd just been something skeevy about him that had rubbed me wrong. But he could carry a beat so I hadn't balked when Gally had brought him onboard. I was easygoing like that.

Oh, you have someone in mind? Fine, he's in.

Well, not anymore. Rock had cured me of that blind naivety when he'd tried to take out one of my very good friends. Turned out, he was a pyro to boot who'd killed a good portion of his family in a house fire years ago (called familicide, by the way). So, he was currently rotting away behind bars and serving hard time, while the rest of us were stuck in the lurch, with four days left to find a new drummer, or we wouldn't be able to play our usual Friday night gig...for the sixth weekend in a row.

This was the second day of tryouts—we'd advertised keeping it open for three—and the three of us had been unable to agree on a single damn drummer yet. Not one freaking person.

I was holding out for talent and, you know, the *non-pyro* vibe—scarily enough, there'd been a couple of those. Gally seemed fixated on image. No dreads, too much face metal, not enough tattoos. Didn't matter how they sounded; he just wanted a certain look...or gender, apparently, since he hadn't bothered to listen to the one girl who'd come in.

And Heath...yeah, Heath didn't give an explanation. He just shook his head yes or no. Maybe he was going on gut feeling alone. Who knew? It was hard to tell with him.

I had to admit, no one had impressed me enough to flip up my skirt either, but there'd been a handful I would've settled for, if my two fucking bandmates hadn't immediately nixed them.

I was beginning to think this little democracy thing we had going was the worst idea ever when Gally flopped into a chair and groaned as he smoothed his hands up either side of his Mohawk—which he'd dyed orange this week—as if to make sure it was still in place.

"This fucking sucks. I say we call it quits for the day."

Yes. That was about the only thing I could agree with right now. I motioned toward Heath. "Clear'em out."

As Heath pulled the strap of his guitar over his head and set his baby down before heading for the door, I unhooked myself from my Taylor and rolled my shoulders to ease knotted muscle. We hadn't had a break in hours, and I could feel it.

"Reconvene here at eight?" I asked the guys when Heath returned from sending all the applicants in the hall away.

"Re-*what*?" Gally asked, sending me a confused scowl with his mouth fallen open and eyes squinted.

I refrained from the long, tired sigh caught in my chest.

"Meet," I said. "Do you guys want to *meet* back here at eight...in the morning?"

Gally shook his head. "Why the fuck didn't you just say that the first time?"

Oh my God, I really needed to get out of here.

This time, I did sigh. After cupping the back of my neck in both hands, to hopefully keep all the veins in it from exploding, I ground out, "See you in the morning."

I zipped my guitar into its case, flung the strap over my shoulder so the Taylor rested against my back, and hurried for the exit.

I'd never really connected with anyone in the band before. After working a night shift alongside Heath for over two years as a package handler at a local shipping warehouse, I'd finally coaxed out of him during a break one night that he liked to play guitar. When I suggested we hang out and jam some time, he hadn't said no.

Starting an actual band had been about the furthest thing from my mind at that point. But Heath's cousin's boyfriend at the time—aka Billy Galloway—had heard us play one night and he'd butted his way into our sessions, saying he knew a drummer, and so...our garage days had begun.

Friends would stop by to listen to us. It still hadn't occurred to me to start an actual band until one of Gally's many women had told us we would be famous someday. From that point on, all Gally and Rock could talk about was getting bigger.

Since neither of them had the wherewithal to actually do anything about it, I'd dug into the research scene and figured out what we needed to do to start.

The naming thing had taken us over a week. That had almost been a bigger headache to survive than finding a new drummer. But we'd finally been able to settle on Non-Castrato. Next was finding a place to perform. After striking out at nightclubs that were well known for taking on new talent and giving them a chance to show their stuff, I took a leap of faith and contacted the newbie owner of Forbidden. The place had never had anything above jukebox music in its bar before, but I'd already been batting zero. I had nothing to lose by simply asking.

After cornering Pick Ryan in his office, I'd blurted out my request, and I have no idea why—I must've caught the guy on a good day or something—but he'd agreed to let us play in his club. It might've had something to do with me saying we'd play for free and that I'd come to work for him as a bartender since that's what he'd needed at the time, but whatever. He'd *agreed*!

So I found myself quitting the package handling job to work for Pick and starting this music venture with basically three strangers. I hadn't regretted it once, though, not through any of the long hours or headaches or pretty much having to set up all the gigs and create any original song we sang. It was a challenge I loved and a place I knew I belonged as soon as I'd stepped into the position.

But yeah, sometimes I thought it would've been nice if we all understood each other a little better, or if my bandmates actually knew what half the words I said meant. I guess we didn't need to be tight to make a group, however. There was no reason for me to be whiny and wistful. I was probably just one of those people who simply wasn't meant to have a great meeting of the minds with others.

Besides, tomorrow was a fresh, new day. I assured myself we'd finally find a fourth band member to agree on and my current frustrations would be moot.

As I pushed out of the studio and into the cool November evening, however, I felt restless. Unsatisfied. Because I still wished I had...fuck, I'm not even sure. Maybe a friend. Just one person I could hang out with and do shit with, or maybe not even do *anything* with. Just someone to be there, to help me get out of my own head for a while. A lifeline of sorts.

I'd told myself for years that I wasn't lonely. But screw it, I was lonely.

And oddly enough, this past year that I'd worked at Forbidden and made more casual friends than I'd ever had before, I was realizing just how utterly alone I was.

Or maybe I was just in a mood because I was still letting what that girl had said earlier bother me. But, dammit, we were *not* a cliché. I'd worked hard to be my own kind of person and write songs that were different from everything else out there. Why had she gone and said the one thing that would bug me the most? Now her words were going to fester until they drove me crazy.

And what was up with calling me a man-whore? Was she for real? She didn't know me. She didn't know how I interacted with women, or that it'd been months since I'd last had sex. It itched at my craw that she would so easily label me like that.

But then, I tried to tell myself she'd been upset, for which I totally didn't blame her. Gally *should've* let her audition (yet another reason I was irritated with him). So maybe it'd only been her anger talking.

Okay, fine...the truth was I was stewing because I was mad at myself. I could've forced the issue and let her audition, except damn...she'd affected me. Instantly.

As soon as she'd walked in the door with her long, tan legs sticking out of her short, short skirt with such a cocky, self-assured saunter, this heat had spread up from my gut and scorched my brain cells. That kind of immediate, intense reaction had only happened to me, like, twice in my life. Once a few months ago, and then...today. I didn't much like it. It turned my hormones into these primitive beasts that wanted nothing but pussy.

I'd been forced to turn away and pretend to take a drink because I feared staring much longer might've caused me to sprout wood. But I just kept picturing myself ripping off that cheap blonde wig to see what she really looked like under there and then pushing her against the first available surface so I could feast upon her.

Seriously, the craving had been that bad.

So busy trying to cool my jets, I hadn't even paid attention to what Gally was telling her until she'd said, "Is this some kind of joke," and her voice...damn, her husky voice had me jonesing big time. It was low for a female but still really, extra sexy.

When I finally realized Gally was rejecting her because of her gender, sadly, I'd felt a spark of relief. There would've been no way I could've concentrated around someone who attracted me the way she did. I knew it was biased, cowardly, awful, and completely sexist of me, but I just couldn't be in a band with her without wanting to jump her...constantly, and probably convincing her even more that I was some kind of man-whore.

And so, I felt crappy and antsy and regretful as I marched to my ride for not giving her the simple audition she'd wanted.

My motorcycle—bless her faithful heart—sat on the

curb, patiently awaiting me. The '72 Triumph might've been badass if it weren't so old and beat to hell. But it'd been cheaper than anything I could find with four wheels and had better gas mileage, so I wasn't going to complain about image. I loved her anyway.

I went about coaxing her to life—turning on the fuel, pushing the tickler, flipping the choke and ignition before kick-starting her—then I was good to go.

The only place I really had to head was home to Mozart, but right now, that felt like a miserable option, so I steered the Triumph toward my favorite place on earth.

I'd known the Forbidden Nightclub existed for a little over a year now, and in that time I'd lived all of my happiest moments there. I'd gotten to perform there for my first time and return every Friday night to play again. My band had grown a name for ourselves and gathered a crew of followers because of that place. It was at Forbidden that I'd experienced that first punch of intense longing the moment I'd seen a stranger across a crowd and wanted to know everything about her. Hell, I'd learned I had a brother within its walls. The place felt more like home to me than the studio basement apartment where I rested my head each night.

When I drove past the club twenty minutes later and scoped out the parking lot to make sure a black Barracuda wasn't on the premises, I came back around the block, pulled in and parked, satisfied the guy I was avoiding wasn't inside.

I wasn't scheduled to work tonight, and I kind of wished Pick would give me more hours so I'd have something to do on my off nights, but a beer and a little company sounded good. I needed some positive chi around me to absorb so I could boost my own morale.

Quinn and Knox were working the bar. Out of all the club's bartenders, they were the two quiet ones. With the mood I was in, I wasn't sure I'd be the best conversationalist tonight, so they were actually perfect choices for companionship.

"Hey, Asher," Quinn greeted with his friendly, boy-next-door grin. "How're the auditions coming?"

"Shitty." I slumped onto a stool. "How're the wife and kid?"

His smile bloomed with pride, and yep, that was exactly the kind of exuberant energy I needed. "Zoey seems a hundred percent better, and the doctor thinks we can take J.B. home in another week."

"That's great, man." His wife had given birth to a severely premature baby a couple months back. It was nice to hear both she and the kid were making a complete recovery. I should've been happier that things were working out for them.

Instead of the cheer, however, a bitter ball of loneliness swelled inside me. Why couldn't I find someone the way Quinn had?

A bottle of Angry Orchard appeared in front of me right before Knox flipped off the lid and strolled away.

"Thanks," I called to his back, grateful he knew exactly what I needed. I picked it up and took a long pull.

God, that tasted good. I sighed and relaxed into my seat. Quinn went to help a customer at the other end of the bar, and I contented myself with my alcohol while both guys milled about me and did their thing.

Behind them, shelves of assorted bottles glinted in the low blue lighting overhead. It gave the atmosphere a calming effect that soothed a restless part of me. If I could've just sat there and lived on that stool for the rest of my life, I would've done it.

I closed my eyes and tipped my face forward as I rested both elbows on the countertop, letting the sound and smell of Forbidden seep through me.

But apparently, my peaceful reverie wasn't meant to last.

"Asher?" A familiar voice had me jerking my head up and my eyes snapping open wide.

Instantly on edge, I swiveled toward the call and gaped in horror at the man who approached.

"Shit! Where did you come from?"

Pick, my boss and as of three weeks ago my older half-brother, slowed his approach and cocked an eyebrow. "Uh...my office?"

Damn, I should've known he'd still be around this early in the evening. It was his club; why *wouldn't* he be around? But I'd been so sure I hadn't seen his Barracuda out front.

"Did you get a new car or something?"

"Actually, yes, I did." He squinted at me. "Why? Were you trying to avoid me?"

"What?" I snorted as if that were a ridiculous suggestion.

"*No.*"

He knew I was lying. Pick had a way of eyeing a person that let you know he could read every thought in your head. I kind of admired that about him, even though it also intimidated the shit out of me. Hell, just about everything there was to Pick Ryan impressed and unsettled me in equal measures.

It was eerie as fuck—as well as astonishing and yet utterly overwhelming—to know I was related to such an intuitive yet pleasant guy.

If I could've handpicked anyone on earth to choose as my biological big brother, it would've been him. He was just one of those personable, laid-back guys who accepted you for who you were and watched your back without you even asking him to.

And yet, the whole brother thing rattled me to the core. Me and "family" had never meshed. I just had this sinking feeling I couldn't shake that if I let him actually *be* my brother, it'd all go to hell.

I had too much to lose if Pick ended up telling me to get lost. This place and what I had here were my entire life. My job, playing on Forbidden's stage with my band, my friendship with him and all the other guys who worked here, and just...well, all of it had become the most important things to me. I didn't know what I'd do without everything he'd already given me.

Pick continued to watch me with those omniscient brown eyes, which he must've picked up from his dad since our mom's had been green, like mine.

"Prove it," he murmured. "Tag along with me."

"Huh?" I blinked at him as if he'd spoken a foreign language.

An amused grin cracked his face. He hitched his head toward the exit. "I have somewhere to be soon. Why don't you come?"

"Why?" I winced as the suspicious-sounding word left my lips. What I really should've asked was *where*. But Pick answered me anyway.

With a careless shrug, he said, "Just to hang out."

The offer was tempting. It was the exact kind of companionship I'd been craving only minutes ago. But I didn't dare hope, wouldn't fall victim to the lure. It would end badly. It *had* to end badly. Any and every familial thing in my life ended badly. Why would this be any different?

"Oh, Jesus." He rolled his eyes and slugged his arm against mine. "Quit overthinking it already. Just get your ass off the stool and come with me."

"But...I have to finish my beer." Yeah. That sounded... lame.

Pick glanced at the countertop in front of me. "What beer?"

I spun to check on my drink, but it was gone, only a wet ring left on the bar where it'd once sat as Quinn tossed a bottle in the trash that looked suspiciously like an Angry Orchard.

"So let's go already." Pick nudged me again.

With a reluctant groan, I slid off my seat. I told myself I was only doing this because he was my boss; he could fire me if I was subordinate. But honestly, I was curious. No matter how certain and afraid I was that starting a brotherly relationship with him would end badly, I wanted to know more about this guy who'd come from the same womb as me. I secretly *did* ache to have him as family.

CHAPTER 4
Asher Hart

IT HAD ALL STARTED WITH a stupid song I'd written about my mom and how she'd given up her first child, abandoning the baby boy at the hospital only hours after he was born and then going on to live a miserable life until some asshole—aka, my father—had beaten her to death. Then I had to go and sing it on stage with my band. And the people who'd heard it just *had* to tell me it reminded them of Pick because *his* mom had abandoned him at the hospital when he was born, which led me to wonder if Pick might've possibly been that child, and then further led me to do the epically stupid move of mentioning the little coincidence to him. He, in turn, ran off and got a blood test done, and boom...here we were. Fucking blood-related brothers who shared a mother but had different fathers.

After working for him for as many months as I had, I thought I knew him well enough, but now...now I realized I barely knew a damn thing.

Like the fact he was into restoring old muscle cars.

As he led me outside toward a maybe 1970s model blue Mustang with a white stripe running down the hood, I let out a low whistle. "Nice ride."

"Thanks." He unlocked my side for me. "It wasn't even running when I came across it. I traded out the original 302 for a 351 and installed a new heating and air system before I got her purring again."

I understood basically nothing he'd just said, but I nodded like I did as I climbed into the passenger seat.

"Next, I'm going to work on the interior and paint job."

Nodding some more, I ran my hand along the tattered seat under me. "I had no idea you knew how to fix up old cars."

He glanced at me as he started the engine, and damn, I wasn't a car expert, but even I knew the melody of this one coming to life sounded good. Pick might've called it a purr, but to me it was more like a deep satisfied growl, like the sound a guy might make while stretching his muscles on a soft mattress after coming hard and deep inside a soft eager woman.

"Sure. It's kind of my thing. I worked at a garage right up until I came to own Forbidden." He canted his head as if he couldn't believe I didn't already know that.

I hadn't. Honestly, it was startling and a little unnerving to learn he'd been a mechanic. His father had been a mechanic. That's one of the few details I knew about his sperm donor, outside the fact the guy had been killed at nineteen on the same day Pick had been born. That, and my mother had referred to him as Chaz.

Okay, fine. She'd told me plenty about Chaz, the guy she'd considered her one true love, but it'd mostly been shit a seven-year-old boy didn't want to ever hear about his mom. So I'd blocked most of her sexually explicit stories from my memory banks. The mechanic thing though, I figured Pick might get a kick out of knowing cars were in his genes. If I were him and knew nothing of my origins, I'd want to know.

But for some reason, I didn't enlighten him. I wasn't ready to go down that road, too leery where it might lead. However, I knew he was all fired about the brotherly bonding idea. He was ready to travel the shit down that road.

And yep, the first thing he said as he put the car into gear was, "I was thinking maybe we could tell everyone."

"Hmm?" I played dumb. It was a stupid, useless stall

tactic that got me nowhere, but anything to prolong the inevitable sounded good right about now.

He didn't pretend to think I had no idea what he was talking about. He carried on as if I knew exactly what he meant...since I did. "I mean, I have a feeling everyone pretty much knows already. I told Tink, of course."

When he glanced at me, I shrugged, completely unsurprised. Tink—aka Eva—was his girlfriend, though most of us called her his wife already. They had one of those rare, close, bonding relationships I'd never seen in play before I'd come to Forbidden. But it was the type where both parties shared everything. So I'd already figured he would've informed her.

"And I'm sure she mentioned it to Reese." Eva's best friend and first cousin. "Who would've blabbed to Mason." Reese's fiancé, who also happened to work behind the bar at Forbidden with me. "And you know he probably told—"

"The rest of them," I finished lamely. Scrubbing my face with my hands, I tried to beat down the panic, since there really was no reason to panic...but I felt panicky anyway. I just couldn't help it; this shit was beginning to get way too real for me.

"Exactly," Pick was saying with a shrug. "So, I was thinking why not make it official and public so everyone doesn't have to keep pretending they don't know."

I lifted both hands, horrified to find they were beginning to tremble. "Look, can we just...I don't know...put off any big announcements for a while?"

Pick's disappointment came with a five-second pause of silence. I bit the inside of my lip, hating that I'd given him an answer he didn't want to hear, but hell...I wasn't ready.

Finally, he said, "Sure," in his easygoing way, but I knew he had wanted more from me. "You need some time to adjust to the shock. I get that."

God, did he have to be so freaking understanding about it? The guy was so noble and nice and had such good intentions; it made me feel shittier because I couldn't get down with all this touchy-feely family shit as freely as he could. I knew I wanted the same thing he wanted. I *did* want to be his brother and have one of those close relationships any pair of good brothers had. I just couldn't—

"I'm sorry. I know I'm wigging out about this more than I should. But I just don't...I don't have the best of luck with the whole...*family* thing. Which..." Damn, I was such an idiot, "I know, sounds really stupid since you obviously don't either."

"Actually...I've had remarkably good luck with the family thing lately." His gaze strayed to his sun visor where a snapshot of a sexy blonde and two little toddlers grinned back at him. A sharp pang of envy ran through me. He had the most devoted girlfriend and two kids any lucky bastard should have. And what was even cooler was that they loved him right back with the same intensity.

Pick glanced at me, his eyebrows raised. "That includes you."

I sighed and sank lower in my seat, feeling even worse and undeserving.

But he didn't let me stew in my guilt. Pulling into the driveway of a nice, suburban home with a For Sale sign sitting in the spacious front yard, he put the Mustang into park and killed the engine. "But we'll keep it quiet for a while if you prefer. No problem."

"Thanks," I answered distractedly as I eyed the place. It was exactly the kind of home I'd always dreamed of growing up in but had never even lived in the same neighborhood as.

When I couldn't stand the curiosity any longer, I glanced at him. "Where *are* we?"

Pick eyed the house with the same kind of yearning I felt inside me. "Tink and I have been house hunting."

I zipped my attention to the yard. Then pointing, I dropped my mouth open, completely incredulous. "And you're considering *this* one?"

He glanced my way. "What? You don't like it?"

"No, I...I do! It's amazing. I just...nothing. That's cool, is all. House hunting. Wow." I couldn't tell him I might commit unspeakable crimes to live in a place like this. That seemed a bit dramatic, so I just pushed open my door, dying to see what the inside looked like. I didn't get to see the insides of nice, suburban homes very often.

"So...why aren't you doing this with your Tinker Bell?" I asked as he followed me with much more reservation toward the front door, where a realtor was waiting to greet us.

I glanced back when he didn't answer. Pick sent me a chagrined, embarrassed wince. "I kind of pissed her off when I vetoed everything we've looked at as soon as I stepped out the back door and saw the yard."

I sent him a curious glance, but he waved me silent. "Long story. To say the least, we're looking for houses separately. After she checks them out, she gives me a list of her favorites until I find...the one."

"O...kay," I said slowly, thinking that an odd way to house hunt with your significant other, but whatever.

"Mr. Ryan?" the realtor asked, eyeing me politely.

"Oh! No, not me. Him." As I pointed toward Pick, I realized we'd probably have the same surname if my mother had never abandoned him.

No, scratch that. We wouldn't, because I wouldn't exist if she hadn't abandoned him. She would've been too busy raising a baby she actually loved and never would've met my worthless, drug-dealing father. They wouldn't have started their unhealthy...whatever it was they'd had, and I never would've come along.

She'd probably still be alive today too.

Rubbing the back of my neck, I glanced across the pristine yard while Pick and the realtor introduced themselves, and I tried not to feel guilty about being alive while my mom was not. She'd been the one to make all the decisions that had led to her demise; I was just a product of them.

I repeated that to myself a lot. Not that it ever made me feel better. But what could I do now? What was done, was done.

"And this is my brother, Asher."

Jolted by the label, I turned back to the conversation at hand and sent the realtor guy a tense smile. "Hey."

He introduced himself as Brian and then led us into the house, immediately explaining every feature.

It smelled...homey. I liked it.

I wanted it.

"As you can see, the trim is a beveled oak stained with—"

"Where's the back door?" Pick cut in, obviously not at all concerned about the trim.

"Uh... The, uh...it's this way," a puzzled Brian answered. As he showed Pick where, I paused to take in the oak trim, deciding, yeah, I even liked that. Having beveled trim was nice. If I ever had my own house, I'd fancy trim the fuck out of it.

Then I turned to follow the other two toward the back.

The three of us crowded out the exit and into a yard that

had me drooling, envisioning barbecues and luaus, swimming pools, maybe a trampoline next to a kid's swing set.

But Pick set his hands on his hips and frowned. "Nope." He turned back toward the house, telling Brian, "Sorry, but this isn't it."

The realtor and I shared a confused glance before I called, "Wait. *What*? You seriously don't like this?" I splayed my hand out to encompass the lush, spacious yard, completely confused. This yard was the freaking bomb diggity. My new brother was completely whack.

Pick paused to shrug. "It's nice, sure. But...it's not the place I'm looking for."

Jesus, no wonder Eva didn't want to house hunt with him anymore.

When he started back toward the back door, I shook my head. "Don't you want to see the rest of the inside?"

"Don't have to. This isn't it."

"Well, *I* want to see it," I insisted.

Pausing again to glance back at me, Pick did another one of his creepy stare things, where he looked inside you and dug around in your head, pulling up all your deepest, most-achiest desires. Finally, he nodded as if he understood. "Okay."

So we checked out the rest of the empty rooms in the house. Brian had long ago given up on feeding us details as he wrote something in a notebook in the front room—probably that his client was impossible to please—and we finished the tour ourselves.

"You're totally insane if you don't like this place," I murmured as we entered the last bedroom.

"Oh, I love it," Pick corrected. "It's just not the *right* place."

I had no idea how this couldn't be the right place. It was fucking awesome. "I'd give my left nut to live in a house like this."

I busied myself by examining the white crown molding lining the ceiling, but I could still feel my brother's gaze on me.

"Never lived in a true house?" he asked.

I shook my head. "Nope. A couple of apartments, a trailer park once, and now I'm in some basement under a storage warehouse that some guy rents out, but never a *house-*

house."

"So why don't you get one?" Pick asked quietly after a short silence.

I snorted. "And live there with *whom*?" I met his gaze and shook my head. "Houses are for families."

When pity and compassion filled his face, I realized I'd said too much. More exposed than I wanted to be with him, I left the room without a word and didn't stop until I was outside and pacing the front lawn. I wasn't comfortable with being so vulnerable and letting others know what I wanted most. To fight off the panicky anxiety crawling through me, I kind of wanted to ninja kick the For Sale sign in half, but I refrained.

Pick emerged a minute later, jiggling his car keys in his hand. "Ready to go?"

I nodded, grateful he didn't try to pry anymore into my head. In the car, we were mostly quiet. As he drove me back to my bike I'd left at Forbidden, Pick searched the radio for something to listen to, but when he couldn't find a decent song playing, he sighed and asked, "Any luck finding a new drummer for your band yet?"

I couldn't answer beyond "Nope," as I continued to stare out the passenger side window, ready for this little field trip to be over. I felt shitty because I knew I was the reason everything had turned awkward and prickly, but I didn't know how to fix it. So I sat helplessly silent, just making it worse.

When Pick parked beside my Triumph, he turned to me, worry in his eyes, and that made my shame double. He had no reason to worry or feel as if he'd done anything wrong.

"I know we're not conventional, Asher, but Eva, the kids and I...we're your family now. And all the guys at Forbidden...they are too. You're not alone any longer."

Fuuuuck.

It just wasn't right how easily he could read me.

"Whenever you're ready to accept us and let us in, we'll be here for you. Just remember that."

Clearing my throat, I stared down at my lap, trying not to get all sissy and emotional. I had to clear my throat a second time. "Yeah," I mumbled, sparing him a micro-glance before quickly turning away and reaching for the door handle to escape. "Thanks."

I didn't give him a chance to reply. I was out of there, slamming the door, and climbing onto my motorcycle before I really disgraced myself by doing something embarrassing, like giving him a hug and telling him he was the best damn brother a guy could suddenly have or that shit, I think I loved him already.

But I held it together, and as I roared down the block, the wind in my face made moisture seep from the corners of my eyes.

I wasn't sure how to handle any of this, because I *did* have a family now. I didn't have to feel so alone.

So why was I too fucking afraid to just...embrace it?

CHAPTER 5
Remy Cullan

I SHOULD'VE KNOWN WHEN I'd drafted Jodi for this job she'd go all out. That was just her way. And wow, go all out, she did.

Making the clay mold had been a bitch. For her, that was. All I had to do was sit still as she caked my face with gunk. Then she'd made another mold. The first was an exact replica of my face and the second was the altered, male version of me. After that, it was easy. For me.

That's when the real work started for Jodi, though. For the mask to work properly, it needed to be an exact representation of the face we wanted to make. Every flaw in the mold would show up in the outcome.

I sat and watched in wonder as she hovered over the mold, chipping and sanding to perfection.

"How old do you want to look?" she asked, frowning at her work as she concentrated. "Lots of wrinkles or a baby face?"

"Uh...about as old as I am now?" I guessed. "Maybe a year or two older."

"Early twenties. Got it."

Pouring the latex in was kind of cool to watch. Jodi moved the mold constantly so the liquid would fill every crease and corner equally.

"It's like watching a cooking show," I said as I munched on popcorn.

The clock hovered at one in the morning, and the clay mold had just dried enough to play with. Nudging the bowl full of liquid latex, I shuddered., "Except I wouldn't want to eat that shit. Smells funky as hell."

"Ooh, don't mention food to me right now, you bitch. I'm starving." Jodi's hands were caked with some kind of concoction I didn't even want to know the ingredients to as she swiveled the mold back and forth.

"Well, then open up, sweetness, I'll feed you."

When I lifted a fluffy kernel, Jodi dutifully opened her mouth wide. On our first three tries, one bounced off her nose, then her cheek and finally her chin. That's when I gave up and scooted off the comfy chair I'd been sitting in to let her grab the popcorn straight from my hand with her teeth.

I hand-fed her until she claimed to be thirsty. Then I fetched her a can of cola from the fridge and stuck a straw in it before holding it up to her mouth for her to drink.

"Mmm, puta, you sure do treat me right." She sent me a smile and sexy wink. It was too late for me to flirt back, so I just grunted out a sound, plopped back onto my chair and tried to stay awake with her by reading funny little things I found in the newsfeed of the Facebook app on my phone.

By three thirty in the morning, I was just beginning to nod off when the timer blared, letting us know the latex was dry. Jodi jumped and rolled off the couch where she'd been dozing, landing on all fours on the floor.

"Shit," she mumbled as she sat up, rubbed her eyes, and let out a mammoth yawn. "Time to decorate your new face. Get up, woman." She slapped me on the ass as she passed.

I wanted to whine, but since this was all for me, I merely yawned too and stumbled out of the chair I'd been curled in.

And even though I was only half-awake for the rest of it, I remained in awe of Jodi's power of creativity. She had given the male me a square-cut jaw and a sloped forehead with a defined brow ridge. But it was her talent with hair that blew my mind. After finding a dark wig, she hand-sewed it to the mask, allotting it an m-cut brow line, slight sideburns and even a five-o'clock shadow.

"Holy shit," I murmured in amazement as Jodi tacked in the last of the mask's eyebrows. "That looks...wow."

"I thought I'd give you a little facial hair to cover as much of your jaw as possible, so it'll be harder to tell you're wearing a mask."

I just nodded, unable to say anything, though seriously, I didn't think anyone would guess it was latex after the expert way Jodi had painted it and applied makeup.

"Jesus, you're amazing."

Preening, my friend grinned as she held up the final product. "I know, right?" She motioned me forward. "Now this might feel a little strange. I tried to make it as comfortable as possible by fashioning the inside layer to conform to the shape of your face, but it'll also get warmer more quickly that way."

"Well then, thank God we're in northern Illinois in November," I teased.

I ducked my head, which Jodi had wrapped with a tight nylon hairnet to contain my natural hair, and the mask slipped over my scalp. The latex tried to stick to and pinch my face but Jodi kept working it, determined to get it into place. And finally we were a go. I opened my eyes, blinked my lashes a few times and peered out from a mini-tunnel.

"Ooh, it makes your eyes look deeper set." Jodi nodded with an approving smile. "Much more masculine. And I've always preferred that in men. Actually...you're kind of hot as a guy." To prove her point, she wiggled her eyebrows and sent me a little wink. "Too bad you're not into girls; I'd *so* turn bi for you."

Rolling my eyes, I turned to study my face in the mirror. "Wow," I said again.

I looked nothing like myself whatsoever. My forehead was more pronounced, the bridge of my nose wider, my chin no longer pointy. Even my mouth had been squished around the edge of the mask to look wider and flatter.

I opened and closed my jaw a few times; the mask never gave itself away. "This is freaking unbelievable. It looks so real."

"Yup. So, let's get to work on the rest of your body." Jodi sounded way too eager and energized for ten in the morning, after she'd been up all night.

I turned from the mirror and lifted my fake, bushy dark eyebrows. "The *rest* of my body?"

"Well, *yeah*, puta. If we're going to do this, we're doing it right. You might not have double Ds like me, but *that...*," she pointed to my breasts, "is clearly a female chest."

Scowling, I glanced at the front of my shirt. "Can't we just bind them with an elastic bandage or something to flatten them down?"

She snorted. "Only if you want to half-ass it. And after all that work I put into your face, you're not allowed to half-ass the rest."

"Okay, fine. But what exactly did you have in mind?"

A large grin spread across her face. "This," she announced before pulling what looked like a tan bulletproof vest from her closet. "It's padding for male actors to make their chests look fuller. But we can use it for you by cutting out some holes on the inside where your boobies can go."

I blurted out a laugh. "Oh, my God. You have the strangest shit in your closet."

Jodi merely shrugged. "No stranger than having molding clay and mask latex on hand."

"Good point."

So we made me a male chest. Then Jodi went as far as to sew in a rolled-up wad of cloth to give my panties a "package."

"Why the hell do I need a package?" I argued. "No one's going to be staring at my crotch."

"You never know, they might. I made you look hot enough as a guy, I'm sure *some* girl off the street will cop a peek."

"Honestly, I really don't care if some girl off the street finds me lacking down there."

"Well, I do. And I'm in charge of this man-body, so you're wearing it."

"Oh, Jesus." I sighed but complied.

"Thank God it's almost winter," Jodi added. "You can wear jeans and long sleeves without anyone thinking you're weird." She shuffled through my drawers, mumbling something about how it was depressing I had so many clothes that could be considered manly. "Here," she finally said, shoving a wad at me. "Put these on."

After pulling on my "man" panties, I tugged up a pair of

loose-legged denim jeans and put on a black AC/DC concert shirt over a white long-sleeved thermal.

When I turned to face her, Jodi was beaming with a huge smile. Then she held out what she called man jewelry, which consisted of black leather straps with silver beads on them for bracelets. And finally, she sprayed cologne in my direction.

Coughing and sputtering over the unexpected stink, I waved my hand over my face. "What the hell?"

"You need to smell the part as much as you look it," Jodi argued as she pulled the cologne bottle to her chest and chirped with pride. "And you look just perfect. I would so throw you down on your bed and ride you right now if I didn't know you were really a girl in there. Hell, I'm tempted to, anyway."

I rolled my eyes but chased it with a smile. "Gracias. I think."

"Now practice your man walk," she demanded, waving out her hand.

I faltered. "My what?"

She sighed. "You're not going to pass for a dude if you stroll in there with your hidden girl hips swaying and flattened tits pooched out on display."

My mouth fell open. "Excuse me. I do *not* walk like that."

She snorted. "Oh...own it, puta. You're a hot piece of ass, you can't help the girly swagger."

"But I don't—"

"Hunch your shoulders over a little more, concentrate on keeping your hips in line, and try to jut your cock forward when you strut."

"Do...*what*?"

"That's how hot guys walk, like they're leading with their junk."

I could only shake my head. I had honestly never seen a guy walk as if he were trying to poke his pecker out ahead of him. "Where do you come up with this shit?"

"Just do it, puta."

I sighed but used her suggestions, trying to overdramatize the cock-and-go strut, as I was thusly dubbing it.

"What do you think?" I asked.

She purred out a promiscuous growl and clawed the air in my direction. "How do you say 'I want to sit on your face' in Spanish?"

"*Jodi.*" I fell to a stop and sighed in exasperation. She was too much sometimes. "Really?"

"No, seriously. I've always wanted to know how to say that to a guy anyway. Ooh, and use your slutty señorita voice."

With a chuckle, I had to oblige her. "Quiero sentarme en tu cara," I cooed, puckering my lips to go with the voice.

Ever since I'd crank called her once in Spanish, putting a sensual little hitch in my tone, she'd been fascinated. Totally intrigued by my impersonation, she'd dubbed it my slutty señorita voice and claimed it didn't sound a thing like me.

She repeated the phrase, butchering it until I made her repeat it enough times that she finally got it right. Once I was satisfied, she seemed satisfied too. Letting out a loud squeal, she jumped in a circle and fisted her hands in the air.

"You are so going to rock this audition. I just know it, puta."

With my new guise in place, I let her confidence consume me. "Yeah," I murmured. And I allowed the hope to swell. I really was going to rock my audition.

I had to. There was too much of my own self-esteem riding on it not to.

CHAPTER 6
Remy Curran

I NEARLY DIDN'T MAKE it in time. It was almost one in the afternoon by the time I skidded into the studio, hoping they hadn't closed the auditions yet. Heading directly to the hallway where I'd waited in line for hours the day before, my relief soared when I saw six guys still loitering outside the auditioning room.

All half dozen of them glanced over to narrow their eyes. It wasn't nearly the reception I'd received from my fellow drummers yesterday, because today, they saw a guy.

They saw competition.

Chauvinist assholes.

"This the line for Non-Castrato?" I asked.

One guy was gracious enough to nod, but that was it. The others went back to ignoring me.

Only two other people showed up to wait in line after me, and this was their last day, so shit, I was the third to last person to try out. For some reason, that felt like a bad omen.

But I stuck it out anyway. I'd gone too far to quit now.

This time, dammit, I *was* going to play with them before they told me to "git."

An hour of waiting later, it was my turn. I entered, not at all nervous. Maybe it was because I was hiding behind my mask. Maybe it was because they'd already rejected me, and things could only go up from there. Or maybe I just felt that confident.

I had no idea what was causing it, everything just seemed...*right* this time around. Even more right than last time.

The room was exactly the same, and the guys were still loitering in their same basic places they'd been the day before. But today, Galloway ignored me and seemed to be sulking as he fiddled with the tuning pegs on his guitar.

Hart took charge and nodded a greeting. "Hey, man. What's your name?"

Score!

I'd already gotten further on this audition than I had in the first one. And the man guise was obviously working; he'd called me *man*!

Jazzed, I cleared my throat and used the lowest voice I could muster, even though it was already low for a woman's voice. "Call me Sticks."

"Sticks?" Galloway snorted, finally glancing up. "Wow. That's original."

Still miffed over the way he'd treated me yesterday, I was tempted to shove my drumsticks up his ass. But I didn't want to do such permanent, scarring damage to my babies—even though they were my non-pink backup pair—so I managed to contain myself enough to send him a bored glance. "About as original as a douchebag bassist."

Holden let out a belly laugh. When Galloway glared his way, Holden only grinned. "Burn," he informed his bandmate.

"Screw you," Galloway mumbled to me...or maybe to Holden, I wasn't sure which. Probably both of us.

Hart cracked a half smile. "Well, you can already take Gally's shit and dish it right back. That's a must. Let's see what you can do with those sticks of yours." He nodded toward the drum set. "You can handle a five-piece, I assume."

What idiot couldn't handle a five-piece? I arched one of my fake eyebrows, still amazed Jodi had been able to rig my mask so I could manage facial expressions too. "Only since I was six."

With a horrified shudder, Hart shook his head. "You'd be amazed by the lack of talent we've seen come through here these past few days."

I nodded, understanding. "Well, I can manage any drum set up you put before me."

He smiled, and damn...*that smile*. I probably shouldn't look at him when he smiled. Way too dangerous.

"Good," he said, thrilling me with his approval. "I want to try a delayed backbeat with a quick blast during the chorus, then double time to finish it up."

Pulling my drumsticks from my back pocket, I saluted him. "I'll do whatever you tell me to, drill sergeant."

With another half-smile, he shook his head. "Forrest Gump. Funny. In that case, we're going to play 'Run, Daddy, Run.' You familiar with that one?"

Was I familiar?

"Pfft." It took everything I had not to roll my eyes. "I'm familiar with every song you guys have ever produced."

Hart smiled. "Well, all right then." He motioned me toward the stool. "Count us off."

After seating myself, I took a deep breath, lifted my hands into position, and began with the ride cymbal, setting the tempo.

When I added the snare and bass drums, the guitars joined me, completely in sync with the rhythm I set. A smile spread across my face, relief ballooning inside me until I was ingesting my excitement with each breath.

Even if I ended up totally bombing this audition, I was here, *right now*, living my dream. I was jamming with Non-Castrato. For a minute, I forgot what jerks they were and that I was supposed to hate them.

It was euphoria.

Forcing my lungs to function, I exhaled and sucked in more air. By the time Hart leaned in toward the microphone and began to sing, I already had an adrenaline buzz going, but the sound of his voice sent another spike through me. There was just something about the way he sang. Made me wet in the panties every time.

Yeah, it seemed all kinds of wrong to soak my man panties with girlish enthusiasm, but there you had it.

The music inspired me, flowing through my bloodstream. I was actually living it, morphing into it.

Becoming one with the drum kit, I switched from the ride cymbal to the hi-hat when Hart changed from one passage to the next, giving the song a little extra punch with the added lean sound. The drummer before had never done that, but I'd always thought it would sound better. So I gave it a try.

I mean, hell, what could they do? Tell me to *git* again? Been there, done that.

Except the overhead ring in the room was growing slightly obnoxious. To reduce it, I yanked a hanky from my pocket without missing a beat and draped it over my knee nearest the drumhead to muffle the snare's reverberation. I smiled as that instantly helped. Bobbing my head, I switched into overtime as Hart had instructed. His voice rose, coming to a crescendo.

Though I'd never heard one in this song before, I hit the crash cymbal when he peaked and added a strong kick to the bass drum pedal.

The other members stopped playing, and it was over. An echo of guitars, drum, and Hart's voice continued to resonate through the room, filling it with a heaviness that made me bite the inside of my lip and hold my breath.

All three band members turned to look at me.

"You brought in the hi-hat in the middle of that second verse," Hart finally said. His stare wasn't exactly accusatory, but it sure as hell wasn't reassuring either.

Shit. Maybe I shouldn't have gotten so carried away, adding my personal touch quite so soon.

But it had felt so right at the time.

I gave a slow nod. "Uh, yeah. It just seemed...fitting." Growing more nervous, I swiped the hanky from my knee to mop my damp brow, only to remember the sweat wasn't showing on the outside of my mask.

"And the crash cymbal at the end," Holden spoke up. "That was new."

"Well..." I cleared my throat. "You know...I thought... why not?"

"Why not?" Galloway repeated tonelessly, shaking his head as he glanced at Hart and Holden. Then he burst out, "Shit, yeah. Why the fuck not! Christ, that was fucking *awesome*."

Holden nodded, agreeing with Galloway.

I nearly peed my pants. "Really? You liked it?" Of course, they liked it. I had totally kicked ass. But to hear them actually admit it aloud... Man, you have no idea how much of a rush that gave me.

"I loved it," Holden said. His grin was goofy but proud. "I didn't think we'd ever find anyone half as good as Rock was."

"But goddamn, if you're not *twice* as good," Galloway exploded. "You got an ear for this shit, Sticks. A fucking brilliant ear."

Thank God for my mask; I was blushing so hard my true face had to be tomato red right now. Glad I could look cool and collected, I lifted my eyebrows at Asher Hart, who had yet to comment.

Narrowing his eyes as if he didn't trust my talent and that one song had been a fluke for me, he murmured, "Let's try 'Sweat.' See how well you handle that one."

Since I'd sat out in the hallway through two days of auditions now, I knew it was rare when a drummer played more than one song with them. This had to mean something.

Something good.

Beyond excited, lightheaded and a little sick to my stomach, I nodded and wiped clammy palms on my jean-clad thighs. "No problem."

"Sweat" was a hard-core track for them with some tricky drum moves, but it wasn't anything I couldn't handle. Ready to show them my mad skills, I dove right into it.

And nailed it.

Bam, I was so good I shocked myself.

As the last beat from my cymbal clanged through the air, Holden and Galloway hooted and hollered while Hart slowly turned to stare at me intently.

I squirmed under the heavy inspection. I knew Jodi had done a damn fine job of guying me up, but what if Hart saw straight through the layers? What if he knew what I really was?

Then he said, "'Stone-Hearted,'" which was pretty much their signature song.

I grinned and began the count off.

After we finished that one, I immediately started the percussion lead-in for "Ceilings," a new one, but my favorite, of theirs. Hart glanced back at me, and I wondered if he'd get pissy about me initiating a new song all on my own. But then a small, impressed smile crossed his lips right before he wailed out the first striking line before joining in with his guitar, on cue.

The others followed, and we played a fourth song together, just pretty much rocking out by this point.

I would've lit into a fifth after Asher sang the last line, but he held up a hand, stopping me.

I set my drumsticks against my knee and held my breath.

He studied me a second, then nodded. "Can you play this Friday?"

"Friday?" I echoed stupidly. Is that when their second round of callbacks started?

Hart nodded. "Yeah, that's when our next gig is. Are you available then?"

Holy shit. "Wait. Are you saying I'm... in? I'm in the band?"

They'd been auditioning drummers for three full days. How could they just hire one of us on the spot? No one was good enough to hire after playing four songs with them. Were they?

Hart lifted his eyebrows. "Sure...if you're interested in joining Non-Castrato."

His green eyes were freaking hypnotizing and the dark lashes framing them made them pop even more. It didn't seem fair that a guy should have such gorgeous eyes to go with such a gorgeous face and gorgeous lean body. But hell, put him on a stamp, and I'd write a letter to everyone I knew just for the chance to lick him.

Did they even make lickable stamps anymore? They totally should. *Asher Hart* lickable stamps.

I blinked, clearing my jumbled brain from all the lust, and what he'd just said finally made an impression in my head. And then, I was filled with a giddy radiance.

Holy shit, they really wanted to hire me after four songs.

I was *in* the band.

"Fuck, *yes* I want to join!" I exploded.

But as soon as the words crossed my lips, reality set in. Oh hell, what had I just done?

This was where I was supposed to rip off my mask and tell them all to go screw themselves. Except the words never came. The mask-ripping never commenced. Because I wanted to play that gig on Friday more than I wanted my next breath. Who cared if I was scheduled to work at Castañeda's? Carmen owed me one. And who cared if I told one little white lie of omission, and just let them believe I was a guy? My gender had no bearing whatsoever on how well I could play. I just knew one thing: nothing was going to let me miss my first performance as a drummer in my first band.

I guessed I was going to have to be a man just a tad bit longer. I could still totally rip off the mask after Friday and make them all feel as stupid and sexist as they were for not giving me a chance when I'd been a girl. So, yeah, that's what I'd do. Wait until after Friday to let them in on my secret.

CHAPTER 7
Asher Hart

THE WORST THING ABOUT being so laid-back was that when it came to the more professional, business aspect of things, I sucked ass.

"Are you sure I didn't pay?" I asked, tucking my cell phone between my ear and shoulder as I knelt in front of the garage door of the storage unit to unlock the padlock.

"I'm looking on the computer screen of your account history right in front of me, Mr. Hart. And there's been no receipt of payment yet."

Scowling because I was so sure I'd already given them my credit card information, I rolled up the metal door and entered the cramped space.

"Okay, then. Just send me another invoice or whatever, I guess. I'll make sure to take care of it this time, I swear."

After the woman assured me she would, we hung up and I set my guitar on a box that had *Christmas Decorations* scribbled on the side. The unit belonged to Heath's family. But they only used half the space, so they didn't mind if we shoved all their things against the walls to make room in the middle for the drum set and sound system. We'd practiced here a couple times each week for almost two years now.

Today was the first chance we had to practice with our new band member. It was also the last opportunity before our first gig to really mesh with him, so I was a bit edgy, hoping he stayed as good as he'd been during his audition. I was almost grateful that Shelly from the studio had called me to distract my nerves.

When I spotted a box that belonged to me, I sat on an old scarred nightstand, settled the box onto my lap, and began to riffle through the scattered pages inside. I'd only glanced at half a dozen when someone knocked on the opening.

I looked up to find the new drummer hesitating in the entrance and gazing around the inside of the unit in half horror, half wonder.

"Hey, you made it. Come on in." I waved him forward and went back to scanning the documents in the box. "The other two should be here any minute."

He stepped cautiously forward as if he feared a piano would fall on him as soon as he entered. "So this is really where we practice, huh? I had to reread the address you gave me about ten times, sure there was a mistake when I pulled in the lot of a freaking storage unit."

"Yeah, it's not much. But it gets the job done."

"You're telling me," he muttered under his breath.

From the corner of my eye, I saw him wander to the drum set and run his hand over one of the mounted toms. Then he gingerly seated himself on the stool in front of the five-piece set and rubbed his hands up and down his thighs as he took in the sight before him.

Wondering if he was nervous, I glanced up and lifted one of the pages from the box. "Oh, by the way, the sheet music for all our original songs is in here if you need go through them to learn any."

Sticks zipped his gaze my way as if I'd surprised him. Then he shrugged. "I'm good. I pretty much learned them by ear when I listened to your records."

I nodded, admiring his ability to do that. "Right on."

I tried to refocus my attention on my task of finding the receipt I was sure I had when Heath and Gally arrived together, Gally being just as loud and rambunctious as Heath was quiet and subdued.

"What up, losers? You ready to rock this garage?"

Sticks didn't respond and I barely gave a distracted "Hey," because I was busy tugging up the sheet I'd been looking for and crying, "Aha! I *did* pay already."

"Pay what?" Gally asked as he and Heath went about plugging their guitars into the amplifier.

"Hmm?" I glanced up from my triumphant grin. "Oh. Someone from the music studio just called, saying I hadn't paid for the three days we rented the room for our auditions. And I *knew* I'd paid." I waved the receipt that had a big red Paid stamp on it as I slid my phone out of my pocket.

Gally's mouth hung half open as he stared at me. "We actually had to pay for that?"

I wrinkled my brow, hoping he wasn't serious, but I was pretty sure he was. "Uh... Don't you think we'd practice there daily if it were free?"

"Oh. Huh, yeah, I guess. I never really thought about it." Then he scratched his head. "I don't remember paying shit for any studio rental."

"That's because you didn't. I took care of the cost."

Instead of thanking me for handling it, he mumbled, "Oh," again and then slipped his guitar strap over his shoulder. "Well, are you ready to play or not?"

I held up a finger. "Not yet. I need to call these people back." As I dialed, Gally sighed, rolling his eyes, so I assured him, "It'll only take a second."

I called the lady I'd just talked to, and once I read her the number on the receipt and the date, she paused a moment before telling me, *Oh yeah, there was my payment.* Huh, go figure.

By the time I finished the call, everyone was already set up and raring to go, just watching me. "Sorry about that." I stuffed my phone back into my pocket as Gally demanded to know if I was *finally* ready yet.

Both Sticks and Heath were silent, but by their expressions, they didn't appear to be as annoyed by the delay. It seemed the new drummer was going to be as quiet as our lead guitarist.

Until I said, "What do you guys want to play first?" as I got my guitar ready.

Sticks was the first to answer, "'Ceilings.'"

I zipped a surprised glance his way, not expecting him to

speak up, but glad he had. "All right." Rolling a finger his way, I told him to count us down since the drumbeat led with this song.

He instantly started in and I was blown away all over again by how good he was. I almost missed my cue when I needed to start singing. But once I got with the program, it was easy to immerse myself in the music. We sounded good together, better than we'd ever sounded when Rock had been the drummer. Sticks had a way of keeping us in sync with the beat he set.

We went through most of our original songs as well as the more popular cover records we usually played, and each one sounded better than the last. I called song title after song title, one right after the other, so into jamming that I hadn't realized how much time had passed until Gally demanded a break.

I checked the time on my phone and nearly pissed myself. "Shit." We'd practiced over three hours. "I need to get to work."

Unplugging my guitar, I glanced at the newest member of the band, who'd not only kept up with us without a problem but had basically led us. I'd been a bit worried he might need more practice, but no...he was ready for stage action now.

Still making sure, I asked, "You sure you're okay with playing live tomorrow?"

Excitement lit his eyes, which made me grin. I remembered the day before my first gig, how it'd felt as the eager anticipation thrummed through me. He was rocking some serious happy endorphins.

But he managed to keep it cool by nodding and merely saying, "Sure. Just tell me where."

"Ever heard of the Forbidden Nightclub? We play there pretty much every Friday, though I'm trying to get us booked at other places as well."

"Sure, I've heard of it. I've even been there once and sang on karaoke night. I saw on your website that you'd been there before, but I guess I didn't realize that's where you guys played regularly. Cool."

"Yep." I eyed him hard because I'd worked every karaoke night we'd ever had, and I didn't remember his face.

I was about to say something, but Gally snorted. "You sang karaoke? How lame is that? Wait...was it 'All About

That Bass'?"

Sticks pulled back in surprise, gaping at Gally. "Excuse me?"

Pissed off because he'd only asked Sticks that to dig at me, I spotted an old basketball sitting in the top of one of the packed boxes and grabbed it so I could heave it at him. "Shut it, fucker."

He laughed and ducked out the way so the ball merely bounced off his shoulder. Hooting even louder as he dodged most of my attack, he bent at the waist and slapped his knee.

Sticks darted a curious glance between the two of us while a silent Heath merely shook his head.

"Okay, there's some kind of inside joke in there, right?" Sticks asked.

I sighed. "It's nothing. Just ignore him."

"Can do. Easily."

He said it so cheerfully that Gally stopped laughing to pierce him with a scowl. "Hey, know your place, newbie."

"Oh? And where's that? Sitting over here, snickering at *you*?"

I grinned and tucked my guitar into its case as the two bickered back and forth. Ripping my shirt over my head, I traded it for the black Forbidden Nightclub shirt I had to wear to work that I'd tucked away in my case. I wadded up the old top and crammed it into a side pocket before slipping the case's strap over my neck so I could settle my guitar against my back. Meanwhile, Gally was trying to prove to Sticks that he was the better man by swearing he'd scored with more women than Sticks ever had.

"Come on," he challenged. "Just give me a rough estimate. How many bitches you ever fucked?"

I sighed, ready to take off and leave this quickly declining conversation when Heath finally decided to speak up, telling Gally, "You're wasting your time on him with that line of questioning."

"Oh?" Gally arched him a curious glance. "Why's that?"

"Because he obviously plays for the other team. Dude just checked out Hart's chest when he pulled off his shirt."

"Say what?" Gally shrieked as he physically leapt a foot away from Sticks.

I whirled to gape at the drummer, shocked to be shoved

into the conversation this way.

Sticks shrank lower into his stool, his eyes darting with fear like a cornered animal before he cried, "The hell if I did."

I lifted my eyebrows. He was acting way too guilty to be telling the truth. "Are you really gay?" I couldn't help but ask, "Because that would actually be great."

"Say what?" Gally repeated, spinning toward me as if I'd lost my mind.

"What?" I glanced between him and Heath, confused by their shock. "It would give us more diversity since we've been accused of being such a *cliché* lately."

And yes, that accusation from the girl *still* bothered me.

"Diversity?" Gally yelped "Shit, if we wanted diversity, we could've just hired that punk rocker chick who wanted to play with us."

I scowled at him for bringing her up.

"What chick?" Sticks asked, suddenly too curious for my comfort.

Ignoring him, I scowled at Gally. "*You're* the one who refused to even listen to her play."

"Like you wanted a girl in the band either." Gally glared back.

I gave a dismissive shrug. "Never know. She might've been good. But yeah, one of us—meaning *you*—probably would've nailed her, and she would've taken off within the week. Then we'd be back at square one, looking for another drummer."

Sticks opened his mouth to say something, but I lifted a hand to stop him. "Doesn't matter, anyway. We've got Sticks now." Smiling congenially at the new guy, I added, "Problem solved."

Sticks didn't seem so flattered, though. He lifted a censorious brow. "So...you didn't even let someone try out just because she was a girl?"

I heaved a sigh, and pointed meaningfully at Gally to pin the blame on him. "He didn't. Not me."

Gally scowled at Sticks. "Oh, shut up, queer. No one asked you."

I was about to snap at him for being so offensive, but Sticks frowned right back. "I never said I was gay."

Gally lifted his hands. "Well, do you prefer cock over pussy or not?"

Sticks winced. Then he ducked his chin and mumbled into his chest, "Yeah, I guess I do."

Hating how Gally was making the newest member to our group feel ashamed, I slapped the bass guitarist hard in the chest with the back of my hand and told the drummer, "Ignore him; the rest of us do. He never did find the wizard to grant him a brain."

As Sticks sent me a small, grateful smile, Gally frowned in confusion, mumbling, "Huh?"

"Never mind." I didn't have time to explain the *Wizard of Oz* to him. "I gotta go. See you guys tomorrow at Forbidden." When I glanced meaningfully Sticks's way to make sure Gally hadn't scared him off yet, he nodded, and relief bloomed in my chest.

The band was back.

Thank God.

CHAPTER 8
Asher Hart

I SLID INTO A PARKING spot with ten minutes to spare before we were set to open, but I was surprised to find as I hurried inside that I wasn't the last to arrive. Everyone but Mason milled about, doing assorted tasks.

It was Thursday, ladies' night, so aside from the doorman and cooks in the back, only us bartenders worked, waiting tables and tending the counter. Knox and Noel prepared things behind the bar, while Ten and Quinn took chairs off tables.

"About time you decided to show, rock star," Ten called to me.

"Oh, hey, Ten," I called back, snapping my fingers, then pointing at him. "Before I forget, could you let Caroline know she left one of her shirts at my place last week?" When Ten narrowed his eyes at me for bringing up his wife, I grinned. "It's that tight, white little number with all the red lips on it. You know the one I'm talking about, right?"

"Fucker, I'll cut you."

I laughed. No one was as fun to rile as Oren Tenning. So I had to mess with him pretty much every chance I got. He had a comeback for everything I said too, which only amused me more.

Right on cue, his scowl morphed into a grin. "Besides, I peeled that very shirt off her last *night*, so ha. I know you're lying."

Then he was off, whistling under his breath, to move a table that had shifted too far into a major walkway. Chuckling, I turned to the bar where Knox was behind the counter, replacing a CO_2 canister at the tap.

God, I loved working with these guys.

"Hey, man." I sent Knox a head bob greeting. "How's Felicity? She give up on you yet, so I can have a turn with her?"

Brown eyes lifted to sear me with a deadly glance. "I won't just cut you," he said in a voice that made me want to piss myself, because I knew he wasn't mere talk; this one backed his words up.

Yeah, Knox wasn't nearly as entertaining to tease. But I still liked him, regardless, because he was a good man to have on your side when you needed help.

I cleared my throat, sent him a tight smile, and quickly escaped to help Ten prepare the customer area.

As soon as I pulled a chair off the table, however, Harper admitted three people into the club. Only VIPs—aka, people close to us bartenders—were allowed inside before opening and after we closed—new rules—so I glanced over, curious to see who'd stopped by to visit. It had to be someone I liked, because I adored all my coworker's other halves. My friends had found the most awesome women to fall in love with.

The lucky fuckers.

The gorgeous brunette in the lead of the trio marched straight to the bar, her face wreathed in anger. The first boy directly behind her hung his head in shame, while the younger one behind him, gaped around him in starstruck wonder.

Aspen Gamble stopped in front of the counter opposite where her husband was counting out bills before he slotted them into the cash register.

"Your brother," she snarled, making Noel's head come up. "Is in so much trouble right now, I can't even deal with him."

Noel immediately scowled at the older boy as the kid slumped onto a stool and glumly set his elbows on the bar top and then his chin in his hands.

"Brandt," he growled. "What the hell did you do?"

Brandt opened his mouth to answer, but Aspen spoke over him. "He got into a fight. At school. The very school where I've been working only *four months*. It was so mortifying; I was called to the principal's office. Oh my God, Noel. I have never in my life been in trouble with a principal before."

"*You* weren't the one in trouble," Brandt argued. "I was."

"But I'm your legal guardian, which puts me in the same boat as you. I seriously cannot believe you. You broke that other boy's nose."

"Totally shattered it," Brandt agreed with smug pride before both Noel's and Aspen's frowns had him slumping back into his seat with shame.

"What'd he do to make you punch him?" Noel asked, still the puzzled outsider.

"Oh, that's the best part," Aspen railed, still glaring at her teenage brother-in-law. "He refuses to divulge that little piece of information, so I have no idea *why* he just walked up to some boy who was merely trying to get into his locker between classes and decked the hell out of him. I heard it even knocked him unconscious for a couple seconds. But all Brandt will say on the matter is..."

When she lifted her eyebrows Brandt's way, he sighed reluctantly and replied, "The cocklicker deserved it."

"He said that verbatim, too, straight to the principal," Aspen wailed.

I'd just settled on the barstool on the other side of Colton, the younger brother, who was staring at all the bottles of alcohol lining the back wall with wide eyes. But at Aspen's words, he glanced at me. "What does verbatim mean?"

"Means word-for-word," I murmured back.

He nodded while Noel sighed and scrubbed his face before sending Brandt a dry glance and repeating, "He *deserved* it?"

"Well, he did!" Brandt cried.

"So this is what Noel's bar looks like from the inside?" Colton asked me.

I didn't correct him that it was technically Pick's bar.

Since this was where his big brother worked, it'd probably always be Noel's in his mind. So, I said, "Yep. Pretty cool, huh?"

He shrugged. "It's okay." Then he slapped the top of the counter to catch Knox's attention. "Hey, bartender. I'd like a beer."

Knox blinked his way. "How old are you?"

"Eleven," Colton proudly reported.

"Yeah..." Knox shook his head slowly. "Cherry limeade is all you're getting from me."

As Colton heaved out a sigh and gave a reluctant groan, saying, "Fine," Brandt thundered, "Why can't you just trust me? It wasn't as if I attacked some poor, innocent, unsuspecting guy. I'm telling you, the douchebag cocklicker fucking *deserved* it."

While both Aspen and Noel railed at him to watch his language, Ten slugged him companionably on the back. "Hey, man, I totally believe you."

Noel sent him a scowl. "You're not a part of this conversation."

"Uh, *excuse* me? I'm just as much his brother-in-law as Shakespeare is," Ten argued, motioning to Aspen.

"Except *Aspen* and I have legal custody over him. You don't. Butt out."

"I just don't see why you're not cutting him any slack," Ten went on mildly. "Since he came to live with you, he hasn't gotten into one scrap. He's been a damn good kid."

"Thank you," Brandt told Ten as Knox set Colton's drink on the counter in front of him.

The eleven-year-old took a big drink and sighed out his satisfaction. "Thanks." Then he eyed Knox a second before tipping up his chin. "Hey, are you the one dating Felicity?"

Knox paused and cocked him a curious glance. "Yeah. Why?"

"You ask her to marry you yet?"

Eyebrows furrowing, Knox narrowed his eyes. "No."

"Well..." Colton puffed up his chest. "She's kind of the woman of my dreams, so..." He sighed as if refreshed by the thought of Felicity Bainbridge. "If she's not married by the time I'm sixteen, I'm making her mine. Just thought I'd warn you, you know, man to man."

"So...you're saying I've got five years to put a ring on it

or I'm going to find myself some healthy competition, huh?"

Colton merely shrugged, and Knox broke out grinning. "You're on, little man." He held out a fist and the two bumped knuckles.

On the other side of them, Brandt was still arguing his case. "Why does it really matter *why* I did it? His nose is still broken, and I'll still be suspended from school for a week. None of my motives will change any of that. Can't we just drop it?"

"I don't understand why you just won't tell us?" Noel growled.

As I watched Brandt clench his teeth in frustration, I decided he was protecting someone else.

Thirty seconds later, I learned *who* when Mason swept in late, two minutes before we were supposed to open.

When he spotted Brandt, he veered toward him, saying, "*You*...I need to talk to you. Sarah told Reese what you did today."

Brandt winced and slowly turned on his stool to face Sarah's brother. "She did? Shit."

Mason nodded. "Reese was over at my mom's when Sarah got home from school, clearly upset. It took some coaxing, but Reese finally pried out of her what had happened. And..." He heaved in a deep breath before holding out a hand for Brandt to shake. "Thank you."

As Brandt turned an embarrassed bright red, Noel waved his hands. "Thank you? What! Lowe, what the hell did he *do*?"

Mason needed another second before speaking, then announced, "Some little asswipe was bullying Sarah, messing with her wheelchair and calling her names. I guess she spent her lunch hour crying in the bathroom. When Brandt here heard about it, he taught the idiot some manners."

We all turned to gaze in amazement at Brandt, who only sank lower and lower onto his stool, looking totally mortified.

Aspen finally covered her face with both hands and groaned. "Oh my God, I am so sorry, Brandt, but..." Lowering her fingers, she scowled. "Why didn't you just *say* that from the beginning?"

The fifteen-year-old growled out a mutter. "Because she was embarrassed and didn't want any more attention brought on her." He scowled Mason's way. "I can't believe she caved and told Reese. I promised her I wouldn't drag her name into it, and that's all she wanted."

Mason only shrugged. "I think the guilt got to her. She didn't like you getting suspended because of her."

"Like I give a shit if they suspend me because of that. She didn't ask me to do anything about it. Hell, she didn't even know I'd found out about it. He deserved it, and I'll go after any cocksucker again who messes with one of my friends."

"You sure the fuck will," Noel raged in agreement. "That little shit-stain bully. I'm going in to talk to the principal tomorrow so he gets just as much if not more punishment than Brandt's getting."

"And I'm going with you," Aspen declared.

"Oh, I've already called him," Mason assured them with a tight, angry smile. "He's well aware that the kid wasn't innocent in any of this, and he assured me he'd do something about it."

"Jesus, you guys." Brandt groaned and clutched his head. "This is exactly what Sarah *doesn't* want. If you make a big deal out of it, a million people are suddenly going to take notice of her, feeling bad and pitying her, or worse, maybe even blaming her. She doesn't *want* that."

Having witnessed enough of their family drama, I slid off my stool and patted Colton on the back as he continued to sip on his cherry limeade, watching the show. Then I made a last round through the customer area before letting Harper know we could open.

Quinn had similar thoughts and was picking up a stray straw off the floor. He grinned at me as he nodded his head toward the bar. "It's never a dull night around here, is it?"

I chuckled. "Not with the drama we manage to stir up."

Motioning a finger toward Harper, I let him know we were good to let customers in. He nodded, and half a minute later, they started trickling through the entrance.

I took my first table full of orders of the night and brought them to Knox to be filled since Mason and the Gambles were still arguing amongst themselves over how to seek justice for their younger siblings. Ten gave up on trying to put in his two cents' worth and decided to help Quinn and me wait tables.

I'd just delivered a tray full and was pocketing the payment when my cell phone alerted me to an incoming text. I checked the screen, surprised to find it was from my new drummer.

I just realized I don't have an exact time or address of where to be tomorrow for the gig. I've only been to Forbidden once and I didn't drive so I'm not sure if I remember how to get there.

I zipped back the time and address and pocketed the phone, only for it to ding seconds later.

Gracias. Me and my two boys will see you then.

After I told him okay, all the while wondering who his two boys were, he spit back another message to me.

And by two boys, I meant my drumsticks, not the pair in my pants.

Before I could even think up a response to that, he messaged me again.

Not that the other two won't be there too, of course. But technically, you won't be seeing THOSE boys, so yeah...I'm only talking about the drumsticks.

I grinned, growing more amused by his rambling posts. I could almost picture him groaning to himself as if he knew he kept saying shit he didn't mean to even as he typed more. And on cue, he wrote.

So, yeah, I'm just going to shut up now before I dig myself any deeper into my humiliation. See you tomorrow.

I laughed outright and typed back that I'd see him then.

"Who're *you* flirting with?" Ten asked, making me jump out of my skin because I'd been so preoccupied with pushing *Send*.

Scowling at him, I shoved him back when he tried to read the screen over my shoulder. "None of your business, nosey ass." Then I tucked the phone into my pocket out of his sight.

He snickered and wiggled his eyebrows. "Just tell me she's hot."

I rolled my eyes. "What makes you think I was even talking to a girl?"

"Because you were grinning and laughing as you read the messages, like a little douche boy with a crush."

"What the hell ever." I shoved at his shoulder again, this time to shut him up. "I was not. It was the new drummer in my band. And *he* said something funny...so I laughed."

"Yeah..." Ten kept eyeing me as he scratched at the

scarred side of his face. "I'm not buying it. You were reading your screen far too long for it to be from another dude."

I stared at him in absolute confusion. "Huh?"

"It took you a while to read the screen," he explained. "Ergo it had to be from a chick. Two guys messaging back and forth to each other will keep it to five words or less per text...or they'll just call. So yeah...you were most definitely sexting."

"Whatever." I shook my head as I walked off. "You're weird. Stop being so weird."

"That's okay if you don't want to talk about her yet," he yelled after me. "I'll learn who she is soon enough."

"Freak," I muttered under my breath. But for some strange reason, what he said stuck in my head. Making sure he wasn't looking, I pulled my phone from my pocket and reread my conversation with Sticks.

Sure enough, everything I'd typed to him had been squeezed into five words or less. His shortest text to me had been ten words long.

"Huh," I murmured, frowning as I shoved the phone back into my pocket. Then I finished my shift and didn't think about the bizarreness of it again.

CHAPTER 9
Remy Curran

"¡Dios mío! I am such a moron." I tossed my cell phone onto the coffee table as if it was infected and swiped my hand across my forehead, utterly mortified.

I'm surprised Asher hadn't called me a freak and told me not to bother coming to the show tomorrow. What I'd just texted him had been beyond idiotic.

I'd started out, trying to be funny, but then it'd sounded like I was being too sophomoric. Yet when I tried to explain what I'd really meant, it'd all just gone downhill from there and splashed right into shit lake.

"Ugh." This was *his* fault, I decided. The guy was just too hot. After spending hours in his company, listening to him sing, I was still rocking too many raging hormones.

But Asher had shocked me today. In a good way. After my first encounter with the group, I'd had it stuck in my head that Galloway was their leader. That had concerned me. I mean, not enough that I didn't want to play with them tomorrow, but it'd still been a distressing, disturbing, depressing thought.

After this afternoon, however, it was apparent that Asher took care of things. He knew where the songs were kept, had paid the bill for the studio rental, he'd made all the suggestions on changing and fine-tuning songs here and there, and he'd been the one to remind us where we were supposed to meet for our next gig. Him, I might be able to get behind as a leader...especially since he had such a nice behind. But Gally? Hell to the no. I would never stick with a band longer than one gig if he led it.

Remembering Asher's reminder about our gig, I'd realized I hadn't gotten an exact time. And thus had begun the ten-minute debate with myself whether I should call or text him...and it *had* to be him I contacted; he'd been the only band member who'd bothered to exchange numbers with me. So, I'd ended up going with a text, since calling would be disastrous; I knew too well what hearing his voice did to me.

And yet I still managed to flub even texting up. I was once again groaning through my embarrassment when the front door blew open and Jodi breezed inside, toting a small bag and a big smile.

"Hey, puta. Damn, do I have some goodies for you!" Then she pulled to a stop as she got a look at me. "You're still in your mask."

"Huh?" I blinked at her before I realized... "Oh, shit. I am. I just got home from band practice." As I slowly peeled my "Sticks" mask off over my head, I grinned, giddy from actually being able to say I'd been to a practice...*with my new rock band*! "You know, I actually dig this whole gay idea." I had already texted her that the guys had caught me scoping out Asher's bare chest and about the whole gay conversation that had followed. "Now I can check out a guy," meaning Asher, since I was sure I wouldn't notice other men while he was around, "and no one will think it's weird. Shit, why didn't I come up with this idea before even auditioning with them? It's brilliant."

Then I scratched at a place right on the inside of my upper thigh where my man panties I hadn't taken off yet were chaffing.

Jodi squinted at me scratching myself. "Sweetie, you do remember you're a *girl*, right?"

I jerked my hand from my crotch. "Yes. *Hush.* Besides, the man panties *you* made me were itching like crazy."

She sighed. "I'll forget you just bashed my clever invention, because I'm still too jazzed about all the awesome shit I just did for you."

"Why? What'd you do?"

Sniffing airily, she fluttered out a hand in a girly, dramatic fashion. "Well... despite the fact I don't approve of this idea and I think you're crazy for actually going out like this in public tomorrow, I decided to show my support for you, anyway. And I bought you a couple things you'll need."

Sitting up straighter, I clapped happily. "Really?" Ooh, *gifts*! I loved gifts. "I knew there was a reason I adored you. What'd you get me?"

"For starters, there's this..." She pulled a small chunk of plastic that looked like a credit card from the bag and waved it with a flourish before stopping to display it for me. "A fake ID!"

Blinking, I slowly slid it from her hand. "Oh, wow. You shouldn't have. This is so awesome, Jodi."

The last time I'd tried to get a fake ID, I was seventeen and my uncle had discovered it before I could even try to go to a bar with it. Surprisingly it was still naughtily thrilling to have one, even at twenty-three.

Jodi had taken a couple pictures of me after dressing me up the first time, but I figured it was for school credit or something...not this. I snickered at my manly mug set alongside my real name and weight and height. Actually, the only thing that wasn't true, was the picture...and honestly, that was me too, just...an altered version. Even the gender was marked the same.

"Wait, this says I'm a female."

Scowling, Jodi ripped it from my hand and carefully tucked it into a brand new wallet. "As if anyone's going to check for an F or an M. Gah." She handed the wallet back, which must be another present from her. "You probably won't even get carded."

"True," I murmured, standing up to test out what it felt like to stash a wallet in my back pocket. My butt cheek flinched in surprise as the billfold slid past it and into place. Interesting. Not painful, or ticklish, or anything; just different.

"And....I saved the best for last." Jodi tossed a flesh-colored chunk of silicone at me.

I caught it against my chest before pulling it away and

turning it at all angles, studying it. It looked like some kind of funky-shaped funnel.

"Uh...thank you. But..." I squinted at her. "What the hell is it?"

"It's a Go Girl."

"I'm sorry, a *what* girl?"

Sighing, she rolled her eyes and strode over to yank it out of my hand. "A female urination device. You know, so you can pee standing up." Demonstrating, she held it up to her crotch so it poked out like a strap-on. Then she made a hissing sound and swiveled her hips as if she were pissing all over the floor.

I would've laughed—because it was freaking hilarious—but I had a bad feeling she actually meant for me to *use* this thing.

"Umm..." I scratched the side of my hair where the wig had left me all itchy. "You're not joking right now, are you?"

She stopped fake peeing and straightened, lowering the *urination device* from her privates. "What? I was just thinking...you're going to be hanging out in a public club all evening and eventually you're going to have to go." She shrugged. "Since you'll be in man drag, I just assumed you'd have to use the little boys' instead of the little girls' room. This way, you won't look so suspicious if you're caught sitting down to take a leak. And look..." She held it up proudly. "I even got you the khaki-colored one so it could look more penis-like."

"¡Dios mío!" I covered my eyes with my hand. "Please don't tell me they come in *different colors*?"

"My favorite was the lavender, but I figured it wouldn't help your cause any to go that route."

"¡Locos!" I shook my head, unable to believe she could act so serious right now.

"Check it." She bent the funnel into a different shape. "The reviews said this was the best brand since it's more flexible for storage."

"And...they're so popular they come in different brands," I murmured in disbelief. *Of course*, they did. "How the hell have I never heard of a Go Girl before?"

"Beats me." She shrugged. "Maybe it's because you're not big into hiking or camping."

Or maybe it was because I squatted and hovered and

hoped to God whatever was tickling my bare fanny wasn't a snake or poisonous leaf whenever I peed in the woods. Like a normal girl.

Jodi appeared to be hurt by my reaction to her gift. I hated hurting her feelings, and besides, it'd been really sweet and considerate to think of me, so I took it gingerly from her hands and said, "Gracias," with all the sincerity I could manage.

I had no idea where she thought I was supposed to stash the thing whenever I wasn't using it. Tape it to my thigh or something? I already had a faux penis in my man panties. How many fake cocks did one pretend dude need?

My roommate did pose a good question, though. How the hell was I supposed to use the public restrooms when I was out and about with the band? All I could hope for was a pooping stall in the men's room at Forbidden.

Twenty-four hours later, it was time to find out. Once again, decked out as "Sticks," I left the Go Girl at home and drove to the address Asher had texted me. It'd been months—back in early summer, or maybe late spring—when I'd last been here. But it looked familiar, so I parked and hiked across the street to the entrance.

The sign said they didn't open for half an hour and the open light wasn't lit up, but a doorman was already hanging out just inside the front doors, so I tapped on the glass to get his attention.

He turned to frown at me, so I motioned for him to open up. When I refused to give up on hand signaling, he finally cracked the door and stuck his head out.

"We're not open yet."

"Yeah, I know, sorry to bother you, but...I'm in the band." When he just stared at me as if he had no clue what I was saying, I carefully added, "You know...Non-Castrato. They're supposed to play tonight, and...I'm in the band." God, it felt awesome saying that. "I need to get in and set up my drum set before we play."

"ID?" He held out his hand with a bored glance.

"Uh...okay." Reminding myself I owed Jodi big time for the fake driver's license and wallet, I fumbled in my back pocket and finally yanked the crisp, new billfold free. When I showed it to him, I bit my lip, hoping he didn't notice the big, glaring F in the gender box.

He barely glanced at the piece of plastic before flipping it back to me and studying a clipboard in his hand. "You're not on the list."

For a brief moment, my heart seized. The band had already rejected me, and my big chance to perform before an audience was over before it had even started. I opened my mouth, but it took a second for words to come. "Oh...yeah. I'm new. Just joined this week."

Dude didn't seem to care. And all he seemed to know how to say was, "You're not on the list."

Anger, fear, and worry slithered through me. I decided to let the anger take front and center. I'd come this far; I refused to give up now. "Look. I need in there so I can prepare for our show that we're getting paid to provide *your* customers." Wait, *were* we getting paid? I hadn't even asked, and honestly it'd been the last thought on my mind. Didn't matter. The point was, "I have to get to the stage and—"

"You're not—"

"On the list!" I boomed. "Yes, so you've said. Repeatedly. But I swear to you, I'm not pulling your leg. Can't you just grab one of the other band members to come out here and vouch for me?"

"Are you going to be a problem?"

I gritted my teeth. "Not if you let me in already."

When he left the doorway and took a menacing step outside toward me, I gulped and backed away from him, suddenly remembering he saw another guy when he looked at me. He probably had no qualms about getting physical and roughing me up.

Oh hell, I didn't want to get the shit kicked out of me the first week I was a dude.

The door behind him re-opened. "Everything okay out here, Grim?"

I peered around the hulking figure in front of me to see another gigantic guy in the doorway, except this one was drop-dead gorgeous and didn't seem nearly as menacing as

Grim—Dios, what a good name for him.

"I'm with the band," I rushed to tell the hottie before the asshole in front of me could send him away. "I need in so I can help set up before we open tonight."

"Oh, are you the new drummer?"

"Yes!" I sent him a thank-you gesture before glaring at Grim for still blocking my path.

"Hang on a second. I'll get Asher."

He disappeared, the door reclosing behind him so I was once again left with the moody doorman who'd crossed his arms over his chest and continued to stand guard in front of the club's entrance.

"He's going to get Asher," I couldn't help but taunt with a smug little smile.

Grim grunted in reply.

Seconds later, Asher popped his head out. When he saw me, surprise lit his face. "Oh, hey. You're early. Come on in." When he opened the door wider, the guy still looming in my path refused to budge, so Asher said, "Grim, man. It's cool. He's with the band. Sorry, I thought I'd put him on the list."

"There's no Remy Curran on the list," Grim told him.

"Remy...?" Asher blinked, confused, before his eyes lit with understanding. "Oh, right. Yeah." He motioned to me. "I never got your real name, so I just put you down as Sticks." Then he nudged Grim aside. "Could you be so kind as to write Remy Curran next to the name Sticks? He can come in."

Grim didn't look too happy about it, but he nodded and reluctantly stepped aside.

Asher waved me forward, and I was finally admitted into Forbidden. I was so tempted to stick my tongue out and send good ol' Grim a raspberry, but I refrained, because raspberries probably weren't very manly...or mature.

"Sorry about that," Asher told me as he led me toward the stage. "Grim's ex-military. He doesn't stray from the rules. Ever. If Harper had been working the door tonight, he wouldn't have given you such a hard time. Still...you surprised me. None of the other band members show up until after we open."

That made me frown. "What about setting everything up?"

"Oh. I usually take care of that."

I blinked. "Every week? By yourself?"

"Yep." He shrugged as if it were no big deal while he bounded up onto the stage. "But since you're here, I'll let you take care of the drum set."

"Sure." Hopping up behind him, I had to pause to glance around in awe, trying to imagine what the place would look like in an hour. I'd been up here once before, singing karaoke, but this felt totally different. Excitement thrummed through me.

I was going to play here...tonight! On the drums.

"So, your real name's Remy?"

I jumped at the question and glanced Asher's way where he was kneeling next to an amp and plugging in guitar cords. When my gaze connected with his curious green one, a tickle in my stomach made all my girly parts tweak to life. "Um...yeah."

Wow, look at me, with my awesome extensive vocabulary around the pretty boy. If I didn't check myself soon, I'd be drooling on him next.

He grinned, and sure enough, I had to swallow some drool. "But you'd rather go by Sticks?"

I shrugged. "Whatever." Telling myself to say more words, I lamely added, "Either works."

His chuckle made my hormones whimper. I tried to ignore him and prepare my area, but everything already appeared to be pretty much in order. All I had to do was lower my stool and hi-hat, move the pedals a tad bit closer, readjust the snare-drum and shift the toms an inch. So I found myself hovering around Asher, asking him if he needed me to do anything else, while around us, down on the ground floor, other bar workers milled about, preparing the club for opening.

"Umm..." He bit his bottom lip as he glanced around the stage. "Actually, I think we're good to go. I'm usually the only one who comes in to prepare so I get here pretty early, but if you want to make a habit of it, I can show you the storage closet where we keep everything and how the sound system works."

I tried not to watch how his lip popped free of his teeth, but it was so freaking sexy, I had to clear my throat before saying, "Sure. That'd be cool."

I had to move closer to him to better see all the features

he pointed out, and man, the guy even smelled amazing. Not fair.

Inhaling deeply, I went lightheaded from the amount of times I breathed him in. Then he sneezed, and por Dios, even that was adorably sexy.

When Asher paused in his demonstration and I said, "This is a pretty sweet setup," my voice went higher than usual, making it sound extra feminine.

I usually had a slightly hoarse, raspier sound to my vocal chords and people over the phone had often confused me for a guy. But right then, I didn't sound like one at all. Snapping a worried glanced to my right, I was relieved when Asher didn't seem to notice.

He grinned proudly and said, "Thanks."

I was too busy stewing over my worries; it took me a moment to realize what he was saying. Finally, I shook my head. "Wait. You just said thanks as if *you* set this up?"

When he nodded, still grinning out his pride, I returned my attention to the panel of knobs and buttons with new awe. "Impressive. And here, I thought it belonged to the club."

"Oh, it does." I glanced at him, frowning my confusion, so he explained. "When Pick—the club's owner—hired me on, he let me have free reign to install any kind of stage and sound system I wanted. So...I did."

I shook my head, even more lost. "You...work here?" Did that mean I worked here too? Shit, was I going to have to turn in legal forms, like social security numbers and such?

It was one thing to fib for one night to get to play drums, but lying to the government—yeesh. What had I gotten myself into?

"Yeah, it's a bit of a long story. I came in one day, trying to beg a night for us to play, but he only needed a bartender. So...we made a deal. I work bar on the nights we don't play, and he pretty much let me build up anything to do with music in this place that I wanted. He gives me two hundred for Fridays, which...I split up between us four members and pay you guys out with cash." He paused to send me an apologetic wince. "Sorry, fifty bucks isn't much, but..."

"Hey, it's more than I ever got for playing before," I said, relieved I was getting cash and thrilled I was getting *any* money.

Asher laughed. "Yeah, that was kind of my mindset

when we began too." Clapping me on the back of my shoulder and scaring the crap out of me when he slightly jostled my foam chest out of place, he grinned big. "I think you're going to fit in just fine, Sticks."

I momentarily forgot that I needed to readjust my fake chest back into place. But really, when Asher Hart smiled at me with such approval, life was freaking perfect.

This was going to be a night I'd never forget.

CHAPTER 10
Remy Cusson

"Good evening, Ellamore. Welcome to Forbidden!"

Asher's greeting into the microphone had a ton of screaming fans—mostly women—rushing the stage, arms waving wildly. I grinned from my safe little stool behind the drum set as Asher had to skip another two steps in reverse to keep grabby girl hands from reaching him.

His nervous laugh echoed through the speaker system right before he said, "It's nice to see all you ladies too, but let's get to some music, shall we?"

The women began to chant something that sounded like "If I Knew," which wasn't the title of any song Non-Castrato played. I frowned in confusion, wondering what the heck they were talking about.

Asher glanced back at us, mouthing "'Counting Stars,'" and then he went and lifted his eyebrows my way, giving me a thumbs-up sign.

I wasn't nervous, didn't usually have a problem in front of crowds. And with my mask on, there wasn't even a twitch of performance anxiety. I guess my subconscious knew that if I flubbed anything up, it'd be fine because no one knew it was really me. But the second Asher sent me that little thumbs-up of approval and support, silently letting me know I'd do fine, a little hitch in my heartbeat sent everything inside me haywire.

So I blamed him completely when I dropped a freaking drumstick.

It clanged against the hollow floor of the stage with a resounding echo that caused all my bandmates to look my way...as well as about half the crowd watching us.

Scrambling to retrieve my fallen stick, I straightened so fast blood rushed to my head and made me instantly dizzy. But I sent out a rueful grin and waved both sticks above me to let everyone know I was good. Everything was just fine back here. No reason at all to gape at me like I was an idiot.

Asher turned back to the microphone. "Guess that was my cue to introduce the newest member of our band. Everyone, please give Sticks, the best damn drummer you'll ever hear, a little bit of encouragement, will you?" Cupping his hand to his mouth, he added more quietly, "This is his first time, so go gentle on him, please."

Some people laughed, more cheered, but boy, did the room encourage me. All lit up inside, I waved my sticks above my head in greeting, then clicked them four times together to set the beat of the song, and boom...we were playing a cover for one of my favorite OneRepublic songs. Live. In front of people. It took a whole verse before I actually got to play, but when my intro came, I nailed it.

It was...

Awesome.

My dream was coming true. I couldn't stop grinning, couldn't stop feeling the rush, couldn't stop playing. Once the song ended, I just kept going, moving straight into the song, "Ceilings."

Asher glanced back at me in surprise. Then he rolled his eyes, as if to say he should've known, and grinned before turning back for his first line. His voice hit me hard, and seemed to vibrate through my bones, echoing along my spine and shivering out the ends my toes.

It was pure nirvana. My heaven.

I didn't even realize how many songs or how much time had passed until Asher said we were going to take a quick break. That's when it suddenly hit me how soaked I was inside my clothes and mask from the sweat that came because of all the heat pouring down from the overhead lights. Then I stood, and my legs and back gave a scream of protest due to sitting for so long.

Working my shoulders and kicking out my legs a time or two, I followed the other three, jumping off the side of the stage and into the crowd. There was no "backstage" so we were instantly swamped, most everyone gathering around Asher to get their hands on him.

A man in a black Forbidden shirt appeared—the same hottie who'd rescued me from Grim, the dick doorman, and fetched Asher to let me in. He helped free Asher from the clingers and then paved a path for us to get to the back hall, where he and Asher led us to a back room with a couch, some lockers, and a small kitchenette.

"Thanks, Quinn," Asher told the gorgeous giant as he swiped the back of his forearm over the sweat glistening on his brow. "You're a life saver."

Quinn's smile was adorable: sexy, shy and sweet all rolled into one. "No problem. I better get back to the bar, though. You really drew a crowd tonight."

As Asher waved him off, Quinn began to retreat, only to feel my eyes on him or something, because he glanced my way.

He sent me a small wave of acknowledgement and said, "Good job. You guys sounded great."

As he disappeared out the door, I stared after the spot he'd been and tried not to sigh. I liked Quinn. There was just something in his aura that made me feel...nice. And safe. Plus he was just so easy to stare at.

That's when Galloway slapped me in the arm. "Dude, did you catch the redhead who flashed us her tits? The one in the tight, yellow top with cleavage down to her belly button. She was screaming your name."

I blinked at him, clueless. "Huh?"

He rolled his eyes. "Oh, yeah, that's right. You don't do chicks. What a waste." He turned to Holden, who was wiping at the pit stains on his shirt, directly under his arms. "Holden, you saw her, didn't you? I am so fucking that bitch tonight."

I groaned in disapproval and sought Asher with my gaze. Not sure why, I just always found myself looking at him when he was around. He wasn't big and classically pretty like his co-bartender Quinn, but checking out his lean frame and deeply angled face caused the same stir in me. Except I didn't feel at all safe when my eyes were on him. I felt...I don't know...challenged, a little breathless, exhilarated, as if I were standing on the edge of a cliff and could already feel the rush burn through my blood before I even jumped.

Ignoring all of us, he leaned down to open a miniature refrigerator and pull out a bottle of water. My gaze lingered on his ass. He didn't wear his pants tight, like a lot of rockers these days—ahem, Galloway—but the material sure stretched nice and snug over his perfect ass as he bent over. Then he straightened all too soon and was turning back to us before I could cut my ogling party short.

He caught me in the act, but instead of scowling for checking him out, he lifted his bottle. "Need one?"

I shook my head, even though my mouth was as dry as sawdust. "Actually, I need to find the john." Which I was dreading. I so did not look forward to entering the men's room in this place. Why, oh why, had I laughed at Jodi's Go Girl and purposely not brought it?

"You can use the private one for workers." He motioned to a nearby doorway, and I nearly wept in relief.

"Gracias." Thank you, thank you, *thank you*.

I hurried into the small room, glad to have it all to myself, and sped through my potty break. All the sweat that had gathered inside my mask was bugging the hell out of me, but I didn't give into temptation and take if off for a quick dry-down. I had a bad feeling I'd probably pull it back on all wrong.

Once I washed my hands and returned to the rest of the group, Galloway was still jabbering about all the different women he felt he could score with before the night was over while Holden quietly listened to him. Asher sat sprawled on the sofa with his head back against the cushions, his eyes closed, and his fingers and toes tapping to a beat only he could hear. His lips moved as he silently sang to himself.

When I shut the door behind me, his lashes came open and green eyes assessed me. "How're you holding up? Your playing's been great."

"Gracias." I shrugged and settled into a side chair. "And I'm good. Definitely feeling the vibe and ready to get back out there."

The excitement seeped from my voice, causing him to

grin like an experienced professional smiling indulgently at a greenhorn and possibly remembering his first time out.

"Well, take my word for it; get all the rest you can now. We're only halfway through."

We were already halfway through? No! We couldn't be that close to being done. I had so much energy still left in me. I wanted to do this for days. And I was so done with this break that seemed to last for days.

Asher went back to his quiet meditation, or whatever he was doing, while Gally just kept talking about his dick and whom he thought he could shove it into before the night was over. Disgusting. Next to him, Holden listened silently to his bragging. I shifted impatiently in my chair, unable to sit still.

Finally, Asher said, with his eyes still closed. "Okay, Sticks. We'll head back out now."

Wondering why he was addressing me and no one else, I glanced his way, frowning. "Huh?"

He unfolded himself from the couch, standing in a sexy way only a hot guy could manage, and sent me a grin. "I swear your eagerness is louder than Gally's chirping."

Galloway stopped talking to glance our way. "What'd you call me?"

"Nothing." Asher spun his finger in a circle over his head. "Let's roll out."

The second half of our performance seemed to go even faster than the first. And at about a quarter until one in the morning, when Asher wished everyone a good night, I was still too psyched to calm down.

I loved this.

I'd always craved the opportunity, watched other bands on stage and wished I could do that someday, but I still had no idea, *no clue* it'd give me this kind of rush. Plus, the fans really loved us, which was...wow.

And damn, it made me love all of them right back.

As soon as we alighted from the stage, they swarmed in, most of them centering around Asher, but some swooped down on Galloway and Holden too. I screamed out a surprised yelp when a pair of arms wrapped around me and squeezed hard.

"Oh, my God, *Remy!*" Jodi shrieked in my ear. "I can't believe you actually did it! You were so great."

"Gracias." I laughed, and we hugged again. When I

pulled away, I saw she was wearing a skintight yellow shirt with swooping cleavage.

Dios, I should've known she was the flasher Galloway had been talking about.

"Oh, shit. *You're* the one who flashed me? I can't believe you flashed me. Really? That's like buying a pack of bottle rockets at a used firework stand. You know you're not getting a boom-boom out of me."

Jodi laughed. "I know, but I couldn't help it. I got caught up in the heat of the moment."

"Don't worry about it, sweetheart." Galloway butted his way between the two of us to throw an arm around Jodi's shoulder and grin down at her. "Us *hetero* members of the band sure as hell appreciated the show. Nice tits, by the way."

Jodi lifted her finely trimmed eyebrows. "Why, thank you."

"You bet." He gave her a slow grin. "The name's Billy. Billy Galloway."

When Jodi lifted her hand to shake with him, I pushed her fingers down. "No." Glaring at Galloway, I growled, "She doesn't want to meet you."

"Yes, I do," Jodi said.

I ignored her and continued to glare at the bassist. "Jodi is my *friend*. You stay away. Got it?"

"*Whaaat?*" Gally's innocent smile wouldn't have fooled a six-month-old. "I was just introducing myself to your friend."

"And guessing her bra size," I muttered.

"36 DD," he rattled off, and Jodi's mouth fell open.

"Wow, he's good."

"I know, right?" Gally preened and asked, "Want me to show you *how* good?" just as Asher joined us.

"Hey, Sticks. Good job tonight."

Forgetting Gally, Jodi gaped at him, her eyes bulging as she slugged me on the arm.

"Holy...shit," she whispered. "Asher Hart is standing *right there*."

"Oh, my God," I whispered back. "You see him too?"

Asher chuckled. "Hey," he said, holding out his hand to Jodi. "You must be Remy's friend."

Jodi whimpered as she shook with him. When she continued to stare and pump his hand up and down without saying anything, I rolled my eyes.

"This is Jodi," I said. "She's my friend who...typically has better communication skills than I do."

"Quiero sentarme en tu cara," Jodi blurted.

Though Asher blinked in confusion, obviously not understanding, I screeched, "*Jodi!*" Unable to believe she'd just asked to sit on his face, or that she actually remembered how to pronounce the phrase right, I gaped at her in horror.

"What?" she asked me innocently. "He can tell me no if he's not interested."

With another laugh, Asher managed to extract his fingers from hers. "Your buddy here saved our ass tonight," he said, obviously having no clue what Jodi had just requested. "I don't know what we would've done if we hadn't found Sticks to join the band. He has some wicked talent."

"Oh, I *know*!" Jodi looped her arm through mine and pulled me close with a proud smile. "Remy's played drums since we were running around in diapers together. She's amazing."

I stopped breathing as Asher blinked. When I pinched her where no one would see, Jodi jumped and let out a squeak of alarm, her eyes going wide. "I mean, he. *He's* amazing."

"Damn, girl." I pulled away to send her a censorious glare. "How much have you had *to drink* tonight?"

Jodi gave a nervous laugh, her eyes glassy with panic. "Too much." She turned back to Asher and gulped. "Obviously."

Asher grinned at her but just as quickly turned to me. "Hey, whenever you have a second, I want to introduce you to the guys I work with."

He was looking right at me, so I guess he was talking to me. I bit back a wince, a little wary of meeting too many more people in this mask. It was a great guise, but I didn't much care for the nip of guilt that came with deceiving more people.

But Asher was still looking at me, and his green eyes were so captivating. Damn gorgeous green eyes.

I ended up nodding and saying, "Sure. Okay. Whenever." So he started to lead me toward the bar, and I guess *whenever* was right then. Mierda.

CHAPTER 11
Remy Curran

I DON'T KNOW HOW MANY times we were stopped by fans, wanting to hug Asher, kiss him, or just touch his shirt. Some were too reluctant to actually make contact but still hovered, crowding as close as they dared and making our trek to the bar seem like the Boston Marathon.

Mostly he was vague and distant with everyone, smiling with them and then setting them an arm's length away once he let them have a hug.

We were only about five feet from our destination when a pretty little blonde squirmed her way through the people to reach him, screeching, "Asher!"

He broke into the biggest grin and swept his up into her arms, kissing the side of her head.

I have no clue why that bothered me. I barely knew this guy, and feeling all possessive of someone just because I thought he was hot totally wasn't my style. Hell, I hadn't even blinked an eyelash when female fans had frenched Fisher right in front of me...when I'd been engaged to him. Yet the urge to pull blondie off Asher by way of all that pretty pale hair hit me hard.

Maybe because he looked so happy when he gazed at her. I liked it better when he smiled at shit *I* said. "Hey, beautiful," he called over the noise into her ear. "Thanks for coming tonight."

I was mentally trying to nitpick his girlfriend's looks apart, but dammit, not finding a single flaw about her, when he turned her my way.

Oh, joy, I realized. I was going to get introduced to the perfect specimen.

"Sticks, this is Caroline."

I lifted an eyebrow as I glanced at him. "The reason we played 'Sweet Caroline' tonight? Twice."

He grinned back. "The very."

Turning to her, I opened my mouth to lie and tell her how *nice* it was to meet her when someone shouted our way. "Okay, fucker. Enough kissy, huggy time. Hands off. Now!"

I glanced over to catch sight of a guy behind the bar giving Asher the finger.

Curious why he was so irate, I asked, "Who's that?"

Asher's grin grew as Caroline slipped away from him. "Caroline's husband."

My eyebrows spiked in surprise, and yes, a little ball of relief welled in my gut. After I watched Caroline skip up to the bar to kiss the man still flipping off Asher, I frowned Asher's way. "So you were flirting with her because...?"

He chuckled. "Because it's fun as shit to fuck with Ten. Seriously, you should try it."

He nudged me forward until I was standing where Caroline had been, because she'd already flitted away to talk to a brunette and a redhead about twenty feet down the counter.

"So that's your wife, huh?" I asked, taking in the guy Asher had called Ten. When I met his gaze, I was surprised to see half his face was scarred. Ouch.

Glancing longingly after Caroline, he nodded. "I know, right? I'm a lucky-ass bastard."

I let out a low whistle. "I'll say, because holy shit...she's got a sweet ass. I bet every man in this joint would give his left nut to tap that."

Ten's smile died flat. "What did you say, motherfucker?"

With a snicker, I nudged Asher in the arm. "You're right. That *was* fun."

He choked on the water he'd been chugging from a bottle and ended up spitting some out onto the countertop.

When he started laughing, Ten pointed at me and demanded of him, "Who the fuck is this douchebag?"

"Ten, meet Sticks. Newest member of the band. He's our drummer."

"Looks like a dead drummer to me."

"Oh, leave him be," Asher told him mildly enough as he grabbed a napkin and wiped away his mess. "I told him to mess with you."

But Ten was already climbing over the bar toward me, looking determined to maim.

Holy shit. I lurched in reverse, my eyes bugging with worry. But damn, one night in public, and two guys had already threatened to beat my ass.

Were men always this punchy?

Asher held up a hand and stepped between us. "Relax," he ordered, his voice harsh. "Sticks is gay. He won't seriously mess with Caroline."

Ten jerked to a stop and sent Asher an incredulous glance before he turned back to me and narrowed his gaze into a suspicious scowl. "He didn't sound very gay with the shit he was spouting about her."

I held up both my hands. "I am. Trust me. I think you're hotter than your wife is. Swear to God." And just because it really had been fun to rile him, I stared after his wife and shrugged. "I mean, sure, she's got a nice rack and all." *The perfect shape and size to drive a girl like me absolutely jealous.* "But I'd rather see what you're packing behind that zipper of yours."

I turned back to send a meaningful leer to the front of his pants and noticed, huh, dude was sporting a nice-sized bulge. Maybe Jodi had been onto something when she'd made my man panties.

Ready for Ten to go all homophobe on me and tell me to back up off him, I was surprised when he merely grinned. "Hell, yes, you'd like to know." He pointed to his fly. "This is a one-of-a-kind, grade-A awesome cock, right here."

"Oh, Jesus," Asher muttered.

Ten lifted an eyebrow and challenged him with a look. "What? Caroline can't keep her hands off it. Or her mouth. Her pussy loves it too." Then he finally narrowed his attention back on me. "And you...don't even get near it, gay boy."

Finally getting the response I'd been seeking, I grinned and winked at him.

He frowned even harder. But a split second later, a new grin broke across his face. Nudging my arm, he coaxed, "You think I'm hotter than Hart, don't you? Come on, you can admit it."

"Ehh..." Not that I wanted Asher to know just how attracted to him I was, but I kind of gave myself away with the incredulous look I sent Ten. So, since I'd already screwed myself, I just went with it and mildly answered, "I wouldn't go that far."

It wasn't my intention to make Asher uncomfortable, but I just couldn't lie about this. Too afraid to glance his way and check his expression, I focused my scowl on Ten for putting me in this position.

"Oh, whatever. I have a way better ass than he does." He turned to let me see his backside.

I looked. I mean, how could I not? A hot guy was purposely showing me his tush bundled up in a pair of jeans, and yeah, he definitely had it going on back there. But even with the nice curvature Ten provided, there was just something about Asher's cute, tight little buns of steel, framed within his narrow hips, that appealed to me more.

So I said, "No. You really don't."

Ten scowled. "Oh, whatever. You suck."

Next to me, Asher roared with laughter. It was one of those open-bodied laughs where a guy had to tip his head back to let all the sound out. Beyond relieved that he wasn't bothered by the things I'd just said about him, I grinned his way.

He smiled back and tapped me on the arm. "Come on. I'll introduce you to the rest of the guys. Don't worry, they aren't quite so...Ten."

"Which means they're lame," Ten called as he hopped back behind the bar and turned to a customer waiting for service.

Asher and I weaved our way to the other end of the bar where a group of couples were gathered, Caroline—who I hated a lot less now that I knew she wasn't Asher's girlfriend—included.

"Guys." He waved his hand, gaining the attention of about half a dozen people. "This is Sticks, the new drummer. I thought I'd introduce all new band members to you from now on, in case he turned out to be related to anyone."

I glanced at him for that odd comment, but it made the others laugh.

And the finger-pointing began. "That's Mason and Reese. Mason also works here, but it's his night off. Same thing with Knox right there. And that lovely thing at his side is Felicity, who is a waitress here. Caroline, you've already met. We're missing three more of the ladies, Eva, Zoey, and Aspen, because they opted to stay home with kiddos this evening. But I think Pick is around somewhere..."

He glanced toward the opening of the back hall before a voice spoke from our left, saying, "Right here."

Asher and I both whirled that way, and I found a hot man smiling at me with a pierced lip and eyebrow ring.

"Sticks, this is Pick, my..." Asher fumbled a second and grabbed at a piece of his hair as if suddenly uncomfortable. But then he finished, "The, uh, the owner of Forbidden."

A brief flash of disappointment flickered across Pick's face before he forced his smile to return.

I held my hand out to him, saying, "Nice to meet you. Awesome place you've got here."

I'm not sure why I shook with him and none of the others, maybe because he was Asher's boss, maybe because he seemed to give me more attention than the others had, or something in the way Asher reacted to him, but it felt as if he needed more...I don't know, notice? Respect?

Something stiff and uncomfortable emanated from Asher as Pick thanked me and told me I'd done well on stage. Then Asher was tapping on my arm to pull my attention from his boss. "And this guy is Noel. The other bartender working over there is Quinn, who you sort of met earlier."

Torn from Pick, I nodded at Noel, who nodded right back. Quinn was at the very other end of the bar in front of a blender making what looked like, oh God...a piña colada. I would die for one of those right about now. Then Quinn went and put a little umbrella in it, along with a pineapple wedge and cherry, and I nearly whimpered.

Piña coladas were my vice.

I was about to go all Jimmy Buffett and start singing about making love at midnight and getting caught in the rain, when Asher told Noel, "Hey, man. Get me an Angry Orchard, will you?" And I suddenly remembered, crap, if I was going to drink anything, it couldn't be a girly mixed drink like piña coladas.

Could it?

No, probably not.

"We're out," Noel called back as he filled a pitcher with Miller Lite at the tap.

Asher scowled. "Are we *really* out, or are you just messing with me?"

"There's none behind the counter. If you want to go back to the stockroom and see if you can dig up a fresh case of warm ones, be my guest."

"Sure, I can do that." Asher turned his gaze my way. "Hey, Remy. You want one?"

I'd never tried the brand before, and I wasn't a fan of malt liquor, but I couldn't go drinking a piña colada, and no way could I say no to him for some odd reason, so I shrugged. "Sure."

"Remy?" Ten repeated with a frown as Asher strolled off. I jumped, surprised he'd appeared out of nowhere on the other side of the counter. Whirling to him, I dragged my stare from Asher's perfect ass and into Ten's hazel eyes. "Hmm? Sorry, what?"

He frowned at me, turned his attention to a departing Asher, and then came back to me. "He just called you Remy."

"Yeah..." I said slowly. "Probably because that's my name."

Just as I said that, Jodi reached my side and slung her arm over my shoulder. "Hey, puta. What'd you order me?"

"Well, well, well," Ten murmured knowingly. "If it isn't *Jodi*."

Jodi whirled to him, her gaze immediately heating with interest. "Oh! Hey, Ten," she purred in her most seductive voice.

Unease stirred through my stomach, but fudge nuggets. If Jodi knew Ten, they'd probably slept together. Shit.

I motioned my finger between the two of them. "You two...*know* each other?"

As I silently begged them both to say no, Jodi licked her lips and skimmed her gaze down Ten's tight black shirt. "Not as well as I would've liked to."

Ten's eyes narrowed slightly. "As well as you're ever *going* to, you mean. I'm married now."

Jodi's smile spread slowly. "Hey, that's fine. I don't mind if the wife watches." She leaned in closer and lowered her voice. "I'm actually better when I put on a show."

"Okay, down girl." I grabbed her arm and yanked her backward, away from the married bartender. "Try to keep your hands off friends of my new bandmates, especially the married ones, *please*."

She sniffed out a sound and scowled at me. "Speaking of *bandmates*, that bastard Billy Galloway refuses to give me my panties back."

I blinked at her, momentarily clueless what she meant before I tipped my head to the side and asked, "How the hell did he get your panties?"

She lifted her eyebrows. "How do you think, puta?"

My mouth dropped open. "¡Dios mío! You had *sex* with him? Just now? But...you...how...Holy Lord, you just *met* him. And you were only gone *five minutes*."

She shrugged. "What can I say? He hit the right spot. Didn't take me long." Then she paused, her eyes growing big. "Oh, shit. You didn't want him for yourself, did you?"

"What?! Eww, no." Wrinkling my nose with disgust, I shook my head, still trying to deny what she was telling me, but...no. I didn't want her to have any kind of carnal knowledge of *any* of my bandmates. Especially that one.

"So...you didn't mind that I...?"

When she lifted her eyebrows, I sighed. "A little too late to ask me that now, but no...I guess not. I just can't believe you actually wanted him." He was disgusting.

With a shrug, she flipped her hair and started to scan the crowds again. "Why wouldn't I take him on? He's like a male version of me."

The hell if he was. Promiscuous-wise...okay, maybe. But other than that, Gally was a bigoted jerk who didn't care about anyone but his dick. Jodi was a fun-time girl who sometimes—or lots of times—didn't think things through or consider other people's feelings, but underneath that, she had a good heart and never set out to purposely hurt anyone. Or maybe I just always made excuses for her because to me, I'd known her long enough, she was more like a younger sister than a friend. I might've possibly put up blinders to her flaws, forgave her too easily, and got a bit protective when anyone tried to bash her.

"Ooh! There he is." She arched up onto tiptoes and peered through the crowd of people before saying, "Those were my favorite pair, too. Excuse me. I have undergarments to retrieve." And she was gone again.

I gaped at the spot where she'd been standing, still stunned that she'd already captured one of my fucking bandmates.

Suddenly, Ten slapped the top of the bar and then pointed at me.

"*Remy*," he nearly shouted. Then he pointed after Jodi. "Jodi, Remy. Remy, Jodi. *Holy shit!*" His eyes went huge and he jabbed his finger in my direction. Then he leaned my way and hissed, "It's you. You're..." His gaze skimmed over me. "Jesus, now I understand why you text such long messages to Hart. You're not a dude at all. You're a fucking chick!"

CHAPTER 12
Remy Curran

" *What?* " I immediately glanced around to see who'd heard him, but fortunately, no one was paying us any attention. So I whirled back to the wide-eyed man who kept staring at my chest and squinting. "How...what...?"

He learned forward. "Unreal. What'd you do with your tits—"

I smacked a hand in front of his face to divert his attention from my chest. "Will you cut that out? I am *not* a girl."

Denying it was pointless, so I'm not sure why I did. I'd planned on telling Asher and Galloway, and Holden after tonight what I was...or rather what I wasn't. There was really no need to put if off any longer, but...I thought it more respectful to tell the band face to face instead of letting Asher find out this way.

Up until this very moment, I hadn't felt any qualms about what I'd done. I'd seen a goal—though goal was such a minor understatement for the ungodly desire I'd had to be in their band—then I'd taken note of the obstacles in my path and I'd done what I'd had to do to get what I wanted. And the tiny little lie of omission I had to tell? Pfft. Those jerks had deserved it for not even letting me audition. I had actually relished the moment of revealing my true identity...until now.

Gally...yeah, I still didn't care about deceiving him. He'd started out a jerk in my mind and still was. Heath...okay, I didn't know him well enough to worry about his feelings. But Asher...he'd been nice and decent to me—er, to *Sticks,* anyway—and the more I learned about him, the more I admired him as a musician and a person.

He was...different. And okay, fine, maybe his level of hotness was affecting some of my thought process there, but still...I was a little more worried about how I'd lied to *him.*

"Yes, you are too a chick," Ten insisted, dragging me back to the problem at hand...one hot, scarred, married bartender who somehow knew too much. "You're Incubus shirt girl."

"No, I...wait, *what?*" Wrinkling my nose, I frowned in confusion. "Who's Incubus shirt girl?"

"You know..." Ten whirled out a finger. "The chick Asher wrote that song about, the one who came here and sang karaoke in the Incubus shirt and totally rocked his world."

Shaking my head, I asked, "Seriously, do you take a shot for every drink you serve, because I think you're wasted, man. You're not making any sense."

"I'm not wasted, and you're a fucking chick," he insisted. "I was here, working with Hart the night you came and sang 'All About That Bass' ...with Jodi. I was standing right beside him when he claimed you were going to have his babies one day and all that lovey-dovey bullshit. Then I watched all his sweet little hopes and dreams crash and burn when you jumped off stage and frenched some other dude."

My mouth fell open as I stared at him. But seriously, how the hell had he known I'd sung *that* song here...with *Jodi?* And Jesus, had I still been with Fisher then? I couldn't remember.

"What the hell?" I murmured, confused and curious to know exactly what he was talking about.

He grinned and waved at my flat chest. "Seriously, I'm not sure why you felt the need to dress in drag and join his band just to get his attention. All you have to do is tell him who you are. I swear to God, he still looks for you every Saturday night. If you want the guy, he's already yours."

"I don't...I have no idea what you're talking about. And I

am *not* a girl."

With a snicker, he challenged, "Yeah, and you totally didn't check out Hart's ass when he walked away just a minute ago."

I stuttered a second before spitting out, "Because I'm *gay.*"

"Or female."

"Listen here, asshole." I pointed at him, but he grabbed my finger and twisted my wrist to examine my palm.

"Yep," he said more to himself. "Total chick hand."

I yanked away from him. "Hey! Don't—"

"Oh, don't worry. I won't tell him."

That caught me by surprise. I straightened and blinked. "Huh?"

"This is how I see it. I owe that fucker one. He knew the one girl I was supposed to stay away from was sneaking into my room to fuck my brains out without my knowing it was her, and he said *nothing.* So I don't feel inclined at all to let him in on the fact that the girl of *his* dreams is actually the new drummer in his band, posing to be a gay-ass dude, which I'm still confused about. *Why* again are you doing that?"

"The...wait, back up. Why do you keep saying shit like *the girl of his dreams*? And what the ever loving hell are you talking about with some...song?"

"Holy shit." He stared at me as if I was insane. "Do you seriously not know?"

I frowned, beyond irritated. "If I knew, do you think I would be asking what they hell you're talking about right now?"

"Jesus, you're sassy. Haven't you heard the song he wrote for you?"

"No." I shook my head stupidly. "Will you please start making some damn sense before you give me a fucking headache? What song?"

Ten grinned suddenly. "Oh, I like you. You'll be good for him."

"Ten," I growled, fed up with this conversation because actually it was already giving me a headache.

With a sigh, he explained. "He wrote a song about you, you know, about how he saw you singing up there on the karaoke with Jodi. Jesus, you're in the band now, why don't you know about this song?"

"Oh, I don't know; maybe because you're talking utter bullshit. No song like that exists. Trust me, I'm familiar with *all* of Non-Castrato's songs."

"No. I really don't think you are. You should look into that." I opened my mouth to disagree some more but he straightened and glanced behind me. "Incoming."

"What?" I glanced back and nearly peed my pants when I found Asher almost upon us, lugging a case of alcohol. He heaved the box onto the counter and extracted two bottles before telling Ten to do something with the rest. Then he popped the caps to both and handed me one.

"To our best performance yet," he toasted.

Warmth flooded me, making me forget everything Ten and I had just discussed. Had tonight really been the band's best performance? Oh God, I loved hearing that.

I tapped the neck of my bottle against his and took a tentative sip, only to lift my eyebrows in surprise. "Holy shit. This isn't half bad."

Asher laughed. "I know. I've become addicted to them."

He slid onto an empty stool and motioned to the free seat beside him. I glanced around for Jodi, only to spot her sitting at a table with Galloway...on his lap as he stuck his tongue down her throat. Eww. I wasn't sure where Holden had disappeared to, or if he was even still in the building. Since I didn't know anyone else and I couldn't think up a good reason to refuse Asher's invitation, I sat on the stool next to him, even though it kind of felt like I was deceiving him to play all buddy-buddy like this.

"So how long have you been playing?" he asked, drawing my attention back to him. I liked his hands—long, slender musician's fingers—and how he always kept them busy, like the way he was idly spinning his bottle on the countertop in the puddle of its own sweat ring. It was as if he had this pent-up energy inside him and he had to use his fingers to expend it.

A shiver and hot trail of lust curled through me, imagining much more productive ways he could put his fingers to use.

God, I was awful. *Concentrate, Remy. He asked you a question.*

I shrugged. "For as long as I can remember. I grew up next door to Jodi's parents, and they owned a music store, not like a place that sold records and CDs either, but an actual music store that has pianos and clarinets and flutes and guitars and such. They always played the coolest eighties music every time I went over there. My family played nothing outside mariachi music, so it was like a whole new exciting world to visit the Maleskys' house."

"And I assume that's where you bought your first drum set."

I winked. "Oh, you know it."

As he grinned, I nodded my chin at him. "What about you?"

"Oh..." He shrugged and picked at the label on his bottle, peeling it free. "I don't know. I've always liked to sing. I think it was an only child thing to help keep myself company. And then, when I moved in with my uncle when I was seven, he was gone a lot, so..." His shoulder lifted again, telling me he wasn't too comfortable sharing his story. But he kept talking anyway. "I found an old guitar in his closet one day. It had this instruction booklet with it, and that was that."

I blinked at him a good five seconds before saying, "Wait, you taught yourself how to play?"

An adorable, rueful expression crossed his face. "I had plenty of free time to practice."

I was still amazed, and I'm sure my jaw hanging open made it obvious. "Shut the front door. You freaking *taught yourself* to play the guitar?"

He finished the rest of his Angry Orchard in one long draw and then sighed in one of those refreshed ways as he tapped the bottle against the bar top and motioned to Noel that he needed another.

When he turned to me, I could tell he was totally going to change the subject.

That intrigued me. A lead singer of a band who wasn't interested in talking about himself. Weird. And not only that, he seemed more embarrassed than puffy-chested and proud that I was impressed by his self-taught skills. Fisher would've been eating up any praise that came his way and making sure I knew the whole story behind his greatness.

Not that I was comparing the two. There was no reason for me to do that, other than, you know, they were both singers in a band.

Still, I really liked Asher's more humble approach on being so awesome.

"So, who's your favorite band?" he asked, almost making me grin because I'd been able to read him well enough to know he'd steer the conversation away from himself.

I snorted and made a face. "As if I could narrow that down to one group."

He laughed. "I know, right?"

"But if I had to name, say...my top ten or so," I went on, curious if he had similar tastes. "I'd go with Metallica, Pink Floyd, Led Zeppelin, Tom Petty and the Heartbreakers, The Stones, Incubus, Rush—but only because of Neil Peart."

Asher grinned and nodded. "The drummer. Of course."

I felt my own lips curve up in amusement and kept listing. "The Beatles, Jimi Hendrix, Joan Jett, Heart, The Bangles—"

Choking on the drink he'd just taken, Asher burst out laughing. "The *Bangles*?"

"What?" I scowled at him for laughing at my Bangles.

He waved a hand. "Nothing. I just wasn't expecting a punk band listed among all the rock groups you were spouting off."

"Hey, they were rock...sort of." Then I shrugged. "They came up with 'Walk Like an Egyptian,'" I argued my point. "That song is fun as shit to play on the drums. For me, it ranks right up there with 'Hot for Teacher,' 'Enter Sandman,' and 'Tom Sawyer.'"

There were more girl bands I loved, but I didn't want to somehow give my gender away by listing too many, so I merely watched Asher continue to chuckle.

"Trust me. I'm not bashing your choices in the least. I agree with every single one of them. And hey, I've been known to listen to Katy Perry and Taylor Swift with the best of them, so don't worry about music genres with me."

"Dude." I leaned in closer. "I wouldn't go broadcasting that to Galloway. I don't think he'd be so—"

"Yeah." He lifted his hand to let me know my warning was moot. "I know." Then he shrugged as if unconcerned. "I just like all kinds of music. As long as it's got a good beat, cool lyrics and resonates in my bones, I'm in."

I nodded respectfully. "I get that." I didn't tell him I was pretty much the same way. Country, rap, alternative, hip hop, classics, I just loved music.

"But I grew up with my parents listening to Nirvana on a loop, so that's probably why most of our songs lean more the way they do."

"Hmm, I wondered about that. I can definitely see the influence." I wondered if this meant he'd had a hand in creating any of our original songs. Just how many hats did he wear in our little group? Guitar player, vocalist, manager and now possible songwriter?

The guy seriously needed to stop saying and doing things to impress me.

He sneezed, and immediately said, "Excuse me," as he reached for a nearby stack of napkins to wipe his nose. And dammit, I even liked his gentlemanly reaction while he tossed the used tissue into a trash can. Ugh! My tiny little crush was getting ridiculous here.

Needing to get my head back into the conversation and away from him being a hot, interesting piece of man candy, I finished my own beer and said, "I've really been getting into Breaking Benjamin lately."

"Mmm." He pointed at me as he took a drink, then had to wait to swallow before saying "And Five Finger Death Punch."

"'The Wrong Side of Hell,'" we said together, naming our favorite song from that group. Then we laughed at the same time.

"Well, isn't this cozy?" Ten asked, appearing in front of us.

I tensed, hoping he kept his big mouth shut. But Asher let out a small moan, and waved his empty bottle in his friend's face. "Don't be a dick. Just get me another drink."

"Dude, slow it down. What is this, your fifth of the night?"

"No, it's my..." He frowned as if confused so I answered, "third."

"Right." He snapped his fingers and pointed at me. "It's my third...and it's my last, *mother*." After a quick scowl to Ten, he asked me, "You want another?"

"Mmm. Okay. Uno más." I slid my empty toward Ten, who shook his head.

"Huh?" Ten only blinked. "What the hell does uno más mean?"

I rolled my eyes. "It's Spanish. Means one more. Por favor. But this should be my last drink, too. I'll probably end up driving Jodi home...if she hasn't already left with someone else." But when I glanced around for her, I was surprised to find her still hanging around Galloway and his table full of women.

"You know, I took like two years of Spanish in high school," Asher said from beside me. "And I learned jack shit."

I turned back to him and was blasted with a fresh wave of lust. Damn, but he was too pretty. And those green, green eyes...so frigging intense.

"Well, my entire family is from México, so I grew up with plenty of people who don't know anything but Español," I explained. "It's pretty common for me."

"Really? Huh. I never would've guessed that about you. You seem so...American."

I arched an eyebrow. "I am American. Born and raised right here in Illinois."

"I mean..." He rolled out a hand and his eyes flared as if he was worried he'd offended me.

"My dad was American," I explained. "But since I don't remember him and grew up with my mom's side of the family raising me, yeah, you could say my heritage is very deeply embedded in all things Latino. I probably fell in love with the type of music I did because to me, it was so much more exotic and exciting than what I was used to my family always listening to. Plus, it was kind of fun to be the rebel in the group."

With a laugh, Asher nodded. "That makes sense." He opened his mouth to say more but two girls approached, one sliding up right against his side and running her fingers along his chest. "Hey, you're Asher Hart, aren't you? We loved your performance tonight."

The smile he sent her was friendly enough as he said, "Thanks," but then he leaned away, obviously uncomfortable with her proximity.

I couldn't keep my narrowed gaze off her red painted fingernails as they kept traveling lower and lower down his chest and over his stomach, steadily making their way toward his lap. "You have the most amazing voice ever."

He caught her wrist before she could get a handful of little Asher but still managed a tense smile. "Glad you liked it."

"Hey! You two." Noel pointed at the two women and waved them off. "This is a VIP area. You need to move along."

The women huffed out their displeasure but Noel narrowed his eyes, and they finally slunk away. As soon as he was relieved of the girl's grasp, Asher spun on his stool so he was no longer sitting sideways to face me but now had his legs tucked securely under the counter space...so no more women could climb into his lap.

"Thanks, man," he told Noel.

"Aww...anything for our delicate little cupcake." Noel went to pinch his cheeks, but Asher slapped his hand away and called him a dirty name.

As Noel moved off, laughing, a blushing Asher slanted a glance my way. "Sorry about that. They can get really...forward."

Again, he surprised me. Fisher would've already been all over those two girls—a very sad fact I hadn't learned until *after* I was engaged to the douchebag. Yeah, it'd been kind of downer to hear he'd slept with a new girl pretty much every time he'd gone out into public without me.

I took a small sip of my beer as I studied Asher's face, watching him glance over his shoulder at the ladies Noel had shooed away. His expression confused me. I saw the flicker of interest; he definitely didn't mind what he saw. But there was also a wariness that didn't mesh with his initial attraction to them.

"And...you don't like forward?" I couldn't help but ask.

He zipped his gaze to me, his green eyes filled with surprise. Then he shrugged. "I don't know. I just..." He shifted his shoulders again. "I guess I just like to be the one pursuing, you know." With one last glance at the women he'd rebuffed, he added, "And I haven't had the chance to do that in a while."

"I can imagine." I'd definitely experienced the same draw to him every other female tonight had. He was probably constantly chased by a horny mob.

Shifting closer, he lowered his voice and admitted, "It's embarrassing as fuck. They all crowd around me as if I'm something, I don't know, *amazing*, and they don't know jack shit about me. I'm just a regular guy, and I can't help but think they'd only be disappointed if they really got to know me."

Oh, I begged to differ on that point. So far, he was turning out to be incredibly interesting...and growing more interesting by the moment.

Thank God Jodi showed up then, before I could say anything, because I might've blurted out that I thought he was by no means dull or regular.

She slid up against me, giggling—obviously drunk off her ass—and almost knocked me off my stool, right into Asher. I had to put out a foot and slam my hand onto the counter to catch myself.

"Hey, puta," she cried, wrapping her arms around my neck and giving me a big sloppy kiss on my masked cheek. "Oh my God, you're so hot tonight. Have I told you how good you look in this get-up? Are you going to drive me home? I could give you fake road head in the car."

I rattled out a nervous laugh, glad she hadn't given my identity away yet, aside from the puta reference and fake road head offer, but I hoped Asher hadn't caught that. Still, she was so wasted she might actually give me away soon. "Looks like I will be," I answered, slipping an arm around her waist to keep her upright. "You are plastered, chica."

"Feels *good*," she answered, tipping her head back, only to catch sight of who I was sitting beside. Eyes flashing open wide, she gasped. "Oh my God, there's that gorgeous lead singer dude in your band again. Don't you just want to lick him?" She started to climb into my lap and crawl across me to reach him. "Hey...Asher Hart? Can I lick you?"

"Jodi!" I hauled her back to the other side of me. "Down girl. No licking my bandmates."

She wrinkled her nose and made a pouty face. "You're no fun. Besides." Her tongue came out to waggle at me. "I just gave that bastard Billy head under the table to get my panties back. And my tongue was *all* over—"

I slapped my hand over her mouth to shut her up. "Eww." Then I remembered where she'd just had that mouth, and I quickly removed my fingers to wipe them on my pant leg. Glancing at Asher, I cringed and mouthed the word, *Sorry.*

He only laughed. "Don't worry about it."

But I kept stressing. "How long do you think it'll take to clean off the stage?"

Waving me away, he shook his head. "Don't worry about

that either. I'll take care of everything. Just get this lovely lady home safely, and we'll be square."

Jodi tittered and rested her head on my shoulder. "Did you hear that? He called me lovely."

"He also called you a lady, so he's also obviously had too much to drink as well."

"Hey," Jodi muttered in outrage and pinched the inside of my arm at the most tender spot ever, making me yelp and squirm away.

Next to us, Asher's phone rang, keeping him from having to respond.

As he answered, my roommate leaned up into my ear and loudly whispered, "Have you told him you're a girl yet? You said you were going to tell him right after the gig tonight. I bet he'll want to jump your bones when he finds out."

"Shh..." I hissed, scowling her quiet as I waved a hand to hush her. "Not yet."

After this evening, my goals had changed. I was still riding some of the giddy rush I'd gotten from playing for people, people who cheered us on and loved what we did for them. And then Asher...sitting here, just talking to him...I realized I didn't want to leave the band.

So I needed a new plan. I needed to approach this delicately, in a way where I could convince the guys to keep me on after I revealed my true identity to them. If I played my cards right, maybe I could coax them into letting me stay on as a girl.

Before I could explain all that to Jodi, though, Asher grabbed my arm. "Holy shit, Sticks, you will not believe this." Excitement radiated from his voice as he continued to shake my shoulder vigorously. "That was some casino owner from Chicago. He was here tonight and saw our show. And he wants us to play at one of his clubs. Next Saturday. He offered us two grand for one night. Can you fucking believe that?"

My mouth dropped open in shock as Asher threw back his head and let out a relieved, happy, excited laugh. "I've been working for over a year to get us an opportunity like this. Then you're with us *one* night—one fucking night—and boom, we've got an offer from fucking *Chicago*. You're some kind of good luck piece, you know that?"

"I..." No words came. I shook my head, feeling some of the same awe as him, but also gaining a load of nerves.

For real, though... Fuck! I couldn't tell him what I was now. What if it pissed the guys off enough that they kicked me out of the band? Then, where would they be? They needed a drummer for next weekend. I couldn't let them down. I couldn't let *Asher* down. He looked so freaking adorable when he was excited like this.

And yes, damn it, I really wanted to play at that bar in Chicago, too.

So, yeah, I guess this meant Sticks, the dude drummer, was going to have to hang around just a little bit longer.

CHAPTER 13
Asher Hart

THAT CALL. THAT WONDERFUL, amazing, life-changing phone call.

Ever since I'd gotten it, I'd been a bundle of anticipation and nerves. The whole thing reeked of Pick, however. I mean, seriously. Why would some big-time casino owner from Chicago be down here in Ellamore and inside the Forbidden Nightclub, of all places, to even hear us play? I had a feeling my new brother had pulled a few strings to get the guy into the building. And yep, when I'd straight up asked Pick about it, he'd suddenly turned too vague and busy to talk.

I wasn't sure what to do about that. Just appreciate it and move on? Somehow try to repay him? Tell him to stop because I knew someday he'd regret helping me? I wasn't sure, so I decided to not even think about it for now.

I concentrated on the positives...like the fact Non-Castrato had just been given the opportunity of a lifetime. Good things were about to happen, I could *feel* it, like some kind of adrenaline rush surging through my veins. It had my muse running wild with ideas for songs, and my chronic insomnia hitting a new high.

The afternoon after the call, I sat on the seat of an old exercise bike, scribbling lyrics in my notebook, and jiggling my knee to expend some of the extra energy still tweaking though me. I paused every few seconds to sing the words in my head, then I marked out a phrase here, or sometimes a whole line there that didn't work, and I wrote in something new above or below it.

I'd just come up with a stanza that made my blood pump eagerly when someone called, "Knock, knock."

Glancing up, I grinned at the new drummer. "Hey, man. You're early again. That's going to be a thing with you, isn't it?"

Sticks shrugged as he strolled into the garage, carrying a restaurant's takeout bag, which *shit*...smelled really good. "And here, I've yet to be earlier than you," he noted.

"Touché," I murmured, watching him plant himself on his drum set stool and open the bag, only to pull out a fried burrito-looking thing that made my mouth water, and reminded me it'd been too long since I'd last eaten.

I never remembered to eat or sleep when I was binge writing.

But when Sticks sank his teeth into the fried breading, I couldn't handle it. "What the hell is that?" I demanded. "It smells amazing."

Pausing mid-bite, Sticks lifted his eyebrows and glanced my way. Then he bit down, chewed a second and finally covered his hand over his mouth before saying, "Sorry. I had to come straight from work and was starving."

"No." I waved my hand. "I don't care if you have to eat. Whatever. That's totally fine. I meant, specifically what is *that* you're eating?"

"Oh. It's a chimichanga." When I licked my lips, he arched an eyebrow and held it higher in my direction. "You want one? I have more in the bag."

"Really?" I instantly came to my feet. "Fuck, yes, I want one."

Smirking, Sticks pulled another chimichanga free and handed it over. I unwrapped it and took my first bite, barely thanking him before diving in, and that was that; I was a goner. We spent the next few minutes in silence, quietly inhaling our food before I could form a coherent word. Finally, I pointed at my mostly eaten chimichanga and announced with a full cheek, "This is good."

"I know." Sticks wiped his mouth with a napkin. "My family owns the restaurant. I grew up on this shit."

"Lucky bastard." I made a small whimper and closed my eyes as I downed the last little bite I had. Taking note of the name of the restaurant on the side of the bag, I decided I needed to go to Castañeda's for a full meal someday soon.

"Seriously, I didn't mean to interrupt whatever you were doing." Sticks motioned to my abandoned notepad across the room.

I shrugged. "No worries. I'd just written down what I needed to. You got any other extra food in there you don't want?"

With a chuckle, Sticks reached into the bag. "I have a couple empanadas."

I had no idea what that was. But when he handed me one, my mouth watered. "You're a goddamn saint."

He watched me stuff my face a few seconds before he lifted his eyebrows and opened his mouth to say something. When he didn't, I motioned for him to talk.

His shoulders fell a fraction before he cleared his throat. "You know the other day when you said I could go through all our songs...?" When I nodded, he cringed. "Is that offer still open?"

"Sure." I dusted crumbs off my fingers and onto the thighs of my jeans, tempted to lick them clean. "The box is over there. I usually keep it here in the garage because it just seems easier that way. Less of a chance to misplace anything."

Sticks nodded and sat his bag on the floor next to his stool. As he wandered toward the box, I returned to the bike and tried to come up with a line to complement the last few I'd written, but nothing seemed to measure up.

"Hey, there are a couple of receipts in here too," Sticks spoke up suddenly, making me glance over to watch him frowning into my box.

"Yeah." I waved my pen. "I put everything related to the band in there. Like a catchall. It's simple and helps me keep track of where things are."

"Really?" His eyebrows rose in disbelief. "Because I don't know how you could find jack shit in here. This thing is a fucking mess."

I had to laugh at the horror on his face. "Feel free to organize it however you like," I said. "Just don't lose anything."

Sticks snorted. "You're worried about *me* losing something? Increíble."

"Oh, shut up, smart-ass." I laughed and reread the last line, finally coming up with a new one.

Holden arrived then. It took Gally another five minutes to show, so while I continued to fiddle with my song, Sticks attempted to drag a conversation out of Holden while he stacked papers on the floor around the box, but he didn't have any more luck than I'd ever had. Holden only answered him with a couple grunts and a nod or shake of the head.

Once everyone had arrived, I put my pen and paper down, and we spent a good half hour hashing out which songs we wanted to sing for the Chicago gig. For the new drummer's benefit, I added "Hot for Teacher" to our list of cover songs since we didn't have enough original compositions yet to last through a full show, and it reminded me Noel, who'd hooked up with his college professor and married her.

Sticks hooted in pleasure when I mentioned that choice, which made me smile. No one really picked on the song choices I'd selected; it was the order in which I wanted to sing them that set Gally off into a tangent.

"Man, 'Stone-Hearted' is our biggest hit. We need to lead with that shit."

"I disagree," Sticks spoke up. "No concert I've ever been to started with their most popular song. It needs to wait until later, so people have time to show up and then make them stick around a bit waiting for it. About three-fourths of the way into the set is best."

Which had been exactly where I'd placed it. I sent Sticks an appreciative smile, but Gally sniffed. "Shut up, queer. You don't have a say in this."

"*Hey!*" Glaring at the bass guitarist, I snapped, "Will you stop with the derogatory remarks already? And yes, he does too have a say. Sticks is just as much of a member of Non-Castrato as any of us are now."

Gally sent us a round of dirty scowls, but at least he shut his trap before he moodily crossed his arms over his chest and muttered, "Whatever."

"I think it needs to come later, too," Holden finally said.

"Three against one," I told Gally with maybe a bit too much glee.

"I said what the fuck ever," he snapped. "But I think we should start with that Kongos song then. 'Come with Me Now.'"

"Actually, we should probably start with an original," Sticks argued.

I knew Gally was going to say something else totally un-called for, and I was fully prepared to come down on him for it, but at the last second, he closed his mouth and smoothed up his Mohawk, which was green today. "Hell, why doesn't *gay boy* here just decide everything?"

"Honestly," I said. "I already had an order planned, and yeah, the first song I put down was 'Ceilings.'"

Sending me two thumbs-up, Sticks mouthed, *Good one.*

I had to glance away to keep from grinning, which I had a feeling would send Gally into an even moodier pout. So I read off the complete list I'd planned. Everyone had their own input, so we tailored it until most everyone was happy. By the time we actually got to practicing any of the songs, I was so ready to drown myself in music I picked the most vocally challenging ones that forced me to put everything into my voice.

By the time we finished, my throat was a little sore from the workout, but I felt better than ever, achieving a high that only came when I sang.

"Shit, man," Sticks said in awe. "You sure can belt out a melody when you want to."

I grinned at him, amused with the way he'd phrased his compliment. "Not so shabby yourself, drummer boy. You weren't lying when you said you did a good rendition of 'Hot for Teacher.'"

"Oh, Jesus." Gally groaned. "I'm leaving before you two start complimenting each other's purses and hair ribbons. Go shopping at the mall together or something, and get it out of your system already. Fuck."

With that, he flung his guitar strap over his shoulder and stomped from the garage.

"He doesn't like it when he doesn't get his way," Holden said in his deep, quiet voice.

"That or it's just his time of the month," Sticks agreed.

I laughed. "Well, I think we have a decent list to play on

Saturday, despite his mood."

"We totally do." Sticks stood and stretched his muscles. "We are so going to rock the fuck out of that club." He returned to the box of music sheets and receipts, picking up where he'd left off in his self-appointed task of organizing.

I packed my guitar, and Holden did the same, waving us goodbye before silently slipping out the opened bay door.

Sticks glanced my way as I found a more comfortable place to sit than the bicycle seat and hiked my ass onto the top of an old scarred nightstand table.

He frowned. "You don't have to stick around here just for me. I'll close the door when I leave."

"It's fine. We have to pad-lock it too, and I haven't gotten you a key yet. So, yeah, I kind of do have to stick around."

"Oh." He stood abruptly. "Shit, sorry. I can go then. I didn't mean to keep you."

"No, really." I waved him back down. "I'm in no hurry. I don't have to be at work for another hour or so. And this..." I motioned to the notebook I was writing in. "I can do here just as easily as I can at home."

He gingerly reseated himself on the floor where he'd been sitting with his legs crossed. "Well, if you don't mind... I think I'll finish organizing this shit then, or it'll drive me batty."

With a laugh, I waved him on. "Knock yourself out, man."

So we worked in companionable silence for a while until he suddenly said, "All these songs are written in the same handwriting."

"Yeah." I glanced up curiously. "Was there a question in there?"

"No, I just..." Sticks looked down at the sheet music, then a couple other pages. Then he whipped his head up to gape at me. "Wait. Did you...?"

I arched an eyebrow, waiting for him to continue.

Finally, he blurted, "How many of the songs for Non-Castrato did *you* write personally?"

I cocked my head to the side, confused. "All of them. Why?"

"All....*all* of them?" he squawked. "Get out. Even 'Ceilings'?"

Unable to help myself, I grinned. "Yeah. Why? You like

that one, don't you?" I knew he did. It was the only one he ever requested.

"I *love* it," he gushed. "I can't believe you wrote that."

"Yeah, I could tell it was your favorite. What makes you like it so much?"

Sticks lifted a hand as if to wipe hair out of his eyes, when there wasn't any hair in his face. "I don't know..." The move made me crinkle my eyebrows because I'd seen Caroline do that to her hair many times. Made me wonder if he'd recently had long hair. "It reminds me of my mom, I guess," he finally answered.

That caught my attention. "Really? *Your* mom?"

With a nod, he mumbled, "Yeah, she uh...she was pretty heavy into drugs for a while there when I was younger."

I understood immediately. "Ceilings" was a depressing song. The lyrics followed the journey of a girl who spent her life looking up at ceilings during her most pivotal moments. She fell in love while staring up at the ceiling of the backseat of her boyfriend's car. Then she gazed up at the ceiling of an auto repair shop where she was hiding when a drive-by shooting took his life. The ceiling of the hospital was what she watched as she gave birth to her dead lover's baby at sixteen. And she cried up at that very same ceiling as she made the decision to sneak out of the hospital and abandon him. When her family refused to have anything to do with her, she hooked up with a drug dealer who turned her into a nasty addict. And she stared up at the ceiling of her bathroom as she tried to abort the baby that drug dealer had knocked her up with. And finally, she gazed up at the ceiling of his living room while the drug dealer took her life.

"It's such a poignant, way-too realistic story that always sends shivers up my arms." Sticks rubbed them now as goose flesh pebbled the skin. "And every time I hear it, I don't know...I automatically think of my mom."

I stared silently at Sticks, experiencing a weird connection with him I'd never experienced with anyone else before. Because what he said...it rang exactly true for me too. I always thought of my mom when I sang it. Probably because it was about her, but whatever.

Remy gave a sudden, self-conscious shrug. "I mean, if her family hadn't kept such a tight leash on her, I could've so easily seen my mom falling into that very kind of life, hooking up with some guy who beat her to death and everything. Hell, if it hadn't been for my uncle and grandma, she probably would've either left me at the hospital or tried to abort me, too."

My heart thudded in my chest, because I totally got what he meant. "That sucks," I murmured. "What ended up happening to her?" But I already knew it couldn't be a happy ending. I didn't know anyone who'd gotten into drugs and then met a good ending.

Sticks glanced down at his hands. "She fried her brain and ended up in a mental institution."

"Jesus." I shook my head, sympathy filling me. "I'm sorry, man."

But he only shrugged. "Not your fault. I'm the one who's the shittiest kid ever, because I can't even stand to visit her. It hurts too much. She never remembers who I am. Last time, she thought I was her sister."

I frowned. Then I said, "You mean, she thought she was *your* sister?"

The expression on Sticks's face froze before he shook his head. "Uh...yeah. What did I say?"

"You said she thought you were *her* sister."

"Oh. Shit. Sorry. Anyway, if it weren't for Abuela and Tío Alonso, it's hard to know where I would've ended up, but I'm pretty sure it wouldn't have been anywhere good."

When he began to play with the necklace he wore, I lifted an eyebrow. "Abuela?"

"Yeah. That's Spanish for grandmother. She, along with my mom's older brother Alonso, plus a couple more of her younger brothers, and all their families came to America two years before I was born. They're a huge, overly religious group that's always in everyone else's business, but...I still kind of respect them for that. It keeps us together, you know, taken care of, which is a hell of a lot better off than I know I'd be on my own."

I continued to watch as he toyed with the necklace's medallion before my curiosity got the better of me. "Is that a family heirloom?"

"Hmm? Oh, this? No. Well... I guess, yeah. Abuela told me it was her mother's but it's actually just a pendant of la Virgen de Guadalupe."

I shook my head. "Who?"

Sticks grinned. "The saint...Guadalupe. She's famous in

México. If you see someone wearing this, they're probably Méxican. Personally, I'm not super religious, but...I don't know. I like to wear it anyway. It reminds me of my roots, my family. It brings me a level of comfort, as if I'm home again. My family... It's strange, but no one can drive me as crazy as they do. They're all, like, complete opposites of me, but...there's just something about them I adore. I love their culture, and Latin pride, and just everything that makes them *them*. They're my heritage. My foundation."

"That's cool." I watched the gold of Guadalupe's image glint in the light and suddenly wished I had some family heirloom too. But, nope. "I don't have anything like that." I glanced down at my feet where I was idly winding a guitar cord around the toe of my shoe. "My mom...she's the girl in the song. So my roots, a family foundation, just sort of got yanked out of the ground with her."

I have no idea why I told him that. It was just...he'd told me about his mom. It only felt right to say something about my own, especially since both of ours had fallen into similar addictions.

He frowned at me a second before his eyes bugged. "You mean in 'Ceilings'? You wrote that about your mom? It's all...factual?"

I nodded. "Every single word."

"But..." He shook his head, and I could tell he was trying to figure out which kid I was; the one she'd left at the hospital or the one she'd tried to kill in the womb.

So, I said, "I was her failed abortion attempt, the mistake she had with the drug dealer."

Remy's mouth dropped open. "Whoa. So, wait... Then, your dad...?"

"Is in jail. Statesburg," I added stupidly.

"Holy shit. Where were you when he, you know...?"

"Killed her? I was sitting on the couch." I have no idea why I answered his question. I didn't want to talk about it. But then I just kept...talking. "Eating a bowl of cereal and watching Power Rangers on TV."

That old familiar weight of crushing guilt swept over me. Not sure how to combat it, I swiped a hand through my hair. "He came in one morning from being out somewhere, probably at some other woman's place, and asked where she was. I just said she was in her room, didn't bother to mention she wasn't there alone. And I didn't bother to run and warn her that he was home. It only got me into trouble whenever I involved myself in the shit those two stirred with each other. But, Jesus, I can't help but wonder...if I'd only done something that morning instead of eating my breakfast and watching TV, things would've turned out a lot different."

"How old were you?" Sticks asked quietly.

I shook my head. It didn't matter. I'd been old enough to know they'd fight when he found her in bed with one of his drug-dealing partners. But I said, "Seven."

"Jesus. What the hell were you supposed to do *at seven*?"

"I don't know." I stared at the wall, seeing nothing. "*Something*. When he finally went back there and found them together, I still did nothing. My dad started shouting and the other dude came running out of the room, pulling on his pants. Then Mom started shouting. I guess she packed a bag and threatened to leave because she came storming into the front room with a suitcase, clothes sticking out each end. When she tried to open the front door—"

"Wait. Did she just plan on leaving you there?" The shock in Remy's eyes made me sniff in amusement.

"It wasn't the first time. But she always came back for more shit to stuff up her nose, so I wasn't too concerned about never seeing her again. When my dad slammed the front door to keep her from leaving and then hit her, I still wasn't surprised. They pounded on each other all the time. And if I tried to help either of them, the other would turn on me and pound on me, so I just continued to sit there like an idiot...as he killed her."

"Fuck, Asher. What he did wasn't your fault. You don't really think you could've stopped him and saved her, do you? He would've just turned on you and killed *you* too."

"I could've run and gotten help," I argued. "But I just sat there and watched as he shoved her into the television and broke it. When it landed on top of her and shot sparks everywhere, she fucking screamed in pain and I just...I just watched. It wasn't until she was already gone and her lifeless glassy eyes were staring up at the ceiling that I did anything. My dad looked at me with shock and panic, and I knew...I was next. I'd seen too much. So...*finally*, that's when I ran."

"¡Dios mío!" Sticks set his hand over his mouth. "Where did you go? Did he catch you?"

I shrugged, suddenly uncomfortable for sharing so much. "Just to a neighbor's place. The old guy who lived there let me stick around until the police showed up, so no...my dad never caught me. I didn't see either of them again that day. The next place I saw him was in the courtroom when I had to give my testimony."

"Damn, that's...intense."

I cleared my throat and glanced at the papers he'd stopped sorting and was still holding fisted in his hand. "If you want, you can just take the box home with you. Bring it back later."

I didn't want to hang around here much longer, not after opening up the way I had.

"Huh?" Sticks glanced down at his hand and then jumped. "Oh, shit. Sorry. But yeah, sure. I'll do that." He started to stuff the sheets back into the box, but froze when he saw something already in there. "What...what is *this*?"

He pulled the single page closer to read it, his eyes growing bigger with each second. "Oh...fuck," he whispered.

"What?" I asked, curious...but also relieved for a complete subject change.

Looking up with a dazed expression, he waved what looked like my hand-printed sheet music for one of our songs. "This isn't...we don't play this song. Where did this come from?"

I took it from his hand and immediately groaned. "Oh, Jesus. I need to burn this damn thing."

"No!" Sticks hopped to his feet and snagged it from me, only to hold it protectively against his chest, gaping at me in horror. "You can't. Just...what *is* it?"

I sighed, my shoulders slumping in defeat. Talking about this was almost as bad as telling him about what had happened between my parents. "It's just a stupid song I wrote after seeing some girl sing on karaoke night at the bar."

"Uh...this is more than just *seeing* a girl." His gaze scanned the page. "You wanted to know everything about her, marry her and give her babies. Make her your one and only—"

"Okay, *thank you*!" I slapped the song out of his hand

with a scowl. "You don't have to read the lyrics back to me. I *wrote* them. I remember what I said...unfortunately." When he gaped at me as if I was insane, I waved out my fingers, implying it was no big deal. "Look, it's just a song some stranger I'd never met before or seen again inspired; doesn't mean anything."

Sticks squinted, letting me know he totally didn't buy that. "Then why're you being so touchy about it now?"

"*Because*." I ground my teeth. "We happened to play it at Forbidden once. Once. One fucking time, and all these women went crazy, trying to convince me they were her. And you want to know the really crazy part? I don't think I'd even recognize her if I ever *did* see her again. I saw her once, all the way across a room months ago for a total of like three minutes. And she had a boyfriend anyway, so I don't know why everyone blew it out of proportion the way they did. It wasn't love at first sight as all my friends tease me. I know that. It was just—"

"Lust?" Sticks guessed quietly.

I winced at the word, immediately repulsed by it. "No. I mean, yeah, there was that too. But this was like...more. Like...I don't even know. A wish. A hope. A..." The right word failed me until I blurted, "A possibility. Like I suddenly wanted to try something I'd never had before."

"A pretty little Latino girl?" he whispered, looking almost hurt.

I blinked, confused. "Huh?"

He picked the sheet up off the floor and pointed to the lyrics. "That's what you called her...in the song."

"I did? Oh yeah, right. But, no, that's not what I'm talking about at all. It had nothing to do with looks, though she *was* gorgeous. This was more like...a feeling. A warmth. Like right there, watching her sing, was where I belonged in the universe. Like I'd just found my place. Everything...fit."

Remy's mouth had fallen open. Realizing I'd once again shared more than I wanted to, I cleared my throat and scrubbed at the back of my head. "Anyway, like I said, it was stupid. Just a momentary blip on my crazy radar. I'll never cross paths with her again, and she'll probably be better off for it."

When I laughed at the joke against myself, Sticks didn't join in. Instead, he became a sudden flurry of motion, stuffing documents back into the box as he blurted, "I have to go."

"Uh..." I glanced around, startled by his abrupt announcement. "Okay." Now I really felt awkward for telling him so much. Shit. Had I scared him out of the band because I'd unloaded a ton of my personal drama on him?

"You sure it's okay if I take this whole box?" He didn't make eye contact as he asked. It was as if he were suddenly too afraid to look me in the eye, which made me feel incredibly self-conscious.

"Yeah, it's fine," I said. "Everything...okay?"

"What?" He zipped his gaze up, his brown eyes wide and far from okay. "Yeah, sure. Sorry, I just...I remembered I have to be somewhere. Like right now. Excuse me, I gotta..."

"Go," I finished for him.

"Right." Pointing to me gratefully for supplying the word he'd been searching for, he surged up from the floor where he'd been crouching. When he plowed forward to flee, he almost bumped the box he was toting right into my gut, so I leapt a step back to give him room, and he finally seemed to realize I was right there.

"Shit, sorry. Uh..." He looked into my eyes again, and I think he saw how worried I was, because he blew out a breath, and his shoulders slumped. "It's not your fault, you know."

I squinted, not sure what he was talking about. Not my fault that I'd brought a whole boatload of uncomfortable into our conversation, making him in such a hurry to leave? Or not my fault that—

"That she died," he clarified. "Your mom. Seriously, just think up every scenario of everything you could've done that day. You know she still would've ended up...where she did. The only thing that might've changed was that you could've died with her."

I took a step back at those words. I'd thought up different scenarios before, and in every alternate reality I'd created in my head, I'd been able to save her. But maybe Sticks was right. In all actuality, I probably wouldn't have been able to keep her alive. Realizing that stunned me.

Sticks blew out a breath. "I really have to go. See you Monday? At practice?"

I nodded, distracted by the thoughts he'd just put in my head. "Yeah. Sure. See you then."

I didn't notice him leave. I slumped onto the nightstand, both my hands buried deep in my hair, and I wondered...was Remy right? Had my mother's death been inevitable? Maybe I hadn't been as culpable as I'd always worried.

CHAPTER 14
Remy Curran

I BURST INSIDE MY APARTMENT, the official Non-Castrato box cradled in my arms, unable to get my mind to stop spinning from everything I'd learned during band practice today...or rather everything I'd learned *after* practice.

Hearing about Asher's childhood and his parents was enough to blow my mind. But then I'd spotted that song. That dreadful, amazing, life-altering song.

Ten hadn't been on crack after all. A Non-Castrato song I'd never heard of before really, honestly, truly existed. And I knew why Asher refused to ever play it again. It was so personal, so revealing, so...

About me.

Well, *maybe* about me. Maybe not. I couldn't be sure. Except all the details fit. Por Dios, how well the details fit.

Thoughts scattered into millions of pieces, I plopped the box on the side table where I always tossed my keys and purse, vaguely aware of Jodi on the couch watching television.

For all I noticed, she might've even greeted me hello. I

have no idea if I replied. I was too busy digging back into the box to retrieve that song. Once I found it, the page trembled in my grasp as I reread the lyrics. Everything seemed right. And yet...I couldn't believe it. The idea that Asher might've seen me once and been so overwhelmed by the encounter that he'd written a...a *love* song about me, fantasizing about an entire future full of what-ifs that could happen between us, was more than I could take.

"Jodi," I started, still staring at Asher's handwritten dreams, as I marched in front of her until I was between her and the television.

"Shh..." She waved me out of her way so she could continue watching the screen. "Check this out." She motioned toward...holy guacamole, was she actually watching the *news*?

Who was this woman and what had she done with my roommate?

"They shut down Statesburg," she said. "You know, that big prison not too far from here. There was some big, insider scandal about the last warden and some current and past inmates. I guess it was bad enough that they're closing the entire place, and apparently there's not enough room in the surrounding jails to house all their inmates, so they're just...letting some of them go."

"What?" I spun to gape at the news too.

"I know, right? Everyone who's up for release or parole this year, is pretty much getting out. That's like *fifty* new felons out on the streets with us. What kind of shit is that?"

"Scary," I murmured, watching the screen as the newsman's camera panned the outside of the state prison where the gates were opening to let out the last busload to convicts they were going to farm out to other prisons. "When did this happen?"

"It's been going on for a couple weeks apparently. But the news just caught wind of it."

"Statesburg's like what, only twenty miles from here, isn't it?"

"However far it is, it's *way too close.*" Jodi shivered and hugged herself. "I'm investing in a fucking Taser." Then she glanced at me and sniffed as she took in my mask. "And if I were you, I'd stay in that form for a while. If there were any rapists in the release, you're far safer as a guy right now."

I rolled my eyes, but the mention of my mask reminded

me...

Sticks.

The band.

Asher and his song.

"Hey." I sat beside her and tried to act causal. "Do you remember the night we went to Forbidden months ago and sang karaoke?"

"Sure." Her attention returned to the television as she chewed on a fingernail. "We sang 'All About That Bass,' right?"

"Yeah." That part I remembered. And it's exactly what the girl in Asher's song had sung...with her redheaded friend...aka, Jodi...maybe. "Was I still with Fisher then?"

She rolled her eyes and groaned. "Yes. The douchebag told me my voice sounded like two alley cats fucking."

"What a dick." I wrinkled my nose, though yes, sadly, that sounded exactly like something Fisher might've said. But all issues with him were over and done. Now...I was too focused on Asher to think about Fisher. "Do you remember what I was wearing?"

"It doesn't really matter." She rolled her eyes. "You never wear anything exciting when we go clubbing. Just those stupid T-shirts you get from concerts."

"I know." I chewed on my lip and returned my gaze to the song, rereading the line about the pretty little Latino girl in the Incubus T-shirt who'd rocked Asher Hart's world.

The news must've moved on to different, less interesting topics because Jodi suddenly focused on me. "What's with all the questions, anyway? And what is that?"

She took the piece of paper from me, and I explained as she began to read it.

After I told her everything and she skimmed over the song again, her mouth dropped open. "Holy shit, Remy. This is us. Asher Hart wrote a song about us." Her wide-eyed gaze landed on me. "About *you*."

I swallowed. "Yeah...it does appear that way, doesn't it?"

"What do you mean, *appear that way*? Puta, this is...*us*."

Shaking my head, I had to deny it. It was just too... much. Way too much. "It might not be."

"Oh, trust me. It *is*."

"Jodi," I whined. "It can't be. What the hell would I do if

this ended up being about *me*? I actually like him."

"Then you tell him immediately and get yourself a ticket to the finest seat on the Asher Hart express, because wow... He wrote you a fucking song, puta. Fuck the boy's brains out in gratitude."

Ugh, of course she wouldn't understand.

"Are you crazy? I totally can't do that. I'm his *bandmate* now. He thinks I'm a guy. Dios mío, if he found out who I really am, he'd think the same thing Ten thought, that I knew about the song all along and this was just some fucked-up attempt to trick my way into getting close to him. Oh...fuck...me." I set my hand against my forehead, the latex of my mask surprising me, because I'd forgotten I was still wearing it. "What am I going to do, Jodi?"

Since I wasn't my roommate and all my answers didn't end with sex, I vetoed the "fuck Asher Hart's brains out" idea. Jodi and I compromised and decided we needed to head to karaoke night again, get some answers and learn the truth...or the constant wondering might drive us insane.

I have no idea why I went as Sticks. Asher had told me he probably wouldn't recognize his Incubus shirt girl even if he saw her again and he most likely wouldn't recognize me as the one girl who'd tried out for his band because of my wig either, but I didn't want to risk it. So I pulled on my mask, fake torso and man panties, then Jodi and I went clubbing.

Grim wasn't working tonight, so I wondered if this doorman was the Harper guy Asher had mentioned. When we reached the front of the line, I was already sliding my hand into my back pocket for my wallet to get our entry fee and ID, but Jodi had to go and point my way. "He's with the band."

I sent her a teeth-gritting glare, but the doorman burst into a huge smile. "Oh, are you Sticks, the new drummer? Hey, man, nice to meet you. I'm Harper." He stuck out a hand to shake with me, so I cleared my throat and tried to get my "guy" on.

"Hey," I said, doing the whole head bob thing men did.

Harper had a much better temperament than Grim had had. He didn't ask for any identification, and he let Jodi and me through without charging us an entry fee.

"I can't believe that actually worked," I said, glancing back, just to make sure no one was chasing us down for money yet.

Jodi grinned. "Of course it did! You're a VIP here now. Let's go see if we can get free booze too." When she hooked her arm through mine, I tried to pull us to a stop.

"No, really. Let's not push it."

I was kind of loath to go anywhere near the alcohol right now. Asher was bartending, and that's exactly where he'd be.

Sure, he was the reason we'd come here tonight, but now that we were actually here and I might actually learn he might've actually been attracted to me—the girl version of me—once upon a time, everything was just...yeah. It all had me repeating the word *actually* over and over in my head, and I had a sudden bout of actual stage fright.

Honestly, I wasn't sure how I'd be able to look into his amazing green eyes ever again.

Jodi didn't seem to care what my nerves were going through, though. She clutched my arm harder. "This is why we're here, puta. Time for answers!"

Dragged by the elbow, I reluctantly followed but argued with her the entire way. "You know, I'm not sure why we came here at all. He put every detail imaginable about his Incubus shirt girl in the song. And it's not like I have a visible mole or tattoo or distinctive feature he might suddenly remember. Hell, he didn't even recognize *you* as the sidekick who sang with me when he met you last night. So, really, what more could we get from him?"

"He didn't say how long her hair was or if she was taller or shorter than said sidekick." She pinched me in the arm, making me yelp. "And that's for calling me a measly sidekick, by the way. *Puta.* I'm no one's sidekick. I am my own force of nature, thank you very much."

True that. But instead of apologizing, I laughed at her offense, because I knew that was what she wanted me to do, until suddenly, we were at the bar and nothing seemed so funny anymore.

"I don't want to do this," I whined, trying to back away while Jodi shoved me forward.

When I finally gave in to her, I went sprawling into the counter, smacking my gut against the edge and causing the nearest bartender to whirl my way in surprise.

He wasn't Asher, thank God. But he *was* gorgeous, and having him see me sprawled like a moron against the bar made my face heat miserably inside my mask. I sent the hottie bartender an apologetic wince and waved. "Hey...sorry, about that."

He squinted a second before pointing at me. "It's Sticks, right?"

I nodded. "Right. And you're...Mason?"

Grinning, he sent me a thumbs-up. "What's up? Can I get you and your..." He glanced at Jodi. "...friend a drink?"

"I want a piña colada," Jodi immediately announced.

Dammit! I scowled at her. Of course, she'd drink one of those right in front of me, when I was trying to be all manly.

"Sure thing," Mason said and glanced at me. "Sticks?"

Since I had liked the Angry Orchard Asher had gotten me the night before, I asked for one of those.

Mason turned away to fill our order, and Jodi lifted onto her tiptoes to call into my ear, "I don't see your man. Are you sure he's working tonight?"

"Shh..." I waved her quiet. "He's not my man, and yes, I'm sure."

"Well then, where is he?"

I scowled at her but shook my head, not sure about that answer myself as I scanned the place too, looking for him and dreading as much as I relished the moment I'd catch sight of his longish dark hair with the corn silk blond highlights. Dios, his hair was amazing. Finger-gripping-while-you-screamed-through-an-orgasm kind of amazing.

"Hey you! Sexy bartender with the scar," Jodi called, making me cringe as she waved down the second guy behind the counter who wasn't Mason. "Is Asher working tonight?"

The guy I remembered Asher calling Knox paused to send my roommate a short frown. "That's classified information, sorry."

I grinned, amused how protective his coworkers were of him. He must get more female attention than I initially thought.

"But I'm asking for her," Jodi argued, hooking her thumb my way before she quickly corrected herself. "I mean, *him*."

Knox glanced at me. It took him a second before recognition hit, but when his face cleared, he nodded. "Oh, hey. I didn't see you there."

"No problem. Jodi, this is Knox, another one of Asher's coworkers. You were...otherwise occupied when I was introduced to him last night. Knox, this is my roommate, Jodi."

She stuck out her hand, cooing, "Well, hello there, precious. Hey, have you two"—she hitched her chin toward Mason as he returned with our drinks—"ever considered being in a threesome together, because I would totally volunteer to be the middle woman in your hottie sandwich."

"Uh..." Mason froze next to an equally motionless Knox as they both stared at Jodi in horror. "We have girlfriends."

"Oh my God," Jodi growled, throwing up her hands in defeat. "Is every fucking hot bartender here already taken?"

"Everyone except Asher," Mason answered, setting our drinks in front of us and waving me to stop when I pulled out my wallet to pay.

Damn, I was just getting the hang of swiping my billfold from my back pocket too. Was no one ever going to charge me anything again?

Cool.

"Where'd he disappear to, anyway?" a voice to my left asked, making me whirl around to find Pick next to me, leaning his arm against the counter as if he'd just arrived.

"Helping someone at the karaoke machine...again," Mason answered as he cleared away a couple empty mugs left on the bar top.

"Of course," Pick murmured, glancing that way, while Jodi practically pushed me aside so she could get in his face.

"Oh my fucking God," she murmured, practically drooling. "I want about five of you. Who the hell *are* you?"

Pick's eyebrows lifted in surprise as he took Jodi in, the ring in his eyebrow glittering against the overhead light. "Well, aren't you the sweetest?" He held out a hand to her. "The name's Pick."

She took his hand, but didn't shake with him and totally didn't let go of him. "Can I have your babies?"

With a grin, he shook his head and lifted her hand to kiss her knuckles. "Sorry, sweetness. I already have a lady for that. But I do appreciate the offer. Does a man good to hear how much a beautiful woman appreciates his looks."

"Oh my God," she whimpered and turned to gape at me. "He just called me beautiful."

"And he also told you he was taken." Grasping her shoulders, I manually tugged her backward away from Pick, forcing her to let go of his hand. She whimpered again when she was forced to separate contact with him.

"But...he's so hot. Just one more touch? A lick? Sniff? Please."

"Hey, is that Carter Lang?" I asked, noticing someone through the crowd that I'd seen sneak from her bedroom multiple times over the years. Knowing how easily distracted she was, I blew out a relieved breath when she glanced over.

"Holy shit, it is! I'll be right back." And she was gone.

Breathing out a breath, I turned to Pick. "I'm so sorry. She..." I had no idea how to describe Jodi. She was sweet and fun as hell, and not at all shy about going after anything she wanted, men included. But...yeah. She could be a handful.

Pick merely chuckled. "Don't worry about it. I was flattered."

So I began to turn to the two bartenders behind the counter to apologize in case either of them had been insulted, when Knox surged toward me...or rather, toward Pick.

"*Pick*, I swear Miller Hart just walked through the front door."

"*What*?" Pick turned, scanning the club. "Where?"

Alerted by Asher's surname in the conversation, I openly eavesdropped, glancing in the direction that Knox told Pick to look.

"Fuck. What the hell is he doing here? I thought he was still in prison."

It took me, like, half a second after that to figure out who they were talking about.

Snapping my fingers, I pointed at each man, remembering the news report Jodi had been watching when I'd gotten home from practice.

"Was he being held at Statesburg?" I couldn't refrain from asking because I suddenly remembered Asher mentioning that, and oh, shit.

Fuck was right. This could not be good.

When both Knox and Pick sent me scowls for butting into their conversation, I cleared my throat. "It's just...they showed something on the news earlier, saying about fifty inmates from Statesburg prison had been set free on early parole because the place is being shut down, and the other surrounding prisons were too crowded to take them all in."

"Holy shit," Knox murmured, sharing a concerned glance with Pick, who also looked worried.

Since I'd already bulldozed my way into this much, I just kept going, because seriously, I had to know. "Who's Miller Hart? He's Asher's dad, isn't he?"

Unease crossed Pick's face before he reluctantly nodded. "Yeah."

"Ah...fuck." I turned back to study the man who'd killed Asher's mother. "This can't be good."

"Do you think he's here because of Asher?" Knox asked Pick.

But I was the one who answered. "Of course he's here because of Asher. Why else would he come here? Asher's his son...not to mention the only eyewitness to seeing the guy kill his wife. It was probably Asher's testimony that put him away. If he's at all vengeful, hell yes, this would be the first place he'd come."

"Wait. How did you know Asher was the only eyewitness?" Pick eyed me with a funny kind of suspicion. "Did he tell you that?"

I shrugged. "It...came up."

"Shit," Knox spoke up suddenly. "He's headed this way. What do we do?"

Pick took control, pointing. "Knox, get Asher to my office. Now. I'll get rid of this fucker."

But Knox shook his head. "Screw that. You're not dealing with Miller Hart by yourself. He's old and pathetic, but untrustworthy as hell."

"I'll get Asher out of sight," I offered.

Pick shot me a surprised yet grateful glance. "Thanks."

CHAPTER 15
Remy Cursan

As Knox leapt over the counter to follow Pick toward Miller Hart, I scanned the stage area for Asher. The karaoke machine started playing a One Direction song, so whatever he'd been helping a customer do, he must've finished. That meant he was probably headed back to the bar. So I started toward the stage to intercept him, weaving and sometimes pushing through people to get to where he had to be.

I ended up almost plowing into him as I dodged around a gossiping horde of women, and suddenly there he was.

We both pulled up short, not expecting to see each other.

His eyes went wide with surprise and what looked like leery apprehension. "Sticks. What—"

"Oh, thank God," I blurted over him, urgently waving him to follow me as I darted toward a huge opening that led down a wide, but low-ceilinged hallway. "Come on, come on, come on. This way."

I was shocked when he actually did come. "Why? What's going on?"

"We need to get out of sight." I clutched his upper arm as soon as we hit the less-crowded hall. "Which door leads to Pick's office?"

Eyebrows crinkling with confusion, he pointed. "That one. Why? Wha...?"

I yanked him into the room with me and slammed the door. Then, panting hard, I leaned against it for good measure.

After stumbling off balance from my tug, he regained his balance to gape at me. "What the hell, man?"

"Sorry. I just..." I waved my hands to let him know I needed to catch my breath. Then I blew out a long, steady exhale and explained, "This is where Pick told me to take you."

"Okay," he said slowly, frowning hard. "And...why did he do that?"

"Uh...you know." I waved his question away. "He'll probably fill you in when he gets here, so...I'll just let him explain everything."

His lips parted as if he wanted to ask more, but with the adorable way his eyebrows kept quirking, he didn't seem to know what he wanted to ask first.

"So, I stopped by tonight to apologize to you about earlier," I rushed out, totally winging it, saying the first thing that came to mind.

Again, he looked thrown off balance by what I had to say. But a second later, he shook his head. "Why? I'm the one who made things weird."

"No, you didn't. You—wait, what? You didn't make anything weird. Why would you think that?"

His shoulders tensed and he turned sideways away from me as if to shield some of himself. Looking totally uneasy in his entire body, he flailed out a hand. "You know," he mumbled, not glancing my way. "By telling you so much shit about myself."

I blinked. "Um...isn't that what you do when you get to know someone; share little things about yourself?"

"Yeah, but..." He finally looked at me. "Those weren't *little* things. And they're not things I share with people...ever."

"Oh." Realizing he'd opened up to me more than he usually did, the significance of the moment took my breath straight from my lungs. A heaviness filled my chest, and I just wanted to...I don't even know. But I certainly wasn't taking Asher's gift of confidence for granted.

So I shook my head, my voice softening, "You didn't make anything weird...not at all."

I didn't realize I'd reached up to smooth my hair back behind my ear until my fingers grazed the short strands, startling me and reminding me I was still in guy mode. So I cleared my throat and stiffened my shoulders, trying for a more manly stance.

Asher cocked his head to the side as he frowned at me. "Then what were you apologizing for, and why did you race away as if I'd freaked you out?"

"Well, I...I was apologizing for having to rush off in the middle of our conversation. And I had to rush off because....because..." Shit, why was my brain so dead right now? I couldn't think up one little lie to tell him.

No way was I going to spill the truth and let him know I had just figured out I was his Incubus shirt girl. I wasn't sure I could let him know that...ever.

So, I sputtered a moment longer before saying, "My roommate! Yeah, Jodi. You know, you met her last night. She had just gotten off work, and I said I'd pick her up this evening, give her a ride." Lie. "I remembered she was waiting on me, so I had to hurry, or she would've been pissed."

Lie.

Lie.

Lie.

All the fibs churned like acid in my stomach, so I turned away, focusing my attention on a bookshelf against the wall, mostly full of small framed photographs.

"So, you *live* with her? With Jodi? Huh. Guess I didn't know that."

"Mmm hmm," I murmured, grateful I didn't have to lie about that at least. Then I reached for my hair again, and nearly growled at myself when I remembered I didn't have long tresses at the moment to tuck behind my ear. Dammit, why did I have to have such a girly nervous habit?

"What's that like?" Asher asked. "Living with a woman?"

"It's fine. Why would it—" Remembering I was supposed to be a gay guy, rooming with a straight woman, I paused. "I mean, other than the fact we fight over all the gorgeous men, it's just...like having any other roommate."

"Oh." From Asher's voice, he sounded more confused by

my answer than clarified.

Glancing back at him and desperate to change the subject before I revealed anything I shouldn't, I waved a finger between him and the pictures. "So...you and Pick. What's up with that?"

Leery suspicion instantly filled his eyes. "Why? What do you mean?"

I shrugged. "No sé, I don't know. It just seems like there's more between you two than just...you know, boss and employee." Then I turned back to the multitude of pictures. A majority of them featured a blonde woman and two adorable little toddlers...except one. "Then there's the fact he has a framed picture of you in his office, while he has none of his other bartenders up here."

"He does?" Asher appeared at my side, and his mouth fell open when he took in the shot I pointed to.

In the frame, Asher stood on stage, singing into a microphone as he strummed from a guitar. The other members of Non-Castrato blurred out to the sides; he was obviously the main focus of the picture.

"Shit," he murmured, staring hard. "I had no idea he had this."

"Looks like this shelf is reserved for family pictures," I mused aloud.

Asher blew out a long breath and ran his hand over his hair. "I guess..." He started slowly. "Yeah. We're family. He's... my brother."

Even though I'd pretty much been leading my guesses toward an assumption along those lines, hearing him actually confirm it had me shaking my head in confusion.

I glanced sideways at him. "Come again?"

He shook his head as if the whole thing baffled him too. "No one really knows yet...not officially, anyway. But, uh, he...turns out, after I started playing the song 'Ceilings,' I learned he'd been abandoned by his mother at birth at the hospital, and..."

"Holy shit," I murmured. "Your boss ended up being your long-lost half-brother? How the hell does that even happen?"

Asher glanced at me, his expression dazed. "I ask myself the same question every day."

"So, wait. How long have you known about this? You've

only been playing 'Ceilings' a couple—"

"Weeks," he finished for me. "We got test results back around three weeks ago. And it's still...really new."

I blew out a breath. "Dude. That's just..."

When I shook my head, he nodded. "I know."

"Why haven't you guys officially announced it?" I wondered, fearing the worst for poor Asher. "Doesn't he want to be your brother?"

He nodded, turning back to the picture of himself. "Yeah. Strangely, he does. I'm actually the one holding back."

I squinted. "So...you don't like *him*?"

"No, I do." He turned to me, his gaze desperate and seeking. "That's the problem. He's this really awesome, stand-up guy, right? And...he's my *brother*. That's just... better than I ever expected it could be. But...he's going to ask about her."

I shook my head. "About who?"

"About our *mom*," he ground out. "It's only logical, isn't it? Wouldn't you want to know about *your* mother if you just met a brother who knew her and you never did?"

When I opened my mouth to answer that yeah, I guess I would, he kept talking.

"You know he's going to want to know everything. He's going to want to know what kind of a person she was, how she died, and I'm going to have to be the one to tell him what a miserable existence she led and *who* killed her. And then what's he going to think of me after that? I'm the son of his mother's *murderer*. He doesn't know *everything* in my 'Ceilings' song is true. What if he learns it is and wants nothing to do with me? I can't..." He shook his head, looking miserable. "I'm just not ready to risk that. My entire life is in this building, and he could take all that away with a single word."

I cleared my throat and scratched my ear. "So...you haven't told him *anything* about your mom or dad yet?"

He shook his head, his green eyes filled with dread.

"And he hasn't asked?"

"No. Not yet. But you know he will."

I blew out a breath and shrugged. "Honestly, I think you should just say something to him because...I have a feeling he already knows what happened to your mom...*and* who killed her."

His expression morphed from concern to confusion. "Huh?"

The door opened, and Pick stepped inside.

When I glanced at his brother and then back to him, Asher must've seen something in my expression. He narrowed his eyes, and his face cleared with some kind of understanding.

He spun toward Pick. "What the hell is going on?" Then he whirled to me, glaring. "What did you tell him?"

I lifted my hands, glad I was free from guilt in this regard. "Nothing. I didn't say shit to anyone. I would never betray a confidence like that." Especially now that I knew what he'd told me really *was* confidential.

Pick cleared his throat, letting me know he'd take over.

When I shut up, Asher darted leery glances between the two of us before demanding, "What?"

"Miller Hart was just in the club," Pick announced.

Color leeched from Asher's face. Then he shook his head. "Excuse me?"

"Knox recognized him from when they were in Statesburg together."

"Wait." Asher lifted both hands, only to burrow them into his hair and clutch his head. His frantic gaze shot to Pick. "How do you even know anything about...him?"

With a small exhalation, Pick sat on the corner of his desk and folded his hands down at his knees. "Come on, Asher, how do you think? I went online and found out everything I could about you the night you left that message on my phone, before I even sent for the DNA test results. It led me to articles about Polly Ruddick...and her death, and her killer, Miller Hart."

CHAPTER 16
Asher Hart

Oh, Jesus. This was more than I could take. Pick knew. He knew everything.

"So...all this time...you already knew?"

He nodded.

I gasped a second for air, scared shitless, and then it dawned on me. He knew...had known a while, and he hadn't fired me or kicked me out of his life yet.

"And you're still okay with..." I waved a finger between us. "Us?"

Pick arched surprised eyebrows. "Were you really worried I wouldn't want to be your...?" He paused and glanced uneasily toward Sticks.

My drummer hunched deeper into himself, totally caught eavesdropping on our very personal conversation.

But I snorted and waved a hand his way. "He already knows."

That seemed to take Pick by surprise. "Really?"

I nodded, not concerned about Sticks. "Why is my dad here? Is he still in the building? Did he—"

"No, he's gone. Knox and I—mostly Knox—escorted him

to the door and let him know he was never welcome under this roof again."

Relief swamped me. "You kicked him out?" Good. But then renewed worry rose. What the hell had Miller Hart being doing inside Forbidden? Wiping a hand over my face, I eased myself down to sit on Pick's couch. "I wonder when he got out. I thought he still had a couple years left."

"I can answer that one," Remy spoke up. When I glanced his way, he explained the closing of Statesburg. And I could only shake my head.

"Well...fuck."

Sticks huffed out a sound of surprise. "Is that all you have to say?"

With a confused shrug, I asked, "What else am I supposed to say?"

"Oh, no sé. How about...where's the nearest place we can get you a restraining order?"

I huffed out a laugh. "Excuse me? Why the hell would I need one of those?"

"Think about it, Asher. He just got out of prison after spending how many years there?"

"Uh..." I did a quick calculation in my head. "About sixteen."

"Sixteen *years* behind bars, and where is the first place he goes when he's released? Here! The very place where the son—who testified against him and ultimately put him in jail—works."

My brain whirled at his words. I hadn't ever thought of it that way. But I had been the only person to testify in that trial with an eyewitness account, hadn't I? The old man probably *was* a bit pissed at me over that.

Huh.

"We need to get you some protection," Sticks stated adamantly, surprising me with how seriously he was taking this whole thing.

I snorted. "Yeah, I don't think that's really necessary."

"¡Dios mío!" He threw up his hands in outrage. "How can you just blow this off as no big deal? He came here...because of *you*. Maybe I'm the only one, but I find that pretty damn alarming."

"No, you're not the only one," Pick murmured.

I glanced at my brother who had his arms crossed over

his chest and was brushing his thumb knuckle over his bottom lip ring in thoughtful consternation.

Jesus, both of them were truly, honestly worried about me.

Yes, my father had been the big bad monster in my life when I'd been young. He'd scared the shit out of me back then, and I'd dreaded every moment I'd been forced to enter the same room as him. But a couple years ago, I'd visited the prison where he'd been held, determined to face my demons.

He hadn't recognized me. After asking me who I was, he wanted to know if I was his new legal representation and he started going on about how he was sure he could still get out if we played the murder off as self-defense. I never corrected him and ended up playing along before I left him with a lie, saying I'd be in contact.

The entire visit had left me...empty inside. No love lost for the man who'd terrorized me, and no fright retained either. He'd aged badly behind bars. He'd just been a weak, pathetic old man who hadn't stirred an ounce of fear in me.

So it was hard for me to summon any now.

"Or maybe he doesn't have a nefarious thought in his head," I told Pick and Remy. "Maybe the guy just wants to reconnect with his son."

"Yeah," Remy agreed with a sarcastic roll of his eyes, and he crossed his arms over his chest. "Because he was just the *soul* of fatherly love and devotion before, raising his precious little boy in a drug house and beating on him and his mother whenever the whim struck. *Right.*"

I scowled at him, deciding I'd definitely told him too much about myself. But, damn it, he did have a point. "Okay, fine, then. I'm his only living relative left. Who else is he going to go to for money or a place to crash? Honestly, if you'd just gotten out of jail after sixteen years, where would you go? He needs shit, and I'm sure he thinks I owe him."

"Well, he's not getting shit *from* you."

Remy's resolute proclamation made me laugh. "Really? And here I was planning on giving him everything I owned."

He didn't seem to appreciate my sarcasm. Spinning toward Pick, he pointed to me. "Talk some damn sense into him."

Pick sighed and scrubbed his face. "Look," he told me as

he dropped his hands. "No matter what his motive is, I don't want him near you either. And just to be on the safe side, I think a couple extra measures of protection would be wise."

"Okay, fine." I held up my hands as if surrendering to their will, but then I gripped my hair. "I will take everything both of you said into consideration, and I thank you for your concern, but honestly, this isn't your problem." When they opened their mouths, looking ready to argue with me, I quickly kept talking. "And if he ever returns, looking for me, just let me *deal* with him. I'll shoo him off myself. He's a weak old man now. He no longer scares me, and I'll be damned before I ever let him spook me again."

With that, I swung toward the door.

Pick leapt forward, panic in his eyes. "Where're you going?"

I sighed. It was kind of nice to know he cared enough to worry about me, but over this particular topic, it annoyed me. "Back to work. If you haven't noticed, we're still open, it's as busy as hell as out there, and I'm on the clock."

Almost daring him to react with the look I sent him, I pulled the door open.

A resigned breath eased from his lungs. "Just...watch your six, will you?"

"Aye-aye, Captain." I sent him a salute, sent Sticks a glance only to see him worriedly chewing on his fingernails, and I stepped into the hall. And what do you know, no Miller Hart leapt at me, intent to kill.

Both Pick and Remy found their way out to the bar a couple minutes later. They stuck around, chatting together over a beer, making me irritable with every minute they lingered.

I avoided both of them, not ready to talk any more about my father, or even think about him.

Except I couldn't get him out of my head. Learning he was free had rattled me. All bound up inside, I wasn't really sure exactly how the news affected me, I just knew it did. I wasn't scared, like some people thought I should be, but I was shocked and...unsettled. I really didn't want to face the old man. After my one and only visit to him behind bars, I'd put that part of my life behind me and moved on. I just wanted it to *stay* behind me.

Both of my self-appointed bodyguards finally left about an hour before closing, but either Pick had given Knox orders to escort me to my motorcycle or yet another person was worried about my safety.

That was weird, having people think about me and worry about me. I wasn't sure how to deal with it, so I just thanked my coworker and waved him off as soon as I started my beast.

When I made it to my place, yes, fine, I checked around a little to see if the old man was there. But the alley that led to my front door was empty. I unlocked all the deadbolts, remembered to lock up behind me, and jogged down the steps into my tiny domain.

Mozart rattling around in his cage was the only thing to greet me.

"Hey, little fella," I said, flipping on the main light, even though I'd left a dim nightlight on for him to see.

My entrance really set him off, racing even faster along the tunnels I'd made him to go from cage to cage until he was in the one closest to me. His excitement made me feel appreciated, even though I'm sure he wasn't glad to see *me* specifically; he was most likely only eager for me to let him loose. So I granted him his wish, and popped open his door.

He shot out past me, a blur of brown fur leaping a good five feet toward the back of the couch. Then he scurried along the backrest and dove onto the floor where he disappeared under my bed.

I sighed. "Yeah, it's nice to see you too, buddy."

Oh, well. He was better company than nothing.

Kicking off my shoes, I strolled into the kitchenette area and opened the mini fridge to pull out a bottle of water. I hadn't eaten since scarfing down half of Remy's food at practice, but I wasn't really hungry. And I didn't feel like sleeping even though I was tired as well. I already knew I'd only toss and turn if I crawled into bed right now, and I hated getting bound up in my own sheets...unless maybe I had company of the feminine variety with me.

But I had no woman around, and thoughts of my dad free and roaming the streets somewhere out there had my head spinning. I might catch an hour or two of sleep later, but not yet. Slouching into a chair at the table, I pulled my notebook I'd left sitting open to me and picked up a pen.

My muse certainly didn't feel as inspired as it had earlier, but this song was the only thing I wanted to work on. Except, shit, envisioning my dad, old and wrinkly at the prison, complaining about how unfairly he'd been treated, was the only thing I could focus on.

Scrubbing my face, I sat back in my chair and opened my mind. The first person to pop to the forefront of my thoughts was Incubus shirt girl, singing on stage and bumping her hip against that of the shorter redhead next to her. She'd been so sassy and relaxed up there, singing with confidence because she'd known she'd had it in the looks and the voice department, and she just wanted to have a little fun with both. It'd made me want to have a little fun with her.

But so much about her was blurry in my mind—I remembered too few actual details other than she'd had long dark hair. So I gave her the legs of the drummer chick who'd come to audition for us. I would've given her the drummer chick's face too, but I couldn't drag that up into my memory banks all that well either. I sucked at recalling faces. So, I guessed the legs and hair would have to do.

I imagined gripping handfuls of that silky, long dark hair while those incredible legs wrapped around me in the hopes of stirring forth a new line for the song.

Only I stirred up something else instead.

My jeans went tight in the lap area, so I slipped a little further down in my chair to make more room. But that didn't help. It'd been too long since little Asher had come out to play, and once I woke him, he only wanted more attention, and he just kept growing, demanding I give him some. So I unzipped and reached down to adjust myself. One of the small perks of living alone; I could sit around with my junk hanging out, and no one cared.

But the thought of no one caring infused that spark of loneliness that'd been claiming me lately, and I had to make myself think of the Incubus shirt girl again with Drummer Chick's legs to get over it. And yep, my dick just grew harder. Before I knew it, I was sliding my hand around the base of my cock and pumping it hard, not thinking about lyrics at all, but closing my eyes so I could daydream of soft, warm skin, long dark hair and a tight wet pussy that had me shooting my load all over my stomach in moments.

With a sigh of relief, I slunk further in my chair and

rested my head against the backrest. But as I panted out the last remnants of my orgasm, I only felt more pathetic than ever. Even though hooking up with some random woman after a gig wasn't my preference, it had to be better than jacking off alone in my apartment. At least I might get a little cuddle time in before she took off, claiming her girlfriends would never believe her when she told them she'd just bagged Asher Hart.

My buddies at Forbidden were right; I needed to get laid. Bad.

A sound from the bed made me glance over and nearly jump out of my skin when I saw Mozart standing there on his hind legs, tipping his head to the side and staring at me, his bushy tail giving the occasional twitch of interest.

I jerked upright in my chair, immediately shielding my dick from him. "What the hell, you little perv? Did you really just watch that?"

At my voice, he darted away and disappeared back under the bed. I sniffed in disgust—more disgusted with myself than my pet—and quickly cleaned my mess, then tucked my cock away before Mozart tried to cop another glimpse of it.

After I picked up my pen and tapped it against my notepad, I sighed in defeat. The adrenaline rush from getting the Chicago gig was officially dead. I wasn't able to write another word for the rest of the night.

CHAPTER 17
Asher Hart

I FINALLY DROPPED OFF TO sleep around eight the next morning after tempting Mozart back into his cage with some sunflower seeds.

By ten, my phone started blowing up. Okay, fine, I got three texts and then a phone call. But for me, that was busy. I ignored the texts but groaned and swatted my arm out blindly for my phone on my nightstand when it just kept ringing.

After I slurred out a hello, Pick's way too awake voice blared in my ear. "Hey, I got another house to check out. You in?"

I wiped my hand over my face, yawned, and then sat up. "Sure. When and where?"

"I'll pick you up in ten."

He hung up on me, and I shook my head, not sure why he kept asking me to tag along. Then I went to erase the texts he'd sent, only to discover they weren't from him. All three were from Sticks.

Hey, just checking in to make sure you made it home okay and your dad didn't sneak in and suffocate you in your sleep last night.

The next : *This is where you answer and tell me you're fine. You can even add a "now fuck off" if my worry irritates you.*

And finally: *Seriously, man. Are you dead or just pissed at me?*

Having pity on him, I typed back. *Not dead, just sleeping.*

He shot back an immediate reply. *Shit, sorry for waking you. Forgot you work so late. But glad you're alive. Try to stay that way. We kind of need you next Saturday for the Chicago gig.*

Grinning, I shook my head and told him I'd see what I could do. Then I tossed my phone back onto the nightstand and rushed to yank on some clothes before Pick showed up. I snagged an apple that I'd bought for Mozart and was just polishing it off when my brother pulled up to my door in his Barracuda.

"So which neighborhood are we going to this time?" I asked as I slid into the passenger's seat.

When Pick answered me as he shifted the car into drive, I gave a low, impressed whistle. "Nice."

A proud grin twitched across his lips. "Nothing's too good for my family."

"Which reminds me," I said, settling deeper into my seat and tipping my head back to close my eyes. "Don't you think you should actually, I don't know, *propose* to Eva first before buying a house with her?" They called each other husband and wife already, as did half the group we hung with, but they'd yet to tie the actual knot. "Or do you not go for that kind of traditional shit?"

"Oh, I've proposed." Pick sent me a smug, secretive smile as he wiggled his eyebrows. "And we've even set a date...in about a month, actually. Which reminds me, you going to be my best man or what?"

I choked on air. After sitting upright and pounding on my chest with my fist, I sent him an incredulous glance. "What? *Me*? What about Mason?"

Mason would be the obvious choice. He was Reese's man, and since Reese was Eva's cousin and best friend, she'd no doubt be the maid of honor. Besides, the four of them hung out a lot, or so I'd heard. He had to be much closer to Mason than he was to me.

But Pick only shrugged. "I'm sure he'd understand that

I'd rather have you stand up with me."

Shaken by such a declaration, I rubbed my hands over my face. "You seriously don't have a problem with who my dad is, do you?"

"What do you mean?" He glanced at me, clearly confused.

I sputtered out my disbelief. "What do you think? He...he killed your mother."

After squinting as if even more boggled by my explanation, he murmured, "She was your mother too."

I blew out a breath. He definitely wasn't the type to put the sins of the father on the son, that was for sure. "I still can't believe you know everything already," I muttered, more to myself than him. "I kept wondering why you never asked about her."

He shrugged and turned down a nice, quiet residential street that had me staring out the window and salivating at all the amazing houses. "I figured you'd tell me when you were ready."

"It's not a pretty story," I said, watching a mother with two small boys open the door to one house and step outside. They looked like a happy, healthy family together.

I glanced away.

"I didn't figure it was."

"She talked a lot about you...and your dad. She told me all kinds of shit she probably never should've." Like how she'd never forgiven my father for stopping her home abortion attempt that he'd walked in on in their bathroom when she'd been pregnant with me.

"But she loved him, if that's any consolation." I glanced his way. From the expression on his face, he was soaking in every word and wanted to hear more. "She was sixteen and he was nineteen. All she ever called him was Chaz, so I don't know his full name, sorry."

Pick gave a small shrug, letting me know that was okay. He was learning more about his sperm donor than he'd ever heard before.

"Her family didn't approve of them being together. He was a high school dropout who drank a lot, and it didn't look as if he'd ever aspire above the mechanic job he had."

Pick glanced at me sharply. "Mechanic?"

I nodded. "Yeah, he was into cars too. So, anyway, when

Mom—Polly—left home to be with him, her family cut all ties with her. She got pregnant almost immediately, and then went into labor on the same day your dad was killed in a drive-by shooting at the garage where he worked."

I rushed the last part, not sure how Pick would take it. His fingers tightened around the steering wheel, but he said nothing. He only slowed the car in front of a two-story with a For-Sale sign in the yard, pulled to the curb and cut the engine.

Then he blew out a breath. "So, he's dead too, huh?"

"I'm sorry," I shook my head sadly. "She was pretty upset and couldn't handle a new baby so soon after what happened, but she always talked about how much she regretted leaving you. She never tried to find you again, though; she was convinced you had to be in a better place."

I didn't mention how many times she'd told me over the years that she wished she'd left me and kept him instead.

"Well..." Pick said slowly, staring straight ahead out the window. "That's something, I guess." Then he glanced at me and lifted his eyebrows. "Ready to look at this place?"

I had upset him. Feeling shitty about that but no with idea how to fix it, I nodded and opened my door. "Let's do it."

I didn't really want to look at houses anymore, so as soon as we met with the realtor and he started showing us features, I said, "You might as well save it, man, and just show us the backyard first."

Pick laughed while the other guy sent me a funny look. But we got to see the backyard first, and as soon as disappointment glinted across my brother's face, I knew he hadn't yet found what he was looking for.

Waiting until we were back in his car and driving away from the house, I finally let my curiosity get the best of me. "So, are you ever going to tell me what's up with the backyard thing?"

Pick sent me a small frown, then groaned and admitted, "You'll never believe me."

I shrugged. "Try me."

"Okay, fine. I've seen it before. In...like, a vision."

One eyebrow shot up. I wasn't as startled by what he said as I was by learning he was actually into that. I never would've taken him as the type.

Lifting a finger, he warned, "Don't look at me like that. I

don't believe that shit either, but it's fucking true."

"I didn't say anything."

"When I was a kid," he went on with a reluctant sigh, "I had an...encounter once, with this witch lady. Like a true witch, who sold potions and shit and told fortunes from her home."

"Okay..." I said slowly.

"I'm not fucking lying," he muttered defensively.

I laughed and lifted my hands in surrender. "I didn't say you were."

"I went to her place to throw a rock through her window because she'd upset one of my friends, but she caught me and put her hands on my face. I don't know what the hell she did, but I suddenly had all these visions, like little flashbacks, but they were flash-*forwards*. I saw Tinker Bell, and Julian, and Skylar in them...ten years before I even met Eva or the kids were ever born. We were living as a family in some house that I only saw from the backyard, and..." He glanced at me. "You were in one of the visions too."

"*Me?*" The hair on the back of my neck immediately stood on end.

Pick nodded. "You were at my wedding reception, in a tux, over by the sound system at Forbidden, exactly how you have the stage and everything set up now. That's why I didn't turn you away when you showed up that first day, asking about playing there. I'd seen you before. I knew you had to stick around long enough to be at my wedding."

"Shit," I said, stunned by everything he'd just told me.

"Oh, and by the way, the first song Eva and I have to dance to is 'Baby Love.' Don't forget that."

"Shit," I said again.

He grinned. "Too much to take in all at once?"

I shook my head but said, "A little bit, yeah." Then I turned fully in my seat to gape at him. "You're not shitting me, are you?"

He shook his head. "Not even at all."

"Huh." I tapped my fingers against my bottom lip to the rhythm of "Baby Love," because now that song was stuck in my head. "So, let me get this straight. You're searching for that backyard you saw in your vision during all these house hunting trips?"

When he nodded, I snorted. "Well, that's just stupid."

"Excuse me?" He shot me a surprised scowl right before he pulled down the alley to my place and stopped in front of my door.

I only shrugged, not apologizing. "The way I see it, you already have the best parts of the dream. The woman and the kids, right?"

"Right," he said slowly.

"So, why don't you just enjoy them and let the rest of it fall into place on its own. Stop trying to force shit to come true, because hell...someone else could still be living in your dream home. It could be years before it even becomes available for sale. Why torture yourself—and Eva—with turning everything else down and upsetting her in the process, when you could just be *enjoying* the best parts together, right now?"

Pick was thoughtfully quiet before he murmured, "Good point." Then he glanced at me and grinned. "It'd sure make Tinker Bell a lot happier if she actually felt as if she had a say-so in deciding where we lived."

"Then...there you go."

"Damn." He huffed out a small laugh. "Why didn't I think about it that way?"

"I guess you just needed your little brother around to slap some sense into you."

He grinned, genuinely pleased by my answer. "So you're finally ready to admit we're related, huh?"

I glanced out the window toward the rusted metal door that led down to my apartment. "I suppose I should, since I'm going to be the best man in your wedding, and all."

When I risked a glance his way, he beamed at me and reached out to ruffle my hair, like he was some kind of older brother.

I kind of wanted to hang out with him some more, but it felt too risky, like something bad would happen if I stuck around him too long, and I'd lose him, so I mumbled, "See you around," as I opened the door.

But Pick grabbed my arm. "Hey, wait."

I glanced back at him.

He turned his attention to my front door as well, but his gaze seemed to linger on the three deadbolts keeping it shut. "You haven't heard from your father again since last night, have you?"

I groaned. "Jesus, you sound like Sticks. No, he never

showed up here, and I never saw him at the bar after you left."

"Good." Then he used his teeth to play with his bottom lip ring. "What's up between you and your new drummer anyway?"

That question caught me totally off guard. "Nothing. Why?"

He shrugged. "Don't know. You two just seem awfully close for just meeting."

I blinked, not sure what he was leading his questions toward. Slowly, I said, "Yeah, I guess. I like him. He's funny, has good taste in music, and can play the shit out of the drums." And he had an uncanny way of making me tell him all my personal drama. Plus I felt a strange connection to him.

"I think he likes you, too," Pick murmured. "A lot."

I began to snort and deny his claim, but then I shrugged. "I don't know. He *is* gay; I guess it's possible."

"Huh. Maybe that's it. He's just gay."

I frowned, confused. "What do you mean? You don't like him?"

"Yeah, I do. He seemed fine. There was just something...different about him."

I straightened, almost defensive of my new friend. "Different how?"

"I don't know," Pick answered with his own confused frown. "There was just something about him when I was talking with him last night that made me want to treat him like he was...a woman."

I laughed. "Yeah, I'm guessing that's the gay thing. I'm not sure."

"So you've noticed his little effeminate qualities too? Damn, we *must* be related then."

Grinning, I opened my door wide. "Leave my poor drummer alone. He can be whatever the fuck he wants to be. I still think he's cool as hell."

"I did have fun talking to him." He leaned toward me as I stepped out of the car and called, "And just so you know, if he ends up turning you toward men, I'll still proudly claim you as my brother."

"Oh...fuck you, man." I slammed the door on him but still had to chuckle and shake my head as I turned away and unlocked my door.

But really. Couldn't a heterosexual man just be friends with a homosexual man without everyone assuming shit?

CHAPTER 18
Remy Curran

I COULDN'T CALM MY NERVES. It was Saturday, we were in Chicago, and we'd be playing in hours—mere *hours*—in front of a new crowd of listeners, a larger venue, pickier fans who were used to having bigger named bands in their club. And we were getting paid ten times the usual amount.

It was as if we were actually on our way to *somewhere*!

Asher had rented a van to take the four of us together plus all our equipment, my drum set taking up the most room. It was cramped, and stunk to high heaven—because Heath had a serious gas problem—when we alighted in the city, four hours after being trapped in one vehicle together. I gasped for air as soon as I pushed out the side-sliding back door. But God, as soon as I got into my room at the hotel where we were planning on staying the night before heading back first thing in the morning, I was taking off this mask and fake chest and lying naked on my bed to just...air out.

Behind me, Gally and Heath began to unload their luggage while Asher headed for the front desk to secure our rooms. I stole another moment for myself, glad I didn't have to listen to Gally degrade women anymore while he bragged about how much pussy he got, or smell any more of Heath's dirty sock farts.

But Gally just had to go and holler, "Sticks, get your shit already. I'm not hauling your gay-ass luggage around for you."

I spun to glare at him; my luggage was a plain, boring black. Dios, he was such an ass. But I tromped back to the van, anyway, because I didn't want his disgusting hands anywhere near my things.

"Sorry, guys," Asher announced as he rejoined us, flashing two key cards. "Looks like we're doubling up tonight."

My stomach immediately began to swirl. "Say what?"

I'd made it explicitly clear I'd wanted my own room; I didn't care how much extra it cost me.

But holy shit, this couldn't seriously be happening. How the hell was I supposed to take my mask off to sleep? Panic clawed at my throat.

"Wha...wha...why are we doing that?"

Asher sent me a small cringe of apology. "We're too close to Soldier Field, and apparently the Bears have a home football game tomorrow. I got us the last two rooms available."

I scowled. Stupid Bears. Stupid football. Why, why, *why* would they do this to me? I was counting on having my own damn room.

Asher tossed a piece of plastic at Gally. "You and Sticks can take 5B. Holden and I will be in—"

"Oh, fuck, no," Gally exploded. "You're not bunking me with the queer. What if he crawls into bed with me in the middle of the night and tries to get kinky?"

I snorted. "As if that would ever happen."

"He'll see me change," Gally whined to Asher, completely ignoring me. "And I sleep naked. I don't want Sticks seeing me naked."

Him and me both. Now, I was turning toward Asher, my eyes begging. "Please, God, do *not* stick me with him."

"Fine." Asher rolled his eyes big enough to encompass Gally and me together. "You take Heath then. Sticks can room with me."

Oh, Dios, *what*?

Me room with Asher Hart?

No! In its own way, that was worse.

I actually *wanted* to see him naked. Crap, what if I saw him naked? Then I probably *would* try to crawl into bed with him in the middle of the night to get kinky.

I felt a little sick to my stomach with worry.

But seriously, how the hell was I going to hide the fact I was a girl from someone sharing a room with me?

Oh, fuck. How was I supposed to take off my mask at all during this trip?

"There's two beds, right?"

Asher sent me a dry look. "Yeah."

I almost passed out from the relief of that answer, but I managed a much more contained nod. "Cool."

So we unloaded our overnight bags from the van, left the instruments inside, and while Heath and Gally wandered off to find 5B, Asher and I stayed on the ground level, looking for 1D. I trudged along after him, rolling my suitcase behind me while he only toted a small duffle bag over his shoulder.

My mind raced as I kept thinking up ways my identity could possibly be revealed. Thank Dios it wasn't that time of the month; I wouldn't have any feminine hygiene products lying around. I'd even gone out and bought all new manly toiletries so I could play the part. But still, it'd take only one peek inside my luggage to see my girly thong or spare mask Jodi had made me, in case this one had a costume malfunction.

I wasn't sure how Asher or the other two would react when they found out, but I was pretty sure I didn't want to risk it happening while I was trapped with them in Chicago.

Trying not to worry or think about that, I said, "I'm sorry you got stuck with the gay guy."

Asher's back was to me as he unlocked the door to our room. Holy shit, I couldn't believe I was going to share a hotel room with Asher Hart.

"Don't worry about it." He glanced over his shoulder to grin at me. "What Gally doesn't know is I've seen Heath fall asleep on breaks when we used to work together. He snores like a freaking freight train."

I chuckled and shook my head. "Burn."

He flung the door open and entered ahead of me. "Do you have a preference of beds?"

And now I was talking about beds with Asher Hart.

Unreal.

"Uh...no. Whatever." *I'd be totally fine with just sharing*, I didn't say aloud.

He flung his bag onto the bed nearest the door and immediate toed off his shoes. I rolled my case to the end of the bed closest to the bathroom and ducked my head inside to see how much room was in there, because apparently, this might be the only space I'd get to peel off Sticks for a couple minutes and actually breathe.

It was small but clean, so I guessed it'd have to do.

When I exited, Asher was shedding his shirt and flinging it onto his bed.

My mouth went dry. Seriously, for such a slim guy, he knew how to pack a few awesome muscles into his lean frame. Then he reached for his fly, and my eyes almost bugged from my head.

"Wha...wha...whatcha doing?" I managed to ask.

He shimmied his jeans down his legs until he was in nothing but boxer shorts. "I'd rather not smell like Holden's ass for the rest of the night so I'm taking a quick shower."

"Oh." I couldn't take my eyes off him as he unzipped his duffle and fished around inside, keeping his boxer shorts on. I should probably look away or do something productive like... I don't know. But I really needed to stop gawking.

Not that I did that either.

I just kept right on staring...and probably drooling.

"Damn," Asher muttered suddenly. "I forgot to pack my bathroom shit." He glanced up. "Hey, did you bring any toiletries? I hate those little bars of soap they leave. It's like they only provide enough to clean your big toe."

It took me a second to actually return to reality and the conversation at hand, and then I blinked. "You forgot *everything*? How can you forget *all* your freaking toiletries?"

As I hauled my luggage onto my bed and opened it, easing my hand inside and afraid of what I might've left sitting on top, Asher snorted. "How can you *remember* all of them?"

Extracting my very manly cosmetic bag, I flung it toward him, where he caught it effortlessly. "It's not that difficult."

He opened my tote and whistled. "Jesus, you really did remember everything, too. What the hell is all this *for*?"

Offended by his question, I scowled. "What do you mean? I only brought what I needed."

"Really?" Arching one eyebrow, he lifted a bottle. "You need this? I don't even know what it is?"

"It's gel. You know, to style your hair."

"Right." He shoved it back into the tote, only to fish out a comb, soap, shampoo, and aerosol deodorant. "*This* is all you need, man. And a razor if you're going to be gone a while."

With a sniff, I rolled my eyes. "Such a caveman."

He laughed. "Shut up." With a grin, he flung my bag at me. Unprepared, I fumbled to catch it against my chest.

"I'm taking a shower," he announced as he strolled into the bathroom with my things. "Thanks for letting me borrow your shit. I owe you one."

"Uh-huh," I murmured, distracted as I glanced into my cosmetics bag. "Wait! Don't you want the conditioner?" Pulling it out, I held it up for him to see.

He paused and glanced back, scowling. "I thought only women used that."

"Oh, gee, would you read this here little label? It says conditioner *for men*."

"Yeah, but only—" He broke off suddenly, as if he knew he was about to say something offensive.

"Only what?" I asked, lifting my brows. "Go ahead and finish that sentence. Only *gay* guys use it?"

He scowled. "That's...*not* what I was going to say."

I sent him a look, letting him know I knew better, and he frowned harder.

Then I sighed. "I seriously can't believe you don't condition your hair." It looked so soft and shiny, as if it was properly taken care of. "With those blond highlights, you must have split ends galore. It's just...what a sad state of affairs is all I can say. And I bet your roots—"

"Oh, brother." He reached out a hand. "Toss me the fucking conditioner."

I did, smiling smugly for some reason. "And when you're done, I'll use the gel on you and show you how to probably style that gorgeous mane of yours."

He froze, staring at me, only his eyelashes moving as he blinked. "You...want to *style* my hair?"

"What?" I asked innocently. "I'm gay, remember?"

A small smile cracked his lips and his shoulders relaxed an inch. "You're fucking with me right now, aren't you?"

"Of course." With a wink, I blew a kiss at him. "How could I resist?"

"Jesus." Shaking his head and chuckling softly under his breath, he began to close himself inside his bathroom as he said, "I knew there was a reason I liked you."

As the latch clicked shut, a broad smile swept across my face. That had been kind of fun.

Note to self: verbally joust with Asher Hart as often as possible.

Sure, he'd treated me like a guy the entire time, but this giddy little bubble inside me kept floating higher and higher in my chest.

Despite his forgetfulness and complete lack of organizational skills, Asher was a cool guy. Not once on the ride up here had he done anything to annoy me, quite unlike the other two, who thank God, I was actually relieved I didn't have to room with. And he had my sense of humor. No one had my sense of humor.

This was just...awesome.

The water in the shower kicked on, and my grin died a sudden death. All I could picture was him...naked and wet, slicking the very soap I'd bought onto parts I'd never get to see...or touch. I wanted to be his hands so bad right now, smoothing their way up his muscled abs, or soaping his hair. Damn. This wasn't awesome at all. He was torturing me without even knowing it.

Asher Hart didn't need some fancy seduction to draw a woman in. He just had to be himself for me to want him. Bad.

CHAPTER 19
Asher Hart

I ended up letting Remy style my hair. I have no idea why; I knew he'd just been joking about that. But it'd been fun to tease around with him, and I needed a distraction, because truth be told, I was a little nervous about tonight.

Performing at Forbidden had become comfortable and predictable. I loved it, but I knew if we were ever going to grow, we needed to branch out. So...here was to new-and-terrifying experiments.

Gel-styled hair included.

Sticks jabbered the whole time, altering his voice to sound like one of those flaming hairstylists from old eighties movies and making his wrist limp when he flung out a hand. "Don't you worry, darling, we'll make you look just *marvelous*."

"Shut up, asshole." I punched at his knee, though he jumped back in time, dodging me. "Just do your thing."

So he'd gooped his hand with that gel crap and sunk all ten fingers into my hair.

I closed my eyes and tried not to enjoy it too much.

But...fuck. For someone who wasn't raised by the touchy-feely kind of parents and then by an uncle who was the exact same way, even the slightest human contact was like complete carnal awareness for me. And he really had to torture me by working slowly, gently tugging at my scalp with these rhythmic pulls that forced me to swallow down a moan of delight.

It reminded me I hadn't really been touched, aside from friendly jostles or pats on the shoulders from friends, in months. It made me crave sex, body against body, hands and lips caressing, mouths full of breasts and fingers buried deep in tight, wet—

When Sticks said something about how amazed he was by the lack of split ends, I jumped in surprise, suddenly remembering *he* was the one touching me.

"You about done?" I asked, moodily shifting my weight around on the closed toilet lid.

His hands in my hair suddenly felt way too personal. Even the women I slept with didn't play with my hair this much. They'd been known to grip it when they were coming, but after that, it was no use to them. I wasn't too sure how to deal with Remy being so familiar with it. And I'd never in a million years admit I liked how it felt when he messed with it.

"Geez, impatient much?" He pulled his hands free, and I almost whimpered from the loss of his touch. After picking up the comb, he did a little swishy thing here and there and then stepped back. "There. Perfection." Grinning proudly, he motioned toward the mirror. "What do you think?"

I stood and checked out my reflection. He'd fashioned it all to flare up and off to one side in a somewhat messy fashion, but it was like a controlled kind of chaos. I looked like a freaking rock star. But then, I guess that was the idea. "It's..."

"Sexy as hell," Remy confirmed, earning a glower from me. But he shrugged, nonplussed. "Yeah, you thought you had a lot of women crawling all over you before. Just wait until tonight, boy. That beautiful mess is going to bring *all* the girls to the yard."

I laughed, but the mention of women made me think of sex again.

It reminded me how long it'd been since I'd gotten laid, and a pulsing heat spread through my dick. Then my mind went into über caveman mode, thinking of nothing but pussy. And thrusting.

Damn. This was getting bad. I really needed to do something about this.

Grunting out something—I'm not even sure what—I escaped the bathroom and gathered up my wallet and keys. "I'm going to scout out the area, find out how close we are to the club. Then it'll probably be about time to head out. Bathroom's all yours, man."

He leaned his shoulder against the doorjamb, watching me. When all he said was, "Okay," a strange unease claimed me, as if I should do more, or *know* more, or hell, I don't even know. I just didn't feel right. So I ran. "Thanks again for...you know." I motioned to my hair and hurried out the door.

I stayed away longer than I probably should have, but at least I learned the lay of the land, and when I returned to gather up the band, I was able to drive us straight to our destination without getting lost.

With Gally's jabbering and Holden's loud silence, the weirdness I'd experienced earlier with Sticks dissipated, and I was able to think about the actual gig. While we waited backstage for our time to start—because this place actually had a backstage—Sticks cracked his neck and hopped on the balls of his feet, as if preparing for a race or something.

I shook my head and grinned. "What the hell are you doing?"

He only shrugged. "Loosening up." Then he rolled his shoulders and kicked out each leg before shaking it. "You have no idea how stiff I get after sitting on that stool for so long."

Made sense, so I turned away, and sucked in a breath when the coordinator waved us forward. "We're up," I announced to the guys and led the way onto the stage, where a crew had already set up our equipment.

I exhaled a rush when I saw the crowd. This place wasn't as packed as Forbidden usually was, but it was easily four times the size, meaning it held at least twice as many people. It was dark out on the floor with about four blue spotlights flaring down on where we were each supposed to stand, already heating the back of my neck.

I jogged to my place, slipped on my Taylor, and reached for the mike, glancing around me to make sure the others were ready. When Remy nodded, I gave him the signal to begin before we even introduced ourselves.

I finally did a little talking two songs later, telling the crowd a little about who we were, where we were from, and where they could find more information about us. By this point, we'd riled them up with our music, and they were more responsive, cheering when I introduced each member.

And then we were playing again, rocking each song. I thought we were going to have a problem when Holden experienced a smidgeon of stage fright and missed a lick on the guitar. But Remy kept the beat steady the entire time, and it was easy for Heath to pick right back up with us.

Relieved, I sang a little stronger to make up for it, and no one seemed to notice. They cheered us on, and danced, and seemed to have fun.

By the time we finished, I was drenched in sweat but riding an adrenaline high that felt freaking incredible. The owner—yeah, the actual owner—met us behind the stage to invite us back again in a month, and I only had to glance at my bandmates for them to agree, so I bobbed my head yes.

After that, we were given coupons for discounted drinks at the bar, and I think all four of us were too wired to crash yet, so we took them and headed out into the club.

Gally immediately disappeared, on the search for a one-night stand, but Holden, Sticks and I found a free table to park ourselves. It took a few minutes for people to recognize us, but soon a trio of carbon copy blondes were gathered at our table, one particularly bold as she slid right up onto my knee and perched herself there to tell me how much she'd liked watching us.

Her perfume was strong, but her body was soft and oh-so feminine, and I had all this excess energy to expend; I didn't send her away. I even set a hand on her waist so I didn't have to worry about her losing her balance and tumbling off my leg. She flirted with me while her friends gathered closer, one of them finally turning to Sticks to talk to him.

I knew the woman on my lap would be willing if I wanted to take this any further. Hell, I had a feeling she'd be willing if I wanted to drag her off to some private corner in the club and take her right then. But something kept stopping me from acting, probably the way she kept calling me by my first and last name together.

Annoying as hell.

We'd been sitting there less than ten minutes when someone approached, calling my name.

I glanced over and nearly fell out of my chair when I met my dad's snickering gaze.

"What the hell?" I demanded. "What're *you* doing here?"

"We need to talk." He leered at the cleavage of the woman on my lap before returning his attention to me. "Now."

"Wha... How did you find me?"

"It's posted on your little band's website. Since they kicked me out of that shithole you usually play at and I haven't gotten your home address yet, this is the only place I could reach you."

"He doesn't want to talk to you," Sticks answered for me, appearing at my side so he could fold his arms over his chest and glare at my dad.

The old man blinked at him before snorting. "What the fuck is this?" he asked me. "Your bodyguard. Little bastard's smaller than I am."

"I'm also younger, faster, and *armed*," Sticks reported, narrowing his eyes.

His posturing amused me, and kind of delighted me since it meant he cared enough to have my back, but it was totally unnecessary.

"Excuse me a minute, sweetheart." I scooted the woman off my lap and then stood before telling Remy, "I got this." Motioning my dad to follow me, I found the quietest place possible to hear whatever he had to say. When I noticed my drummer had followed us and stopped a few feet away, I rolled my eyes. He really was worried, the weirdo.

Then I faced the guy who used to be my living nightmare. But yeah, I couldn't summon my old fear of him. I was a head taller and wider than him now. He just looked shriveled and crude, and bitter. I couldn't even think of him as a killer. I'd been there, I'd seen his shock. He hadn't meant to take her life.

He was nothing but a nasty, washed-up bully.

"What do you want?" I asked, folding my arms over my chest.

"I want to know where my stash is," he snarled, moving

intimidatingly close, which was also a joke.

I shook my head, clueless. "What stash?"

"The fucking stash I had hidden away when they arrested me."

Barking out a laugh, I shook my head. I hadn't seen the guy in sixteen years, and all he cared about were his drugs? No *sorry for murdering your mother, for all the split lips and black eyes, for raising you like a slave.* Just *where's my drugs*?

It figured.

"And you honestly think I know what happened to that shit?" I kept swishing my head back and forth. "They never let me back into the apartment. I don't know what happened to *anything.*"

Growling out his disappointment, the old man gnawed on his bottom lip. "So you think the cops found it?"

I lifted my hands. "I have no idea. And honestly, I don't give a flying fuck what happened to your drugs. You're on your own with this one."

I started to walk past him but he grabbed my shirtsleeve. "Hey, I'm not done talking to you, you little cocksucker."

Sticks shifted toward us, sliding his hand into his pocket. My dad darted him a scowl but immediately eased up on me. Leaning closer, he snarled. "You owe me. I kept that bitch from killing you I don't know how many times, from drowning you in the bathtub or suffocating you with a pillow. I kept you breathing and provided for you."

I glanced at him impassively. "And yet I have no idea why." He'd never shown me an ounce of compassion himself.

"Because you were supposed to turn out like me." He started to step even closer but then remembered Remy and sent him a cautious glance. When he turned back, his lip curled into a sneer. "But you had to go and turn out like *this.*"

I shook my head and sighed, focusing on Sticks because I couldn't look at the waste of space that was supposed to be my father. "I told you I don't know where your stash is, and I don't. So...we're done here."

I started off again, but he called, "I need some money to start back in again. Damn, kid, don't you fucking walk away from me. You'll regret it."

Without even glancing back, I spoke to Remy out the

side of my mouth when he immediately moved to my side. "See, I told he wasn't out to kill me."

"Oh yeah, sure; that *you'll regret this* wasn't threatening at all."

I laughed. "Relax, man. I'm sure that's the last time I'll ever see or hear from him."

"I think you're wrong, but whatever."

With a glance his way, I asked, "Are you really carrying a weapon? What the hell are you packing in your pocket?" I just couldn't picture him tucking a gun in his luggage between his conditioner and hair gel.

So when he reluctantly answered, "Mace and a whistle," I threw my head back and laughed.

Gripping his shoulder, I had to admit, "Man, you crack me up."

"Hmm. Well, looky there," he muttered, falling to a stop before we reached our table. "Your harem of sluts was kind enough to wait for you."

His bitter tone only made me smile. "What? Jealous because there's no dude in the group for *you*?"

He glowered at me. "Mmm hmm. Yes, that must be it."

When I shrugged and started back to the table again, he caught my forearm. "I can't stick around. I'm going to see if I can catch a cab and get a ride back to the hotel. Are you sure your dad won't come back? I could leave my mace and whistle with you."

I flipped him off. "I think I can manage without a freaking rape-prevention whistle."

He shook his head and eyed the women watching and waiting for us to return. "I don't know, Hart. That one looks like she's ready to tear your clothes off any second, whether you're willing or not."

With a chuckle, I shoved him away. "Whatever. Get lost already. I'll see you back at the hotel."

A miserable expression crossed his face, but then he nodded and turned away. I watched him walk off for a second, then I shook my head and turned back to the women.

CHAPTER 20
Remy Curran

Fine, yes, I admit it. Seeing that skank crawling all over Asher had turned me into an evil jealous troll bitch. But I couldn't help it. She just kept touching him. And *I* wanted to touch him.

It was no fair. I couldn't even freaking put my bid in, since I was pretending to be a dude and all.

Unable to watch her maul him a second longer, I had hightailed it out of there and slumped back to the hotel, miserable, when I should've been pumped and happy. We had rocked that performance. It'd been awesome, right up until that slut had crawled into Asher's lap, and he'd actually wrapped his arm around her waist. Had me so worked up I couldn't even worry about his dad showing up.

Ugh.

I tried not to wonder what would've happened if I'd been in full girl mode, decked out in my makeup and tiny black dress. Could I have competed for his attention, stolen him away from lap slut?

And why did it even matter? I was never going to get that chance. I'd shot myself in the foot the moment I'd stepped into the auditioning room as Sticks.

After taking an extra-long shower, then cleaning and blow-drying my sweaty, sticky mask, I put it back on because I had no idea when Asher planned on returning. I just knew I couldn't sleep with all my dark long hair spilling out over the sheet.

I reluctantly crawled into bed, flipped off my nightlight, and then tossed and turned for what felt like forever, wondering just what he was doing with that other girl, where he was touching her, where she was kissing him, how many clothes were being removed.

Damn. I punched my pillow. This was stupid. I was his bandmate. That was all. He could do whatever he pleased with whomever he pleased. It shouldn't be any of my business or concern.

So why the hell did I want to cry so badly?

Finally, what felt like hours later, my consciousness dragged me into a fitful sleep. It felt as if I'd barely drifted off when I was jerked awake by the opening of my room door.

Hoping Asher was alone and hadn't brought his *friend* back with him, I froze, even tried to stop breathing.

Oh, Dios. What if he had brought her back, though? Would I have to lie here and pretend to sleep while he screwed some other woman only a few feet away?

No way in hell could I handle that.

My face itched like crazy inside my mask, but I refrained from scratching or moving a muscle as quiet footsteps—just one pair, *whew*—shuffled across the floor. Mattress springs shifted behind me as Asher sat on his bed.

My body instantly responded, heating uncontrollably inside my already warm disguise. But then the reek of feminine perfume hit me and I went cold. He'd taken that other girl home then. The blonde.

I really hated that blonde.

Asher let out a long, tired sigh, and I could picture him rubbing his weary face, maybe running his talented fingers through his silky dark hair. Hair I'd had my fingers in and gotten to touch and play with, hair that I wanted to experience again.

He stood. The soft swish of clothing told me he was undressing.

Oh, man. My internal thermometer soared, spiking off the charts with a horny heat.

I shouldn't look. I shouldn't look. I totally shouldn't look.

I really was being a good girl and not looking, but then he walked into the bathroom, and in order to get there, he had to pass my bed and right where I was staring wide-eyed into the darkened room...well, mostly darkened until he turned on the bathroom light and gifted me with a view of his perfectly formed bare ass.

Sweet baby Jesus.

His toned, tanned cheeks were...they were...yeah.

Sweet baby Jesus.

All too soon, he closed the bathroom door, disappearing inside and shrouding me back into the darkness of the hotel room. The shower kicked on and my imagination ran wild, thinking of all the places he had to be touching his wet, naked body right now, running my soap over warm, sculpted skin and slicking a sudsy trail down his taut stomach to between his legs, where he was probably cupping his testicles and palming them clean.

Damn. A shower had never seemed so freaking dirty before.

I wanted to be under that steamy spray with him so bad.

My body ached and my nipples burned with the need to be touched. Closing my eyes, I breathed through my mask's nose holes, each shallow breath highlighting my arousal as my hand wandered down inside the waistband of my flannel pants and into my panties.

God, how I loved sexy silk panties. They were perfect for self-pleasure, for sliding them against your clit to create friction for a maximum experience.

But tonight, it didn't matter what I was wearing down there. I could've gotten off to the mere sound of Asher Hart singing George Ezra's "Budapest" in the shower.

I was inches from fondling myself, my hips already straining to lift off the bed, when the water shut off in the bathroom.

Damn it.

Why couldn't he have dawdled a little longer?

I yanked my hand free of my clothes and squeezed my legs together just as the bathroom door opened. Automatically, my eyes flew open.

Asher stepped out, dripping wet, with a towel slung around his waist. I gaped at the beauty that was his bare chest as he skidded to a surprised halt.

"Shit," he said, wincing. "Sorry, Rem. I didn't mean to wake you."

"S'okay," I slurred, trying to act half awake, when honestly I was freaking *wide* awake. With a yawn, I stretched and rolled to face away from him.

But that actually solved nothing. He strolled to his side of the room, which I was now turned toward.

And then he dropped his towel.

On purpose.

"You been asleep long?" he asked in a conversational manner as if nothing earth-shattering at all was happening. Glancing my way as he dug a pair of his own flannel pants from his duffle bag, he lifted his eyebrows curiously.

"Uh..." My eyes refused to blink as I watched him tug the pants up his legs without putting on any underwear first.

Oh, Christ. Did he always crawl into bed commando? This was not something I should know. Technically, I wasn't supposed to know how well hung he was either. But, wow, *was he ever*. How could such a slim guy be so thick where it mattered most?

Licking my lips, I had to turn away and roll onto my other side as he pulled back his sheets and crawled into his bed.

"Not long," I finally answered once I was facing away from him.

Not long? *Whatever*! That was probably one of the longest dicks I'd ever seen. And the girth. Hot damn, it'd take more than one hand for me to wrap my fingers all the way around it.

"Oh, good. Hey, you mind if I turn on my light until I settle down for the night?"

"Knock yourself out," I grumbled. I certainly wasn't going to be getting back to sleep any time soon. Too many well-hung dicks floated around the insides of my eyelids every time I tried to close them.

"Thanks."

I heard shuffling and the sound of paper crinkling, but I refused to look. Not until a certain scent caught my nose, anyway.

"Ugh. What is that gawd-awful smell?" I demanded, rolling back to face him again.

Sitting upright in his bed and bare-chested with his back propped by both of his pillows and his legs stretched out on top of the sheets, he poured a handful of treats into his palm, then popped them into his mouth.

"Corn nuts," he announced, holding them up for me to see. "Ranch flavored. I saw them in the vending machine in the hall and couldn't resist. This shit and orange-flavored Tic Tacs are my vice."

I wrinkled my nose. "Well, I hope to God you bought some of the Tic Tics too. I bet your breath reeks to high heaven."

Completely unoffended, Asher laughed. "Whatever, asshole. I was going to ask if you wanted some."

I immediately held out my hand over the space between our beds. "Hell, yes, I want some. If I'm going to be forced to smell them all night, I may as well eat 'em, too."

With another chuckle, Asher leaned out to pour a healthy amount into my hand. "You really are funny as shit, Sticks."

"Yeah, I'm a regular comedian. Don't be stingy now."

He wasn't, which surprised me. He was probably too generous, actually, with something he admitted was his favorite snack, because the mound in my palm grew so tall a couple kernels tumbled off the side and fell onto the carpet.

"Oh, shit." I let out a cry of dismay. "Corn nut down."

"Five second rule," Asher called and dove off the side of his bed.

"Hey, those are my nuts." Indignant, I jumped off my mattress after him. Shoulder checking him out of my way, I snatched up the three nuts on the floor and shoved them into my mouth.

Then while I was still chewing, I yelled, "Ha!" right in his face, probably fumigating him with my ranch-flavored breath.

Not my most attractive moment, but he thought I was a guy, so...who cared? I'd beaten him to the corn nuts. Booyah!

"Fucker." He jabbed his fist into my calf and I gasped more in surprise than from pain.

Damn, I was really going to have to get used to this guy camaraderie thing of beating the shit out of each other.

"Ow." Scowling at him, I rubbed the sore spot, even though I was reassured in the fact that yeah, he definitely thought I was male. No way could I picture him doing that to a girl.

I kind of liked it, even though it stung like a son of a bitch. At least I knew he was completely okay with me and relaxed enough to be himself and fool around.

I was seeing the true Asher Hart, his guard completely down.

He narrowed his eyes at me, his sexy lips twitching with mischief. "Watching you eat those makes me wonder exactly what's happened on this floor. You're eating all that, you know."

I paused chewing, then shrugged. And swallowed. It was such a guy thing to do, I was proud of myself, even though I made a mental note to gargle three times as long in the morning and brush twice.

Grumbling aloud, Asher crawled back onto his bed and picked up a notebook he'd been writing in.

"You're always writing in that thing," I said, more than curious what he was scrawling away so madly about.

"Hmm? Oh, it's just lyrics," he murmured in his distracted, concentrating-hard-on-something-else voice. "I pretty much always have to write something before I go to bed each night, otherwise I can never get to sleep with my brain constantly running."

"No fucking shit?" I said in surprise, feeling more connected to him than I knew I should. "I do that too."

He glanced over, surprise making his eyebrows lift. "Really?"

To prove it, I leaned off the other side of the bed where my luggage was and unzipped it before tugging out my notebook. I waved it at him before fluttering the pages open to show him it was three-fourths full.

"No way," he murmured, reaching out as if he just expected me to hand it over.

With a scowl, I slapped it back to my chest. "I don't think so, Scooter." I'd learned the hard way to never show my lyrics to another living soul. After Fisher had stolen my lines and used them to make Fish 'N' Dicks's one and only hit song, I was never going down that road again.

But Asher blinked at me as if I was insane.

So I cleared my throat. "I just...they're all awful. So there's no point in wasting your time even looking at them."

"Whatever, man. I'll be the judge of that. Besides, ninety percent of mine suck ass too. Now...gimme."

When I merely shook my head stubbornly, he sent me a sexy grin. "I'll show you mine if you show me yours."

I snorted. "Honey, I just saw yours and let me say...holy fucking wow. You win."

Asher's mouth fell open before he shook his head and murmured. "I can't believe you just admitted that to me."

I shrugged. "What? That you're bigger? You're the one who had no qualms of flashing your junk at me. So I'm just saying that was one impressive cock. Seriously, you should be proud of that monster. I mean, the first moment you came out of the bathroom, swinging it around, I just wanted to...you know, *suck* on it."

When I wrapped my hands around air as if gripping a ginormous invisible penis, I realized what I was doing and what I'd just said. "I mean..." Oh holy hell, that had to be going too far, even for a gay guy.

I gaped at Asher, bracing for him to kick my ass or throw me out of our hotel room, or something, but he only threw back his head and laughed. "Holy shit, you are so fucking funny. That has to be the gayest thing you've ever said to me."

Gulping, I cringed backward. "Yeah, sorry."

"Meh, don't worry about it." Still laughing, he wiped tears from his eyes. "But, wow, you are definitely one hundred percent gay, aren't you? I mean, you *really* prefer guys."

"Um...*yeah*," I drew out the word as if that shouldn't be so hard to believe.

He shook his head. "That's just so strange. You don't even like boobs? I mean...*boobs*, man." He feigned squeezing a pair. "They're just so..." He made a hungry sound in his throat. "Breastly."

I shrugged. "Eh."

Still with the head-shaking, he studied me as if I was some odd, unnatural specimen. "Okay, fine. What about pussies then? Seriously, no way can you have a dick and turn your nose up at one of them. They're all wet and warm and tight. They were freaking *made* to hold a cock, and they feel like heaven when you slide into one. And the flavor.

Have you ever even *tasted* a pussy?"

I wrinkled my nose. "Eww. *No.*"

He lifted his hands. "Well, there's your problem. You have no idea what you're missing."

Narrowing my eyes, I said, "Are you trying to turn me hetero?"

"No." Then he laughed as if laughing at himself. "Well, I didn't think I was. I was just trying to figure out what you didn't like about women. They're freaking perfect, all soft and feminine and good-smelling." He sucked in a breath and closed his eyes. "There's nothing like sinking into one while you're sucking a nipple into your mouth. And then warm, smooth legs go and wrap around your waist until she's digging the heels of her feet into your ass. It's just...nirvana."

CHAPTER 21

Remy Cullan

Heat traveled up my thighs until my pussy was so wet and aching I had to squeeze my legs together under my covers.

Asher opened his lashes and glanced at me from glossy, lust-covered green eyes, letting me know the vision he described affected him as much as it had affected me. I wondered how big his monster cock was now, and how it'd feel if he was on top of me, sliding it deep between my legs as he sucked on *my* nipples.

Dios.

I shuddered, noticing he was doing the same thing.

"Sorry, I just...love women," he murmured before glancing away as if suddenly uncomfortable.

Which made me think of the stench of perfume that had clung to him when he'd entered the hotel room only half an hour ago.

My lust soured, then died completely.

"Yeah, I can tell," I muttered. When he glanced at me with a confused frown, I said, "You smelled like a dozen whores when you came in. I'd have hopped into the shower first thing to wash off all that reek too if I'd been you."

Chuckling, Asher didn't take offense. He merely shook his head. "That actually came from only the one woman. The blonde. Monique."

I snorted, wishing Monique an awful untimely death. "Well, Monique has quite a habit of rubbing her perfume off on other people."

Asher rolled his eyes and muttered, "You're telling me."

My mouth fell open as I stared at him. Finally, I said, "Oh, I'm sorry, man. Did Monique not do it for you in the bedroom?" The skank's pussy had probably been so well-used it hadn't been nearly tight enough for him.

"Huh?" He glanced at me as if I was insane. Then he shook his head. "No. We didn't have sex."

"Uh-huh," I mumbled, not buying it.

He scowled. "I'm serious."

I rolled my eyes. "So... What, then? You just smell like her because—"

"Because she wouldn't stop rubbing against me like some kind of cat in heat," he snapped, glowering hard.

"Right. So you're saying you love everything there is about women but when one rubs against you *like a cat in heat*, you don't take her up on the offer? Gally certainly would."

"Do I fucking look like Gally?"

When I realized just how pissed and irritated he was with this line of questioning, I blinked and pulled back, amazed. "You're really serious, aren't you? You *didn't* screw her."

"No, I did not."

My breath caught in my throat, and hope flared in my chest. "Why not?"

"Because..." He seemed too flabbergasted to continue.

Unable to let this drop because I was dying of curiosity, I pressed, "Because...?"

"I was tempted, sure," he relented on a shrug. "Feels like it's been forever, and I've been craving sex like you wouldn't believe lately, but..."

No way could I drop this issue, so I said, "But what?" Then it hit me. Oh dear Lord. "You have an STD, don't you?"

"Jesus. *No!*" He sent me a dark look, then pointed

threateningly. "Okay, fine, I'll talk, but if you ever repeat anything I'm about to say to Gally or Holden, I will kick your ass to Ellamore and back. Got it?"

I sniffed out a laugh. "What do I look like? Some kind of gossiping girl desperate to tell everyone else your personal business? *Please*."

His shoulders relaxed before he rolled his eyes toward the ceiling and reluctantly admitted, "It's just...I'm not really a fan of one-night-stands."

My mouth fell open. Leaning his way, I cupped my hand around my ear and said, "Say again?"

He narrowed his eyes. "Laugh it up, fucker. It's just not my thing. Okay?"

I lifted both hands. "Trust me, I'm not laughing. I'm just shocked is all." And really impressed.

He glanced away, looking humiliated. "Pathetic, isn't it?"

"I didn't say it was pathetic either. It's just...*unusual* for a guy in your position." A very good, amazing unusual. "Which makes me extremely curious as to...why?"

He sighed and rolled his gaze to the ceiling. "I knew you were going to ask that."

"Well?" I lifted my eyebrows, letting him know I still wanted the answer regardless. "For someone who *loves* women so much and is craving sex..." I started.

"I do love women," he insisted. "I just want one to want *me* instead of..." He rolled his eyes. "Asher Hart."

I opened my mouth to respond, but nothing came. After a second, I said, *"Aren't* you Asher Hart, though?"

He growled and frowned at me. "Yes, but...Christ, I don't even know how to explain it." When he grabbed his hair in supreme frustration, I took pity on him and decided to stop playing dumb.

"You want someone who appreciates the man within, not just a groupie wanting to score with the lead singer of a band."

Dropping his hands from his hair, he gazed at me as if he'd just discovered a kindred soul. "Yeah," he murmured. "Exactly."

I nodded, letting him know I understood. "So you don't just want a physical connection. You want something...deeper."

He looked down at his hands. "Oh, trust me. I love the physical connection. And I've done the one-night-stand thing because it seems to be the only thing women want from me. It's just...I don't know. All my friends at Forbidden have these incredible women that they're all devoted to and completely crazy about. And when I watch them together, it just looks so..."

"Nice?"

He blew out a breath and glanced at me. "Makes me wonder what a real relationship would be like."

That confession had me blinking. "What? You've never been in one?"

He shook his head. "No. You?"

My lips quirked. "With a woman? No."

Snorting out an amused sound, he muttered, "With a *guy*, then?"

"Well...sure. A couple times. I mean, not tons but...three or four meaningful enough ones."

Focusing on me as if he'd just discovered I knew the secret meaning of life, he asked, "What're they like?"

I crinkled my brow. "Relationships?"

"Yeah."

Blowing out a breath, I ran my hands through my hair, startled when my fingers met the short fake tendrils of my wig. For a minute there, I'd forgotten I was Sticks, the guy drummer. I'd just been Remy...talking to Asher.

"It's..." Mentally reminding myself I was a guy here, I tried to think up a male way to describe it, but a second later, I just blurted out, "At first, it's nerve-wracking as hell. You're always afraid to show your true self. You just want them to see what you think they'll like, so you're always on edge, hoping to impress him and trying to figure out if you even like him in return. Even though it's kind of thrilling and exciting too. But then...then something finally clicks, and you realize you have this...thing...this amazing thing in common with each other that you don't really have in common with anyone else. Pretty soon, you're opening up more of yourself and discovering that more parts click, and before you know it, life is amazing and you're thinking about them night and day. You can't wait to see them again, and you love everything about everything."

Asher cracked a dreamy grin as if he were imagining what I described, and he liked the visions it produced. "Really?"

I nodded. "And then he turns into a fucking lying bastard who rips your heart out, shatters your trust and leaves you a bitter hardened bitch of a human being."

He blinked and pulled back. "Wow. Uh, I was not expecting you to end that way."

"Well..." I shrugged. "It's not happily ever after for everyone."

He studied me a moment before murmuring, "What did the bastard do to you?"

I shrugged and began to play with the sheets that had bunched down to my lap. "He just...I mean, besides making me come to feel as if he was doing me a grand favor by being with me, he cheated on me with every woman who'd take him on and—"

"He slept with other *women*?" Asher tipped his head to the side in confusion.

Shit, I'd forgotten the gay thing again. *Grr.* Clearing my throat, I mumbled, "Yeah, he, uh, he's bi." And strangely, that lie felt really good to spew. Fisher would hate being called bi. *Ha!*

Nodding as if understanding, Asher winced in sympathy. "Well, that had to suck. What else were you going to say he did?"

"Oh. He, uh...I wrote him a couple songs and...he stole them, sang them in his band and claimed they were his own."

"Shit," Asher murmured, compassionately. "No wonder why you didn't want me looking at your notebook."

I shrugged and held up the pages of lyrics I'd created. "Sorry, I wasn't accusing you of being a plagiarist. I just...you know what? I know you're not like him. Here."

I tossed the notebook across the beds and into his lap. He picked it up, hesitation glimmering in his green eyes. "Are you sure? I totally respect your privacy, man. And I get why you're—"

"Just read," I mumbled. "If you even think about stealing any of my lines, I'll just cut off that huge cock of yours and force-feed it to Gally."

He laughed. "Fair enough." Before opening the pages though, he tossed me his booklet.

A knot formed in my throat at his return trust in me. When he flipped open my notebook, I did the same to his.

A second later, I gave a low whistle. "Damn, these are

amazing."

"Ditto," he murmured distractedly, too busy reading my work to talk.

I flipped the pages, growing increasingly stunned that he hadn't already turned some—okay, *most*—of them into songs.

"Seriously, Asher. You have some wicked, awesome talent."

"Hmm?" Distracted, he glanced up and right back down. Chewing on the end of his pen—something I totally did when I was stuck on a line—he returned his attention to my notebook. "Thanks, but I'm not writing worth shit these past few days. I keep getting stuck on this one line."

"Oh, yeah?" I flipped to the last page. "Let's see what you got."

"Wait!" Tossing down my lyrics, he leapt off his bed and snatched his own from my hands.

I blinked at his sudden reserve. Then I grinned. "Oh, come on. Don't hold out on me now. Sing me what you have so far."

He shook his head. "I've never...I usually can't sing my stuff aloud until I have an entire song fleshed out. It feels...weird."

"Then speak it in words, because seriously, how the hell am I supposed to help if I don't know where you're stuck?"

"You don't have to..." He must've read something in my expression because he gave a long-suffering sigh before he flipped through pages and silently read through the words. Then he shook his head. "Yeah, I don't think I can just read it either. I'd have to sing it."

I lifted my eyebrows. "Then *sing*." I knew the man wasn't afraid to sing in front of an audience, but he suddenly looked uncertain.

He sent me an uncomfortable glance. "Don't carp on me if it ends up sounding shitty, all right?"

I rolled my eyes. "Try trusting me a little more than that, will you? I know nothing's perfect the first time though."

"Okay, fine."

And he started to sing.

In a cappella, his voice was beautiful. I wanted to crawl onto the bed with him, right into his lap and let him sing to me for the rest of the night...or my life.

But I was a good girl. I stayed back and merely bobbed my head to the beat, then reached out and tapped the rhythm with my bare hands against the top corner of the nightstand.

He grinned, obviously getting into the grove, and began to sway to the tune as he continued the song until he stopped suddenly and shook his head.

"And that's all I got. That's where I'm stuck."

His words were still flowing through me, the melody catching fire in my blood. I kept tapping out the beat and sang, "Until the stars fade away and the day swallows the dark."

Gaping at me, Asher blinked and jerked backward. "Holy shit." If I hadn't seen the shock so clearly on his face, I definitely would've caught it in his voice. "That's...that's perfect. How...?" He shook his head.

I gave a loose shrug and was glad he couldn't see my blush from under my mask. "I was just finishing what you started."

"Well, get your ass over here, Curran. We're going to finish this song. Tonight."

When I hesitated, he lifted an eyebrow as if to say, *Well? What're you waiting for?*

So I heaved out a big sigh as if it were such a hardship, when really, I had to restrain myself from hopping over there too fast. Grateful I'd left on my man torso too—despite how uncomfortable it'd been to fall asleep in—I slipped out of my covers and eased gingerly onto the mattress beside him until we were sitting with our backs to the headboard and our feet stretched out in front of us.

I stole a second to watch my bare feet next to his at the end of the bed, poking out the ends of our surprisingly similar flannel pants. Except his feet looked decidedly larger—and male—next to mine, so I burrowed mine into the covers under me.

He noticed none of this, thank Dios, too busy frowning down at the notebook he was scribbling in. So I leaned in closer to study the lyrics with him, amused by how many times he marked stuff out, only to rewrite the same line and then mark it out again.

"Ooh, you could say something about everything being a lark to rhyme with dark."

He tapped his pen against his chin as he glanced at me.

"Yeah, that might wor—"

A loud sneeze cut off the rest of his sentiment.

I shook my head. "Do you realize you *always* sneeze when I get close to you? Geesh. It's like you're allergic to me or something."

He chuckled as he leaned away toward his nightstand to snag a tissue from a nearby box. "Only if you're made of latex."

I froze, blinking at him. "Uh...what?"

"That's the only thing I know I'm allergic to," he answered between sneezes and nose blowing.

"Oh, shit." I immediately scooted to the edge of the bed away from him, worried I'd kill him any second with my deceitful proximity.

He lowered a tissue from his nose, eyeing me curiously.

I gulped, not wanting the guy to end up dying around me or anything. So I blurted, "I'm wearing a latex mask."

"Really?" His eyebrows shot up in surprise and he leaned closer to examine my face.

I reared backward. "What're you doing? Don't get *close*."

He sniffed and rolled his eyes. "It's not going to kill me from just being near it. Just a couple sneezes here and there. I need skin-to-skin contact before it really does any damage with a rash and swelling. Unbelievable," he murmured. "I had no idea. That thing looks so real."

"I know. Gracias." I patted at my face, still keeping a few feet between us but remaining on the same mattress. "So, latex, huh? That's an usual allergy. I'm all boring with a common one: peanuts."

He winced, making me edgy with how heavily he was concentrating on my mask. "No peanuts? That's gotta suck. You know, if you'd be more comfortable taking it off, it's okay. It's only me around; I promise you I won't freak out."

Damn, that was a sweet offer. He didn't try to pry and find out why I was wearing a mask or ask what kind of deformity I was hiding. He immediately tried to reassure me.

"Thanks, but..." I cringed. "Not tonight, okay?"

He nodded immediately. "Yeah, no problem. Whatever you want. I was just trying to tell you, you didn't have to worry about me doing anything to upset you."

"Gracias," I repeated, touched by his compassion. I cleared my throat, feeling extra guilty about lying to him.

Maybe I should just take the mask off and let him see the real me.

But then I remembered all the things he'd told me tonight; he'd feel extra betrayed if he knew I was really a woman now.

And I was too scared to find out how he'd respond.

Damn it. How the hell had I gotten myself into this predicament? Putting on a little disguise to get my dream to come true should never have had the power to hurt anyone else. But I had a sinking feeling it just might upset the one person in this entire situation whom I didn't *want* to hurt.

I watched Asher as he read through our song, silently lip-syncing the words, and I tried to think up a way to tell him without him thinking I was a big fat liar. But nothing came to mind. Instead, another idea hit me.

"What about sex?"

He glanced up, startled. "What?"

"Condoms." I rolled out my hand. "You know, your allergy. Don't you have safe sex?"

Amusement lit his face. "They make non-latex condoms."

"Do they? Oh."

Shaking his head as if my shock was the most amusing thing he'd heard all day, he tapped his pen against the paper and glanced over the song as he said, "What do you think of this idea?"

So I concentrated on the new line he read off to me, trying not to pay attention when he ran a hand through his hair. But damn, I loved when Asher's hair was all tousled and sexy. Made me want to sink my hands into its softness all over again, then rip my mask off, straddle his lap and experience some non-latex fun with him.

I didn't, though. I kept my fingers to myself, made my own suggestion and didn't mention a thing about my gender while we spent the rest of the night *platonically* on his bed, pounding out the rest of his song.

CHAPTER 22
Asher Hart

I'D JUST SAVED MY WORK on my laptop when Sticks mumbled something in his sleep. Around four this morning, he'd crawled back to his bed, grabbed a pillow, and curled around it, closing his eyes as he helped me come up with a final line. Then he'd passed out a few minutes later.

But I couldn't sleep. I was too psyched because we'd just finished something that had been taking me weeks to work through. So I'd dragged my laptop out of my duffle bag and pulled up my music program, hoping to concoct the perfect melody for the words.

Sticks had slept peacefully for the past three or four hours, but as he flailed out a hand and banged it against the headboard, he began to come to.

"Wha...?" he finally yelped and jerked his head up to gape at me from bloodshot brown eyes. His hair was full of bedhead, sticking out everywhere, and I had to wonder why he'd brought so many products for it now that I knew it was a wig connected to a mask. But hell, I knew nothing about wigs. Maybe you washed and gelled them like normal hair.

Then I wondered what the hell had happened to mess

him up so bad he thought he had to wear all that. Poor guy.

"Shit, sorry," he mumbled, wiping a hand over his face as he sat up. "I can't believe I fell asleep on you."

"No problem." I saved the file I'd been working on and then clicked into the play option so I could have him listen to it. "Want to hear what I've come up with so far?"

"Huh?" He blinked at me, still clearly half-asleep. "How long have I been out, what time is it, and how the hell can you still be this awake?"

I shook my head. "It's a little after eight. You dropped off not long after four. And I suffer from insomnia, so...I don't typically get more than a few hours of sleep at a time, anyway."

He shook his head as if reeling and completely disoriented. I couldn't hold in a grin as I said, "Listen to our song."

I pushed play, and as the melody began on the digital program I had, Sticks squinted and cocked his head to the side as he studied the wavelengths playing across the screen. When I began to sing the lyrics we'd hashed out, his gaze veered to mine.

His mouth fell open as I made my way through all the verses. And as the last note rang through the room, he shook his head. "What...how...that was totally freaking amazing."

I shrugged, even though the compliment made my chest compress with pride.

"No, really," he told me. "How the hell were you able to come up with the entire melody in just a few hours?"

"It wasn't a very complicated one, plus it still needs tweaking," I assured, "and I still have to add other instruments. But this is a start."

"You're damn right it is," he sputtered. "You're a freaking genius. A musical genius."

His praise made me feel funny, so I closed the laptop and stretched my arms over my head. "Actually, I'm starving. Want to head across the street with me to that Denny's and load up on pancakes?"

"Hell to the no. I'm going back to sleep." Hugging his pillow, he flopped back onto his mattress and yanked his sheets up to his chin. "I doubt Gally or Holden will be ready before noon, either, so don't wake me until then."

"Uh...we have to check out by eleven," I reminded him.

He grumbled a curse and then mumbled, "Ten thirty then." I thought he'd fallen back to sleep, but he added one last, "Love the song, by the way. I think it'll be our next hit."

I grinned and shook my head as his heavy breathing filled the room. I liked Remy Curran. He was strange, but funny as hell. It'd been nice writing with him last night. I'd never tried that with anyone before. He hadn't been afraid to disagree with me, but unlike Gally, he didn't get huffy and rude and push for his own way when I had another idea; he listened to my opinion and took it into consideration.

Non-Castrato had struck it rich when he'd showed up to audition for our band.

Whistling the melody of the new song under my breath, I dressed for the day, grabbed my key card and headed from the room, readjusting the blinds to the window so the ribbon of light coming through didn't bother my roommate. Then I shut off the bedside lamp I'd kept on all night and left him to sleep while I sought food.

But no sooner did I cross the street and enter the restaurant than I remembered I'd left my wallet back at the hotel. Heaving out a sigh, I scrubbed my face with my palms. Thinking maybe I should've taken a little cat-nap too to recharge my brain, I scooted out from my booth, told my waitress I'd be right back, and then hurried outside into the crisp morning air.

It woke me up as I waited at the busy crosswalk for my light to turn, and then I jogged to the hotel and retrieved my key card from my pocket as I approached my room.

The light was still off as it'd been when I'd left a few minutes earlier, but the bathroom door had changed. It was shut most of the way so only an inch of a crack showed, revealing the light was on inside. The sounds of a shower and singing filtered out into the hotel room.

"...And a hug around the neck. A hug around the neck...," a clearly feminine voice serenaded from the bathroom.

I froze, frowning hard, as the lyrics to Doris Day's "A Bushel and a Peck" continued. At first, I wigged out, afraid I'd just entered the wrong room. I began to backpedal, afraid to be caught in someone else's room, but then I wondered why my key had gotten me in. So I flipped on the light.

My laptop sat on my bed and the blankets on Remy's side were rumpled and unmade. Plus his familiar suitcase and my duffle sat on the floor, so I knew I had the right room.

But who the hell was in our shower? From the sound of it, I would've thought Sticks had snuck in a woman, except he wasn't *into* women.

Wrinkling my brow, I inched cautiously toward the crack in the bathroom door. Using the tips of my fingers, I reached out, standing as far back as possible, and gently nudged the entrance open. Steam exited, clouding around me as the woman's voice grew louder.

"...You make my heart erect," she continued to wail with a pretty decent set of pipes. I lifted my eyebrows, intrigued.

I have no idea why, but I said, "Remy?" I already knew that wasn't him in there.

In answer, the woman screamed.

"What the—" Confused as all get-out as to what was going on, I reached for the shower curtain and yanked it open.

Inside, the naked, wet woman yelped again, instantly shoving one arm over her breasts and splaying her free hand between her legs to cover herself.

"Holy shit!" I gasped.

We gaped at each other, the water spraying down on her and forcing her long dark hair to clog into her face.

Rationally, I knew I should turn away, but yeah...for some reason, I'd kind of lost the ability to think rationally. Instead, I shook my head, and demanded, "Who're *you*?"

She shoved her hair out of her face so she could see me, probably forgetting that she had to uncover her breast to use her hand, because suddenly, I was being flashed some very nice tits indeed.

My gaze instantly dropped to her chest, and she gasped, slapping her arm back over herself. A split second later, she snatched the shower curtain and wrapped it around her, concealing all the best parts.

"No hablo inglés," she panted in this super-hot sexy voice that had my hormones raging even harder.

Ah, shit. I shook my head, still completely flabbergasted. "You don't know English?"

"No." She shook her head. "No hablo inglés."

"Fuck." I wiped my hand over my face, glad I hadn't

started drooling or anything, because...wow. There was a very hot Spanish-speaking chick in my shower. "Well, I know crap Spanish." Glancing behind me, I muttered to myself, "Where the hell is Remy when you need him?"

Behind me, shower girl repeated, "¿Remy?" I spun back to her and she babbled something in Spanish, her hand waving the entire time.

I blinked, understanding absolutely nothing. But she'd said Remy's name, so I slowly asked, "You know Remy?"

She nodded, her eyes lighting with recognition. "Sí. Remy." Then she spouted off something else. I was sure I caught the word *amigo* in there, so I snapped my finger.

"Amigo," I repeated. Yes, a word I understood. "Friend. Okay. So...he let you in to take...a shower...alone?"

I squinted because there was no way that sounded as if it were even plausible.

"Dios," she moaned, clutching the shower curtain closer to her breasts. Then she bit her lip and waved me away with a free hand, sputtering something in Spanish that went way over my head. But the shooing motion and desperation on her face made her plea obvious enough.

"Shit, sorry." I suddenly realized how badly I'd been gawking. Lifting my hands, I backed up a step toward the half closed bathroom door behind me until I nudged it with my spine. "I'll...let you finish." But I couldn't seem to take my gaze off her. She was just...stunning. "And I swear, I'll look away...soon. Once the blood stops rushing to my dick and returns to my head and I can think rationally again, because...wow."

Ah, hell, I'd just said that aloud, hadn't I? Thank God she didn't know English, though I swear she blushed as if she did. But then her eyebrows twitched with irritation and she blasted me with more Spanish, this time most definitely scolding me for being a creeper and still staring at her.

So I blew out a rattled breath and stumbled back into the hotel room, closing the bathroom door all the way to give her privacy.

But Jesus, that had been... Actually, I wasn't quite sure what that had been, but it had definitely been intense. I wondered if I should be upset or indignant that some stranger was making herself at home in my hotel room, but then I remembered all her gorgeous nakedness, and yeah...I could summon neither emotion.

I paced the floor, running my hands through my hair, wondering what the hell was going on. Where was Remy and why had he let a hot chick into our room so she could shower...alone? Finally, I realized I could just ask him, so yanked my phone from my pocket and dialed his number. Across the room, The Bangles began to sing "Walk Like an Egyptian," which must be his ringtone, because as I followed the source of the sound with my gaze, I spotted his phone sitting abandoned on his nightstand.

Damn it. He hadn't taken his phone with him...wherever he'd gone.

Where the hell *had* he gone?

When the shower water in the bathroom turned off, I spun that way. Then I realized I was probably still being a creeper. So I plopped onto my bed to wait. But I didn't really have to wait at all.

The bathroom door eased open and big brown eyes peered out.

I waved my fingers at her. "Hi again."

"Hijo de puta," she muttered, scowling. Then she seemed to draw in a deep breath before she pushed the door open wide. She'd grabbed a towel and had it wrapped around her, tucking it in tight around her breasts and barely covering the tops of her water-splattered thighs so that she showed off just how long and lean her tanned, gorgeous legs were.

Clutching a bundle of clothes to her, she tiptoed barefoot from the bathroom and murmured, "Gracias," as she motioned behind her, thanking me for the use of my shower, I guess. Then she waved and added, "Adiós."

What? No way was she leaving just like that. I swung off the bed and leapt to my feet so quickly she jerked to a halt and eyed me warily.

"You don't have to leave yet," I told her, pointing toward her clothes. "You *can* change into your things first. It's fine."

She shook her head and pointed toward the door, rattling off a whole string of shit I didn't understand.

When she started to flee again, I eased into her path and set my hand on the door. Skidding to a halt, she gaped at my fingers with wide eyes before sliding her skittish gaze to me.

I knew I was freaking her out, but I kind of liked that. She'd definitely freaked me out when I'd discovered her in my shower.

"I'm Asher," I said, leaning mildly against the door and effectively barricading her way out.

She drew in a deep breath, stared at the floor a moment, then looked up, meeting my gaze head-on, without fear as she gestured toward the door. "Por favor," she murmured, requesting I let her out.

I only grinned and shook my head. "I don't think so, beautiful. It's your turn. What's your name? ¿Nombre? ¿Cómo te llamas?"

Her eyes flared. Then she shook her head adamantly and whispered, "No."

I leaned closer, my grin only stretching wider. "No, what? No *is* your name, or no, you can't *give me* your name?"

"N-no," she repeated, her breathing picking up as I dipped my face closer to hers. She definitely no longer appeared afraid of me. Her eyes glossed with heat and she didn't even try to pull away. From the entranced way she studied me, I wondered if she was going to kiss me. I kind of really hoped she did.

Raw, hot lust stirred inside me, prickling my skin and hardening my cock.

Unable to stop smiling, I eased closer, halting only when I was a mere inch from pressing my mouth to hers. "Yes," I argued softly, playfully.

She shuddered, blinking rapidly. Then she jerked her head back and forth, refusing to give in. "No," she insisted on a husky whisper. "Por favor."

Disappointment filled me, but I hadn't really expected her to do anything differently.

"Well, whoever you are," I murmured, dropping my arm from the door before I stepped back and even opened it for her to leave. "It was very nice to meet you. I hope to find you naked again in my shower. Preferably soon."

"Tha..." Her eyes wide with shock, she suddenly shook her head and sputtered disjointed sounds before gasping, "Adiós," and escaping through the door. She fled into the hall, grabbing the door from me so she could slam it shut behind her.

Once I was alone in the room, I ran my hand through my hair and twirled in a slow circle, trying to make sense of what had just happened. This urge to race after her enveloped me, but what the hell would I do if I actually caught her? She had refused to give me her name, and it wasn't like we could actually have a conversation, so there was no way I was going to find out how she'd really gotten into my room or why she'd been there.

And tossing her over my shoulder so I could drag her back to my bed and fuck her senseless was probably a bad idea.

Maybe if she'd left something behind I could snag it up and have a reason to track her down, return her items to her, so I could...what? Bask in her presence a few seconds longer?

Lame as that idea was, it was the only one I had, so I hurried into the bathroom, praying to find panties or hell, anything, to give back to her.

But I found nothing. The small room was still misty and the occasional droplet of water dripped from the showerhead, reminding me how recently she'd been naked in here. It smelled like Remy's soap, but I didn't even care.

A vision of shower girl filled my head and before I knew it, I was stripping off my clothes and stepping into the same place she'd just stood naked. I imagined her still here, wet and gorgeous. As I turned on the water full blast, I pinned her to the wall in my mind's eye. Gripping myself, I wondered what it would've felt like to push inside her, feel the warm give of her flesh wrap around me, suck her breasts into my mouth and drive my hips repeatedly between her wide open thighs.

"God." I picked up the pace, practically jerking my dick off as the orgasm raced down my spine between my legs, tightened my nutsack and then shot out the end of my cock. I bowed my head and pressed one hand against the wall, stroking myself to completion.

But as the relief of satisfying myself began, so did the self-disgust. I was so pathetic, jacking off alone in a shower merely after seeing a pretty girl. I needed sex so bad I was probably going to wank myself blind soon.

I should've never turned Monique down last night. What the hell was I waiting for, anyway? So what if a woman wasn't my soul mate; a couple intimate minutes with a complete stranger had to be better than nothing, because right now, I had nothing.

CHAPTER 23
Remy Curran

Oh shit, oh shit, oh shit.

I couldn't believe I'd been stupid enough to let him catch me in the shower. But he'd just barely left to get food, and even as tired as I was, I knew that had to be my last opportunity to take a shower before we left, so I'd leapt out of bed and tried to hurry, except, damn it, he'd caught me.

And then I'd gone and used my slutty señorita voice on him.

Jodi would be so proud.

I, on the other hand, was horrified.

But he hadn't pieced the truth together, and when he asked me who I was, the Spanish just came pouring out because I knew he wouldn't understand me. I had told him that I hated lying to him, but someday I was sure he'd know the truth, just not right at that moment while I was naked in a shower and he was staring at me as if he found me attractive.

And then he went and admitted he found me attractive.

I almost melted right then.

Asher thought girl-me was hot. That was just so... amazing. Not only that, but he'd flirted with me. Freaking-fracking flirted...*with me!*

I'd never seen him so bold or engaging with any female before. Ever.

But then...he had once admitted to me he liked to be the pursuer, hadn't he, and I'd definitely retreated enough to heat the predator in him. Not intentionally. At the time, I'd just wanted to flee, but damn, watching him on the hunt was erotic as hell.

Rocking a whole boatload of nerves and fear and excitement, I raced along the halls of the hotel in nothing but a towel, my mask and sleep clothes clutched to my chest until I found a public bathroom at the end of the hall. Darting inside, I dropped the heap I'd been carrying on the floor at my feet. Good thing I'd been naked when he walked in on me; it had successfully distracted him enough that he hadn't noticed Sticks's wig-mask sitting pretty as you please on the bathroom vanity.

Cursing myself for my stupidity in leaving the door cracked, I peeled off the towel and dug through my heap to find my man panties. But I hated showering with a door closed; it just felt so humidly, smotheringly cloistering to me. Still...

"Stupid, stupid, stupid," I muttered, jerking on my foam chest and then the rest of my clothes.

My hair was dripping wet and I didn't have anything to comb it with, so I used the towel to squeegee as much moisture as possible from it. Then I ran my fingers a couple times through the damp locks before winding them into a bun and tugging on my mask. I checked out the mirror for glitches and straightened my left ear when I saw it was wonky. Then I blew out a breath and turned to leave the bathroom. That's when I realized I was barefoot.

I couldn't return to the room barefoot; Asher would wonder why I didn't have any shoes, and I was sure he was going to bombard me with enough questions I needed to come up with some answers for.

So, while I scampered barefoot around the hotel, searching for something that might pass as shoes, I tried to come up with a plausible story.

But really...why would I have let a girl into our room and then left her there alone to shower? Maybe I thought she needed some privacy. But then, he'd want to know who she was. Just some random girl who'd knocked on our door, begging for the use of our bathroom? Meh, I couldn't see him buying that story. If I'd trusted her alone in our room, then I'd have to know her, and if I knew her, I'd have to come up with a name for her, possibly a life story if he got really curious.

I was already lying to him enough with the whole I'm-a-dude trickery, I didn't want to lie any more than I had to. So I decided to go with the clueless route. Yeah, that sounded good. After miraculously spotting a pair of Chicago Bears flip-flops with one strap broken sitting on the closed lid of the dumpsters outside, I trudged back to the hotel, holding my breath as I let myself into our room.

Asher pounced immediately. I barely opened the door before he was in my face, demanding, "Where the hell have you been?"

I lurched a step back, a bit concerned by the anger flashing in his eyes. "I...I was looking for you. I thought you said you were going to eat breakfast at Denny's across the street, and when I couldn't go back to sleep, I hauled my butt over there, but you were gone."

"Because I forgot my wallet in the room and came back to get it. Who was the girl?"

I swear, I deserved an Academy Award for the way I furrowed my eyebrows, squinted at him and asked, "What girl?"

"The...the..." He sputtered a second longer, motioning wildly toward the bathroom. Finally, he was able to blurt, "The fucking chick in our shower!"

Mouth gaping, I glanced toward the opened door of the bathroom and then back to him, sending him a look that told him I thought he was straight-up tripping.

"There's a chick in our shower?"

"*Yes!*" he boomed, then swatted a hand toward me. "Well, not now. But there *was* when I came in."

"No way." Letting him know I totally didn't believe him, I strode toward the bathroom and peered inside to see that the shower stall was still wet. I swerved back around. "Who the hell was she? How'd she get in here?"

"That's what I'm trying to ask you, asshole. She said she knew you."

"She did?" I scratched at my head, perfecting the confusion bit.

Poor Asher, he was really baffled by all this. "Well...damn it," he muttered, running his hands through his hair. "I think she did. She only spoke Spanish."

I lifted my eyebrows in offence. "Oh, so all us Spanish-speaking people must know each other?"

"No...I didn't mean it like *that*." He scowled at me for even assuming as much. Then he blew out a breath. Once he was calmer, he explained, "I said your name and her face lit up with recognition. Then she rattled off...something that had the word amigo in it, which means friend, right? She had to have been one of your friends."

Damn, he seemed really bothered by all this. I was tempted to break down and tell him everything, but then the fear of how he'd react scared me back into silence. "Well..." I frowned, hating this game more with each second. "What'd she look like?"

"Fucking gorgeous," he said immediately, making my heart rate jack faster. "Long, straight black hair with these stray purple streaks in it. Eyes the same color as yours, but like fuller. Thick, dark eyelashes that seemed to go on forever. Heart-shaped face, flawless features. Perfect tits and legs, and..." He drew in a deep breath before adding, "A banging body. I shit you not; she was...beautiful."

I blushed and was tempted to thank him. Hell, I was tempted to push him down onto his bed and crawl on top of him so he could appreciate everything he'd complimented up close and personal.

Instead, I shook my head and murmured, "Weird."

He nodded. "So, you really have no idea who she was, or how she got in here?"

"No. Sorry. Do you...think we should say something to the hotel about it? It's kind of freaky that just anyone could break into our room like that."

"I don't see why we need to. She only took a shower. And I don't think she stole anything—except a towel—I mean, my laptop's still lying right there."

"Huh. That's just...strange."

My guilt for lying grew as Asher scratched his temple and murmured, "Yeah," in an equally perplexed tone.

Because I couldn't keep looking at him in all his confusion, I hurried to my side of the room. "I'm going to check my shit, anyway. See if everything's still here."

We made it back to Ellamore early that evening. Asher, of course, had to tell Heath and Gally about "shower girl."

Gally's first question was, "Did you fuck her?"

Asher had declined to answer that aside from a roll of his eyes. He also downplayed how pretty he thought I was. I found it adorable, like his way of keeping me to himself and protecting his shower girl from the likes of a perv like Gally.

The next day—Monday—we didn't have band practice, which was good because I had to work through the lunch hour. But I couldn't get Asher off my mind. The thing with his dad, the song he'd sang for (possibly) me, how much fun I'd had writing lyrics with him, all the guilt I was packing around for continuously lying to him. It all swirled through me until I just had to see him.

I'd finished organizing the Non-Castrato box. I had planned on bringing it to practice the next day, but I couldn't wait that long. I was going through Asher withdrawals. So after I got off work and showered, I texted him to learn he was working at Forbidden. And half an hour later, that's where I found myself in my Sticks outfit.

The place was fairly dead...well, it wasn't packed wall to wall with people. There were actually some tables free and I could walk directly to the bar without having to murmur "excuse me" to anyone. It was kind of nice. Almost peaceful. I felt the urge to slide onto a stool at the bar, order a beer, and sigh in total contentment. The entire atmosphere made me want to watch some reruns of *Cheers*.

I scanned the room for Asher, but didn't spot him. The coworker who knew I was a female was the only one working. Crap. What had Asher called him? It'd been some number. Eight? Nine?

Ten. That was it.

Dreading the encounter, I plunked the box in my arms onto the bar top and sent him a scowl. "I have some shit for Hart. He around?"

In the middle of drying a glass he'd just taken from a tub

of freshly cleaned mugs, he glanced my way. "You know, you don't have to talk dude to me. I'm onto your chick status, remember?"

Damn, I hadn't even realized I'd been talking like a guy. This was bad. It was becoming habit now as soon as I put on the suit. What if I completely lost all my girlishness soon? What if—okay, I might be overthinking this. With a scowl, I grumbled, "He said he was working tonight, and I could drop this box by for him."

"Oh, yeah?" Ten set the dried glass aside and leaned forward, resting his forearms on the counter, to get a look inside. "What is it? Kinky sex stuff?"

"You wish." I moved it back so he couldn't see the boring file folders I'd organized and arranged.

He shrugged, nonplussed, as he straightened again. "Eh, no matter. Caroline's and my collection is already complete, so I'm good, anyway. It was Hart I was thinking about. That boy's *long* overdue."

I frowned, confused. "Overdue for what?"

He blinked as if he couldn't believe I had no idea what he was talking about. Then he said, "Sex," adding a silent *duh* behind that.

Oh, brother. I should've known better than to ask.

"Seriously," he went on. "I don't think it's healthy for a guy to go as long as he has without any."

"Wait, he talks about all his...exploits?" This I did *not* want to know. It disappointed me to learn Asher was a kiss-and-teller. I didn't want him to disappoint me. I was just starting to think he was okay.

Fine...*better* than okay.

Ten lifted his eyebrows. "Exploits? Yeah, there she is. *Now* you're sounding chick again."

I rolled my eyes and turned away, deciding to look for Asher myself and get out of here.

But Ten called after me. "Of course he doesn't talk about that shit."

I shouldn't have stopped, but I did. And when I turned back, Ten sent me a smug smile, knowing I was more interested than I should be. "I just know when he's been laid," he explained. "Hart has a definite tell."

"What's his tell?" Dios, why had I asked that? I didn't want to know...except, okay, I totally did.

Ten chuckled. "Why don't you go find out for yourself? He's alone in the storeroom right now, sorting through a load of inventory that just came in."

I sniffed and frowned. "You're an ass." Then I whirled away to find the storeroom.

"Watch out, *Sticks*. Your girl's *really* showing now."

Knowing I wasn't going to win against this guy, I ignored him, wondering where the hell to look for the storeroom, until he called, "Down the hall, last door on the left."

I went that way, and could hear the muffled singing before I reached the last room on the left. The door was cracked, so I nudged it the rest of the way open and paused just inside the entrance where Asher was belting out a kick-ass rendition of Hozier's "Take Me to Church."

He really did have the most amazing voice, and I was coming to realize he liked songs that challenged his vocal chords. He loved to let it loose. And God, I loved to listen to him. I propped the box against my hip, leaned a shoulder on the wall, and enjoyed the show.

He'd just emptied a cardboard crate of bourbon bottles onto a shelf and was beginning to tear down the empty box when he hit the round of Amens in the song. So he paused to tip his head back and really wail the chorus. Mesmerized, I shook my head.

Didn't matter if he was alone or in front of a crowd, he put his entire heart and soul into it, didn't he?

Once he started the next verse, he kept singing but returned to work, straightening the row of bottles on the shelf. Then he stepped back to inspect his work, only to step forward again and nudge one bottle an inch to the right until he was satisfied.

I laughed because I couldn't help it. He was just too adorable. The guy was as easygoing as they came, acted as if nothing ever bothered him, messy and forgetful on occasion, and yet he had this small perfectionist side that totally contradicted the rest of him.

Startled, he stopped singing and spun toward me.

I shook my head and said, "Te amo," blurting out the first thing on my mind.

CHAPTER 24
Remy Cursan

I DIDN'T REALIZE WHAT I'd said until Asher sent me a confused grin. "Te amo? What does that mean?"

I froze, my mouth opening, but no words coming. I totally hadn't meant to say that. He'd just been so cute with his OCD bottle arrangement and his voice flooding me with a happy, content feeling; the words had poured out.

"Uh..." Thinking way too slowly for my own taste, I said, "You know...good job...with your stocking abilities. I think you could win some kind of award with such damn fine alcohol shelving."

The tops of his cheeks brightened as he strolled toward me. But then he shook his head and grinned. "Shut up, smart-ass."

I loved the way he walked—that unintentional swagger in his hips was just so incredibly male. It was nothing like the cock-and-go Jodi had tried to teach me and had nothing to do with hip movement. It was in the arms, his posture, and even the way his thighs were spaced. It was just so confident and slow. There was no way "Sticks" could ever cop a walk like that, and thank goodness; I'd probably want to do myself if I could.

"Did you get it done already?" He reached out to take the box from me.

I didn't answer, could only watch as he pulled out a folder and started flipping through the spreadsheets I'd made. "Hey, these are awesome. Thanks, man."

I studied his expression, the eager appreciation making something heat in my belly. I cleared my throat, noticing he'd gone back to humming "Take Me to Church" under his breath as he looked over my work.

"You really love to sing, don't you?" I mused.

"Yeah. Sure." A grin split across his face. "I definitely didn't go the rocker route because I wanted a mob of women to attack me everywhere I went."

I laughed.

"Actually," he shrugged, "another reason I was so determined to be in a band was so I could piss off my dad."

Now he sounded like me. I'd recently gotten my purple highlights pretty much just to piss off my uncle, who hated unnatural hair colors.

Splaying my hands out as if reading a nameplate on an office door, I said, "Asher Hart, rebel singer."

He smiled lightly. "My old man used to knock the shit out of me every time he caught me singing when I was a kid. I didn't even realize I was doing it. I'd just be playing with my Tonka trucks, you know, minding my own business and trying to stay out of his way, when wham...out of nowhere I'd get a wallop on the back of my head. He'd tell me to cut the singing shit out because it was gay."

"Shit," I murmured. I'd known he'd been abused, but to hear actual details tore me up. Tío Alonso had been a strict motherfucker and never seemed to hold back on punishments, but he'd never physically struck me aside from a couple slaps on the back of the hand with kitchen utensils.

Asher sent me a sudden, mischievous grin, which told me his bad childhood hadn't kept too tight of a hold on him. "If I didn't love boobs so much, I probably would've turned gay too, just to piss him off even more."

My breasts tingled at his words, making me wish I could unleash them on him and let him enjoy *my* boobs. But then I remembered I was in guy mode. *Gay* guy mode. So I said, "Well, that's a damn shame," and I wiggled my eyebrows as if to tempt him to the other side.

He let out a full laugh and bumped my arm. "Sorry," he offered with an amused grin that was so freaking adorable it sizzled my hormones.

This guy was going to be the death of me. The more time I spent with him, the more I liked him and the more attractive he grew.

"I should probably get back up front." He hitched his head toward the door. "You want a beer or anything?"

Totally not ready to leave him yet, I nodded. "Sure."

I followed him from the storeroom, then waited in the hall as he dropped the Non-Castrato box off in the break room. Once we made it back into the main area, he slid behind the bar and went to fetch me an Angry Orchard, which gave his coworker a moment to slide up across the counter from me and whisper, "Learn his tell yet?"

I scowled. "Shut up."

He only laughed as he moved to the other end of the bar to serve a customer.

"What was that about?" a curious Asher asked, glancing between the two of us as he opened my bottle and set it in front of me.

God bless my mask; he couldn't see my blush. I was able to play it off by shrugging and lifting the malt liquor to my lips. "How should I know? I'm only fluent in Spanish and English, not Asshole."

Asher laughed. "Good one."

Had I mentioned how much I loved his laugh? But I loved even more how I seemed to always be able to *make* him laugh. He liked me, not just as some pretty girl he'd seen in a shower or someone singing on stage. He liked me, the person.

That made me feel better than I could ever verbalize.

The first moment his back was turned as he tended to a customer, I tapped the bar top to get Ten's attention.

"Hey," I hissed. He scowled suspiciously at me but wandered closer. "Just how sure are you that it was me he was singing about in that song?"

"Oh, so you finally heard your song, huh?"

I growled. There was no time for him to crow with a load of I-told-you-so's. "Ten," I warned.

He rolled his eyes and sighed. "Incubus shirt girl was singing with Jodi. I know that for certain. How many fucking chick friends named Remy does she have?"

Just me. I gulped. "Did she have longer, straight black hair? Taller than Jodi? A black, tighter, form-fitting, instead of loose, Incubus shirt?"

He nodded. "Yep, yep, and yep."

Damn. I bit my lip. That sounded exactly like me. But I didn't want to admit without a doubt yet. "Any other distinguishing features? Tattoos? Birthmarks? Anything?"

He sighed, clearly growing weary with my interrogation. "No, but..." Snapping his fingers, he pointed at me. "Tattoos. The dude she kissed after singing had this tattoo on the left side of his face of a—"

"Fish," I finished for him. "¡Dios mío! It *was* me. Oh...my...God." I buried my face in my hands and leaned forward, unable to handle this. "What the hell do I do?"

"Tell Hart the truth," Ten said on a careless shrug as if he thought it was as easy as that. Then he narrowed his eyes. "Wait, you're done with fish-face, right?"

I scowled at him as if he were insane. "Yes! He turned out to be a lying, cheating, thieving asshole, so yeah...that's over. Way over."

"Good. So then come clean with my boy, and all will be okay."

All would just...*be okay*, huh?

Yeah, right.

Leveling a get-real stare at him, I said, "You really think it'd be that easy? He'd just...*forget* I'd been lying to him for almost two weeks?"

"Yeah, I never did catch why you were lying to begin with? There's, like, a good reason for that, isn't there?"

I sighed. "They wouldn't even listen to me audition when I went in to try out as a girl. So I had this stupid crazy idea to dress up as a dude to see if that made a difference, and obviously it did. Things just snowballed from there. Every time I had a nice little opportunity to come clean, something would happen to make me keep up the act just a little bit longer, until now...now it feels too late to say anything without causing a huge problem."

Ten nodded as I talked as if he understood and sympathized with my dilemma perfectly. But then he lifted his hands. "So, wait...you went in as a chick to try out first?"

When I nodded, he shook his head. "Why didn't Hart recognize you then?'

Embarrassed to admit the truth, I ducked my face and mumbled, "I kind of went a little overboard to dress the part. I had on a blonde punk rocker wig and fishnet hose and—"

"And you obviously like to go around incognito," he concluded.

My shoulders slumped. "Not really. Just...those two times."

"Which was enough to completely dupe my boy."

"Hey," I muttered, scowling. "I never meant to dupe, or deceive, or hurt anyone."

But Ten wasn't paying attention to me any longer. A wistful smile had flitted across his face. "You know, my woman went incognito to catch me, too. It was really hot...and a most effective way to win the guy."

Or lose him, in this case, I said in my head.

"What'd I miss?" Asher said, coming up to us from Ten's left side as he tapped a beat onto the bar. "What're we talking about?"

"Remy has something to tell you," Ten announced before clasping Asher on the shoulder and strolling away.

I scowled after him, wishing I could strangle him. But Asher was already turning to me. "What's up?"

"I..." I gazed into his green eyes and...totally chickened out. "I really should get going. It's late." I actually looked at the time after that and, wow, it *was* late. Almost closing time.

"Okay." Asher grinned at me and waved a farewell. "See you tomorrow at practice then. And thanks for organizing that box."

I slipped off the stool. "You bet." Then I hurried from the bar so I could cry all the way home. After making it to my lonely apartment—no clue where my supportive roommate was to mope all over—I had a pity party in the shower, obsessing over the fact that nothing I did from this point on was going to have a nice happy ending.

I'd auditioned as a way to find myself, be accepted into a band for who I was, and stick it to my ex. But none of that had happened. I'd had to fake it the entire time, pretending to be something else entirely just to fit in, and Fisher couldn't even know what I was doing.

Now I had no idea what I was striving for.

Wait, yes I did. Now, my main goal was not to hurt Asher.

Except I had no idea how to avoid that except to keep on keeping the truth from him.

Damn it, I'd fucked up. Big time.

My fingers were pruned and white by the time I shut off the water, telling me how long I'd dawdled and moped. But I just couldn't help it. Asher was never going to want to see or talk to me again after he found out.

I'd just dressed in some comfy pants and camisole, pulled a pint of ice cream from the refrigerator, and was dipping my spoon straight into the carton when my phone rang.

It was Asher.

Of course. Because my guilty conscience needed to hear his voice so I could feel even worse.

"Hey, I didn't wake you, did I?" he asked as soon as I answered.

"No. Not at all." I returned the spoonful to the container and slapped the lid back on as if to hide all evidence of a sulk fest.

"Good." He blew out a breath. "I was hoping you might still be up, because...I need a ride...if you're in the area."

"A ride?"

"Yeah, my bike started and then...died, so I'm stuck here alone in the parking lot, and Ten's already left. I would've called and bothered him, but I just had this horrible mental picture that he wakes Caroline up whenever he gets home from work, and I didn't want to interrupt, you know, any of that."

I lifted my eyebrows. "Oh, but you knew you wouldn't be interrupting anything if you called *me*?"

He was quiet a second before hissing, "Shit. I'm sorry. If you're busy, I'll just call—"

"No, *no*." I laughed and waved a hand. "I'm just fucking with you. I'll be there in a few minutes."

I hung up on him and leapt into action, taking longer than I wanted to get into my Sticks gear. This shit was definitely not made for speedy dressing. In my hurry, I tore a little bit of the latex on the back of the neck, but hoped my hair would cover it.

Not that it mattered; he knew I wore a mask now. He just thought I was grotesquely disfigured under it. Shit...

another lie I'd added to my plate.

Fifteen minutes later, I pulled into the empty parking lot across the street from Forbidden where a lone figure leaned against a badass-looking motorcycle directly under the spray of a streetlamp.

¡Por Dios! He rode a motorcycle. Okay, yeah, he'd said bike when he'd talked to me, but it took me until I was actually looking at it to really process the words. Asher Hart drove a motorcycle.

In that second, he got, like, five times hotter.

Trying to cool my jets, I blew out a breath and pulled up next to him, rolling down my window. "Still won't start?" I asked.

He pushed upright away from the bike and reached for the door handle of my car. "No." After he slid inside, he slumped low and moodily into the passenger seat. "I discovered the problem. The fuel line was cut."

I blinked and stared at him. "Cut? You mean, like, cut-cut?"

He arched an eyebrow, letting me know there was no other kind of cut.

My mouth fell open. "Holy shit. Who would..." Then it hit me. "*Fuck*. Do you think it was your dad?"

That idea made him pull back in surprise. He flashed me a strange look. "No." Then he shook his head and made a face as if to reassure himself his answer was still no. "Why would it be *him*? We already had our confrontation. All he wanted from me was his stash, which I didn't have. So I doubt I'll ever hear from him again."

I sighed. "Your testimony put him in jail, Asher. For *years*."

"Yeah, right. My testimony did shit. There was enough proof and evidence to put him away without me ever taking the stand."

That made me frown in confusion as I put the car into gear, leaving his lovely dead beast behind. "Then why did you have to testify at all?" Seemed like a lot of undue stress to put on a kid.

He shrugged and turned to stare out the side window. "I don't know. Guess the lawyers thought my seven-year-old self wasn't traumatized enough after I saw my mother murdered."

"Bastards," I hissed with agreement.

"It certainly wasn't reason enough for the old man to carry a sixteen-year vendetta against me."

I bit my lip, taking that option into consideration. Then I remembered, we were sitting at the opening of the parking lot because I had no idea where he lived. "Which way?"

He glanced up. "Oh, sorry. This way. Then hang a left when we get to Grand."

I nodded and turned onto the street. "Then who do you think did it?" I pressed. "Because, you know, fuel lines don't just go cutting themselves open. *Someone* obviously has it out for you."

He arched an unimpressed eyebrow my way. "So they went after my fuel line? That's like...a thirty-dollar fix, and the worst that could've possibly happened to me from this is that my bike wouldn't start, which...it didn't. If someone really had it out for me, they could've done so much worse. This was probably just one of the guys fucking with me."

I made a face. "That's not a very funny joke."

He blew out a frustrated breath and scrubbed at his hair before admitting, "Yeah, I'm not laughing about it either. Go north here."

I turned, frowning at his directions. We were not heading toward any kind of residential area. The only thing in these parts was a couple of dying factories and condemned-looking warehouses.

Just where the heck did he live?

When he said, "Turn here," I faltered.

"That's an alley," I argued.

"Yeah, I've noticed."

Finally, I turned, shaking my head slowly. "You live in *an alley?*"

"I rent the basement of this place. And the only entrance is in this alley."

"Creepy," I murmured, squinting out my window at the total darkness surrounding Asher's home.

"Right here," he said, and I stopped, then killed the engine. He sent me an amused glance. "Seriously, man. I'm fine. You don't have to walk me to my door. My old man isn't creeping in a corner, waiting to off me."

"We'll just see about that," I answered, taking off my seat belt and opening my door.

"Whatever," Asher answered, sighing in defeat. "You can

come on down if you want. There's not much to look at, though."

My curiosity about this basement apartment of his, plus my worry over his cut fuel line, prompted me to follow him through the dark to a rusted metal door. A streetlight at the opening of the alley showed how dented in the entrance looked, as if multiple people had tried to kick it in, multiple times.

"Watch your step. There's no light in the staircase." After he swung the door open, he disappeared inside. I took a breath, and glanced in to see a soft glow from the other end, helping to light my way some, so I cautiously stepped down. The steps were steeper than I was expecting and made from a wood that liked to creak and groan, but from the way Asher was plowing down them, they must be sturdy. Once he reached the ground floor, he turned on another light in his apartment and called, "Better?"

"Yeah. Gracias."

I reached the opening of his snug, tidy studio basement apartment and stopped dead so I could gape around me in amazement. But holy shit, it wasn't a dump down here. Everything was small, but the kitchenette in the corner looked relatively new, as did all the furniture and—

A banging of metal above me about made me pee my pants.

"¡Dios mío!" I yelped, clutching my chest as I jumped away from the wall and spun around to gape up at what I'd heard. Then I realized how girly I'd just sounded, so I cleared my throat and muttered, "What the fuck was that?"

But I could already see for myself what had caused all the racket. Asher had taken half a dozen metal mesh cages and somehow attached them high to the wall above the doorway. Then he'd attached short aluminum pipes between them so the creature inside could travel from one cage to the next.

"That..." Asher announced, leaning up on tiptoes so he could reach for the opening clasp of the closest cage. "Is Mozart."

A flash of brown fur darted past him as soon as the door was open, and the animal inside leapt out, landing about ten feet away on the back of Asher's couch before bounding along the length and leaping to the floor so it could disappear under the bed.

I pointed toward the bed, squinting because I couldn't be absolutely certain I'd just seen what I'd really just seen. "That was a squirrel."

Asher grinned with pride. "I know, right? Pretty cool, huh? I went to all the pet shops in town, looking for one until I came across him. I guess he was a rescue case they found with a broken leg in the park one day. After fixing him up, it didn't seem safe to let him back out into the wild, even though he seems to have healed okay. He'd been returned three times by customers before I came along, because he scratched the hell out of all the other owners." Asher shrugged as if he couldn't figure out why a squirrel would scratch anyone. "But I've learned that if you just don't try to touch him and give him his space, he's fine."

I shook my head, trying to get over the fact that Asher Hart had a pet squirrel. But then I flared out a hand and said, "I mean, yeah...why would anyone buy a pet, thinking they could actually *pet* it."

"Shut up, smart-ass." Asher grinned and shook his head as he moved to the kitchen to open some cabinets and pull out a handful of peanuts. Immediately, Mozart's head appeared from under the bed, his nose twitching as he watched Asher toss the nuts into various parts of the room. "I like him because he's cool as hell to watch. Squirrels are geniuses. Just watch."

Darting out from his hidey-hole, Mozart jumped and shimmied his way into retrieving every single peanut, all the while making it impossible for any humans around to get close to him.

"Pretty cool," I had to admit, setting my hands on my hips as I watched Mozart disappear back under Asher's bed, a really comfy-looking queen-size with the blankets rumpled out of place as if he'd just crawled from those warm white sheets.

Damn, I shouldn't look at his bed. "Personally, I would've gone with a dog or a cat," I said, forcing myself to stop thinking naughty thoughts about what I'd love to do on that bed with its owner. We could totally shock Mozart into having a heart attack with all the thoughts that ran through my head. "You know, something I can actually touch, but yeah, okay."

Asher shook his head. "Just because I can't touch him

doesn't mean he still can't be taken care of and loved," he argued. "I swear, those are the souls who need a little TLC the most."

I blinked at him, realizing he was talking about himself. Maybe. It fit, though. After he admitted to me in Chicago that he would like to be in a relationship with someone, it struck me that he had no one to touch...and that seemed to be what he wanted most.

I wasn't lucky enough to ever be able to touch him—really touch him—but I decided right then and there, I would give him a little TLC, because I could still be his friend.

"Why the name Mozart?" I asked.

"Because the original Mozart was a genius too. You know, he was only fourteen when he wrote his first opera. A freaking *opera*."

I wrinkled my nose. "Why would you even know something like that?"

He shrugged. "I cruise the web a lot, looking at music sites. And I was reading an article about him one night when I clicked on his music. Put the squirrel right to sleep...so, I named him Mozart."

I eyed the tree rat warily as he peeked out from under the bed to watch us as if he knew he was the topic of discussion. His beady brown eyes stared back with a wise yet nervous certainty.

"Okay, I can see how he might grow on you." Then I glanced at Asher, frowning. "You said he, right? It's a boy squirrel?"

Asher wrinkled his brow before admitting, "Oh, hell, I guess I really don't know. He's never let me get close enough to actually look."

"So, *he* could be a *she*?"

He rolled his eyes. "I'm just going to go with he. It...fits."

I shook a finger at him. "You should never assume shit like that, you know." I was living proof.

Asher laughed and waved a hand at me. "Whatever, dork. As you can see, my dad isn't hiding out with a machete, or gun, or chainsaw. I'm perfectly safe down here with my wild pet squirrel. So..."

I knew that was my cue to leave. But I felt bad about abandoning him, even though it was late and he probably wanted to go to bed...on that snuggly-looking mattress. I just kept replaying his words in my head, feeling as if it was a call from a lonely guy. So when I glanced down and saw the Play Station game sitting on his coffee table, I gasped and clutched my chest. "You have the new Black Ops 3 edition. Holy...shit. That's so sweet. I only have the original and zombie versions."

Asher's eyebrows arched with interest. "You play Call of Duty?"

I sent him a look to let him know he was insane for even having to ask. "Oh, hell yes. My cousin Big T—Tomás—he has officially refused to play against me. Little crybaby whiny boy. I've kicked his ass one too many times, I guess."

"Oh, so you think you're good at it, huh?"

"Think?" I snorted and sent him a get-real glance. "Honey, you don't know what a real whoopin' is until you're beaten at Call of Duty...by me."

As soon as I said the words, I remembered that he *did* know what it felt like to be whipped...by both his parents. Gulping, I glanced at him to make sure I hadn't hit a sore point, but he only grinned. "Challenge accepted, asshole. You're on."

So we gamed for the rest of the night and into the early morning. He wasn't bad, and since I'd never played this version before, I had some learning to catch up on. But as soon as I got with the program, I smoked his ass. And every time, he would demand a replay.

I have no idea how long we played. After a while, he fetched us snacks and drinks. But I had so much fun, just hanging out with him, I forgot to check the time. After a while, I passed out exhausted on his couch.

CHAPTER 25
Asher Hart

I WAS CRUNCHING INTO an apple for breakfast—one I'd bought for Mozart—when the call came through the next morning. I knew I should stop eating all my pet's fruit. Everything I'd read said squirrels needed a balanced diet of fruits and vegetables, along with plants and nuts. But nuts seemed to be his favorite, so I overindulged him in that area. Besides, some of the fruit was beginning to go bad, so...I figured I might as well eat it before it was too late.

I'd never really been a fruit eater before. It was kind of growing on me, though. I might actually get into some healthy foods.

"Hello?" I answered the unknown number around a mouthful.

On the couch, Remy stirred and sat up, his fake hair sticking up everywhere as he peered at me from over the back of my couch with bloodshot eyes.

I waved at him, only to pop to my feet and turn my back to him after the man on the other end of the line introduced himself. Excitement lit through me.

"Are you serious?" I blurted out without meaning to.

The man chuckled before letting me know just how serious he was. After that, we hashed out a few details before I hung up and swung around to share the news with Sticks.

"What?" he asked immediately, hopping up from the couch with a look of eagerness. "We got another gig, didn't we?"

I nodded. "Here in town at the Grenada. Next Saturday. Holy shit." That was the first place I'd tried to get Non-Castrato a gig over a year ago when we'd just started. Now, the guy was calling *me* and begging for us. Oh, this was sweet justice.

"Hot damn," Sticks cried, doing a little dance that made me laugh.

"And so it begins," I said dramatically, wondering how many spots we'd score after this. Things were definitely looking good for the band.

I offered him a fist bump and he blew it up before sighing as if refreshed. "This is so cool. It's like...a dream come true for me. I still can't believe you guys let me in the group sometimes. It's all just...surreal. And amazing."

I waved his praise away. "Honestly, you've got pure talent. I'm sure you could've gotten into whatever band you wanted."

He snorted. "Think again. This has been a yearning of mine for years. I've tried for more places than you can imagine."

I frowned. "Then why haven't you...?" My eyebrows rose. "Are you saying you've been turned away because you're gay?" What idiots all the other bands had been.

An uneasy look crossed his face. Then he bowed his head and scratched the back of his neck before saying, "More or less, yes...it's because I prefer guys." He looked up, and deep appreciation filled his gaze. "Really, Asher, you have no idea what a gift you've given me, not only for the chance to be in Non-Castrato, but...just by accepting me."

"Hey," I said softly, wanting to clasp his shoulder or, I don't know, somehow convince him he was very important to me. "Screw all those other people who refused to look past the surface and see what a truly awesome person you are. Actually, you know what, I'm glad they were all idiots, because their loss was our gain. Playing in the band with you and getting to know you has been...it's been nice."

Remy's eyes glazed as if he were going to cry.

Shit, I hoped he didn't cry. I got uncomfortable enough around girls who cried...no way did I know how to handle a weeping dude.

But all he choked out was, "Thank you," before he cleared his throat and glanced around my apartment. "But damn, I can't believe I fell asleep on your couch. What time is it, anyway?"

"It's a quarter after ten."

His eyes bugged. "Shit! I'm late for work. Ah...I gotta go." He started to back away, then paused as if he needed my permission or something.

I laughed and waved him away. "Go, man. And sorry about that. I would've woken you sooner if I'd known. I should've asked."

"No biggie." Scooping up his shoes he'd kicked off at some point in our Call of Duty wars, he raced toward the stairwell, waving his fingers at Mozart once again cooped up in his cage as he went.

"See you at practice," I called after him, grinning over his flurried departure.

"Yeah, see you," his voice echoed back down the stairs.

Once the door slammed after him, my smile died. The room suddenly felt a lot...emptier. Not even my squirrel rattling around in his cage could fill the void.

Blowing out a breath, I decided I had other things to worry about. A fuel line to replace, a new gig to plan for, music for our newest song to compose.

Busy, busy, busy. I had no time to feel alone.

"Dude," Remy hissed in my ear, clutching my arm hard. "You didn't say anything about Fish 'N' Dicks being here tonight."

We'd just arrived at the Grenada where the band Sticks had named was on stage, already performing.

"Yeah, I did. I said two other groups would be playing tonight before us," I called over the blaring sound.

"But you didn't specify that *Fish 'N' Dicks's* would be one of them."

I frowned at him, wondering why he sounded so pissed. Then I shrugged. "I don't see the big deal. Their song 'Tomorrow's Promise' is kick-ass."

That comment seemed to catch my drummer off guard before he said, "Really?" as if I'd just complimented his outfit. Then he suddenly straightened his shoulders and cleared his throat. "Their lead singer's an asshole."

I only laughed. "If assholes bugged me, I never would've made a band with Gally in it."

"Huh?" Gally glanced over, only hearing his name.

Remy glanced at the bass guitarist and promptly turned back to me. "Good point." And he shut up about it from that point on...until we actually ran into the other band backstage as they were coming off and we were preparing to go on after the second group sang.

Yeah, I said that right. We were the grand finale performance. Boo-yah.

"Well, well, well, if it isn't Non-Castrato," the lead singer said as he spotted the four of us together. I think his name was something Fisher, but at the moment, his given name escaped me. "It's Hart, right?"

When I nodded, not letting him know I didn't remember his name in return, I simply said, "Hey, man. What's up?"

He slid his gaze to Remy, who I felt tense beside me. "Not much. Heard you guys had to get a new drummer. The last one did...what again? Went to jail for burning his entire family in a house fire, was it?"

"He was asking where you lived, too," Remy spat back.

Gally started hooting at his burn, which got Holden to chuckling too.

I sent Remy a *behave* glare, but he was ignoring me, narrowing his eyes on the guy with the fish tattoo taking up half his face.

"Who the fuck are you?" Fish Boy demanded, scowling at my drummer.

And my drummer scowled right back. "None of your fucking business."

The two stepped toward each other as if to start brawling then and there, so I put up my hand between them. "Hey, hey, hey. We're here to play tonight, fellas. Not brawl."

Remy immediately blew out a breath and retreated, but

the other guy kept glaring.

"Your drummer has a serious attitude problem."

"He's fine," I assured him, patting his chest to send him on his way. "Good job tonight."

Finally pacified, Fish-face sniffed at us and whirled away to storm off.

"What the hell?" I hissed to Remy as soon as he was gone. It was usually Gally I had to worry about acting up and getting into a fight.

He shrugged and glanced away. "I just hate that bastard," he mumbled.

I lifted my eyebrows. "And you actually know him, because he didn't seem to know *you*."

Remy glanced at me. "I...I know a girl who dated him...and royally got screwed over by him. To say the least, I'm not a fan."

"Okay, fine," I relented. "Just warn me next time you're going to get mouthy with an opposing band so I'll be prepared."

"Well, if I'd known he was going to be here—"

"Fine. *Fine.*" I lifted my hands. "And I'll warn *you* if we ever play in the same venue with them again."

"Thank you." He sent me one last pouty glance and that was that.

We had our turn on stage, played our hearts out, and left the crowd screaming and begging for more. As Gally, Heath and Remy started for the back room that had been assigned to just us for the evening, the owner of the club stopped me with a cash payment.

I grinned at the money and told him we'd love to come back again when he invited us. I tried not to worry about my Forbidden friends. All the guys had bitched and moaned when they'd learned I wouldn't be there again for another karaoke night. They hated having to deal with all the technical issues that I usually took care of.

Pick had told them all to shut up because my new gigs were big opportunities for me, but I worried about him too. He'd helped me get started, given me more opportunities than anyone, and here I felt as if I was abandoning him.

I knew he wouldn't want me to be that way, though. It was strange having a family member who only wanted what was best for me. Made me wish I could do more for him.

Shaking those thoughts away, I hurried back to the guys, who looked as if they were already plastered as they passed around a complimentary bottle of Grey Goose that had been left in our room.

"And there's the man of the hour," Remy called, lifting the bottle in cheers. "Everyone give it up for Asher Hart." He made the sound of a roaring crowd before taking a big slug.

"Watch it, you greedy bastard," Gally complained, stealing the vodka mid-gulp so that Remy ended up spilling some down his chin.

"Fucker," he told Gally as he wiped the back of his hand over the leak. Then he grinned glassy-eyed at me. "What's up, boss?"

No idea why he called me boss, but I lifted the cash we'd made and fanned my face with it. "It's payday," I announced.

"Damn straight," Gally hooted, fisting his hand into the air. "Gimme my *money*!"

Since the only open spot to sit was an end seat on the couch next to Remy, where he'd sprawled out, practically taking up the whole damn thing, I nudged his legs aside with my knee and sat next to him.

He grinned at me and stuck a Twizzler between his teeth.

Yanking the dangling part of the Twizzler stick free, I took a big bite from the opposite end and began to chew. "The manager invited us back next month if we're interested. I said we were."

"Hell yes, we are," Gally called while Holden nodded.

Remy was too busy scowling at the string of candy I'd stolen from him. Jabbing out his hand to steal it back, he growled when I was faster, taking it from my own mouth and holding it tauntingly away from him. Then I really did it; I licked the entire length, spreading my germs so he couldn't take it back without being gross.

"Ha," I crowed triumphantly. "I licked it, so it's mine." That was payback for his kicking my ass at Call of Duty.

He scowled. "Really? How mature is that?" Then, he wiggled his eyebrows. "Now, I just want it back more."

While I sputtered out a laugh and nearly choked on my Twizzler, Gally hissed, "Sick, man. That's disgusting. No flirting allowed here, queer."

"Whatever," Remy muttered, leaning forward to find the bag for a new Twizzler stick. "You're just jealous because I didn't hit on *you*."

"Wow," Gally said as he yanked his share of cash out of my hand. "That was totally not the case. Seriously, though, you two lovebirds sure got chummy since rooming together in Chicago."

"Yeah." Letting out a big, dreamy sigh, Remy pressed a hand to his chest and fluttered his lashes my way. "We bonded. It was beautiful."

"Jesus, Sticks." I scowled at him. "Just how drunk are you?"

He gave a husky laugh and blew me a kiss. "I'm three sheets to the wind, baby."

"Yeah, I can tell." I waved at Heath, motioning him to toss the bottle of vodka that was now in his possession my way. "Looks like I'm going to have to guzzle to catch up."

CHAPTER 26
Remy Curran

AFTER ASHER TOOK A healthy gulp from the Grey Goose, and then another, he divided the rest of the cash out by three, so Heath, he and I got equal shares. It struck me that he should take more. Not only did he do double time in the band, singing, playing an instrument, and writing all our songs, he also acted as our manager, setting up all our gigs and taking care of the business end of Non-Castrato.

I hated to admit it, but I admired the hell out him.

Half an hour later, I didn't hate to admit it so much. I was damn eager to as I slung a plastered arm over his shoulder and slurred, "Man, I admire the hell out of you. Awesome singer, awesome musician. Amazing songwriter and even more amazing body with an ass I want to sink my teeth into. Is there *anything* you suck at?"

He leaned heavily against me, having just as much trouble sitting upright as I was. After squinting as if deep in thought, he admitted, "I can't tell my left from my right."

"Damn." My grin was sloppy and proud. "You mean, I actually know something you don't?"

"You should've seen him trying to Hokey Pokey at this

wedding reception once."

I grinned over at Gally while he laughed over the memory. "It was at the wedding where Holden here's cousin tied the knot and..." He grinned at Heath. "Hey, remember when I used to bang her, back in the day. Man, she was a hot piece of ass."

"Yeah," Holden said with a dry scowl. "I remember."

"She had a mouth made for fucking. Plus she liked to swallow."

"I think I'm going to be sick," I told Asher, who laughed.

"I'm serious." Gally scowled, kicking at my knee. "Just shut up, gay fucker. Women's mouths were made for a man's dick. I'm telling you...because you wouldn't know, nothing is as fine as a well-given blow job. And...now I want some pussy."

He stumbled to his feet. "Who's with me? Why are we still sitting back here like a bunch of losers when there's some grade-A, half-naked bitches out there? Let's find us some pussy."

Heath stood first, and Gally cheered him on, slapping his back in congratulations. Then he turned to Asher.

"What about you, Hart? Go pussy hunting with us. Just this once."

Asher actually seemed to consider the request before he shrugged and started to crawl his way off the couch. "Okay."

"What?" I snapped my gaze to him, but he wasn't paying me any attention, too busy trying to stand straight.

Gally clucked his tongue at me. "Sorry, gay boy. Guess that leaves you out."

"No, Remy can still come along," Asher argued, waving me to follow them. "He can be our wingman."

I winced, suddenly not as drunk as I'd been seconds ago. But the idea of helping Asher score a chick left me sick to my stomach, wanting to puke all the alcohol I'd drunk.

"Or maybe he can find his own dude to score," Asher added, sending me an encouraging grin.

I sent him a small smile. "Sure, count me in."

Count me in? What the hell was I saying? I didn't want to watch him pick up chicks. And yet I couldn't *not* come along. I'd worry all night, wondering who he'd chosen, how pretty she was, how funny and—

"All right!" Asher cheered, slugging me on the back before he slung his arm over my shoulder and crookedly steered me out of the room.

As Heath and Gally continued on ahead of us, I leaned in, wincing when I made Asher sneeze. But I still had to mutter into his ear, "Thought you said you didn't like one-night stands."

Though my voice had been discreet enough, he hissed, "Shh," and slapped his finger to his lips. "I don't. But I'm horny and desperate and just drunk enough not to care about how shitty and more alone I'll feel afterward."

I wrinkled my brow and opened my mouth to argue, but the look he sent me was full of an aching craving I knew I couldn't fill with a couple rounds of Call of Duty.

"I need this, Sticks," he confessed. "I need...something."

I knew exactly what he needed. He needed to be touched.

Then, as if to wipe away all the misery in himself, he grinned and bumped his body into mine. "And who knows. Maybe I'll actually meet my soul mate out there."

Good Lord, I hoped not. Watching him take home a one-night stand would be bad enough; watching him fall into a committed relationship with some other woman...yeah, just kill me now.

I swear, all the females in the building could smell his need, too. As soon as we cleared the back hall and entered the main portion of the bar, they flocked to him, touching him, praising him, smiling their evil, witchy skank smiles at him.

I was torn away from him as they crowded in, and while the space between us grew from one foot to ten, I knew he was lost to me. I wanted to drown myself in more alcohol, but then...I just couldn't. I went to the bar and ordered a water before returning to the fringes of his crowd of fans, watching helplessly.

After a couple sips, I started to think luck would be on my side. Asher was politely turning them all away. And as the disappointed, rejected flock slunk away one by one, my spirits lifted. If this kept up, his own pickiness would save my entire night.

Asher slumped down next to me, scowling. "What're the odds that some woman in the place *doesn't* know I'm in a band?"

"Oh, about zero to nothing," I assured him, feeling better by the second.

He scowled at me. "Thank, asshole," he hissed. "That makes me feel so much better."

I laughed and slapped his arm. "Just being honest, my friend."

"Well, I could use a good lie right now. So if you could be so kind—umph." He went sprawling toward me as someone bumped into him from behind.

"Oh, I'm so sorry. I didn't see you there," A girl gushed, her eyes wide and hand covering her mouth. "Are you okay, sir? Did you spill your drink?"

"No, it's fine. We're good." Asher glanced at me to make sure I was good, then turned back to the woman. "Are you okay?"

She preened and held out a hand. "Well, I am now. The name's Tamra."

"Asher," he greeted, shaking with her.

She scrunched her eyebrows before leaning forward and saying, "Archer?"

"No. It's *Ash*er," he called a little louder.

"Oh, okay." She smiled and kept her hand in his. "Did you come to watch the bands play, Asher?"

His eyebrows lifted. Then he sent me a smug little smile, as if to say *zero to none, huh?* And he turned back to Tamra...the whore.

"Something like that," he answered. "Did you get to hear them?"

As they started a conversation about the bands from tonight and music in general, I rolled my eyes and turned away, sick and disgusted and freaking hurt.

He was going to pick this one. I just knew it.

I hated it, and yet there was nothing I could do about it.

I should've left then. I *knew* I should have. But I just had to torture myself. I had to watch it all play out.

They were totally hitting it off. Asher was laid-back, but I could tell he was into her. I mean, he didn't flirt with her or look at me the way he had me when he'd caught me in the shower—a small consolation I played up in my mind—but it was enough. He was drunk and desperate enough to take her home.

When she announced she had to go the ladies' room and would be right back, he spun to me and flashed me a thumbs-up as well as a grin that seemed to say *we have a winner.*

I didn't smile back. Instead I hopped off my barstool. "I gotta take a piss too."

His grin died. "Uh...okay."

Turning away from him and unable to keep looking at the hopeful, excited expression on his face, I hurried toward the bathrooms. There was a little alcove before it separated into the men's and ladies' rooms. As I entered it, I completely ignored the men's side. Instead, I bent down and peeled off my mask.

When I straightened and shook out my hair, some guy had just entered the alcove and had stopped frozen, gaping at me. "Dude," he said, raising his hands and circling around me before he could escape into the lavatory.

I didn't even care that I'd been caught. I was too drunk, or jealous, or something, to think it through. I hurried into the women's room and pulled to a stop when I saw Tamra with a few friends, fluffing their hair in the wall of mirrors above the sinks.

"You lucky bitch," one said, slapping Tamra's arm. "I can't believe you're about to score Asher Fucking Hart."

"I know, right?" Tamra giggled and bit at her lips to plump them

I drew in a breath and pressed my back to the wall just inside the doorway.

But I couldn't believe this. She already knew who he was. He'd never told her his last name.

God, of course she already knew who he was. She was just better at the game than all the other clueless women out there.

This was exactly what Asher didn't want. And yet a groupie was about to trick her way into his pants anyway. I needed to warn him, except...how?

Oh, you'll never believe what I just heard in the ladies' room, Ash?

Yeah, that'd go over real well.

Wanting to cry, I pushed from the wall and started for an empty stall. Tamra and her group spotted me and offered me tentative smiles.

"Love the purple streaks," she had the nerve to tell me.

I sent her a sickened smile. "Gracias." My hair was a disaster, I knew. It'd been trapped under the mask for hours and was probably matted and sweaty, sticking to my head in a most unnatural way.

Escaping into a stall, I sat down and hugged my ribs, wanting to cry.

Outside my door, one of the skanks asked, "Do you think he'll take you back to his place or rent a motel room somewhere?"

"Like it matters. I'd settle for the backseat of his car if that's what he wanted."

It's a motorcycle, bitch. He drives a motorcycle, not a car.

And then I pictured him taking her on his motorcycle and had to squeeze my eyes closed and press my lips together to keep from crying.

"Just as long as we don't go back to my place," Tamra cooed, beginning to sound way too smug.

Both of her friends laughed before one said, "Yeah, I'm sure your husband and two kids would have a small problem with you banging Asher the rock god Hart on the living room couch."

My eyes popped open as the other two joined in, laughing.

Say what?

Oh, no fucking way. The skank was *married*? Surging to my feet, I tried to barge my way from the stall, only to find it locked. So I fumbled a second before I could escape, and yep, by the time I was free, the three women were gone, only their snickering, married-ass laughter echoing around the bathroom behind them.

I started to follow them, pushing my way from the bathroom. But no sooner did I charge from the bathroom alcove than I spotted Asher headed my way.

And he saw me. At the same moment his eyes went big and his mouth rounded into a surprised O, I remembered that I'd forgotten to put my mask back on.

Moving quickly, I ducked behind a group of three guys passing by just as I heard Asher's voice call, "Hey, wait."

I crouched down behind my unknowing shield until we passed a door, which I reached out and tried. When it opened, I popped inside the dark space, with no idea whether it was an office, supply closet or what. Afraid to shut myself fully inside alone, I kept the door cracked and was able to peek out from my dark hiding place.

"Hijo de puta," I hissed when I saw a determined Asher striding my way as if he knew where I was hiding.

But Tamra found him, grasping his arm and asking him where he was headed.

He glanced at the cracked doorway I was peeking out of. "I...I thought I saw someone I knew. Did you see a girl? Um...maybe Latino, long dark hair, purple highlights."

"Purple highlights?" Tamra said, her smile freezing. Then she shook her head. "No, I sure didn't. Sorry."

Gasp!

Liar!

Okay, so I was a worse liar than she was. But she was trying to trick him into bed. That was just wrong.

After she urged him away, grasping his arm to steer him back toward the direction of our table, he tossed one last wistful glance to my door but then turned away.

I blew out a thunderous breath, counted to ten, then whipped on my mask as fast as was humanly possible, hoping to God I didn't have it on crooked. Then I eased out of my hidey-hole and hurried back to the table as well.

No way could I let that whore get away with doing this to my Asher.

I reached them just in time. They were both standing, Tamra was slipping her purse strap over her shoulder as if getting ready to leave, and Asher was tossing some cash onto the table to take care of the tip. Then he set his hand on the small of her back and turned her toward the door. But I popped in front of them, right into their path.

They pulled up short, so I had to pretend to pull up short in surprise too. "Oh, hey. You guys leaving?" I asked innocently enough.

"Yeah." Asher sent me an odd look. "I just tried to find you, but you weren't in the bathroom."

"Oh...yeah. I...." Crap. I spotted the bar and quickly ad-libbed. "I went to get another drink, then decided against it."

He nodded. "Well, we're going to go. This is Tamra, by the way."

I turned to her, sending her a pleasant smile, if I did say so myself.

"Tamra, this is my friend, Remy."

"Hey," she greeted, holding out her fingers in one of

those lame, limp-wristed ways that drove me crazy.

I took the tips of her hand anyway. "Nice to meet you." Then I snapped my fingers and pointed. "Oh, hey. You're that chick who was tucking her wedding ring in her purse just outside the john a few minutes ago, weren't you?"

"Say what?" Asher whirled toward her, his eyebrows lifted.

Shock clouded her face. "I...I...I most certainly was *not*."

"Yeah, that was definitely you," I cooed, unable to hold back a grin as I shook my finger at her. "You were bragging to your friends about how you were about to score Asher the rock god Hart, weren't you?"

"What? How..." She shook her head, gaping at me, trying to figure out how I knew as much as I knew. Then she whirled to Asher. "That did *not* happen. Not like that."

Maybe not exactly the way I'd described it, but oh, it had definitely happened.

Asher didn't seem to care how the conversation had gone down. "Are you really married?" He took a decisive step away from her.

"I..." The guilt spreading across her face told us both she was.

"And you lied about not knowing who I was," he further accused before lifting his hands. "That's just...not cool." Then he turned and walked away.

Tamra's mouth dropped open. "What the hell?" she cried.

When she glanced my way, I shrugged. "Hey...life's a bitch and then you die, huh?"

"You..." She narrowed her eyes. "You're such a fucking liar. Thanks for ruining my night."

As she stomped away, I was about to call after her, something about a pot calling a kettle black, but then I stopped myself.

I *was* a liar, and I was probably a worse liar than she was. She'd only planned on tricking him for one night. I'd been tricking him for weeks, and would keep on for who knew how much longer. There was no end in sight to my deception, because I just didn't know how to tell him the truth.

Feeling like crap times ten, I scoured the place until I found him at the bar by himself a couple minutes later, nursing some water, probably trying to sober up. His shoulders looked tense as he hunched over the counter, consoling himself.

I slumped down beside him.

For a couple seconds, no one spoke. Finally, I said, "I'm sorry."

He blurted out a harsh laugh and sent me a weary glance. "What the hell are you sorry for?"

"I just...I cock-blocked you," I mumbled. Because I was an evil, jealous bitch who hadn't been able to stand seeing him take another woman home.

"No. You just saved me from fucking a married woman. I should be *thanking* you...not you apologizing to me. Idiot."

"Still..." I blew out a long sigh. "If only I'd kept my big mouth shut, you could've found a little relief."

"Or ruined a marriage," he argued. Turning to me, he looked me dead in the eye and set his hand on my shoulder. "You saved my ass just now. Thank you, man. You're a true friend."

Except I didn't feel like a friend at all. My deception pierced me to the depths of my soul and I felt like the biggest fraud ever.

A true friend would've just wanted him to be happy.

In that moment, I swore to myself I'd help him find a woman before the end of the night if it was the last thing I did. And who cared if I cried myself to sleep afterward. I deserved it.

Asher, on the other hand, deserved the human contact he so craved.

CHAPTER 27
Asher Hart

WELL, THIS SUCKED ASS. The evening had started out great and quickly nosedived into crappy. All because I'd been thinking with my stupid dick.

I was practically sober again as I finished off the last of the water I'd ordered. Next to me, Remy was pensive. He hadn't said much since trying to apologize to me for saving my ass. He sat with his back to the bar so he could watch the crowd. I thought I knew what his mood was about, and I'd just been ignoring it for the past so many minutes. But now, now, it was time for me to do something.

After setting down my empty container, I tapped the bar top next to him to get his attention. I hadn't seen Holden or Gally for quite some time, but that was fine. Sticks was really the only one I wanted to say goodbye to, anyway.

"I think I'm going to head out."

He jerked his attention to me, alarmed. "What? No. Where're you going?"

"Home." I slipped off my stool, patting my pockets to make sure I had my wallet and keys. "I'm just...I'm going to go home."

"Why?" Sticks shook his head, confused as he popped off his stool. "You're not just going to give up after one dead end, are you? What about your...your need?"

I sighed, feeling like an idiot for confessing that to him in the first place. "I'm fine. It's okay. I have a hand; it knows my cock well."

That answer seemed to stun him. "Look." I sighed, deciding to get real. "I just...I have a feeling it'd...*bother* you if I went home with a woman tonight. And you're my friend. I don't want to upset you by flaunting some chick in your face."

There. I'd said it.

And boy had saying it gotten me a reaction.

Remy jerked backward, his eyes flying open and mouth gaping wide. He shook his head for a second before sputtering. "Excuse me? What do you mean by *bother me*?"

He sounded so affronted I immediately realized I'd fucked up. "Shit." I lifted my hands, trying to restore the peace. "I shouldn't have said anything. It sounded a lot less arrogant in my own head."

"Un-fucking-believable," he muttered, gawking at me as if I'd called him a liar and a cheat. "You seriously think I want you for myself, don't you? Well, fuck you, man. I don't care if you take home ten women tonight. Fuck whomever you like. I don't give a shit."

He started to turn away, but I grabbed his arm. "Hey. Shit. I'm sorry. Seriously, Rem." I lifted my hands again. "I'm sorry. I don't...I was being an idiot."

He stared at me a full five seconds before muttering something in Spanish and then scrubbing his hands over his face. After lowering his hands to eye me wearily, he muttered, "Damn it. You're right, though." When I tipped my head to the side, he reluctantly admitted, "It would've bothered me."

Hanging his head, he looked so guilty and contrite; I wanted to reassure him. I even reached for his shoulder. But then I stopped myself, not wanting to send the wrong signal.

So I blew out a breath. "I suspected as much."

"But the thing is," he went on, finally looking up. "No matter how I may want you and how freaking sweet and considerate your worrying about my feelings is, you're my friend too, Asher, and I want you to be happy. So don't go turning into some miserable monk on my account. I assure you, I'll live."

I nodded, watching him closely. When I was confident he really was okay with it, I said, "All right then. From here on out, I'll just...I'll be discreet about it."

He winced. "Actually...I'd rather know."

"Huh?"

With a rueful shrug, he explained, "If you hid it, I'd drive myself insane, always wondering. Every time you'd smile or seem unusually happy, I'd think it was because you got laid. I'd always be stressing myself out, my mind coming up with the worst possible scenarios. But if I *knew*...well, then I'd know. And then I could deal with getting over it."

I nodded. "Okay. Strangely, that makes sense. I won't hide it from you, then."

With a grave return nod, he answered, "Thank you."

"So...how're we going to work this then?" I rubbed my hands on my hips. "I really don't want to cause you any undue distress."

Chuckling, he shook his head. "I have no idea. Maybe, like, don't stick your tongue down a girl's throat in front of me. That'd be great. Though I can't picture you as the PDA type, anyway."

I shrugged. "I never have been before."

Sticks nodded. "Then it'll be fine. I mean, I get to vet them, right, throw out the rotten ones I don't approve of?"

I threw back my head and laughed. "How about you just set me up with someone who passes your muster, and if I like her, we'll go from there."

"Nope. Sorry." He winced. "That would be an impossible task. Frankly, I doubt I'd find a woman good enough for you."

Shaking my head, I sighed. I wasn't sure about anyone not being good enough for me, I hadn't even been able to find someone actually *willing* to be with me...for longer than a night. But I wasn't going to think about that. Glancing at my bud, I had to admit, "You know this is the strangest conversation I've ever had with a guy, right?"

"You're telling me." He rolled his eyes. "I can't believe I admitted *aloud* I had a thing for you."

I shrugged, not sure how to answer. I'd had dudes hit on me before and it had wiped me clear out of my comfort zone. But for some reason, knowing what Remy thought about me was okay. Maybe because he didn't come on strong or actually expect me to reciprocate. He was chill and laid-back about it, almost making light of his feelings so we'd ended up laughing instead of turning uneasy about it all.

So I said, "Honestly, man. I'm flattered."

He swiped a hand my way as if to hit me in the arm. "Shut up. It's embarrassing."

Chuckling, I said, "It's not that bad."

"Whatever. Now you're going to have to tell me something embarrassing about you."

"The hell if I do." When he scowled, I gave in. "Fine. It says Ashley on my birth certificate."

At first, the words didn't seem to sink in. Then he frowned and tipped his head to the side. "No way."

"Oh...yes way. My mother was so determined I was going to be a girl, she named me Ashley Jean. Had it on my birth certificate and legalized it before my dad found out. He was so pissed off. He refused to call me that, so I eventually morphed into Asher. And when my uncle got me under his custody, he helped me get it legally changed."

Remy's mouth fell open. "Holy shit. She really named you Ashley...and not after Ashley Wilkes from *Gone with the Wind*, but Ashley because she wanted you to be a girl?"

"Yep. And I suspect, she would've raised me as if I were a girl in frilly pink dresses if my father had let her."

"¡Dios mío! That's just..."

When he shook his head as if dazed, I sighed and said, "Fucked up. Yeah, I know. But go ahead. Laugh it up, asshole."

He chuckled but waved his hands as he did so. "No. Actually, it's kind of sad." He blew out a breath. "And here, I grew up miffed because I had such a guy name."

I sent him a strange frown. "Huh?"

He started to open his mouth when a strange expression hit. After a second, he stuttered, "I just...you know, because of the gay thing, I kind of always preferred the more universal names that could go either way, like Alex or—"

"Remy could go either way," I argued. "Actually, Remy for a girl would be pretty kick-ass."

"You think?" he asked, his voice wistful.

When I frowned at him, he quickly cleared his throat.

"So, about this chick we're going to find for you tonight." Rubbing his hands together, he scanned the crowd for possible targets, but I held up my palm.

"No. Let's just give it a break for tonight. Besides, I'm starving. Let's get something to eat instead."

Remy blinked as if he'd never heard of such an idea. "Food?"

"Taco Bell," I declared. "Only place to go after a night of drinking." Then I grinned and quoted their slogan, "Yo quiero Taco Bell."

"No." Wrinkling his nose, Remy shook his head. "No, no no. *No* quiero Taco Bell. The only Méxican food I eat is made at Castañeda's."

Remembering the chimichanga he'd shared with me, I rubbed my stomach. That did sound good. But... "I'm guessing they're not open this late."

He shook his head. "But I could call my cousin Big T and get him to fire up the grill. He makes the best tostadas de tinga. Ooh, or chicharrón preparado if you just want a cold snack."

I sighed. "Meh. Don't bother him. Let's just find an all-night cafe or something."

So half an hour later, we found ourselves sitting across a diner booth from each other, scarfing down bacon, and eggs, and biscuits and gravy.

"We totally rocked tonight, huh?" Remy said, brushing crumbs off the corner of his mouth with his thumb. "Better than we did in Chicago, I think."

"Yeah," I agreed. We were definitely developing our talent and learning to play better as a group. But the word Chicago struck a memory in me, making my mind veer in a different direction. Snapping my fingers, I pointed. "Hey, I forgot to tell you earlier. I saw shower girl at the Granada."

Remy lowered his fork and blinked at me. Then he slowly said, "Shower girl?"

I rolled my eyes, because, really, who else could I be referring to? "The stray woman I found in our shower in Chicago...in the hotel," I added when he continued to stare at me as if he had no clue what I was talking about.

Finally, he licked a crumb off his top lip and slowly responded. "And she was...at the Granada? Tonight?" When I nodded, he squinted. "Are you sure?"

"Absolutely one hundred percent positively sure," I answered. "It was her, same purple streaks in her hair and everything."

"That's...that's..." He shook his head and sent me a sly smile. "That's actually a little hard to believe, man. I mean, the *same* exact girl was in Chicago *and* here in Ellamore?"

He had a point. The idea was a little out there. I chewed on my bottom lip, certain it had been her, but doubting myself nonetheless. "You don't think I'm going crazy, do you?" I finally asked. "I mean, not enough sex, jerking off too much lately... What if it's making me delusional? Oh shit." I sat back in my booth, stunned. "What if there wasn't even a girl in our shower? What if she doesn't exist, and this little obsession turns out worse than that thing I had for Incubus shirt girl, and I end up drooling and rocking in some corner because I've lost my damn mind?"

"Uh..." Clearly at a loss for words, Remy moved his mouth a few times but couldn't come up with anything to say.

"Never mind," I told him, letting him know he didn't need to say anything. "You're probably right. It couldn't have been the same girl. I probably just wanted it to be her because there was, you know, so much chemistry there when I saw her in Chicago."

"Chemistry?" Remy lifted his eyebrows in interest. "Oh really? Do tell."

I sighed and rolled my eyes. "Shut up, fucker. I'd rather talk about *your* infatuations than mine."

Murmuring out a sound of pity, he tipped his head to the side. "Ah, but we already know who my current infatuation is, don't we?"

I gulped, remembering *I* was. Shit. I hadn't meant to go down that road again. I opened my mouth to apologize, but he swished out his hand.

"Besides, that's old news. Let's get back to you. This shower girl. Be honest. More or less chemistry than what you felt for Incubus shirt girl?"

I opened my mouth, stunned when I realized I didn't know the answer to that. "I'm not sure," I spoke honestly. "Strange. Both encounters were just...different, but probably held the same intensity. Does that make sense?"

"Sort of," he murmured, "not really."

"You know," I spoke over him, frowning in thought.

"Now that you mention Incubus shirt girl, the two of them did have a lot of similarities. Same basic figure, long dark hair, that certain Latino look. Too bad I never got a good up-close glimpse of Incubus shirt girl's face."

Remy slapped his hand on the top of the table as if an idea had just struck. "Maybe they're the same girl."

I snorted. "Right...because she just happened to show up at Forbidden, the Granada *and* in Chicago all on the same nights I was there. That's totally possible. Sure." Then I rolled my eyes.

"It's...slightly possible," Remy hedged.

I smiled and shook my head. "Yeah, and mix those two in with punk rocker chick, and we'll have my dream woman...right there. Boom."

Straightening, Remy said, "Punk rocker chick. Who's punk rocker chick?"

Damn. There went my mouth. "No one. Just...some girl who auditioned for your drummer position the day before you did."

Remy brought his hand up to his chin. "I thought only *one* girl had...had auditioned for that."

"Yeah...and she dressed in this punk look with a spikey white Tina Turner wig, and I just had this brief little kinky vision of ripping it off and..." When I realized where I was going with my confession, I stopped cold and lifted a hand. "You know, I'm going to stop right there, stop thinking about sex, stop talking about sex, and women, and just...all that shit. Let's go to my place and slaughter some futuristic zombies. What do you say?"

Remy opened his mouth and then shook his head. "No sé; it's late. And *some* of us don't have insomnia. I'm one of those rare breeds who needs more than two hours of sleep a night, so...yeah. I'm going to head home and crash."

Disappointment hit me hard. I didn't want to go home alone. But I nodded and forced a smile. "Fine then, loser. I'm going home to practice so I can finally kick your ass the next time we play."

He snorted. "Dream on, fucker. You should just face the facts. You'll never beat me, because I am...a legend."

When I made it home from the diner with Remy, I felt lonelier than usual. I let Mozart out of his cage to play, so he ran and hid under the bed and was lousy company. I ended up practicing the lyrics of my new song as I cleaned out his cage.

I finally dropped off to sleep around five in the morning, and Pick called at eight.

"Hey, I got another house to check out this morning. You coming?"

Yawning as I sat up, I ran my fingers through my hair. "Yeah, sure. But I thought you were going to go back to looking at them with Eva."

"She refuses. Says she wants me to check out this one last house. So...pick you up in ten?"

"Sounds like a plan." I hung up and dragged my ass out of bed. Mozart banged around in his cage, reminding me I had to feed him. But after I tossed some broccoli in for him to munch on, he only looked at me, letting me know he wasn't even about to eat that healthy crap. So I sighed and gave him some of my old stale corn nuts, which he promptly pounced on.

When Pick showed up, the first thing he asked me after I slid into the passenger seat was, "Heard anything else from your dad?"

I groaned and sank lower into my seat. "Jesus, you're as bad as Sticks."

"Sticks?" He lifted an eyebrow. "How's that?"

After I told him about my run-in with the old man in Chicago and how Remy had threatened him with his mace and whistle, Pick threw back his head and laughed. "I like that kid. You need to keep him around."

I shrugged, declining to mention how my motorcycle's fuel line had been cut and the theory Remy had about that. I'd fixed it the next day, so no harm done. No reason at all to mention it to Pick.

"So which fancy-schmancy neighborhood are we headed to today?"

Pick sent me a look for making fun of his possibly new

neighborhood, then he said, "Glendale."

I nodded, deciding it wasn't as ritzy as the last neighborhood we'd been to but it was a good modest, decent family-oriented type of area.

"Tinker Bell's aunt and uncle—Reese's parents—live around here."

"Ahh," I murmured. "Cool."

This time around, neither Pick nor I beat around the bush. As soon as we saw the realtor, we spoke in unison. "Backyard?"

As I followed Pick out the sliding glass door, I asked, "So when's your wedding anyway?"

"The Sunday after next."

I froze on the back patio as Pick moved toward the middle of the yard and spun in a slow circle.

"I'm sorry, did you say the Sunday after next?" I asked, shaking my head, sure I'd misheard him. "Because that's only—"

"Eleven days away," Pick answered. "Yeah, I know."

"Shit, man. What's the rush?"

He shrugged. "We just decided we didn't want to wait any longer. We're doing it at Forbidden, so...there's not going to be a lot of decoration or party planning. And it's going to be small, mostly just everyone who works at Forbidden, their families and maybe Tink's aunt and uncle. But that reminds me." He finally looked my way. "Since you're going to be the best man, am I going to have to find a different deejay to take care of the reception?"

I shook my head. "Nah. I can ask Remy to do it. He's learned the setup already; I'm sure he'll agree."

"Cool." Pick nodded, distracted as he squinted at a huge old tree in the corner of the yard.

I hooked my thumb over my shoulder, motioning back to the house. "You ready to head back in yet?"

But my brother just stood there, staring at the tree, then he glanced around as if looking for something.

I blinked. "Holy shit. Is....is *this* the place?" I pointed to the ground under me; it suddenly felt as if I were standing on hallowed grass.

"I don't know," Pick finally murmured, wiping his hand over his face. "It looks...different." He motioned to the wooden fence, separating this yard from the neighbors.

"That fence was white, and there was a small tree...right over there. A huge swing set here with a row of purple and yellow tulips to the side."

A big grin spread across my face as I clapped him heartily on the shoulder. "Well, it looks like you have some painting, planting and building to do then, because congratulations, big brother, you just found your dream house."

"Holy shit," he uttered, looking stunned speechless as he pushed his fingers through his hair and gaped at the yard around him. "I did." Then he turned dazed eyes to me. "I don't know how to plant a fucking tree."

I laughed. "Then I guess you're going to learn. Come on. Let's check out the inside. How many bedrooms does it have? You going to have a spare one for Uncle Asher to come crash in every once in a while?"

"I don't even know." Pick's voice sounded hollow as he remained rooted to the center of the yard. "I didn't bother to check how many rooms it had."

When I realized he was still too discombobulated to move, I retreated to his side, grabbed his arm and hauled him toward the back door. "Come on, old man. Let's see what the master bedroom where you're going to make sweet love to your wife for the rest of your life looks like."

That got him to move. We thoroughly checked each room, and with each one we entered, this smile would spread across Pick's face as if he couldn't believe his good fortune. He'd make little comments about which one would be Julian's or Skylar's room, or Chloe's, though I had no idea who Chloe was. But I didn't really need to understand—it was the growing excitement emanating off my brother that was awesome. He had a future, family, and now the perfect home to look forward to. I was happy for him.

And extremely jealous.

I kind of didn't want to go back to my apartment after that, and I didn't have to work that evening. There was no band practice. It was as if I had nothing.

After Pick dropped me off and I jogged down the steps into my basement, I texted Remy to see if he wanted to grab something to eat with me. It was nearing the noon hour and I'd skipped breakfast. My stomach was growling. It sounded like the perfect plan to me.

But he wrote back, saying he had to work, so I called him

a loser, and tossed my phone onto my coffee table. Slumping onto my sofa, I stared at my television, not really in the mood to watch anything. I didn't even want to play Call of Duty, because it'd been more fun when I'd done that with Sticks.

Ugh. I needed a life. Dropping my head back, I stared up at the ceiling as my stomach growled again. I wasn't in the mood to prepare my own food so I decided now was as good a time as any to check out that family restaurant of Remy's. Castañeda's or whatever it was called.

Slugging back to me feet, I gathered my phone, wallet, and keys and was out the door.

CHAPTER 28
Remy Curran

"ELISA!"

Tío Alonso's voice jarred me from the daydream I was having. Hands buried in a bowl of floury dough, I spun around.

"Lo siento," I immediately apologized before he could even scold me for whatever he was going to scold me for this time. "I'll have these in the oven in five minutes."

I'd been distracted ever since getting the call from Asher. He'd sounded lonely. I had no idea how I could tell that from one little text, but I still felt guilty about having to tell him no. I felt guilty about turning down his offer to hang out longer last night, too, and I felt guilty about lying to him, and falling for him and—God, I was just really extremely guilt ridden, okay?

But it would've made everything worse if I'd followed him home from the diner last night. I needed space from Asher. I was growing too many feelings, and it was only making things harder for me to handle.

"That's not what I needed," my uncle said, waving me forward. "I mean, yes, we need them, but you're required out front now."

When I only frowned in confusion, he sighed. "Juan and Diego couldn't make it in today."

I nodded, then scrunched up my eyebrows because I still wasn't sure how this related to me. My mother's two younger brothers Diego and Juan only came in once a week on Wednesdays to play with Big T and Luis—Diego's son—in their special live mariachi music band. They liked to move from table to table to serenade the customers. While Tío Diego and Big T played guitars, Tío Juan strummed a harp, and Luis shook maracas.

Clapping his hands at me impatiently, Tío Alonso waved me to follow him. "Come on. We need some live entertainment. It's Wednesday. The people are expecting music."

I gasped with excitement, totally not expecting him to ask me. "And you want me to play the extra guitar? Or the harp?" Because, really, I could do either.

But my uncle scowled. "No, no. You sing. You have a beautiful voice. Tomás can accompany you on his guitar."

My shoulders slumped. Of course he'd want me to sing...and probably something like "Ave Maria" or "Don't Cry for Me, Argentina," too, something all soulful and depressing. He never let me play an instrument. The man was so freaking old school, he didn't believe in females being in a mariachi band to play instruments. They could only sing.

Blah.

Not that I hated singing. I just despised his outlook on life sometimes.

"Come." He clapped his hands as if beckoning a dog.

I sighed and turned back to my dough. "But what about my sopapillas?"

He scowled at my project for a second before waving me forward again. "Bring it with you. You can finish preparing them on the big worktable out front. Put on a cooking show while you sing."

Heaving out another sigh, I picked up the bowl, then grabbed a baking sheet, a few other things I'd need, and followed him out the door with my flour-speckled apron and hairnet still on.

The dining room was crowded and loud, and no one paid me or my uncle any attention as I followed him to the large wooden worktable, where he took off a vase of flowers and began to clean the surface before I could use it. Standing just behind him and clutching my cooking supplies to my chest, I waited like a good girl until someone moved up behind me and murmured into my ear.

"I knew he'd talk you into singing."

I sent a glare over my shoulder and told Big T, "Cállate," as I lightly rammed my elbow back into his gut. Only the sound of his lightly pained grunt made my lips quiver into a mini smile.

"Prima, you are mean."

My smile grew a bit larger.

"So what're we performing?" he asked. "'Cielito Lindo'?"

I pulled my bottom lip between my teeth, thinking about it. "No...something different."

In my back pocket, my phone buzzed, letting me know I had a new text. I pulled it free out of habit and saw that it was from Asher.

Holy shit. I found her.

Scowling, because I had no idea what he was talking about, I began to ask him who he'd found. But another text from him came through.

What's the name of the girl who—

"Elisa!" Tío Alonso boomed, making me jump out of my skin and look up before I could finish reading Asher's question. He splayed out his hand, letting me know he was ready for me to begin. I stuffed my phone away just as it buzzed again with a third text.

Drawing in a big breath, I concentrated on laying out my supplies, while Big T positioned himself behind and a little to the left of me. As I worked, a couple patrons glanced my way as they kept eating and talking, probably realizing I was about to do something to entertain them.

Just as I got everything set out where I needed it, my phone buzzed against my butt for a fourth time. Big T leaned forward, murmuring, "¿Prima?" wanting to know what I was going to sing so he'd know what to play.

I knew Tío Alonso expected something purely Spanish, but I decided to do a little mix of both English and Spanish. And besides, Doris Day was one of my mother's favorite singers before she went crazy. So I murmured, "Que Sera Sera," over my shoulder.

A couple seconds later, the guitar started to strum the

melody. Some tables of people stopped eating to watch us. But not until the introduction was over and I began to sing did we really gain the attention of everyone.

I ignored everyone and acted as if I was self-involved in my menial task of peppering the table with a cupful of flour. Once I had a fine layer covering the wooden slab, I plopped down my ball of dough and began to iron it into a flat circle with the rolling pin I'd brought in. Flour sprayed everywhere.

More people stopped their conversations to watch me work. I kept up the oblivious act, purposely smearing a trail of flour across my cheek when I brushed at a stray hair that had come down from my hairnet.

It wasn't until I picked up the rolling pin and began to roll the dough flat that I hit the chorus and really lifted my voice.

I swear, everyone in the joint stopped what they were doing just to listen to me.

It felt almost electric. Yes, drumming was my heart and soul, but in that moment, I could see why Asher loved to sing the really powerful songs where you had to put your everything into it. Because this right here felt good.

Centering my focus on a place deep inside me, I let the guitar's melody pour through my hands and my diaphragm until the twang in my voice rose to a crescendo and my last note echoed into the silent parlor. I finished the last line and then...applause.

At all the whistling, clapping, and cheering, I blinked and smiled at my audience. But my attention landed on one pair of green eyes watching me from a corner booth with intense scrutiny.

Oh, shit.

Asher was *here*.

Frozen, I could only gape at him as he rose from the booth where he was sitting alone.

He stepped toward me, and my heart leapt into my stomach. Dios, he was coming over to talk to me.

What the hell was I supposed to do?

"Bien hecho, Elisa," Tío Alonso said, patting me on the shoulder as he passed by.

His praise jolted me from my rigor mortis and I swung around to blink up at him. Then he motioned to my worktable and told me to get the cut sopapillas back to my second cousin Frida at the fryer.

I told my uncle I'd get right to it as I glanced toward Asher. He was still coming my way, so I picked up the sheet to flee. When he just kind of froze in his step as if not sure what to do, I whirled away and rushed back into the kitchen.

But as soon as I was behind the swinging door, I stole a glance out one of the round windows. He was still standing where he'd stopped in his tracks, watching the place where I'd disappeared. But as soon as he saw me peeking back out at him, a smile spread across his face and he waved.

Dios. That smile. That smug, I-know-you-see-me-and-remember-me smile did things to me.

If this man caught me in girl-mode again, I wasn't sure if I could resist him...and I really needed to resist him. Lying to him and pretending to be a guy was bad enough. But actually falling into bed with him while I was still lying and pretending to be a guy at other times would be the ultimate deception.

Whatever happened, I could *not* ever run into him as a girl again. Not unless he knew the truth.

So I was able to avoid running into Asher at the restaurant. I dawdled long enough at the fryer that he was gone by the time my uncle called me back to the dining room for another song, and I dragged myself in front of the customers again.

But he knew where I worked now, so this could be bad.

I was going to have to do some serious damage control to keep him away from girl-me.

By the time I finished my shift, I'd forgotten that he'd text-bombed me right before I sang. So when I started to call him, I was surprised to see all his old messages awaiting me. They went a little something like:

1. Holy shit! I found her.

2. What's the name of the girl who works at your family's restaurant? The one with the purple streaks in her hair?

3. Never mind. I just learned it.

I frowned, trying to recall anyone calling me Remy, but then I remembered... Tío Alonso had called me Elisa. A few times.

4. Call me as soon as you get off work.

Blowing out a breath, I dialed him, not sure what to say but determined to throw him off the scent of...well, *me*.

Yeah, I couldn't believe I was going to do that, either.

"Hey," he answered, and I swear, the cheer and smile in his voice lit me up from the inside.

"Hey," I murmured right back, still not sure what to tell him because I knew he was going to ask about her... I mean, me.

He was going to ask about me.

"So..." And here it came. "I know someone you can set me up with."

"Hmm?" My throat went immediately dry. I played dumb. "What?"

"That girl at Castañeda's, your family's Mexican restaurant. Elisa, right?"

Oh...hell. He really thought my name was Elisa. "Elisa?" I said slowly.

But seriously. *Me*? He wanted me to set him up with *me*? For a split second, I envisioned it. I could use my slutty señorita voice, pretend I was someone named Elisa, and I could finally get my hands on Asher Hart, the way I'd been craving.

But then reality set in.

No, I couldn't do that to him. I absolutely could not. I just...I wouldn't.

"You'll never believe this. But she's shower girl. From *Chicago*."

Words failed me. What the hell did I say now? Finally, I stuttered, "No shit?"

"Yeah, and she's related to you, right? You said everyone who worked there was related. What is she, a cousin or something?"

"Sure," I said, not knowing how else to answer.

He gave a laugh. "You don't sound too certain of that."

I shrugged and flailed out my hand. "Well, you know...complicated Méxican family trees and all that."

"Ahh," he murmured as if he understood but was honestly more confused than ever. "So, you really don't know what she was doing in Chicago? In our *hotel* room?"

"Well, uh, I... I guess I *did* know she'd be there that weekend, and I told her where I was staying, but I hadn't thought she'd stopped by to see me. Maybe, uh, maybe when I went to meet you for breakfast, I left the door unlocked or something, and she stopped by then and just...needed to borrow the shower. I...I'll have to ask her about that."

"Yeah...definitely do that. And...why didn't you realize who I was talking about when I mentioned the purple streaks, since you were obviously expecting her?"

Damn it, Asher, I almost growled. *Stop making me think up more lies.*

"*Are* they purple?" I asked, then laughed. "I thought they were a grayish color."

Big T always teased me that they looked gray instead of purple.

"No," Asher's voice echoed through my ear. "They're clearly a light purple."

Thank you, I almost told him. I was glad *some* people didn't see gray.

"So you think you can do it?" he pressed.

I blinked and shook my head. "Do what?"

He sighed. "Set me up with her?"

He seemed so eager...to meet me. Me! This powerful zap of energy bolted through me and I suddenly felt more alive than I ever had before. Asher wanted me. Female me. I kind of wanted to scream and dance and hug the entire world.

But yeah...reality and all that.

My own disappointment crashed through me as I slowly said, "No....I can't do that, sorry."

Silence.

He wasn't expecting that answer. He honestly thought I'd help him out. Then he slowly asked, "Because of your own feelings for me? Or because she's your cousin?"

Since hurt laced his voice, I quickly assured him, "No, no. It has nothing to do with...either of those things."

When I floundered, trying to come up with an answer that might appease him, he said, "Does she already have a boyfriend?"

"No." Crap! *Yes!* I should've said yes, and that would've

stopped him in his tracks. Damn it, why was I so stupid?

"Then....?"

"You don't want to go out with her," I blurted, not sure what else to say.

He laughed. "Yes, I do. I just told you I did."

"No..." I shook my head adamantly, even though he couldn't see me. "You don't."

"Why?"

"Because..." *Yeah, Remy, why?* "Because you don't even *know* her."

Again, he chuckled, but this time, it sounded more strained. "Which is the reason I want to meet her. So we can get to know each other, see how things flow."

But I continued to shake my head. "No."

Finally, irritation flooded his voice. "Just what the hell do you think I'd do to her? I realize she's family to you, which makes you protective, but I thought you and I were good enough friends that you knew I'd never—"

"That's not it," I broke in before he could really work himself into a tizzy. "That's not it at all."

"Then what *is* it?" He seemed so affronted.

I shrugged, feeling shitty. "Maybe it's the other way around," I said before I could stop myself. "Maybe it's *you* I'm worried about getting hurt. *Not her*." Because honestly, this was all because I didn't want to hurt him.

A couple seconds of silence followed. Finally, he settled with a perplexed, "What?"

"Please just...trust me," I told him softly. "I can't...I can't tell you the particulars, but I know you don't want to get tangled up with her."

He sighed. "Okay. Fine."

But I knew it wasn't fine. He'd really wanted to meet girl-me. And when he tersely told me he had to go a few minutes later, I crumbled into a chair and hugged myself, wondering how the hell I was going to fix this.

CHAPTER 29
Asher Hart

I THINK I FUCKED UP.

I never should've asked Remy to set me up with his cousin. I wasn't sure if it was because he didn't trust me to treat his kin right or because he liked me himself. He'd insisted it was neither, but I knew it had to be something.

Like a woman telling you she was fine; he wasn't fine.

The *whole thing* seemed oddly like I was dealing with a chick. With other dudes, I never worried about hurting their feelings, or even *what* they were feeling. Never so much drama. You either knocked another dude on his ass for pissing you off or told him the fuck off. Five minutes later, you were friends again.

Not so with Remy Curran. I wasn't sure if it was the gay thing or what, but it'd been three days and there was this *distance* between us.

I wasn't helping things, either. I was still miffed because he'd so adamantly shut me down and not only refused to help me with a girl I wanted to meet more than...probably any other girl I'd ever seen before—probably even Incubus shirt girl—but he'd then gone and cock-blocked me, telling me he didn't want me near her at all, so now I couldn't even try to get to her on my own. Felt like a pretty shit move to me, frankly. He knew better than anyone that my intentions were actually honorable. I wouldn't fuck her and drop her. I legitimately wanted to get to know her.

The jackass.

And if it was because he wanted me for himself, he needed to cut that out too. I mean, I liked the guy. He'd probably become my best friend in the few weeks we'd known each other, but I wasn't going to trade sides, not even for him. I couldn't help it that I preferred women. Damn it. The whole fucking thing irritated me to no end. Kind of made me want to drop him and his drama completely.

Except I missed hanging out with him. He was entertaining and competitive, had similar tastes as me so we always had plenty to talk about, and I knew I could rely on him for probably just about anything. He was the perfect friend, except for the part where he wanted my dick. But I could look past that.

There'd been so many times in the last few days I'd picked up the phone to call him up so we could hang out, only to stop myself. Because he was avoiding me too. He'd left straight after practice on Thursday without bullshitting with me like usual. And we always hung out together after our Friday night gig at Forbidden. But he'd gone home as soon the show was over, pleading a headache.

Total chick move.

If I didn't know better, I'd swear he was a girl.

"You're quiet today."

I glanced away from the window I'd been staring out to glance across the car toward Pick.

I also was getting tired of always being in the passenger seat, riding bitch. I needed to get my own set of four wheels so I could be in the driver's seat every once in a while. I don't know if it was lack of sex lately, or what, but I could almost feel my nads shriveling up into ovaries. I was sitting here, stressing about my friendship with another guy and upset because I hadn't even been able to just *talk* to some girl. I had the sudden urge to rip a loud, foul fart or belch or something equally guy just to prove I wasn't losing it.

"I'm fine," I mumbled, and immediately realized I'd just

pulled the purely feminine *I'm fine* line. Not cool, so I quickly added, "I need to get laid."

Pick chuckled. "The way the women flock to you after all your shows, I wouldn't have thought you had a problem with that."

"Yeah, but all they want is some singer in a band. I'm just...I'm over that shit. You can only handle so many meaningless, empty hook-ups before you want..." I didn't bother to finish the sentiment. It sounded lame and whiny to my own ears, and besides, two guys did not talk about this. But not only had I confided in Sticks about it, but now Pick too. What the hell was wrong with me?

"Aww....is my baby brother growing up?"

I scowled at Pick, not sure what he meant by that. "Huh?"

"It's a sign of a maturing male when he's ready to stop sowing his wild oats and settle down with a good woman."

Maturity? Huh. Was that what this was? Because I still felt like a clueless, bumbling kid most of the time. But maturing did sound better than becoming a chick.

"Got you all restless and edgy, doesn't it? Feeling lonely and kind of pathetic because you keep turning down sure things that you really have no reason to turn down at all?"

Holy shit. How did he know that?

The stunned expression must've revealed my feelings because he sent me a knowing smile. "Been there. Suffered through that. And damn glad I found my Tinker Bell when I did."

"Lucky bastard," I mumbled, scowling.

Which only made him laugh. "I know, right?"

When he pulled into the entrance of an auto repair shop, I sat up straighter, forgetting about my own issues.

We'd just come from my uncle's place. He was the only family member I had any contact with, even though it'd been three or four years since I'd last visited him...or called. After my mom had died and my dad was arrested, the authorities had gotten hold of my mom's family to see if they would take me in. None of them were interested in raising Polly's little crack baby, except her older brother Stan.

He hadn't been the loving, nurturing type. In fact, he'd rarely been around. Since he had worked for a trucking company, he would be gone for days on end. The most interest he'd ever shown in my life was a "how's it going?"

whenever he'd see me. But he never hit me or even yelled at me. He was just kind of there...sometimes. If it wasn't for him, though, I would've been put into foster care and who knew where I would've ended up.

Anyway, since Stan had been Polly's brother, that made him just as much Pick's uncle as mine. So when I'd asked Pick if he wanted to meet Stan, he'd been all for that idea. And that was why we were hanging out today.

The visit with Stan had gone about how I'd expected with one small surprise.

I hadn't called before visiting. He wasn't a fan of answering his phone, so I hadn't even bothered. So he'd been mildly startled to see me when he'd opened the door of his trailer house.

"Asher? Is that you? Shit. How long's it been? You've finally filled out some. Thought you were going to be a stick for the rest of your life. Well, come on in. Who's this?" He eyed Pick warily before glancing at me. "You turn to men, or something?"

Jesus. Not Uncle Stan too.

"No. This is Pick. Patrick Ryan. He, uh...well, he's your nephew too."

Stan's perusal of Pick's tattoos and piercings turned into a scowl before he glanced at me and hitched up an eyebrow. "Come again?"

After I explained how Pick was the baby Polly had left at the hospital and how we'd stumbled across our discovery of being related, Stan scratched his fraying beard stubble. "Well, hell. I didn't even realize that kid had survived. I just assumed Polly'd had a miscarriage."

"Well..." I shrugged. "She didn't."

"It's nice to meet you." Pick held out a hand, and Stan stared at it as if he didn't know what to do with it, before he finally took hold of Pick's palm and returned the shake.

"You do have the Ruddick chin, I guess," Stan murmured thoughtfully.

"We came not only so he could meet you, but to see if you had any information about his dad, so he could maybe research his paternal side too."

"Your dad's dead," Stan announced abruptly, making me cringe. Thank God I'd already told Pick this so it wasn't too startling, but fuck. Our uncle had never bothered with subtlety, and he sure didn't now, either.

"Didn't know his real name, just what Polly called him. Chaz."

"Yeah," Pick murmured, disappointment at the dead end glimmering in his eye. "That's what Asher told me."

"There wasn't much worth knowing, anyway; he was a no-account drunk," Stan went on. "He was never going to go anywhere past that repair shop where he worked on Bullview Road."

Pick suddenly perked to attention. "You mean *Murphy's* Repair Shop?"

"Yeah." Stan snapped his fingers. "That place."

The oddest expression entered Pick's face. "Holy fuck," he murmured, sounding stunned.

"What?" I had to ask. "Have you heard of it?"

He turned to me, more looking through me than at me. Shock made his pupils dilate and lips part. "I used to work there," he said.

So that's why we'd driven to Murphy's Repair Shop. Pick told me the owner had run the place for nearly forty years; he'd probably remember an employee named Chaz.

As we exited the Mustang, I followed Pick to an opened bay door where Luke Bryan's voice wailed from a radio about stripping it down and returning to the simpler life. Pick nudged a pair of ragged boots that were sticking out from under an old Chevy truck.

"Hey. Murph around?"

The boots moved and rolled out until we could see the grease-stained face of the worker. "Well, hey. The prodigal son returns. You coming back to work for us again, Pick?"

Pick merely shook his head. "Just looking to chat with Murphy today."

The mechanic tipped his head to the right. "In his office. Go on in."

"Thanks, man."

Pick strolled that way, so I followed. The door to the glassed-in office was open, and even though it was cold outside a small oscillating fan whirled slowly on top of a paper-stacked desk. The man sitting behind it looked to be slimmer and taller with stooped shoulders. He had his glasses perched on the tip of his nose as he read something on a clipboard in his hand.

Rapping his knuckles on the doorframe, Pick called,

"Hey, Murph. You got a minute?"

The older man looked up, his bushy gray brows arching in surprise. "Hey! If it isn't Patrick. Come on in, kid. I always have a minute for you."

Pick stepped in far enough to allow me room inside with him. After glancing at me, he turned to his old boss. "You've owned this place a long time, haven't you?"

"Forty years next summer, why you asking? Want to buy it from under me? Hell, shoot me a decent price, and I'll consider it. Eh?"

"Aww." Pick chuckled and waved a hand. "No. I'm too busy with the club to tinker with cars anymore."

A fond smile layered itself across Murphy's face as he sat back in his seat. "You used to love tinkering with cars if I remember right."

"Still do. But just my own now. I don't want to make a business out of it."

"Then what'd you come down here for if you don't want to work for me again, or buy me out, and you can take care of your own automobiles?" He glanced at me, and leaned back deeper in his chair as he considered me. "You want me to hire this thing here?" When his gaze landed on my hands, he snorted. "Doesn't look like he's had grease under his fingernails a day in his life."

"No. He..." Pick glanced at me. "This is my brother. He's been helping me with a little research, finding someone, and oddly enough, our trail led us here to one of your employees back...twenty-five, twenty-six years ago."

Something odd flashed across Murphy's face before he sat forward, suddenly interested. "Oh?"

"Yeah." Pick wiped his hand off on his thighs. "All I know is the guy went by the name Chaz, and he was killed here, or near here, by a drive-by shooting possibly."

Murphy's hand fluttered to his mouth as he stared at Pick with a sudden intensity. "Well, I'll be damned," he murmured, blinking as if tears were clouding his eyes.

"Do you remember him?" Pick asked softly, but eagerly stepping forward because it was obvious Murphy did remember Chaz.

After clearing his throat, Murphy answered, "Chaz was short for Charles. Charles Edward Murphy...Junior."

When Pick sucked in a breath I glanced at him, but he

was busy staring at his old boss. "You mean...are you saying he was your *son*?"

With a nod, Murphy said, "He was. Why're you asking about him?"

My brother turned to me, and I think he was too stunned to talk, so I tried to smile at Murphy. "He, uh...well, we just discovered my mom, Polly Ruddick, was also Pick's mom."

"My God," Murphy croaked, unable to take his eyes off Pick. "I thought you looked like him. The first day you came here, looking for a job, I could see so much of Chaz in your eyes. Probably why I hired you without a reference to your name, but I...I never would've dreamed you were that baby."

Pick blew out a shuddered breath before shaking his head and asking, "So you knew...you were aware my mother was pregnant with Chaz's—"

He broke off when Murphy nodded. "Sure. They were shacked up together, living in my garage while she was pregnant with you. She'd come into the kitchen every morning, and I'd feed her a hearty breakfast so you'd grow nice and strong."

"Did you know she gave birth to me the same day—"

"I did," Murphy said on a choked nod. "Took me a couple days, after the funeral, before I got around to go see you. Polly had already taken off by then, but they let me look at you through a window."

"And you didn't..." Pick shook his head, his eyes glazed with shock. "You didn't try to get custody of me?"

Guilt lined Murphy's eyes before he glanced away. "Shit, Pick. I'd just lost my son. My wife had been gone for years. I was trying to run my own business by myself; there was no way I was equipped to take care of an infant."

Both Murphy and I watched as devastation lit Pick's features. But he gave a noisy swallow and nodded. "I understand, Murphy. It would've been tough."

As if realizing what a mistake he'd made, Murphy's face took on a pleading expression. "They told me they'd find a real nice foster home for you, people who'd gone through classes and been trained on how to take care of a baby. I thought...I knew it'd be the best thing for you." A wavering smile lit his face. "And hell, look at you now. You turned out just fine."

With another nod, Pick mumbled, "Yeah. Just fine."

I kicked at a spot on the floor, nearly biting my tongue in half because I wanted to tell Murphy so bad that Pick had not been fine...not for many, many years. But I figured if Pick had wanted him to know that, he would've said something himself. It wasn't my place.

"If it's any consolation," Murphy went on. "Your mama loved you something fierce."

I glanced up and watched the fond smile on the older man's face as he nodded to Pick. "She was young—shit, they were both too young, but her in particular. And yet...none of that mattered. She talked and dreamed and envisioned the day you were going to arrive. She would've made a damn fine mama for you if Chaz hadn't..." After another clearing of the throat, Murphy went on. "They were going to name you Dugger."

"Dugger?" Pick murmured, glancing me with a slight wince. "Dugger Murphy."

"Nice." I flashed him two thumbs-up, refraining from telling him what our mother *had* actually named me.

Pick flipped me off before turning back to his grandfather.

Even as I chuckled, I tried not to let the bitter jealousy in, but it stirred within me, anyway.

I wanted so bad to tell Pick what a gift it was that our mother had loved him. Because she'd never loved me. She'd hated me, and told me so often. She'd gone on and on numerous times, complaining how much she'd wished I had died, how she resented Miller Hart for making her keep me, how she wanted her true baby boy back. I'd always known she'd loved Pick and not me, but listening to his grandfather back that fact up only dug the pain in deeper.

"I think we're done here," Pick said, tapping my elbow to get my attention. Then he nodded stoically to his former boss...his grandfather. "Murphy, thank you for your information. I'm going to...I'm just going to mull this over awhile, then I'll probably be back to catch up on...things, if that's all right with you."

Murphy nodded immediately, and a smile lit his face. "I'd like that. Thank you."

As Pick turned away abruptly and strode off, needing space, or to think, or whatever, his grandfather glanced at me. After a long blink, he said, "Now you...you have your mother's eyes."

Then he smiled fondly as if that was something I should've been proud of.

I nodded, twitching my lips to make him think I was smiling, but all I could remember was how much Polly had hated the fact I'd gotten her eyes. Almost as much as she'd hated me.

CHAPTER 30
Asher Hart

WHEN PICK RETURNED HOME, I was done being an insecure coward. If maturity was what Pick was calling this, then I was going to do the mature thing and just call Remy. Besides, I wanted to kill zombies with my friend again.

But as soon as I pulled my phone from my pocket, it rang. When I saw *Sticks* on the screen, I grinned.

"Hey, loser," I answered, relieved to talk to him again. "I was just about to call you."

"You were?" He sounded surprised, which made me laugh.

"Hell, yeah. I don't have to go to work until five this evening, so I was curious if you were up for some Call of Duty."

"Sure. I was actually going to see if you were around because...I have something for you."

I nodded and waved him on, even though he couldn't see me over the phone. "Well, then get your ass over here, man."

Ten minutes later, there was a knock on my door, and you'd think I was waiting for a hot lady to visit, I was a bit too eager to answer it. But I didn't care, and as soon as I pulled it open, this ball of relief eased inside me.

"This is for you." Sticks held out a small brown paper sack as soon as we jogged down together into my apartment. When I only arched an eyebrow, curious, he jiggled the bag impatiently. "Well, go on and take it. It's not poisonous, I swear."

I took the sack and unfolded the top so I could peer inside.

"What the hell?" Staring incredulously, I gaped at the new box of condoms that had the words "Use Me Please" written out in thick black marker along the side.

"And I remembered to get the non-latex kind too." Remy sounded way too proud of himself, so I squinted an incredulous glance his way.

He sighed as if disgusted that I wasn't happier. "This is me proving to you that I'm perfectly okay with you going out and having sex with...whomever."

"Just not your cousin," I had to add, trying not to sound bitter and hoping I hadn't just stuck my foot into my mouth and made things worse between us. But I was sort of hoping he'd say he was okay with me pursuing Elisa after all.

He didn't. Of course.

He scowled a second before shrugging. "Yeah. Just not her."

I wanted to mope and scowl and argue, but...this was Sticks extending an olive branch. Strange method, but he wanted to make amends, so I accepted it.

"Well...thank you, I think," I said, tossing the box onto my bed. "So you want to kill shit now?"

His shoulders eased and a relieved smile slid across his face. "Sure."

"So...Dugger Murphy, huh? Yeah, I can't see Pick being named that either."

As I gave my controls a rest to snatch my bottle of Angry Orchard and take a couple gulps, Remy finished off the small invasion of enemies closing in on us.

Damn, he really was good at this game.

"I know, right?" I set the drink back down to back him up as he entered a nearby building, guns drawn.

With a snort, he grinned my way, "God, your mom had sucky taste in names."

I shot a guy in the head that was about to take him out.

"Shit, I didn't see him." Remy gritted his teeth in frustration. "Gracias."

His gratitude came begrudgingly. It cracked me up how competitive he was and how he hated missing something or getting help.

I acted blasé about it. "Mmm hmm." But he still flipped me the bird for my answer, and I had to laugh.

"So, this guy who owns the garage and who Pick actually used to work for ended up being his paternal grandfather? That's some crazy shit."

"Yeah, about as crazy as me finding out *my* boss was my brother." I didn't mention that I was a little jealous Pick had ended up discovering a new family member who didn't outright hate him, resent him, or just not give a shit about his life. But then I reminded myself, I'd gotten a new family member out of Pick, hadn't I? So I was technically no longer batting zero in that regard.

"Hey, I keep forgetting to ask. Will you deejay his wedding reception? It's going to be at Forbidden next Sunday."

"Next Sunday? You mean, like in eight *days*, next Sunday?"

"Yep. I would've thought Eva would've been more into the big, drawn-out grandiose planning thing too, but apparently they're ready now and don't want to dawdle. So, what do you say about deejaying? You're really the only other person I trust with the sound system."

"I am?" The crack in Remy's voice told me he was honored by my announcement. After clearing his throat, he sounded much less emotional and more nonchalant. "Okay, sure. No prob. How's Pick handling it, anyway?"

"The wedding plans?" I sent him a short frown. "Like I know." *Or care.*

"No." He snorted and waved a hand. "How's he, you know, dealing with the shock of learning so much in one day. Met his uncle, then his grandfather. How's he doing with that?"

I sent him another strange glance. "No idea. He seemed okay to me. Why?"

"Oh, Jesus." Remy rolled his eyes. "You hetero men. I swear. Always too afraid to talk to each other about your feelings."

Now I was really stumped. "What the hell was I supposed to ask him?"

"No sé." Sticks sighed as if I was impossible. "Ask if he was bien, maybe. If he wanted to talk about it. If—"

"I'm sure Eva will take care of all that. He doesn't need me to give him a hug or pat on the head."

From the corner of my eye, I saw Remy glance my way. "And what about you?"

Huh? "What *about* me?"

"You don't have an Eva to talk to or hug."

I sent him an incredulous glance. "Yeah, and I'm not the one who met my grandfather for the first time today, either." I'd just gotten confirmation how much my mother had truly despised me.

"Yeah, but you had to face your uncle again after not seeing him for...how long now? And you spent the entire morning with Pick, when a month ago, the idea scared the shit out of you."

"Christ," I groaned. "I tell you way too much." When he just smirked, I rolled my eyes. "My uncle's still completely impartial about anything to do with my life, and Pick...I don't know, I'm growing on the idea of him being my brother."

"Really?" That seemed to please Remy. "That's great."

"Yeah, ever since he told me he'd already researched Polly online and knew what had happened to her and my dad, I haven't been so freaked."

"Speaking of your dad—"

"Don't." Holding up a hand in his direction to cut him off, I sighed. "I haven't seen him again since the run-in at the bar."

Remy was quiet a moment before saying, "Well, I still think he's following you. Keeping tabs on you."

Of course, he did. "And I told you, I couldn't give a shit less if he was." Which I highly doubted he was. "As long as he stays back and I don't have to face him, it's all good."

"But what if he—"

"Sticks." I sent him a sharp glance. "I'm not worried

about him. He has no reason to come after me. From the moment he realized I couldn't help him score any drugs and I wasn't going to give him any handouts, he probably forgot I existed. And I say good. Goodbye and good riddance."

"Well, I'm going to stay paranoid and keep an eye out for him."

I shook my head, even though it felt kind of nice that someone was so worried about my welfare. "Suit yourself. I hereby and from henceforth make you my official bodyguard." When I made a sign of the cross in his direction, he snorted.

"A sign of the cross? Really? What the hell was that about?"

I snickered. "No idea. It just seemed fitting."

He laughed back. "Man, you are so weird."

The way he shook his head as if perplexed by my weirdness made me laugh, too. I was about to tease him and tell him he was the idiot who had the big ol' man crush on me, but I don't know, I decided to just roll with it.

"You think *that's* weird? Well, did you know..." Remembering something I'd read online the night before when I'd been unable to sleep because I'd been stressing about my friendship with him, I asked, "that when they used to cut off a boy's nuts to make him sing castrato, the lack of testosterone in his body would then make his—"

"Bone joints not quite as hard, ergo they grew longer and gave him more rib capacity to sing with stronger lung power. Yes, I actually *did* know that."

My mouth fell open in shock. But damn, how did he know that? I blinked, not sure if I was impressed or irritated that he'd showed me up...again.

Before I could decide, my phone rang.

I tossed my controls aside to reach for it, because once again, Remy was cleaning house without my help. "It's Pick," I said, frowning and wondering what was wrong. *Did* he really need to talk about feelings and shit? I had no clue how to do that, but for Pick, I guessed I'd try.

"What's up?" I asked in answer.

"Man." Pick heaved out a long sigh. "Jesus, Asher. You'll never believe this, but I just got a call from Reese. Mason's mom died like...an hour ago."

"*What*?' I sat up straight on the couch. "That's crazy.

What happened?"

"I don't know. Didn't get the particulars. But she said Mason's pretty upset. They just picked up his little sister Sarah and she's not taking it well either. We're headed over now." He paused and then added, "See you there?"

"Uh...sure. Yeah. I'll be there as soon as possible." After I hung up, I continued to stare at the phone as I murmured, "Holy shit."

Remy paused the game and sat up, concern on his face. "What's going on?"

"My friend Mason..."

"From the bar? Yeah." Nodding, he rolled out a hand, urging me to continue. "What about him? He okay?"

"No. I mean, yeah, *he* is. But his mom...fuck, I guess she just died."

"Whoa." Sticks pulled back, blinking. "What happened? Car accident?"

"No idea. Pick didn't know and Reese didn't say when she called him." I pushed to my feet, feeling disoriented as I glanced blindly around the room. "I need to go. Pay my condolences and, I don't know, shit...just be on hand if they need anything, I guess."

I should've moved, then, but a wave of dizziness assailed me. All I could see were the dead eyes of my own mother, staring sightlessly at nothing. What if Mason's little sister had seen *her* mother die?

"Hey. You okay?" Remy clutched my arm, grounding me back to the present.

"Yeah. Fine," I mumbled. "Just remembering shit from back when. Pick said Mason's sister Sarah was pretty upset. I couldn't help but wonder if she was there. What she saw."

Remy's intrepid gaze dug into me. "What did *you* see," he murmured softly, "when your mom died?"

I sniffed out a sound and shook my head. "Everything," I answered without really meaning to. But Sticks had a way of prying things out of me with a mere stare.

"That must've been pretty shitty. Did you ever talk to anyone about it?"

I glanced at him. "Yeah. Sure. I had to repeat my account of the events about twenty times to the cops and lawyers and judges."

"No, I mean, like a psychiatrist? Emotional help."

With a snort, I sent him a get-real glance. "You think my

uncle was willing to shell out extra cash for something like that? Yeah, think again." Stan had thought he'd done his duty plenty by letting me live in his trailer. He hadn't expended any more effort than that, except to occasionally ask if I needed money to buy my own things.

"You should've gotten some help for that directly after it happened. It's not good to—"

"Sticks." I held up a hand to shut him up. "It happened years ago. I think I'm past it. And I know you'd love for me to open up and share all my feelings and shit with you, but I'm going to go see my friend now and be *there* for *him*."

Except when I glanced around the room, feeling totally lost and not sure what to do next, Remy clutched my arm. "I'll drive you," he said quietly.

I blew out a breath, feeling pathetic because I needed him. Pick's news had affected me strongly. That surprised me. So I nodded at my friend's offer and murmured, "'K. Thanks."

Without making a big deal of my admitting I did indeed need him, he snagged his keys, wallet, and phone off the coffee table and motioned toward the door. Since my head was still messed up, I followed his directive without question.

But as soon as I opened the door, he hissed, "Shit. Food. We need food."

I glanced back, frowning. "Huh?"

"You know." He snapped his fingers and waved out his hand. "When the close loved one of someone you know dies, you bring them food, like casseroles and shit."

I arched an eyebrow. "You're whack if you think I even remotely know how to bake a casserole."

Remy laughed. "It doesn't have to be a casserole per se. Just...anything. Something helpful." Then he brightened. "When Big T's madre died, all these people poured in with different foods, but this one single old guy, Jorge, he brought paper plates and napkins, and plasticware, crap like that. It was the most used thing anyone brought over. And I always told myself, since I can't cook either, that's what I'd do if I ever visited the family member of someone who died."

I blew out a breath. "All right then. We'll stop by the store and pick up some paper plates and such along the way."

Half an hour later, we knocked on Reese and Mason's door. Eva answered, and her face brightened when she saw me.

"Asher." She pulled me in for a tight hug, murmuring into my ear how much it was going to mean to Mason and Reese that I'd come. Then she noticed the guy behind me. "Oh! Hi, there." I introduced her to Remy, and he waved a respectful hello before following us down the hall to a kitchen where Pick and Reese were hovering over a phone book, debating which funeral home to contact.

"Look who I found at the door," Eva announced.

Reese looked up, and though her face was red and puffy from some obvious crying, she smiled when she saw me. "Asher. Thank you so much for coming." She swept around the table toward me and pulled me in for a hug.

Afterward, I heaved the grocery bag at her.

She peeked inside and brightened. "Oh! Thank you. That was so thoughtful. This'll probably come in handy more than anything else."

I glanced back at Remy, ready to give him the credit, but he nudged my elbow and whispered, "Your line is *you're welcome.*" So I dutifully turned back to Reese and shrugged.

"No problem. So...?"

I wasn't sure what to ask. But Reese leaned in and quietly murmured, "She overdosed."

Shock spread through me. "Mason's mom? Shit. I wasn't aware she..."

"She wasn't. Not really. I guess she'd had a problem with prescription pills a long time ago. She used to filch some of Sarah's medicine to handle...well, life, I guess. But she'd stopped long before I'd come along. Mason didn't even tell me about it until after we'd moved here from Florida. But I guess, lately, these last few months...it became a problem again." She shook her head as tears filled her eyes. "Sarah's the one who found her. After she called us, she hasn't spoken a word."

"Shit," I murmured, feeling for Mason's poor sister.

"And Mason...my God." More tears filled Reese's eyes. "He's been busy on the phone, calling lawyers and social workers, so hell-bent on making sure we can get custody of Sarah he hasn't stopped to think about what really just happened. I don't think he *wants* to think about it."

I didn't blame him. Before I could say anything, offer help—just anything she needed—two small children scampered into the room. "Mama, Dada," they called, going to their parents.

Watching what I guessed were my niece and nephew now run to Eva and Pick for attention, I shook my head. They were so damn cute, and so damn lucky they had two parents who cared, who wouldn't overdose and abandon them, who just...loved them.

From the hallway, more people appeared: Noel and his family, and Quinn and Zoey, toting a super-small baby.

As Reese went in to snatch baby J.B. from Zoey's arms, saying she really needed a dose of cuteness right now, Brandt glanced around the suddenly cramped kitchen and asked, "Sarah's here, right?"

Pain clouded Reese's face as she jiggled the baby. "Yes, but I'm sorry, Brandt." She shook her head. "She's not talking to anyone right now. Mason can't even get her to respond to him. She's pretty upset."

Determination glittered in Brandt's eyes. "Can I go see her anyway?" I had a feeling he would've found a way, even if Reese denied him access.

But she nodded. "Of course. She's lying down in Mason's and my room."

He took off, and hushed, respectful voices filled the kitchen as Aspen and Quinn handed food dishes off to Eva, who packed them away in the refrigerator. When Mason entered the room, looking pale, worn-out, and a bit shellshocked, the ladies gathered around him for a round of hugs, while us guys stood back, giving him one of those sorry-for-your-loss nods.

Julian and Skylar kept trying to scream and run around the kitchen, so Pick gathered them both up under his arms, announcing, "I can take them home. Tink...go ahead and stay here as long as you need, be with your cousins. And call when you're ready to come home."

I about spoke up, and volunteered to take her home so he wouldn't have to come back, thinking Remy had a car Eva could actually ride in, but then Remy lifted his hand. "Oh, hey. I can watch them. No problem. If you have an extra room here we could hang out in, you all could stay."

Reese laid her hand on his arm. "Thank you so much, Sticks." Then she glanced my way. "Could you show him where the office is? There are some kids' DVDs and toys in there to occupy the kiddos."

I nodded and helped Remy gather up Pick and Eva's little heathens.

We started down another hall, but when we passed Mason and Reese's room, Brandt's murmured voice made me pause at the half opened door and glance inside.

"It's going to be okay," the kid murmured as he lay spooned up behind Sarah on the bed and stroked her hair. "Living with your big brother isn't so bad. It's actually been better for me since I have. You'll see."

Sarah grabbed hold of his shirt at his shoulder and squeezed it tight. "Please...don't...leave me."

"I'm not going anywhere," Brandt assured her. "I'm staying right here with you."

Behind me, Remy nudged me on, silently telling me I was listening in on a private conversation, but as soon as we reached Mason and Reese's office, he grinned and said, "Well, if that wasn't the sweetest shit you've ever seen. I think I just fell in love with that kid."

I grinned and shook my head. "Yeah, Brandt's a good seed." Then I glanced around the room that had obviously been set up to entertain Julian and Skylar. The two toddlers immediately sought their toys and began to play. "You sure you're okay with watching them?"

"I grew up babysitting younger cousins. I got this." He nudged me toward the door. "Now go be with your friends."

I nodded and started away. "Thanks, Rem. You're a true friend."

CHAPTER 31
Remy Cullan

So I hung out with little Julian and Skylar. Neither of them really watched the movie I put in; they just kind of played around me, occasionally climbing over my legs to get from one side of me to the other. Sometimes a loud or particularly active scene would catch their attention, but mostly, I was the only one glued to the actual plot.

By the time the final credits rolled, they were passed out asleep, each one resting a head on either of my thighs while tears poured down my face, some inside my mask, some trickling down the outside.

"Oh, God," I sobbed, mopping at my cheeks with the backs of my fingers. "This shit is sad."

"Yo, Rem." Asher appeared in the doorway, grabbing onto the side of the frame so he could swing his upper body into the bedroom. "You ready to head out? I need to get to work. Aspen said she'd take over watching Skylar and Ju—" But upon seeing me, he stopped short, and blinked. "Are you crying?"

"It's fucking sad," I nearly bellowed, making Julian stir in his sleep so I had to pat his curly hair to soothe him back into deeper unconsciousness. "I mean, what the hell? It's a *Disney* movie; I thought all Disney movies had happy endings."

He laughed. The bastard actually laughed at my heartache. "Which one is it?" He let go of the door to step deeper into the room so he could see the screen.

"*Tinker Bell and the Neverbeast*, or something like that. Can't remember. He's never going to see her again," I motioned to a picture of the beast as it flashed across the screen. "And that fairy Fawn, she *loves* him. They should get to stay together. This is just...it's *so wrong*."

And God, it was so good.

Asher became entranced watching the credits. Finally, he asked, "What song is this?"

"It's '1,000 Years' by KT Tunstall and Bleu. Haven't you ever heard it before?"

"No," he murmured, his gaze stuck on the screen. "But I like it."

It was perfect for this movie too. Dios, this sad, beautiful, amazing movie.

Easing the babies off my lap and shifting them so they were resting on nearby blankets, I patted their precious little heads, then pushed to my feet. My back was stiff and legs ached from sitting on the floor for so long, so I stretched them and dusted off my backside.

"You said you needed to go?" I asked Asher.

"Huh?" He glanced from the movie and blinked at me before shaking his head to clear it. "Oh yeah. It's Saturday, karaoke night. So I need to get there early too. We'd better go." Then he smiled toward the kids. "I guess they ended up liking you. Thanks again for watching them. Mason and Reese really needed Pick and Eva today."

"No problem. They're good kids...and cute as all get-out." I followed him from the room, where the rest of the apartment was a lot quieter than it'd been in the bedroom with the kids and the movie playing.

Though I loved my spot in Non-Castrato, always having

to dress up as Sticks, the male drummer, was wearing on me. I just really, *really* missed being a girl. I mean, I could still be me when I was home and when I had to go to work at Castañeda's, but it seemed like other than that, I was stuck in my mask and forced to act manly almost around the clock.

I know, know. Why the heck was I whining? I'd gotten my own damn self into this predicament. I'd made my bed, and so forth.

Didn't mean I didn't have regrets though. I still probably would've tried out as a guy if I had to do it all over again. I loved being able to play with the band. And I loved this chance to get to know Asher. The verdict was still out on Gally and Heath. Heath might be okay, but it was hard to tell. Gally, I feared, was a straight-up irredeemable asshole.

I probably would've come clean to them sooner, though.

Now, I was just too chicken-shit and worried I'd destroy everything if I exposed my true identity. It would definitely upset Asher. And I'd do anything *not* to upset Asher, even continue to dress up as Sticks.

I'd never been the girliest girl on the planet, but three nights after I babysat Pick and Eva's kids while Asher helped console Mason and Reese, I felt the need to indulge my feminine side. I took a long, hot bubble bath, gave myself an avocado facial, plopped two cucumber slices over my eyes and didn't budge from the water until all my fingers and toes were pruned and colorless.

After that, I strolled barefoot around the apartment in a fuzzy terrycloth robe with a towel turban on my head as I raided the kitchen for ice cream, chocolate, and a mug of pumpkin spiced tea.

A mini pedicure followed along with fingernail painting and then eyebrow tweezing. By the time I was done with all that, I felt refreshed and ready to take on the world again.

I didn't plan on going out, but I slid on one of my favorite little black dresses and fixed up my face and hair—just because I could—before returning to the kitchen to, ugh...do the dishes.

It'd been a few days and they'd piled up. What was worse, the waffle maker I hadn't used for over a week was still sitting on the counter, waiting to be scrubbed clean. I was sure both Jodi and I had done a round of dishes each since we'd used that damn waffle iron. But it was such a pain in the ass to wash, we'd both put it off.

I narrowed my eyes at it, wondering if it'd be wrong to just pitch it and buy another. It was kind of a cheapie brand. I could buy something nice and self-cleaning. Did waffle makers come in self-cleaning brands?

Well, they totally should.

Bluck, okay. I'd clean the stupid thing.

I had the soap and every possible scrubber on hand, working at it, when I heard Jodi come in, home early from her Tuesday night class. I called a greeting and went back to the waffle iron as I sang "Anaconda." I had my hips swaying and booty popping as I rapped out the Nicki Minaj part, because hell, isn't that what you were supposed to do when you got down with Nicki?

I'd just gotten to the verse when someone laughed from behind me. Yelping out my surprise, I whirled around, the suds clinging to my hands flinging everywhere.

"Oh my God, I'm so sorry. I didn't mean to scare you." The girl leaning against the doorjamb of the kitchen and holding her stomach with one arm as she continued to laugh held up a hand. "I just heard the singing and had to check it out."

I gaped at her, blinking and unable to believe my eyes...because I knew her.

"What the hell are *you* doing here?" I blurted out, shaking my head in confusion. As soon as I realized how rude that had sounded, I slapped my hand over my mouth. "I mean...sorry. I just...I wasn't expecting anyone. I thought my roommate had just come home and—"

"You mean Jodi? Oh, she did." The blonde hooked a thumb over her shoulder, motioning out of the kitchen and toward the rest of the apartment. "I take Theatrical Design class with her, and when we got out early tonight, we decided to go somewhere to eat, but she wanted to stop by her place first to change, so voilà. That's why I'm here, waiting on her. I'm Caroline, by the way."

"Re—" I automatically started to answer before I caught myself, wondering if I should give her my real name. She was friends with Asher, married to his coworker. How safe was I in getting to know her as a girl? Then I decided, screw it. I didn't feel like lying for the rest of the evening, so I smiled and said, "Remy."

She smiled back as if pleased with my answer. I wondered if she knew the truth. Her husband knew; but had he told her?

"So do you want to get something to eat with us?" she asked, looking eager as if she really wanted me to go along.

"Uh..." I glanced toward the dishes, which I really didn't want to finish. But spending too much time with Asher's friend might get me caught up in some lie I didn't want to tell.

Before I could regretfully decline, though, Jodi burst into the kitchen, saying, "Yes! Of course, you do. It feels as if I haven't seen you in forever. You're always busy, spending time with—"

"Sure," I butted in before she could say Asher's name or his band's name. "I'll tag along, if you don't mind."

"Not at all," Caroline answered brightly.

"Great." My smile was forced and my heart was pounding with stress. "Let me just go change into something a little more suitable."

"Oh, hell no." Jodi grabbed my arm, stopping me. "It's been ages since I've seen you looking so nice. You are totally wearing that." Then she crinkled her eyebrows into a confused frown. "Actually, why *are* you wearing that to do the dishes?"

I flushed hard as I shrugged. "Just, you know... sometimes you want to feel pretty when you're slaving away at menial tasks."

Caroline laughed at my answer. "I think I'm going to like you."

I sent her a small, sick smile. *Swell*. I'd probably have to lie and deceive the girl all night, but she liked me. Nothing else for me to feel guilty about there.

No, not at all.

"You know, your singing reminds me of one of my friends. He's always singing to himself when he's absorbed in things like cleaning."

"Hmm," I murmured, trying not to act interested in such a coincidence because I had a feeling I knew exactly which friend she was referring to. "So, if I'm not allowed to change, should we go now?" *Get this night over with already.*

It ended up that I actually really liked Caroline, even though I tried not to so I wouldn't have to feel so guilty about my deception. But she was just so personable and friendly, and she kept involving me in everything she and Jodi discussed.

Once we made it to the restaurant and were seated, I ordered a piña colada as soon as the waiter approached our table and before he could even ask for drink requests.

What? It'd been way too long since I'd been able to indulge in one.

Jodi laughed, while Caroline just sent me a curious glance. As soon as the waiter was gone again, Jodi asked, "Missing the girl life, huh?"

I nudged her under the table with the tips of my high heels.

But Caroline had already lasered in like a heat-seeking missile. "Girl life?"

I waved a hand and shook my head as if it were no big deal, but Jodi immediately started explaining, "Remy's the girl I've been dressing up as a guy."

I kicked her again under the table, but she just kept talking. "You know, the project I'm doing my term assignment on?"

When I walloped her again, she whirled to me with a frown. "Why the fuck do you keep kicking me?"

As I glared at her, Caroline laughed. "I think she's trying to get you to shut up so I won't figure out who she really is," she told my roommate.

With a groan, I slunk lower in my chair. "Except you already know," I concluded. "Right?"

She laughed. "Yep. I figured it out a few days after your first performance at Forbidden when Jodi brought a picture of *Sticks* to class and explained how she helped transform you to get you into Asher's band."

"¡Dios mío, *Jodi*!" I cried, gaping. "You told an entire classroom full of people about it?"

My roommate winced, realizing she might have messed up. "Well, I..."

"She totally did," Caroline gleefully informed me.

"Great," I muttered. "Now, you, your husband, *and* an entire classroom full of strangers know."

"Wait," Caroline demanded. "*Oren* knows?" just as Jodi whirled to her and squawked, "You're *married*?"

I shook my head, confused. "Oren?"

Caroline rolled her eyes. "Well, you didn't think his real first name was Ten, did you?"

"Uh, well, I guess I never thought about it."

"How can you be married?" Jodi butted in, gaping at Caroline as if she'd never seen her before.

I rolled my eyes. "Jodi, you *know* her husband. Hell, you flirted with him and tried to get into his pants at the bar a couple weeks ago."

"You flirted with my husband?" Caroline gasped, blinking at Jodi. "I mean, not that I blame you, but damn...aren't you already sleeping with two members in Asher's band?"

It must've been my turn to be utterly flabbergasted. I swung to Jodi. "*Two* members?"

"Oh yeah," she said, grinning blithely as if she'd forgotten to mention such a major detail. "I went home with the big, bearded one last weekend after you ditched out on us as soon as the show was over."

"You..." I shook my head, still not comprehending. Then I screeched, "Heath? You slept with *Heath*?"

"Yes, and mmm, girl, let me tell you, that one is hung. I mean, like huge. Like the biggest I've ever seen, not just had, but *seen*. I still walk funny because of that night." She leaned toward me, wiggling her brows, before confidentially confessing, "He really likes it from behind too, and I mean, like way back there, in the—"

"Oh!" I yelped, instantly covering my ears, not wanting to know that. "I can't believe you. What about Gally?"

Jodi frowned, clueless. "Who?"

"*Gally*," I growled. "Galloway. Billy Galloway. The bass guitarist in my band. I thought you'd slept with *him*."

"Oh, right." She sighed out a smile. "Yeah, I'm still boffing him, too. He's not as big, but what he lacks in size, he definitely makes up for in freaky. The toys he owns...let me tell you—"

I gagged, just a little, because really...more information about my bandmates I totally did not want to know. "But..."

She winked. "Looks like I'm making my way through your entire band, puta. So by rights, I should get Asher next, right?"

My shock morphed into an immediate scowl. "Over my dead fucking body."

Damn it! I knew she'd only said that to get a rise out of me, and I'd totally obliged her.

When Caroline laughed, I realized just how possessive I'd sounded of poor Asher, too. "I mean, I just..."

Jodi nudged Caroline in the elbow. "I think Remy doth protest too much." Then she smirked at me. "You have such a thing for him."

I snorted. "Do *not*."

"You *love* him," my roommate taunted. "You want to have his babies. You—"

"Shut it," I growled.

"Asher is a really sweet, amazing guy," Caroline said thoughtfully. "You could fall for a lot worse."

I sighed. Yeah, I already knew that.

"Okay, fine," Jodi announced, lifting her hand into a pledge. "I'll refrain from seducing the hot one. But I have to tell you, if he comes onto me first, I won't be held accountable for rocking his hot little world."

"He won't," I assured her, even though I knew she would never do what she claimed. Hell, she'd been the one to clue me into Fisher's cheating ways when *he'd* come onto her.

But seriously, Asher wouldn't hit on her...would he?

No. He was looking for something meaningful. Jodi was allergic to meaningful when it came to guys. She wanted to taste test all of them, not settle down. She liked experimenting and seeing what was out there.

"I can't wait until he meets the real you," Caroline murmured before sucking on the straw of her own piña colada.

I stared at her as if she were insane, because really, she had to be whack for even suggesting such an idea would be anything to look forward to. "Yeah, because it's going to be *so* exciting to see how he reacts to my *month's* worth of deception."

Caroline shrugged. "Not if you tell him at just the right time. Like right before he puts his clothes back on."

"See, I told you; you just need to fuck him," Jodi said.

I groaned as I scowled at the two women across the table from me. "No way," I announced. "I'm not adding *that* to my deception as well. He'd hate me for sure when he found out."

"I don't know," Caroline murmured, smiling mischievously. "A guy will forgive a lot more right after he just—"

"Don't even finish that sentence," I warned her. "Because it's never going to happen. End of discussion. Let's talk about something else."

So, Caroline moved the topic to Pick and Eva's wedding. "I can't believe it's only five days away. They tried to postpone it after what happened to Mason's mom on Saturday, but both Reese and Mason insisted they go ahead."

"How *are* Mason and his little sister?" I asked.

Caroline's expression crinkled with sympathy. "They're still pretty upset. Reese says Mason blames himself because he thinks he should've known what was going on. And Sarah..." She shook her head. "The only person she'll respond to is Brandt. So she's been spending the last few nights at their house so Brandt can get her to eat and sleep. I have a bad feeling it's going to take her a while to get over it."

"Poor girl." I'd seen my mother overdose once. But after calling Tío Alonso, we'd gotten her to a hospital in time to pump her stomach and save her. I'm not sure how I would've reacted if she'd never recovered.

The three of us chatted on until I had to pee. Since I could, I forced both Jodi and Caroline to go with me, as a group. It felt nice too. As I entered the ladies' room, I sighed and petted the sign on the door.

"I can't believe I can actually use the *ladies'* room again. Isn't it lovely in here?"

Jodi laughed as she found an available stall and disappeared inside. "I swear, I've never heard someone sound so excited to be able to use the ladies' room before."

"Well, I'm tired of having the use the men's room all the time. Those things freaking reek. I'm telling you, it is not pleasant. I swear, every guy that uses a public urinal aims to *miss* the actual toilet. The floors...oh, my God, you guys. The floors are toxic."

Caroline clutched her stomach as she laughed. "You are so going to have to write a memoir about this when it's over. *My Life as a Man*." Then she pulled her phone from her purse and started to text someone.

I grinned, wondering if she was sexting her hubby, until

the words "when this is over" actually struck me.

Shit, I really couldn't do this forever, could I?

I was living my dream come true, playing drums for a kick-ass band on tour, and I was doing it all on stolen time. Once the truth came out, I'd be kicked out so fast my head would spin. No way could I keep this a secret forever.

Growing serious, I swallowed down my dread and watched Caroline tuck her phone away before moving to the mirror to check her face.

I finally stumbled into a bathroom stall and did my business, but when I exited, I could no longer be as cheerful. But I really frowned when I found the entire bathroom empty.

"Guys?" I asked.

Both Caroline and Jodi were gone.

"Well, there went all the fun of group peeing," I mumbled as I washed my hands then dried them all by myself. After tossing the paper towels, I checked myself in the mirror, straightened my dress, corrected the lipstick on the corner of my lip and left the ladies' room.

I fully intended to charge toward my table, but as soon as I whipped around the corner of the hall and into the main part of the restaurant, my gaze collided with none other than Asher Hart.

And he was only ten feet away, leaning against the bar as if waiting there for someone to take his order.

As soon as he saw me, he straightened, and seemed to catch his breath. "Hi," he murmured in surprise.

I clutched my small purse to my stomach and gaped back, frozen in my four-inch heels. "Hola," I was finally able to respond.

His gaze fell from my eyes as he scoped out my favorite dress, then my legs, and pumps. As his stare moved back up, I felt stripped bare.

"It's Elisa, right?" he finally said, after we eye-fucked for a good ten seconds.

I bobbed my head stupidly. And then for some reason I said his name.

His face lit up as he smiled at me, and Dios mío, that smile melted my hormones to mush. "Asher, yes," he said. "Good memory."

I didn't know what to say to that, so I just stood there, unable to move or look away.

The bartender interrupted us then, bringing a drink to Asher and forcing Asher to turn to him. "Thanks," he told the guy as he paid. "Hey, you haven't seen a pretty little blonde around, have you? I was supposed to meet her here."

I swallowed as I listened to the bartender tell him he'd seen too many blondes tonight. All the while, my heart began to pound and I swear my eyes teared.

But, shit, holy hell, and goddamn. He was meeting a *woman* here?

He was on a freaking date.

I started to move away, but Asher swung back to me. He opened his mouth to speak, the apologetic, wistful expression on his face telling me he might rather be here with me instead of his blonde bimbo. I fell to a stop, pretty much trapped by the yearning in his green eyes.

Then he sighed, shook his head, and respectfully said, "Buenas noches."

My shoulders collapsed with disappointment. But really, what had I expected him to do? Forget about every other woman on the planet and pant after me?

I was such an idiot.

Besides, guy-me had made him promise to leave girl-me alone. He was respecting his friend's wishes by stepping back.

Mumbling a goodbye to him, I bowed my head and started to move away, except since I wasn't looking where I was going, I plowed into some other guy who looked as if he'd been headed toward the bathrooms.

"Disculpa," I told him, making sure to speak in Spanish.

But when I tried to step out of his way, he only grinned and moved with me. "Wait, what's your hurry, señorita? I've been craving a little Mexican lately."

I scowled at the disgusting bastard and began to step the other way around him. But yeah, he went that way too. So I drew in a deep, calming breath to keep from cussing him out right then and there and maybe kneeing him in the family jewels. Except...since Asher was watching, I wanted to handle this diplomatically.

Until the jerk-ass touched me, running his hand down the side of my bare arm so I threw up just a little in my mouth. "Why don't you come to the bathroom with me, honey? I'll show you what real white meat tastes like."

Eww. I filled my lungs to give him a piece of my mind, not even caring that I was about to give away my knowledge of English, but Asher stepped between us.

"Or you could just get out of her fucking way, asswipe."

He was shorter and not as wide as the other guy, but whatever expression he flashed the jerk, it had the asshole backing away and lifting his hands. "Hey, sorry. I didn't know she was here with someone. You know, a woman out and about, dressed like that, is just asking to be— "

"Treated with the same proper courtesy and respect as every other woman on the planet," Asher growled, his fingers curling into fists at his side.

"Look, I get it," the jackass conceded, his hands still lifted in surrender. "She's yours. I'm backing off." Ignoring me, he veered a wide berth around Asher and escaped into the men's room.

Asher turned to me, but I couldn't...not right now. His coming to my aid so sweetly was more than I could take. As soon as his pity-filled green eyes met mine, I whirled away and raced off. I wasn't even sure where I was going. Jodi and Caroline were both gone to who-knew-where, while poor Asher was probably confused as hell by my reaction. And I just wanted to bawl.

Not because the bully had bothered me. I so could've taught him a lesson. But because Asher just completely overwhelmed me in that moment. I hated, hated, *hated* lying to him.

When I burst through a nearby doorway, I found myself in a small outdoor nook where smokers could come out and have a cigarette before rejoining their parties inside. Except no one was out here smoking. Relieved to find a moment to myself, I rubbed my arms in the chilly night and then unzipped my purse to find my phone and discover what the hell had happened to Caroline and my roommate.

Before I could pull it free, however, the door opened, and yep, Asher stepped outside.

CHAPTER 32
Asher Hart

SHE WAS SO GODDAMN beautiful. And in that dress, those heels, yeah...my mouth watered as soon as I followed her outside. But even as I called myself ten kinds of stupid for racing after her like a lovesick idiot, I asked, "Are you okay?"

Then I remembered she didn't know English. So I said, "¿Bien?" and lifted my eyebrows with the question.

She dropped the purse she'd been digging in back to her shoulder and nodded, then rubbed her hands up the sides of her arms.

She didn't look okay. She looked rattled. Cold. Distressed. Which made me glad I'd stopped by the bar before following her out here.

I lifted the bottle of water I'd bought for her and offered it to her. "¿Agua?"

She took it with a quiet, "Gracias." As she unscrewed the cap and swallowed a long drink, I stepped back, giving her space. But holy hell, she even looked good drinking. As I watched her throat work through each gulp, I just wanted to crowd close and lick that long, graceful neck.

Except I'd sworn Sticks I would keep my distance. So I took another step back.

"Well...I'm sure you came out here to be alone and just get some air. So I'll just..." With another backpedal, I rammed my spine into the doorway to return inside. "Adiós."

She leapt toward me, lifting her hand as if begging me to stay. "Espera."

I froze. "Yeah?"

She fell to a stop too. Then she dropped her hand, and an oddly guilty expression crossed her face, as if she hadn't meant to stop me.

I blew out a breath. "God, you are so lovely."

I was glad she couldn't understand my pathetic confession, even though her eyes changed as if she did.

"Solo un beso," she said and stepped toward me. Her eyes were full of longing, which made the nerves in my stomach jump with hope.

"What—?" I started to ask, but she grasped my shirt and tugged me forward. Then her arms were wrapping around me and she was...shit, she was hugging me.

I couldn't remember the last time I'd been hugged. Hell, I couldn't remember the last time I'd been touched.

She was so soft and feminine, with curves in all the right places. She smelled like heaven and her hands...They kept petting my back as if she couldn't stop touching me, feeling more of me. As all the sensations went straight to my head, all the blood rushed to my dick, and I only wanted to get closer, soothe her...then *soothe* her.

"It's okay," I murmured, sliding my fingers up her back—God, her spine felt marvelous under my hands. Then I petted her hair and kissed her temple.

She drew in a deep breath against my neck, and I swear she was smelling me, then...yeah, was that her *mouth* on my throat?

Or maybe her tongue?

I wasn't sure, but it made me groan, made me tug her just a little more snugly against me and tip my head down until my breaths fell on her chin. She looked up, and bam, our faces were right there, aligned, lips only inches apart.

Vaguely, I knew I shouldn't kiss her. There was a damn good reason, but for the life of me, I couldn't remember what it was.

Her eyes were like brown pools of temptation and I was a drowning man. I tried to resist, I even pressed my forehead to hers, but I already knew it was too late.

This woman owned me.

So when her mouth lifted a fraction of an inch, mine lowered, until our breaths were one. My hand swept up to cradle the back of her neck and her silky dark hair drifted over my knuckles, making me shiver with desire. And in the next instant, our lips were sealed.

I have no idea why, but it felt as if I'd been waiting for years to kiss her. The only thing I knew about her was her name and yet nothing had ever felt as right as just setting my mouth against hers.

My body surged with awareness, skin prickling with a knowledge that the person touching me and pressing against me was the one person who was supposed to. I opened my mouth, tentative at first, and scared to death of scaring her away, because I wanted nothing as much as I wanted this moment to continue.

I damn near wept when her lips parted as well, and her tongue met mine.

With a hungry groan, I took things deeper. She whimpered and stretched up onto her toes, burrowing her fingers in my hair and pressing her chest against mine. My baser needs taking over, I lifted her up and walked her a few steps before setting her on a nearby table. Her legs instantly wrapped around my waist and while one hand stayed in my hair, the other wandered down my back until she was clutching my ass hard and encouraging me to move deeper between her thighs.

When my erection nudged the heat between her legs, the skirt of her dress sliding up to her waist, we both groaned. I palmed her exposed thigh and brought her leg up higher so I could smooth my hand down warm, soft flesh until I encountered the edge of her panties.

"¡Ay por Dios!" she gasped, clutching me as she threw her head back and moaned.

My finger slid under the edge of the silky cloth and across her perfectly formed bottom.

Panting, she leaned forward again to rest her forehead on my sternum. I followed the globe of soft warmth around until I hit pay dirt.

She was wet, so fucking wet that we both sucked in a breath when my finger slicked through her moist heat and tunneled inside.

"No puedo esperar," she mumbled in a high voice. "Más... Más."

Her fingers found the top buttons on my jeans and I lost it. "Holy shit." I pressed my face to the side of her head as she fumbled to free me. And meanwhile, I snapped the crotch of her panties in half, needed nothing in my way.

She gasped and whimpered and couldn't seem to get my jeans opened. I batted her hands away so I could help her when the door behind us burst open.

The slap of ice-cold reality, reminding me where the fuck we were and how I wasn't supposed to be touching her at all, had me spinning around with supreme guilt and making sure to cover her from whoever was coming out.

Caroline skidded to a halt in the doorway. "Oh my God!" she yelped, her eyes huge as her gaze immediately went to the parts of Elisa's legs I couldn't quite conceal from view. So I shifted a step that way to shield her more, even as I growled.

"Caroline? What the fuck? Where have you been?"

"Uh..." She didn't seem to know how to answer as she gaped at Elisa's legs, and then shifted her gaze to my jeans that were partially undone.

As I rushed to button my pants together, I scolded, "Next time you text me to come pick you up and give you a ride home since Ten's working, try not to just...disappear before I get here, huh?"

"Oh...yeah. Sorry, I...I must've been in the bathroom when you showed up."

Elisa grasped the back of my shirt, and I held a reassuring hand behind me to hopefully let her know everything was okay. The move seemed to spike up Caroline's eyebrows, though.

"Doesn't seem like you missed me too much, though."

I glowered. "Are you finally ready to go now?"

I needed to get out of here before I forgot again that I wasn't supposed to even breathe in Elisa's direction.

But Caroline shook her head. "Oh, you know....*actually* the girl I came with is ready now, too, so I'll just leave with her, and besides...I just remembered you drive a motorcycle."

That made me frown. "You're afraid to ride on my bike?"

"No...but I just figured if I'm ever going to ride with a guy on a motorcycle, and you know, wrap my legs around his thighs and smash my breasts to his back, I think I'd rather experience that with Oren the first time, instead of you."

Well, when she put it that way. "Yeah," I said. "Then you should definitely ride with your friend if you can."

"I will," she said brightly, too brightly, as if she had some kind of ulterior motive. "You guys have fun."

Behind me, Elisa tensed, and I realized how truly lame it was to keep trying to hide her from view. Caroline obviously knew she was there. I stepped slightly to the side and yet kept just as close to her.

"Caroline, this is Elisa," I introduced.

"Elisa?" Caroline echoed slowly before nodding and waving. "It's nice to meet you." Then she turned to me. "You know, maybe you can give *Elisa* a ride home since I just saw the person she came with leave without her."

Elisa tensed against me again but said nothing.

I frowned. "Really? That's awful." I glanced at Elisa, not sure how to tell her she'd just been stranded here. Then I asked Caroline. "Hey, do you know any Spanish?"

"Huh?" She blinked at me, then shook her head. "Nope, not a word, sorry." She waved and backed toward the door before reopening it and beginning to leave. "Don't you two do anything I wouldn't." And she was gone.

"Dammit," I muttered, panicking a little because I had no idea how to tell the girl next to me that she'd been left behind or even ask how to get her home.

She breathed out a small sigh as she slipped off the table and straightened her skirt down around her legs.

Realizing I had a whole heap of other problems, I ran my hands through my hair. "Christ, I am so sorry," I told her. "I can't believe I just...right here, in public like this. And I broke your underwear. I swear I'll replace them. And..." The words stalled on my tongue when she looked up.

"Jesus," I murmured. "I still want to fuck you so bad." Quickly, I lifted my hands. "But I won't. I'll behave. I promised a very good friend that I'd keep my hands off you. So...*Remy!* That's it." I snapped my fingers. "I bet he knows where you live. Don't worry. I'll call him, and I'm sure he'll come pick you up and get you home safe and sound."

As I tore my phone from my pocket, Elisa opened her purse and yanked out her own cell phone as well. I'm not sure what she did, but she didn't call anyone. Seconds later, Remy's phone went straight to voice mail.

"Fuck," I whispered. Didn't he know I was trying to be a good boy and not touch his cousin...any more than I already had? I ran my hand through my hair. "How the hell am I supposed to get you home if neither of us understands a word the other says?"

She must've sensed the distress on my face because she stepped toward me and lifted her hand to touch my cheek. I closed my eyes and bowed my head, trying to resist it. But her fingers were so soft and gentle. When she reached up on tiptoes to kiss my cheek, I shifted my face so that our lips brushed instead.

Closing her eyes, she clutched my shirt at the shoulders. "Tu casa," she whispered.

Remembering *casa* meant *house* from my high school Spanish class and *tu* was *you*, I figured she'd just asked to come home with me.

Resistance was futile. I wanted her too damn bad, so I nodded. "Okay. You can come home with me."

I had no idea if she understood any of what I'd just said. But she came willingly when I took her hand. We continued to interlock fingers as I walked her out to my Triumph. I wasn't sure if I'd ever held hands with a woman before. It felt nice. Warm. Cozy.

I kissed her knuckles when we reached my bike. If she was surprised to see that she had to ride on a motorcycle, she didn't show it as I swung my leg over the side and got it started. Then I pointed out the parts she needed to avoid and where she could rest her feet.

Her high heels posed a problem, but she soon solved it by slipping them off and climbing on behind me barefoot. She snuggled up against my back, tightly trapping my hips between her thighs, and enfolded her arms around my waist before smashing her breasts to my spine as if she were born to ride this way. I figured she'd done this before, which reassured me.

I didn't have a helmet for either of us; I never wore one when putting around town. But she didn't seem to mind, so I covered her hands at my waist briefly before putting us into gear.

The breeze was cool and she shivered against me, making me feel crappy since I didn't have a jacket to offer her.

Thank God I didn't live too far away. But it still took me longer than I wanted it to since I drove easy. By the time I pulled down my alley, she was an ice cube, her teeth chattering and arms quivering from trembling so bad.

"Don't worry," I assured her, waiting for her to slip on her shoes before helping her slide off behind me. "We'll get you warm soon."

Then I took her hand again as I led her to the dark opening of my place. My stairwell and her shoes concerned me, but I kept close and led her down each step. "Last one," I breathed, growing nervous as she stepped into my apartment.

But fuck. I shouldn't have brought her here. I kept remembering how the last person who'd been in my place was Sticks and how I'd assured him I'd stay away from this very woman.

I was breaking that promise all to hell, probably even breaking our friendship in the process. But even as I worried about his reaction, I swiped a blanket off my bed and brought it to Elisa so I could wrap it around her shoulders.

She gazed up at me and just like that, I was swept under again.

Damn it, I wasn't usually this easy. I knew how to say no, and I'd done it a lot lately. But all those months of no sex, of not being able to thrust into a hot willing pussy, of needing to be touched...it wore on me. And besides, this was *her*, the very girl who'd caused me to jerk off more than usual lately, ever since I'd first seen her in my shower. Naked. The chemistry I experienced around her was off the charts.

I had to get her naked again.

A rattling from above us caused her to whirl around and look up at Mozart, who was trying to free a stuck peanut that had become wedged in the wires of his cage.

"Oh...yeah." I flushed, wondering what she'd think of me having a pet squirrel, hoping it didn't freak her out. "That's Mozart."

Instead of shying away in horror, though, she grinned affectionately and reached up.

"No, wait!" I leapt forward to stop her so she didn't get scratched to hell, but she merely reached for the peanut, causing Mozart to race away and then stop and watch as she shimmied the nut free. Then he twitched his tail, tempted when she eased the peanut through the wires, offering it to him.

I knew exactly how he felt.

He inched forward and stopped. I held my breath, curious if the squirrel would actually take the nut straight from her fingers. I wanted to warn her to be careful, but from the cautious way she moved, she already knew.

When Mozart snagged the peanut and took off, I gasped, "Holy shit. He really took it from you. Straight from your hand."

Elisa spun to me, beaming and proud. Her smile stole my breath and before I could stop myself, I was cupping her face and kissing her.

"I love that smile," I admitted. "I want to steal it all for myself so you'll never be able to smile at anyone else the way you're smiling at me right now."

Her gaze softened and eyes glittered as if filling with emotion. Then she touched my cheeks gently and pressed a soft kiss to my mouth.

Afterward, she pulled away and tugged at my long-sleeved shirt. Realizing she wanted to peel it off me, I lifted my arms and let her remove it. As soon as I was bare, she sucked in a breath, her gaze darting crazily around my chest before she reached with tentative fingers and began to touch me, touch me as if this were her one and only chance and she wanted to absorb every moment of the experience.

I caught a piece of her hair and watched her face, the awe and the thrill controlling her expression. She looked up at me again, grinning that grin I was going to steal. So I kissed her and picked her up, then carried her to my bed.

Laying her gently on the mattress, I took a second to stand over her and simply enjoy the view of her on my sheets. But she sat up, kicked off her heels and scooted to the edge so she could reach for the zipper of my jeans. This time, she was more successful, and I stepped out of them when she pushed them down my hips until I was in nothing but my boxers.

She reached for my cock, tenting out the front of my shorts, but I caught her wrist.

"Not yet."

Instead, I coaxed her to lift her arms so I could slip her dress up and over her head. Then I helped her out of her bra and grinned as she flung aside the scrap of material at her waist that had once been her panties.

Panties *I'd* destroyed.

Then I nudged her to lie back as I climbed over her. Her brown eyes swirled with yearning as she watched me settle on top of her. When she grinned, I had to grin back.

"Hi," I whispered, to which she whispered back, "Hola."

Noticing the necklace she wore when gold glinted from the base of her throat, I paused, taking in the familiar pendant. "Guadalupe," I murmured, remembering the name of the saint in the image.

She smiled as if proud of me for getting it right. And that smile...damn. I leaned in and kissed her, deep and wet, open-mouthed with tongues swirling. She moaned and arched up under me.

Hard nipples gouged into my chest and compelled me to investigate them. I tore my mouth from hers so I could shimmy down and lap up the beaded tip of one breast with my tongue. Crying out, she grasped the sheets under her, and I drew more of her into my mouth, sucking. All the while, my fingers sought her curves, learning every dip and swell.

When I moved to the second breast, she began to pet my hair and down my back, mapping out just as much of me as I was of her.

"Te amo," she whispered, strumming her fingers down my ribcage.

Remembering how Remy had told me that meant *good job*, I lifted my face and grinned. "Thank you. But you haven't seen anything yet."

She blinked as if confused. But I was quick to show her what else I had in store for her perfect body. I kissed my way down, over her navel and to the apex of her thighs. Catching her breath, she clutched my hair, preparing for me to start.

I grinned up at her. Her chest heaved as she breathed hard and her dewy brown eyes looked glossy and unfocused. She was so turned on I knew I had this.

"That's it, baby," I encouraged, patting her grip in my

hair. "Hold on tight, because this is going to be one intense ride."

CHAPTER 33
Remy Cusan

I LIT UP THE SECOND HIS tongue touched me. Flicking it in a quick, gentle tease, he stirred me up in less time than it took me to cry out some dazed Spanish phrases. I belatedly blurted them out anyway, probably ripping some of his gorgeous dark hair out by the roots as overwhelming wet heat consumed me. He finally stopped playing and stroked boldly between my pussy lips to find my quivering clit.

"Hijo de puta," I gasped. "¡Chinga! ¡Mierda! ¡Oh, Dios mío!"

He slid two fingers into me, and I cried out his name as I contracted almost painfully. The spasms were so severe they took my breath. I could only arch under him, shocked, electrocuted, dazed as wave after wave flooded me, sizzling every nerve ending in my body until I collapsed onto the mattress, panting and drained.

I suddenly knew why the French called this the little death, because I'd certainly just passed through a whole other realm of existence.

Seriously. Best orgasm ever.

I stared up at the tiled ceiling of Asher's basement

apartment, not sure how I was supposed to go on from here. Life as I knew it had just altered completely.

"Damn, you look so good right now," he murmured in one of those smugly satisfied male voices when he sat up.

I slid my gaze to him, not sure how he could call me beautiful when I was still half deceased, not yet fully resurrected from my little death. But his grin only grew as our gazes met. Oh, yeah, he knew exactly what he'd just done to me. Then he went and cockily wiped the back of his hand over his red, swollen lips. Beautiful, magical lips that housed the most perfect tongue ever.

I whimpered and my sex quivered wanting him back on me.

But Dios mío. Who knew Asher Hart would turn out to be a freaking sex god?

Still riding my high, I grinned as he stooped over me, licking my erect nipples playfully as he leaned past me to reach for his nightstand and pull open the top drawer. My body lit up, realizing he was searching for a condom. Oh, goody. I glowed in eagerness. More sex.

Then he sat up, a familiar box in hand with my own handwriting on the outside, the words *Use Me Please* written out with a smiley face beside them. I glowed, happy to see he hadn't used any yet and was struggling to tear open the box.

It took him a second to see my message, and when he did, he stilled, his determined smile falling.

"Shit," he whispered to himself as this crestfallen depression blanketed his expression.

Realizing he was remembering his promise to me—boy-me—I gulped, suddenly not so glowy. I was making him feel guilty.

The last thing I wanted to do was cause him any distress. This was all on me. The guilt should be mine, mine alone. Not his. He'd done nothing wrong.

Damn it, what had I done to my beautiful, sweet Asher?

Reaching up, I cupped his face, trying to convey that he was innocent, guilt-free, and fine. His tormented gaze moved to me.

"I'm sorry," he said softly. "I promised a very good friend I wouldn't do this."

Tears rushed to my eyes, not only because I hated doing this to him but because he'd called boy-me a very good friend. I sat upright and rested my cheek against his, trying to let him know it was okay, I understood. Even though the girl parts of me were throbbing and ready to keep going, I didn't want to torture him with any undue guilt.

His Asher-smell filled my nostrils and I breathed him in, realizing this was probably the last time I'd ever get to be this close to him. I smoothed my cheek along his, relishing the soft rasp of beard burn I gave myself. I touched my lips to his temple, and he let out a tortured sound as he squeezed his eyes closed.

I pressed my forehead to his and he pressed back, clasping a hand around the back of my neck to keep me from leaving.

"What the hell am I doing?" he bit out harshly to himself, shaking his head back and forth. "This shouldn't be so hard to stop. I don't know the first thing about you. You don't understand a fucking word I say. And why am I sitting here talking to myself while you're naked in my bed when I just want to bury myself so deep inside you I can't remember my own name?"

Opening his lashes, he pulled away and searched my gaze as if he was trying to get inside my head. "And yet," he murmured. "Whenever I look into your eyes, I feel like there could be more, so much more. Like there could be everything."

I kissed him. Seriously, there was no helping it. The man couldn't say shit like that to me and not expect me to molest him senseless. My tongue spiked deep, and he was right there with me, pushing me back onto the mattress and ripping off his shorts before opening the condoms and putting one on with a savage intensity that only made me wetter. Knowing all that intensity would be focused on me soon—inside me—I arched into him, tugging at his shoulders desperately.

Then I glanced down, and my mouth went dry as I watched him roll the non-latex over his length. But shit. He'd been big when I'd spied him limp in the Chicago hotel room. But erect, Asher's cock was massively enormous. Without a doubt, I'd never had one that big before.

It kind of worried me, and I shied back as he leaned down on top of me. He looked so predatory, I knew I was going to be taken hard, not gently. It thrilled as much as it scared me.

He must've sensed my wariness because he paused and crinkled his eyebrows as he looked into my eyes. "What's wrong?"

I gulped. "Grande."

"Grande," he repeated, confused at first. Then his eyes cleared and he translated, "Big." Then that smug male grin reappeared. "Why, thank you."

I scowled because I hadn't been trying to compliment him, the goober. God, he could be such a guy. But then he seemed to realize I was more worried than amazed.

The backs of his fingers feathered across my cheek as he whispered, "Baby, don't even worry about that. It'll fit. I promise you."

Yeah, easy for him to say. He wasn't about to be impaled by the Empire State Building of male appendages. But then he pressed the head of himself against my opening and I spread my legs wider, eager to be filled despite his size, because damn it, big suddenly seemed very appealing. My mouth watered as he thrust forward, and the delicious feel of my inner walls stretching, and then stretching some more, to accommodate him had me moaning, "Yes! Yes!"

Then he thrust deep, and powerful, and I'd been so right. He did not go gently into that good night. No, sir, he did not. He plunged with, I swear, everything he had in him.

I cried out from the invasion, but not from any kind of pain.

Damn, but he'd been right. He did fit. Perfectly, blissfully snugly. And it felt so good.

The pleasure was so shocking my inner muscles seized and I came all over his monster cock before he could even begin to pump. He held still inside me, watching my face as I orgasmed around him. Then he grinned as I finished and tried to catch my breath.

"See," he said. "Perfect fit."

The show-off!

I loved it.

Pulling out, he shoved back in, making me gasp from the impact. The man then commenced to fuck my ever-loving brains out. I could only hold on for dear life as he pumped his hips, pistoning into and out of me, driving me out of my mind from the pleasure.

"Goddamn," he hissed, pressing his forehead to mine as

his powerful hips slammed against mine. "This is not just sex," he panted.

My lashes fluttered open, but I could barely focus on him. The world was too blurry, my body was still experiencing too much bliss.

"Feels more like a reaping," he gasped, burying all ten fingers in my hair so he could hold my head steady and stare into my eyes. "What the hell are you taking from me, woman?"

I wasn't sure if I was taking as much as he was giving, or more aptly, we were exchanging. My soul for his. It was so beautiful tears filled my eyes.

"Te amo," I told him.

But all he did was nod. "I know. It's good. So damn good. The best ever."

He bowed his head and buried his face against my shoulder as his body tensed. When he came, I felt the charge from the tips of my toes to the roots of my hair, and it was as if I was forced to ignite with him.

Grasping hold of each other, we rode the storm together until each of our bodies settled.

He collapsed on top of me, heavy and so deliciously warm. I burrowed against him, relishing this moment, enjoying it while it lasted.

"Te amo," I admitted again.

But all he said was, "Yeah, it was good."

I furrowed my brow, wondering why he kept saying that in answer to my big declaration, until I remembered—oh, yeah—Sticks-me had been the one to tell him *te amo* meant good job.

I blew out a breath, relieved and yet also disappointed he had no idea what I was really saying. It was just as well he never knew. Maybe this way I could still preserve some of my dignity after he found out the truth and dropped me flat.

But the idea of losing him made tears sprout from my eyes. I wiped at my wet cheek just as he mumbled something and rolled off me, falling heavily onto the mattress beside me. I blinked, stunned as he literally passed out seconds after coming.

"Well, I guess he does sleep," I announced aloud, a bit disappointed, but also relieved I had a moment to be myself.

Asher didn't reply, his lips parting as he drew in long drugging breaths.

He looked kind of cute, worn out and expended like that, yet satisfied and content. I reached out and gently took a piece of his hair to brush it across his forehead.

Murmuring sleepily, he said, "Sorry. Can never stay awake after sex."

I grinned. "It's okay," I told him in English, and he was so out of it he wasn't even aware I was no longer speaking in Spanish.

Taking advantage of the moment, I stroked him all over, every line of his face, his shoulders, each rib, around his belly button. When I came to the mass between his legs, I took care of his condom for him, sure he'd be grateful for the lack of a mess when he woke up. And while I was in the bathroom, disposing of it, I peed and washed my hands, basically freshening myself.

I was still naked when I came out of the bathroom. Clanging from the cage made me glance at Mozart, who was watching me a little bit too alertly.

"Hey, stop staring, you perv." I slapped my hands over my breasts. Then I decided, "Yeah, you're definitely a boy squirrel."

Realizing I wasn't going to provide him with any more of a peep show, he turned away and scampered off, deeper into his cage away from me.

Then I returned to the bed so I could sit on the edge and watch the insomniac rest deeply. "You really are special," I told him, reaching out to run my fingers through his hair again. But as I tried to pull away, he grasped my wrist, making me gasp.

Bleary green eyes fluttered open. "Don't go," he slurred, tumbling me onto the mattress and right up against him.

Unable to deny such a request, I wiggled a bit to get comfy, and then I let him spoon around me with my ass tucked into his lap and his arm wrapped around my waist. Together, we gave a contented sigh.

I closed my eyes as he stroked his hands idly up and down my hip. But then his fingers moved higher, and he slid them around to cup my breast. When he thumbed my nipple, making it immediately harden, I tensed and didn't mean to, but I pressed my bottom back into him.

His dick twitched against me. Moisture collected between my legs, and before I knew it, I was panting for more as he rolled me onto my stomach and pushed into me from behind.

The thrust caught me off guard and made me cry out...in a very good way. He pumped a few more times before hissing a curse and jerking out.

"Shit, sorry. Condom." I gaped in shock as I glanced back to watch him dive for the spilled box of condoms on the nightstand and roll one on.

He'd felt so good; I hadn't even remembered. This was scary as much as it was powerful. Whatever was happening between us wasn't just normal sex; he'd been right about that.

When he pushed back into me from behind again, I was ready this time, but the shock of his dick inside me was still a delicious rush. I pushed back into him and he surged forward. His groan of satisfaction told me he liked my eagerness. Then he gathered a handful of my hair at the base of my neck and kept my head pinned to my pillow while I lifted my ass to give him deeper access. In return, he groaned. I started to come in hard heaving pants.

I blurted out broken Spanish, because for some reason that was the language that came to me when I was in the throes of passion.

But he seemed to know I was blurting out how much I enjoyed this because he muttered "Fuck, yeah," before slamming into me to release himself.

This time, he actually had the wherewithal to get his condom off and thrown into a nearby trash can before he curled up onto his side and gathered me close to cuddle with him. With a lazy yawn, he mumbled, "Good thing we don't understand each other and can't talk after sex, anyway, because you'd get a really shitty conversation out of me if we could."

I grinned, not minding how I could put his butt to sleep so easily. He needed all the rest he could get.

When he began to breathe heavily behind me, I closed my eyes and rested.

I have no idea how long we slept, curled up together like that. I just knew a phenomenon had taken place because I could never cuddle with a guy for the full night. Five minutes with Fisher, and I'd been squirming away because he'd been too hot and stifling.

With Asher, it felt too nice to move.

But I had to get out of here...unless I wanted to confess everything to him, which I so didn't. Not right now. Not while his apartment still smelled like sex.

I'd done the ultimate. I'd slept with him on top of all the rest of my deception.

I was like the worst of the worst now.

Still...I couldn't regret it a full hundred percent because, well, damn...last night might've been the best night of my life.

Glancing back at him one last time, I crept out of his bed before I hunted up my purse, called my roommate and whisper-hissed-demanded she come pick me up this very instant.

Twenty minutes later, wearing my heels and dress from the night before, I stood outside Asher's apartment, hugging my purse to my stomach as Jodi's car pulled into the alley. I barely gave her time to stop next to me before I was pulling open the passenger side door and muttering, "Go!"

The bitch wouldn't stop grinning at me as she put the car into drive. "Well, he must've been good if the rat's nest in your hair says anything about it."

"Fuck you," I muttered, immediately brushing out my hair with my fingers. "This is all your fault. I did not want to sleep with him, Jodi. Jesus, what were you and Caroline thinking? You orchestrated this whole thing, didn't you?"

"Oh, calm down, will you, puta. We merely arranged a happy coincidental meeting between the two of you. We didn't put his penis in your pussy. That was all you."

"Jesus, God," I sobbed, tears instantly pouring down my cheeks. "I slept with him. I can't believe I slept with him."

"Really, sweetie." Jodi sighed. "It's not that big of a deal. It was just sex."

To her, the joining of two bodies was just sex, yes. But to me...it meant something. I couldn't program my body and heart and head into thinking it was just a good time. And besides, nothing that had happened the night before could ever be classified as just sex. So I wailed, "No, it wasn't. I've just compounded my betrayal to him by double. Fuck, *triple*. He'll never forgive me for this when he finds out. He's going to hate me."

"You never know," Jodi argued. "Just how good was it last night?"

"The best ever," I muttered miserably, wiping at my running mascara with a tissue I found in my purse.

"Well, then maybe it'll be easier for him to get over the lie...if he wants more from you." When she winked, I only groaned.

"No. He'll hate me. It was that good, Jodi. I freaking fell in love with him. I mean, I honest to God love everything about Asher Hart. He's the best man, best lover, best friend I ever had."

I vaguely realized I'd just said he was a better friend to me than she was, but not even Jodi took umbrage with the slight. Suddenly, not so cavalier to my misery, she gulped and said, "Oh. Well...that may change things."

"You think?" I sobbed. "What am I supposed to do now?"

But not even Jodi had any sage advice for me.

CHAPTER 34
Remy Curran

By two that afternoon, I'd calmed myself so that I didn't burst into tears at the drop of a hat, but it took a lot of coaxing from Jodi to get me to go to band practice.

"Why are you so adamant I go?" I whined. "You never wanted me to stay in the band in the first place."

"Well, you didn't listen, so now you're a full-fledged member and it's your duty. Besides, Asher would wonder why you didn't show up, and if he puts too many one plus ones together, he might figure out the truth. You want him to find out this way?"

"No." I totally didn't. So I got my ass in gear and showed up to practice. I was the second-to-last to arrive—only Asher was later than I was, which was unheard of all by itself.

But then he acted all lethargic and tired, yawning and repeatedly drawing in a deep breath to waken himself. He was always a bundle of activity, even needing to drum his fingers whenever he had to sit still. Seeing him like this was just—

And that's when I realized what "the tell" was that Ten had been talking about. Sex made him sluggish and tired.

I grew warm realizing this was all because of me. But then I scolded myself for even thinking about last night.

Asher wasn't just listless though. He was also worried...about Sticks. He wouldn't make eye contact with me throughout practice and when he needed to say something to his drummer, he usually just said it in my direction, not directly to me.

Realizing he felt guilty about breaking his promise to boy-me, I closed my eyes and shook my head. I hated doing this to him.

As soon as practice was over, I loitered, knowing I needed to do something. Confess, or...no sé. Just make things right.

Heath and Gally took off, and Asher sent me a wary glance. I pretended to tinker with things on the drum set before giving up and directly asking, "Everything okay?"

He jumped and set his fist against his mouth before whirling to me. "Huh?"

Damn, he couldn't hide his guilt for shit, the poor guy.

I opened my mouth to...I don't know, maybe tell him the entire truth, when he suddenly blurted, "I had sex last night."

Blinking because I seriously hadn't expected him to say *that*, I opened my mouth, then shut it before I managed to answer, "O...kay."

"It's just..." He waved a hand my way. "You said you wanted to know, so...I'm letting you know."

Oh, right. I'd forgotten about that conversation. "Well...okay then. Gracias for letting me know." And before I even knew what I was going to say next, I added, "I had sex last night, too."

There. We'd both confessed half-truths. It seemed only fitting. But even as I internally cringed, he brightened. "Really?"

I nodded, and his shoulders slumped in relief. "Oh, thank God," he said. Then he waved a finger between the two of us. "So...we're okay?"

I shrugged, "Sure. Absolutely."

Inside, I wailed, *No!* I was still a big fat liar, and I didn't deserve a minute of his friendship.

But he looked so happy as he said, "Cool," I couldn't tell him then.

And the guilt only grew heavier as I drove home. I really, really, *really* needed to tell him. Everything.

Last night, I'd gone too far, and now every time I saw him, I was going to want to jump his bones or bawl all over him for lying.

Jodi wasn't around when I blew inside my apartment, and I really I needed her to talk me out of this because after I took off my Stick's costume, I dressed as Remy—girl Remy—and I drove to Asher's apartment...as a girl.

His bike wasn't in the alley when I showed up, so I kept driving. But a few blocks later, I cursed my lack of courage and pulled to the side of the road. I walked back to the opening of his alley, keeping my face down against the cold blowing wind and practicing everything I was going to say when he made it home.

A full, honest confession; that was what I'd do.

I couldn't fix what I'd done. A lo hecho, pecho. *What was done was done.* But I could make it right from here on out. Más vale tarde que nunca. *Better late than never, huh?*

I'd just entered the alley, hugging myself when the familiar rumble of his motorcycle entered from the opposite end. We made it to his front door at about the same time. He killed the engine and leapt off his seat as I lifted my face and pushed my hair out of my eyes, encouraging myself to speak to him...in English... in my Sticks voice.

But he spoke first. "Thank God you came back. I just went to your restaurant, but they said you weren't working today."

I opened my mouth to tell him no, I had the day off, but he grasped my face and kissed me.

I loved Asher's lips. I mean, seriously, his mouth killed brain cells. Mine certainly short-circuited until I was leaning against him, clutching his strong arms and opening for him when he sought entrance into my mouth with his tongue.

He groaned and lifted me, and I wrapped my legs around his waist. Pinning me to the wall next to his door as he fumbled to unlock all the deadbolts, he continued to kiss me until he pressed his forehead to mine to admit, "I haven't been able to stop thinking about you since I woke up alone in bed with nothing but your smell surrounding me."

Damn it, I hadn't been able to stop thinking about him either. I crushed my mouth to his.

He got us inside the stairwell of his apartment, but he only made it a few steps down with me in his arms because he almost went tumbling and broke both our necks.

"Shit, sorry." He set me on my feet a step above him, but I continued to cling to him, kissing his neck and biting skin to memorize every freaking centimeter of his flesh.

"Jesus," he groaned and pinned me to the wall of the stairwell. I wound my legs back around him, and he humped me a few minutes before we both needed more.

I was able to open his jeans and get a handful of monster cock, but he only cursed when he got to my yoga pants and couldn't tear them off me as fast as he'd been able to ruck up the skirt of my dress last night.

We made it down a few more steps. Then he said, "Fuck it," and laid me on the stairs. Grasping my breasts in each hand, he lowered his mouth to my waist and caught a teeth-full of the elastic band of my pants before ripping them down. I kicked my legs to help wiggle out of them, and thank God my panties came down with them, because I wasn't sure I could afford him tearing every pair I owned off me. And with the hungry mood he was in, they would've been snapped in half a second.

He pulled his wallet from his jeans that were sagging around his knees. Then he had a condom in hand. Then he had the condom in place. The next moment, he had the condom in me.

I threw my head back, relishing the hard thrust of him meshing with the soft give of myself. We fit so right together.

I blurted out Spanish, not able to care about the stair steps gouging into my back. With Asher buried so deep inside me, nothing else mattered.

My release came quickly and so did his. Our simultaneous combustion had us clutching each other through our orgasms, and then he gasped out a sound of shock before rolling off me and skidding down a few steps to collapse on his back, fling his arm over his face and pant.

Though I felt like putty myself, I didn't want him passing out on the stairs. What an awful place to fall asleep. So I shimmied down until I was beside him. I took his arm and helped him wrap it around my shoulder. Then I pushed to my feet, heaving him up with me.

He groaned in dislike but latched on to the railing to help pull himself up.

"Thank you," he mumbled. "You're too good to me."

I rubbed his chest and kissed his cheek.

"Don't leave this time, okay?" he begged, dragging me down with him as he collapsed onto the bed. "Just...stay."

So, I stayed. Yawning, I closed my eyes and napped with him for a while, until I woke at some point in the evening to his mouth between my legs, his tongue massaging my clit, and my body bowing up, already prepared to explode.

"Hi, there." He grinned at me, his green eyes still droopy with sleep but his smile full of life.

I mumbled something, not sure if it was in Spanish or English, but whatever garbled sound came from me, it made him chuckle. Then, he was lifting my legs up to my chest and sitting upright so he could push into me from that angle.

He watched me squirm as he tortured me with his cock, sliding deep and at just the right angle to hit the perfect spot.

"I love watching you come," he admitted, before lifting me up so we were both sitting upright, me still in his lap as we faced each other. "Now come again."

I shook my head, still not fully down from the last high, but Asher didn't care. He slipped his thumb over my clit, heaved more powerfully inside me and had me screaming in moments.

The rest of the night followed a similar pattern. We fucked, we slept, occasionally we cuddled, once he left the bed to get us a snack of apples and cheese. Mozart became quite the voyeur and at some point, Asher had to climb out of bed to throw a blanket over his cage. But he returned immediately to cuddle and hold me close.

The next morning, I woke first, still swaddled in his gentle hold and pleasantly sore between the legs. I knew I should go. Two nights in a row of this was just...it was twice as wrong. But as soon as I tried to sit up, his arms banded tighter around me.

"Oh no, you're not. You're not sneaking out of here so easily this morning. I don't care if I have to handcuff you to the bed. In fact..." He rose behind me and hopped off the mattress to stroll naked across the room until he got to his table, where he had a gift bag sitting. After he dug a hand inside, he turned around, grinning.

My mouth dropped open when I saw the fuzzy, leopard-printed handcuffs dangling from his fingers. "I was going to give them to my brother for a gag wedding gift," he explained. "But now I think I'll get him something else. Come here, beautiful."

Not sure if I wanted to be bound, I screamed out a laugh and skittered away from him as he dove at me. He chased me across the mattress, grinning the entire time before he stopped with a heaving sigh and said, "No?"

I shook my head. "No."

But then an idea hit me. I reached for the handcuffs. Asher lifted his eyebrows at the request but handed them over easily. My smile spread big as I wiggled my eyebrows and motioned him to put his hands up by the headboard.

He furrowed his eyebrows in confusion a second before they shot up high in realization. "Oh...you want to handcuff *me*?"

I nodded and bit my lip, unable to stop grinning at the idea.

And damn, but he was a good sport. Green eyes heating with lust, he said, "Okay." He moved into position, stretching onto his back and lifting his arms over his head to allow me to bind him to his bed.

Damn he looked good like this, staring up at me in eager anticipation as I licked my lips and tried to decide what I wanted to do to him first. The giggles that had been rising inside me died as the lust pooled deep in my abdomen.

God, he was gorgeous, spread out naked like a feast for me alone. I just wanted to lick him.

So, I did. I leaned forward, set my tongue against his navel and moved up, lapping my way over his abdomen, which quivered and tightened under me, and right up along his sternum until I reached the base of his neck. Then I sank my teeth into his throat, sucking at the softness of his flesh, inhaling the aroma that was purely him, delighting in his groan as it vibrated against my teeth.

He shifted his face to the side to look at me, and that look in his green eyes, so full of trust and affection...I wanted to trap this moment in my memory banks forever. I stroked the tips of my fingers along either side of his face, memorizing each detail, how it felt, smelled, tasted. Then I leaned forward and gently pressed my lips to his. He pulled as far away from his cuffs as he could to meet my kiss and try to take it further, but I stopped him, wanting to explore more all by myself. Grinning, he leaned back into the cushions, watching me.

I spent a few minutes playing in his hair. He groaned every time my fingernails skimmed his scalp. Then I pressed quick tender kisses down each arm, determined not to miss a single mole or freckle. And what my mouth missed, my fingers followed along behind to gobble up.

"Christ," he murmured, closing his eyes and tipping his head back as he enjoyed my administrations. "That feels good."

With a smile, I sprinkled a little loving across his chest and down his stomach. He sucked in a breath when I reach the V at the base of his abdomen. I grinned up at him and he blew out the breath he'd just drawn to let me know I was torturing him.

Keeping eye contact, I slid my fingers around the base of his cock and lifted it from his stomach, then I leaned in to take the head between my lips. I watched his eyes dilate as the salty flavor hit my tongue.

"Holy..." he tried to say and then gave up. A droplet of sweat slithered down his temple.

Not taking my gaze from his face, I sucked him in deeper until he hit the back of my throat. His lips parted and he couldn't seem to do anything past breathing as I drew him in an inch deeper. I still couldn't take all of him, but that didn't stop me from pulling and drawing him back in.

"God," he gasped, his eyes fixed on mine only to occasionally drift to my lips still wrapped around him, and then return to my eyes again.

I fondled his sack for a few seconds and his scrotum tightened under my tender loving care. He was getting close. But I didn't want him finishing in my mouth.

When I pulled off him, he groaned but didn't argue. He only watched, his eyes heating as I picked up the condom box, which was way more than half empty by this point.

"You are so beautiful," he murmured as I rolled the prophylactic over his massive length. I knew he had to mean it, too, because he had no idea I could understand every word he said.

Instead of facing him, I turned my back to him as I

straddled his lap. He hummed his approval and tried to lift his lap before I was ready. So I set a hand on his hip, restraining him to the bed, and twisted with a warning smile as I shook my fingers at him.

"Okay," he told me, breathing hard as another trail of sweat rolled off him. "I'll behave, I swear. But fuck, I love this game."

I laughed, loving it myself. Then I grabbed hold of him and positioned myself above him so he rubbed up against the opening of my anus.

"Oh, you've got to be fucking kidding me." His voice was high with surprise and an overload of lust. "This is too good to be true."

But at the last second, I glanced back at him, winked and moved him to my pussy. "Damn, you little tease...." But the word tease came as a groan because that's when I sat on him, impaling myself completely. "Shit. Okay. This way's not so bad either. Fuck."

I threw my head back and laughed as I rode him. He cursed some more, and I started spouting shit off in Spanish because I just couldn't help myself. When my womb began to contract, squeezing an intense orgasm out of me, he shouted his own release and surged up his hips.

As soon as we finished, I crawled off him and took care of his condom for him.

"Thank you," he murmured, eyeing me as if I'd handed him a million bucks or something. Then I curled up next to him and rested my head on his shoulder so I could look into his eyes.

Neither of us mentioned taking off the handcuffs yet. I think we both equally liked being this way. His lashes fluttered, telling me he was getting drowsy. I smiled and stroked his jaw, and his lips tipped up under the caress.

"You don't know this yet," he told me, his voice full of sleep. "But I'm going to keep you. We're going to make this work, language barrier or not. Because nothing has ever been that amazing."

His green eyes were full of so much sincerity, I had to close my own and press my face against the side of his neck. "Te amo," I told him, ashamed and guilty that I couldn't confess it in English, that I couldn't confess anything to him.

I didn't deserve this wonderful, amazing man. Everything I'd ever had with him was founded on a lie of my own making and he should have more, so much more than that.

"Ya no puedo hacer esto," I admitted, because I *couldn't* do this to him anymore. He'd just closed his eyes as I crawled off him, needing to go, needing to escape before I burst into tears.

Behind me, he mumbled, "What're you doing? What's wrong?" as I quickly tugged up my panties and grabbed my bra.

I couldn't face him, couldn't say anything. So I rushed faster to escape.

He tried to talk me into staying, even came up with the worst pronunciation for the words *sit* and *stay* known to man.

"No! Don't go. Please, don't go. I'm sorry. I don't know what I did wrong, but I'm sorry. Shit," he muttered, as if he thought he was messing everything up and didn't know how to make it right. "What's sorry in Spanish?"

I told him, not that he knew that was what I was doing. He just kept begging, kept trying to coax me to stay, which only made me feel worse for every lie I'd ever told him and made me more determined to flee.

Wiping back tears, I finally stopped at the door and glanced back. He blinked as if stunned to see me crying. Then he whispered my name...the wrong name, and I blurted, "I'm so very sorry, but I have to do this," in Spanish before I heaved myself into the stairwell and sprinted up the steps.

Once outside in the cool day, I jogged to my car, blocks away, where I'd left it the day before. Tears blurred my vision as I started the engine, but I kept going anyway. I made it all the way home before I realized—shit—I couldn't just leave him handcuffed to his bed.

So I dug my phone from my purse and called him. I knew he wouldn't be able to answer, but I figured "Sticks" could try getting hold of him, and then drop by his apartment to check on him, make sure his dad hadn't killed him or something.

And fuck, now that I was thinking about his dad, I cursed myself. What the hell had I been thinking to trap him to one spot when his psycho father was still on the loose? What if his old man found him like that, and hurt him? I *had* left his apartment completely unlocked.

I was about to hang up and rush into my room to change into my Sticks gear when Asher actually answered, surprising the hell out of me.

"Hey, man," he answered, sounding breathless and yet casual, as if he wasn't trapped naked to his own bed. "What's up?"

Okay, so maybe he'd gotten loose already.

"Not much." My voice sounded stiff to my own ears. I wasn't sure how I was doing this, why I was still playing this off as two different people. I just wanted to end the charade, and yet the consequences of my actions remained too big for me to face. He was going to hate me so much.

"I..." I had to pause and clear my throat. "I was starving and thought pizza sounded good for lunch. Want to come with?"

"Sure," he answered, still mentioning nothing of his predicament, but I knew he was going to have to tell me...soon...if he was still trapped, anyway.

"Cool," I said. "I'll swing by and pick you up in a bit, then."

"Sounds good. But, uh, quick question first."

Great. Here it came. "Okay," I murmured, bracing for his take on what had just happened.

But after a small hesitation, all he said was, "You don't happen to have...handcuff keys, do you?"

"Um..." Damn, I wasn't ready for that question, and it was probably the most logical one for him to ask. But I didn't have the keys. I didn't even know where they could be.

"Never mind," he said suddenly. "I know I have some here. Somewhere. Could you just...come over and give me a hand?"

"Of course. I'll be there in less than twenty."

I hung up on him before he could say anything. And I made it back to his place within fifteen minutes, my mask, fake torso, and man panties firmly in place.

When I parked in front of his apartment entrance, I cursed myself again for leaving his door unlocked in my escape. His father could've just moseyed right on in and hurt him. A little scared his dad *had* beaten me here, I rushed to the door and immediately called, "Asher?"

"Down here."

Relief sagged my shoulders and I took the steps two at a time. He'd managed to use his legs to cover his lap with sheets, but I'd forgotten just how very exposed I'd left him.

But...holy damn. The boy was pure art. My mouth watered as I remembered everything we'd done together on that bed.

Except the wary way he watched me and the blush climbing his cheeks because he couldn't conceal more of himself from his gay friend shoved me back to reality.

He opened his mouth, probably to explain, but I held up a hand. "I'm not even going to ask."

The air rushed from his lungs before he gratefully murmured, "Thank you."

I nodded. "The only question I have is, where do you think the key is?"

"Fuck, I'm not sure," he muttered, sounding pissed at himself. "But it's got to be somewhere around that gift bag on the table."

I hurried to the bag that had tipped onto its side and had crinkled tissue paper spilling out the top. After burrowing through the mess, I found the box the cuffs had come in and, yes, success! Two little keys were still inside.

I tipped the box so they slid out into my palm. "Found them!"

"Thank God," he moaned as I turned toward him. But when I started toward him, this leery look crossed his features. His eyes were no longer full of trust and warmth.

It was the sharp slap of reality I needed.

"I'll only be a second," I promised as I hurriedly knelt on the mattress next to his upstretched arms and popped the key into the lock. After a small turn and click, he was free and yanking his arms down, grabbing more sheets to cover himself as he scooted away from me.

I backed off the bed to give him room. Then I watched as he closed his eyes and concentrated on breathing before he rubbed his wrists. When I realized the skin was chaffed raw, I lurched forward.

"¡Oh, Dios mío! You're hurt."

But he held up a hand, warding me off. "I'm fine," he snapped.

He so wasn't fine. He looked defeated and lost.

"So...?" I asked, not sure what he wanted me to do now.

Not sure what I *should* do. I jiggled my leg, trying to calm myself and failing.

He sighed and shook his head, not making eye contact. "So you were right. I shouldn't have gotten tangled up with your cousin Elisa."

My mouth fell open. I didn't think he'd confess that to me, and for a startled moment, I didn't know what to say. Then he lifted his face; he looked so guilty and apologetic, my own guilt and need to say sorry rose in my throat.

I shrugged one shoulder. "Well...I guess now you know."

And maybe now he'd stay away from "Elisa" for good, though the very idea made me want to weep inside.

He shook his head, frowning. "Is that all you have to say?"

I glanced at him, not sure what else I could say, unless I blurted out some big long confession. Which, of course, I didn't do.

He shook his head, obviously confused. "Aren't you pissed I went behind your back and hooked up with her anyway?"

Blowing out a long, tired breath, I shook my head. "No," I said honestly. I was actually very, very glad he'd hooked up with me, anyway. Our two nights together were going to be a few of the best memories I'd ever have. "I mean, like I said, *you're* the one I was worried about from the beginning. If you wanted to go ahead after that and take your chances anyway, it's..." Not sure how to say this or even if I *should* say anything, I mumbled, "Besides, I have a feeling you didn't...instigate it." When his eyebrows crinkled as if confused, I rolled out a hand. "I mean, I could picture you trying to stop and she just...pushed for more."

He glanced away, refusing to talk about it. Honored that he hadn't turned me into any kind of trashy locker room talk, even after what I'd just done to him, I glanced away too.

Mozart was still up in his cage, tipping his head to the side as he studied me. I wondered if he knew I was the same person from last night or not.

"If you don't want to go eat now, that's fine," I said, hoping he'd decline. I needed a couple hours away from him to get my head back on straight.

But he said, "No. Let's go. I need to get out of here for a

couple hours."

Guess he needed to clear his head as well. I wanted to ease his peace of mind more than I wanted to ease my own, so I drove him to the nearest pizza parlor because just then, I'd do anything for him.

We both ate quietly, lost in our own thoughts. He didn't talk about what he was thinking or what he planned to do about "Elisa," which I was grateful for.

When I dropped him back off at his place, he told me thanks before he climbed out of the car. Then he called me a true friend.

I felt numb after that. I couldn't do this anymore. I couldn't keep secrets, couldn't lie, couldn't lead a double life. He needed to know, and he needed it more than I needed to keep it from him.

It was going to hurt when he pushed me out of his life, but I was just going to have to deal with it. I just really, really didn't want to be there when he learned the truth, even though it would be best if he heard it from me.

Tomorrow, I promised myself. I'd call him in the morning, and I'd tell him everything.

CHAPTER 35
Asher Hart

I STILL FELT WIPED CLEAN of energy and ready to crawl back into bed to hibernate for the rest of winter when I arrived at Forbidden that evening. I really wanted to skip my shift and find Elisa. I'd stopped by her workplace, but didn't ask about her this time, not wanting to look like a total stalker. But that was the only place I knew to find her. I'd probably have to wait a couple days before going back again.

Damn it.

Yawning as I pushed through the front doors, I nodded a greeting to Harper and wondered if I could maybe play the brother card with Pick, take some time off just for tonight. But then I remembered Mason would already be absent. He'd buried his mother only two days ago, plus he had a younger sister to move into his apartment.

So, we were already shorthanded.

Bummed because nothing since the moment Elisa had crawled out of my bed this morning had gone my way, I yawned again.

"Hole-ee *shit*," Ten exploded, popping in front of me,

right in my face, so I had to jerk to a stop to keep from running into him. "Rock star finally got himself laid, huh? It's about fucking time, my man." He pounded on my shoulder in congratulations, making me scowl because I hated how he always freaking knew when I'd been with a woman.

I started to move around his annoying ass until he said, "I didn't think you'd ever figure out little drummer chick was your Incubus shirt girl. Or wait, did she finally grow a pair and just fess up?"

Pausing, I blinked at him, trying to make sense of what the hell he'd just said. Finally, I shook my head. "What?"

"What?" Ten said right back as if confused by my confusion.

"Jesus," I muttered. "I swear, you only make sense like five percent of the time. Why are you talking about Incubus shirt girl? And who the hell is little drummer chick?"

Ten's eyes flared. "Aww, shit. You didn't bang your drummer last night, did you?" Then he actually looked affronted as he demanded, "Just who the hell did you fuck?"

"None of your damn business," I growled. "Now explain yourself."

"Oh, you know." Ten shrugged and started to move away. "It's nothing. Just ignore me." But I gripped a handful of his shirt and dragged him back.

"I don't think so, fucker. Explain."

He sighed and scrubbed his face. "Jesus, I can't believe she's still too chicken shit to just *tell you*."

"Ten," I warned.

"Okay, fine," he grumbled. "It's not like it can be kept a secret forever. That drummer in your band—"

I blinked, really confused now. "*Remy*? What about him?"

"Not him," Ten said. "Her."

I squinted, not getting it. "Huh?"

"Christ on a crutch." Heaving out a disgusted breath, Ten shook his head and gazed up at the ceiling. Then he told me, "Your gay pal Remy isn't actually a gay guy at all. In fact, he's not even a guy. He's really a *she*, with tits and all that other equipment chicks come with."

I immediately opened my mouth to call bullshit, but the words didn't come. My mind spun, remembering all the times I'd thought Remy had possessed a feminine way about him, all the times he'd encouraged me to "talk," and

Jesus, the moment he'd confessed to me that he wore a mask.

Holy shit.

All these strange little pieces started to align into place until it suddenly made sense. But I still wasn't ready to completely commit to the idea. Remy couldn't be a girl. He just...*couldn't.*

Frowning, I was still trying to make sense of Ten's declaration when he up and dropped another bomb on me. "And not only is she a she, but she's also Incubus shirt girl, who you wrote that song about."

That one made me shake my head, instantly denying it. But then I had to ask, "If...if Remy's really a girl, what the hell makes you think she's *Incubus* shirt girl?"

"Because the night she sang karaoke, she sang it on stage with her friend, Jodi. And I knew Jodi then, so I asked her about her friend for you directly after their little duet that night, but all Jodi would tell me was that her friend's name was Remy."

I kept waving my head back and forth because really, I didn't even want to consider this. But had the redhead on stage with my Incubus shirt girl really been *Jodi*, Remy's roommate? I guess it could've been. I hadn't paid much attention to the redhead. Hell, I couldn't even clearly remember what the girl I'd written the song about had looked like.

"...so when Remy, your drummer, showed up here with Jodi on her arm, I put two and two together and bam, figured it all out myself. And it helped that she admitted that's who she was when I asked her, so *ha*! Pretty cleverly awesome, aren't I?"

Awesome? Awesome wasn't exactly the word I would've used. "You're pretty fucking dead is what you are," I growled right before I wound back my arm and jacked him in the face.

"Fuck," he yelled at contact, clutching his eye and swinging away from me. "What the hell, man?"

"What the hell right back at you," I roared, advancing on him so I could grab the front of his shirt and hit him again. But suddenly too many people were there, Quinn dragging me backward away from the bastard I wanted to kill and Noel helping Ten remain upright.

"How could you not tell me any of this *months* ago when

you first learned her name?" I demanded, struggling against Quinn so I could get back to Ten. "You knew how long I looked for her. You knew how much I would've given just to know her name."

Ten only sneered as he wiped his face and shook his head. "Yeah, well...payback's a bitch, isn't it?"

"What?" I had no clue what he was talking about.

"Caroline," he hissed. "You knew what she was doing when she was sneaking into my room without me knowing it was her. And you said *nothing* to me. You just kept letting me unknowingly betray my best friend on earth. Well, fuck you. You got what you deserved."

My mouth fell open as shock speared through me. I'd had no idea Ten held a grudge for that. All this time, I'd thought we were friends who teased, but now—

"What in God's name is going on out here?" Pick rushed from the back hall, followed by Knox, who must've fetched him.

Pulling free of Quinn because I no longer felt the urge to pound Ten's face in, I sniffed and motioned toward the bastard prodding at his red eye. "Ask *him*. He obviously knows more about what's going on in my life than I do."

"Ten?" Pick said, turning to him.

As Ten mumbled something in response, I wiped my hands over my mouth because I still couldn't believe what I'd just learned.

I started to whirl away, but Pick caught my arm. "Hey. Where're you going?"

I shook my head, not exactly sure myself. I just knew I needed answers, and only one person could give them to me. "I just... I gotta go."

He nodded, too much understanding and concern in his eyes. "Okay. Whatever you need. Everything all right?"

"No," I snarled and ran my hands through my hair. "I don't know. I just gotta go. I need answers."

Pick waved me off. I sent one last glance toward Ten, shocked and hurt I'd been so off about him all this time. Then I was gone.

I didn't call Remy. I wasn't sure if I could talk to him—her—right now and listen to him lie to me a second longer.

Instead, I rang Gally and coaxed Jodi's number from him with the promise that I wouldn't have sex with her.

She answered on the second ring. "Hey, who's this?"

I blew out a breath. "Hey, Jodi. It's Asher. I just tried to get hold of Remy because I have some stuff to drop by for him, but he's not answering. What's your address again?"

"Um...oh... Well, Remy's not here right now."

"That's okay," I assured her. "I can just drop it by to you if you're home, and you can give it to him when he gets there."

"Oh! Well, sure." She suddenly sounded relieved, and I narrowed my eyes because I knew she was lying to me. "In that case..." As she rattled her address off, I climbed onto my bike. "Thanks. Be there in a bit," I told her before cutting the line and starting my ride.

I made it to Remy's building in record time. After jogging up the stairs to her second-floor apartment, I drummed on the door until her roommate answered.

Jodi flashed me an uneasy smile as she poked only her head out into the hall. "Hey, sexy." Then her eyebrows crinkled as she glanced at my empty arms where I had my hands buried in my pockets. "Uh...what did you have to drop off for Remy?"

"Nothing," I answered. "I lied." Then I slid a hand from the pocket to push on her door, letting her know I was coming in.

She didn't try to stop me but stumbled backward, letting me barge right on in as she gaped at me with wide eyes. "Oh, um...*what*?"

"Is she really not here or did you lie about that too?" I asked.

Her mouth fell open. Then she whispered, "Shit. You know."

"Yeah." I nodded slowly, glancing around the place for signs that the drummer I'd come to know actually resided here. But it looked like a typical living room that anyone could live in.

So I strode to a nearby hallway and started for the first half opened door I saw.

"Um...whatcha doing?" Jodi asked, scurrying behind me and trying to keep pace.

I wasn't sure. I'd never bulldozed my way into a woman's apartment before and just started searching it. I was going at this blind, half of my conscience telling me to stop and behave, the other half needing answers.

The first doorway I peered into was a bathroom, a clearly feminine bathroom with hair products and jewelry and all kinds of girly shit splashed all over the counter, though I did spot the spray-on deodorant I'd borrowed from Remy when we'd stayed together in Chicago.

Shit. Chicago. We'd done a lot of bonding in that hotel room. And the entire time, he'd never once thought it prudent to tell me he wasn't a man.

I pushed toward the next door and reached inside to flip on a light. The breath caught in my lungs when I realized this was definitely his—*her*—room. Decorated in brilliant magenta, electric blue, and lime green colors, rock and drummer posters were splashed catawampus all over the walls. Posters of Neil Peart, posters that said "Keep Calm and Drum On," posters that said "Stick to your dreams" with a pair of drumsticks on them, pictures of bands like Metallica, Iron Maiden, Alice in Chains…Incubus.

This was so Remy's room. And yet a girl's room. I swallowed when I saw a lacy white bra on the floor at the foot of her bed.

Jesus, she really was a female.

And that's when I spotted it. A latex mask hanging from the footboard of her bed. A mask with Sticks's face on it.

I snatched it up and immediately sneezed. But instead of flinging it aside, I curled my fingers around it, holding on tight.

In the doorway, Jodi had gotten her phone and was pounding out a text.

I sniffed and shook my head. "No," I told her. "Oh, no you don't. I didn't get any fair warning about this, so neither does she."

Jodi guiltily dropped the phone to her side. "She never meant to—" she started, but I held up a hand, stopping her.

"I don't want to hear it from you. I want Remy to explain…*everything*."

Worry lit her face as she bit her lip. "What're you going to do?"

With a harsh laugh, I shook my head. "No idea."

My mind wouldn't stop spinning. I didn't think I was pissed exactly. Well, some pissed, but mostly just confused.

I couldn't figure out why…*why* would she pretend to be a guy? It didn't make any sense. And why hadn't she felt like she could tell me? I thought Sticks and I had gotten close enough that he—*she*—could confide in me the way I'd confided—

Oh, hell. I suddenly remembered all the shit I'd told her since we'd met. Most of it was probably stuff I wouldn't have admitted to a woman, like how much I love eating pussy and—oh, Jesus! I'd treated her like I would one of my guy friends, calling her fucker and loser, and asshole. Holy mother, I would never call a woman any of those names.

And then I remembered telling her about Incubus shirt girl. My head really went all over the place with that one. I'd talked to her about *her*! Why hadn't she said anything? She knew how I'd reacted to Incubus shirt girl, how I'd looked for her for months. Or, wait. *Had* she known how I'd looked for her? Maybe I hadn't mentioned that part. I'd only tried to convey how much I wanted to be over the entire ordeal, so maybe I'd made her feel as if she couldn't tell me because I'd made her believe I'd wanted nothing to do with her—as a woman.

But none of that explained why she'd gone incognito as a man in the first place.

Down the hall, the apartment door came open and someone called, "Hey, hooker. I'm home, and I come bearing food. Double chocolate fudge ice cream. You are so helping me eat this."

I blew out a breath. That was definitely Remy's voice. All my questions were about to be answered. Jodi and I silently watched each other as we listened to footsteps move to the kitchen, probably to drop off the ice cream.

Then Remy called, "Jodi? Hello? You home?"

"Uh...yeah." Jodi cast me a leery glance as if she thought I'd slit her throat or something if she answered wrong. "In your room, puta."

"What're you doing in *my* room? Doesn't matter. I'm glad you're there. You need to help me come up with a way to tell Asher—"

She rounded the corner to enter her room and gasped when she saw me, skidding to a halt and clutching her chest.

I had no idea what I'd been expecting, maybe that she'd be dressed as Sticks with the mask on, even though I held the damn mask in my hand.

But the very last thing I did expect to see was...Elisa.

My mouth fell open, my jaw worked, but no words came.

Her wild-eyed panicked gaze darted to Jodi, then back to me. When her attention fell to the mask I clutched in my hand, she turned back to her roommate.

"He already knows," Jodi whispered with a sympathetic wince.

Remy, Elisa, or whoever the hell she was, whirled back to me. "Asher..." she started softly, her eyes crinkled in apology as she took a step toward me.

I lurched backward and held up a hand, warding her off, trying to make sense of what was going on.

But, shit, fuck, hell, and damn. This changed everything. When she'd merely been a girl, masquerading as a man, that was one thing. I hadn't been too awfully mad then. But tricking me as Elisa too, deceiving me until she'd tumbled me right into bed with her...

"What the fucking hell is going on?" I demanded. "I go into work tonight and learn you're not only a girl, but THE girl I wrote a song about and had been seeking for *months*. And now I see you walk into this room, and you're *Elisa* too? Who the hell are you really?"

Oh, Jesus, I hadn't realized until that moment, I honestly didn't know her real name.

"I...I'm Remy," she answered in a small voice.

I narrowed my eyes, silently commanding her not to fuck with me right now.

She lifted both hands. "I swear. My full name's Remy Elisa Curran. Elisa is my middle name, but only my uncle at the restaurant calls me that."

"And you apparently understand English perfectly fine," I sneered. Then it hit me. *Fuck*, she knew English. She'd understood everything I'd told her when we'd been together, things I never would've admitted to a girl I'd just met.

Jesus, how the lies were piling up.

I ran my fingers through my hair, tugging at my scalp, trying to calm down, but I just...this blew my mind.

She reached out toward me, concern lacing her features. "Do you need to sit down?"

I cast her a killer glare. "No, I don't need to fucking sit down. I need a fucking explanation. *Why*?"

"I just..." Her lashes blinked rapidly, and I could see tears glaze over her eyes. Then she hugged herself and admitted, "I just wanted a chance to be in the band."

I shook my head, confused and not at all expecting that answer. "What?"

"Non-Castrato," she said. "I went to audition for the drummer spot as myself...but that bastard Galloway wouldn't even let me play one song with you guys."

My mouth fell open. "Punk rocker girl?" I whispered in horror. She was punk rocker girl too? "That was *you*?"

When she nodded, I threw my arms into the air and snorted. But of course. It was just my luck that the biggest liar on the planet would end up being all three ladies I'd been daydreaming and fantasizing about lately. Fucking perfect.

"What was up with the Tina Turner wig?" I demanded.

She shrugged and looked a little ill. "Nothing. I just thought it looked badass for the part."

The part? Yeah, she'd definitely been playing a part...all fucking month long.

"How many other secret identities do you have?"

She shook her head and bowed her face. "That's it." When I sniffed, she looked up, scowling. "It *is*!"

"Whatever." I rolled my eyes and ran my hands through my hair, trying to straighten everything in my muddled head. "So you made up 'Sticks,' the gay male drummer, to get into the band—" I broke off abruptly to wince because it suddenly struck me...Sticks didn't exist. All the rounds of Call of Duty we'd played, the teasing, songwriting together, all the shit he'd helped me with and times he had my back. I recalled the night in Chicago when he—*she'd*—been ready to defend me with nothing but mace and a whistle, and an arrow of pain passed through me. Sticks, my friend, was gone forever.

And why the hell hadn't it thumped me right over the head that mace and a whistle were the classic rape preventatives—*lady* protection. I was such a fucking dumbass. How many times she must've laughed over my idiotic cluelessness.

I narrowed my eyes on her as she said, "I actually didn't even mean to join the band. I was just so pissed after you wouldn't listen to me; I planned on ripping off the mask afterward and telling you, ha, a woman could play drums just as well as a man could. But then you went and invited me to play with you guys *that* Friday. I'd never played in front of an audience before. I wanted to know what it was like. And then that very night, we got the gig for Chicago and you sounded so excited, I couldn't let you down and tell you I was a girl then. What if Gally kicked me out and you'd never gotten to go to Chicago?"

"Oh, so this was all to help *me*?" I snarled.

She flushed and let out a small sigh. "Of course not. But it did contribute to the reason I didn't tell you immediately, until I passed the point that I could tell you without causing a huge ordeal, and then I was just too afraid to...because I knew you'd react *this way*."

This way? So she thought I was overreacting, huh? I rolled my eyes. Nice. "Where does Incubus shirt girl fit into all this?" I had to know.

She blinked, confused. "She doesn't."

When I only lifted an eyebrow, telling her to try again, she gritted her teeth and growled out a sound. "I didn't even know that song existed until after I joined the band, and Ten told me about it."

I growled. Fucking Ten. "But you knew it was about you?"

She cringed. "After I read the lyrics, I knew it was a distinct possibility I was that girl, yes."

"Un-fucking-believable."

I wiped my hands over my face and had to spin away because it was so hard to look at her and not see Elisa, not remember every detail of everything we'd done in my bed.

"I can vouch for that part," Jodi spoke up. "She really had no clue she was the girl in your song until—"

I whirled to glare at her, promptly shutting her up. "You know..." She hooked her thumb over her shoulder as she backed toward the doorway. "I'm just going to leave you two alone to hash this out." And she shot out of the room.

I glanced at Remy, who seemed to shrink smaller into herself as if she expected me to physically attack her.

I'd been inside this woman, seen her naked, touched her, tasted her, had the best sex of my life with her. I'd dreamed of some kind of future with her and had actually thought we'd been starting something big.

But it'd all been a lie.

I wasn't sure if I bought her story about Incubus shirt girl, but I figured she was going to stick to her tale, so I proceeded to the issue that meant the most to me...and hurt the most to ask about. "And Elisa?" I whispered.

Tears filled her eyes as she shook her head. "You were never supposed to meet her. You weren't supposed to return to the hotel room for your wallet and discover her in your shower. You weren't supposed to go to Castañeda's and see her at work. And you were never supposed to take her home with you. I told you—dammit—did I or did I not warn you to stay away from her?"

I snorted and shook my head. "A little hypocritical of you, don't you think, since you *are* her? Why didn't you just fucking pull away when I first kissed you?"

Her mouth fell open as if that was the most ridiculous question anyone had ever asked her. "Have you *met* you?" she cried. "You're freaking amazing. No hetero woman in her right mind could even remotely resist all that."

When she waved her hand to encompass me from head to toe, I hissed out a harsh laugh. "Right."

"I'm serious." Her face fell as she watched me, as if she knew then that no matter what she said, everything between us was over. "The last thing I wanted to do was fall for you. Hell, after one dipshit lead singer of a band crushed my faith in men altogether, I fully expected to despise you. But then I got to know you, and I...well, it's just a testament of how amazing you are to break through the stereotype I'd set up against you, and you actually got me to *like* you."

"Well then it must suck to be you, because right now, I'm not very fond of you in return. Jesus, I actually don't even know a goddamn thing about you. You're a complete fucking stranger to me."

"Asher," she whispered, pressing her fist to her chest as a couple of tears slid down her cheek. I hated to see her cry, but the tightness in my own chest made it impossible for me to go to her and try to soothe her. She was breaking my damn heart here.

"You *do* know me," she entreated. "You know everything there is to know about me. Everything I told you when I was Sticks, that was all me."

"Except that you're not really a man, you're not really gay, and oh yeah...you understand English perfectly. Jesus." I gripped my hair. "How many times did you *laugh* at me because I was too stupid to figure it out myself?"

"Never," she swore, shaking her head adamantly. "I never once laughed at you."

"I'll bet," I muttered. "I treated you like a guy. Jostled and joked, called you things I'd never call a woman."

Remy hugged herself. "I didn't mind. It let me know we were friends."

"Yeah," I murmured, nodding in agreement. "We *were*. You'd probably become one of the closest friends I'd ever had. And you just...you just took that away from me. Then you walked through this doorway and let me know Elisa, the one woman who rocked my world, doesn't exist either."

"No." She shook her head some more. "They both still exist. Sticks and Elisa are still here." She tapped her hands against her chest. "They're just one person now. It's just Remy."

This time it was my turn to shake my head and say, "No. The only person I'm looking at is a fucking liar."

I turned away to storm out the door when she called, "Wait! What about tomorrow?"

I paused and glanced back, frowning. "*What*?"

"It's Friday. The band," she reminded me. "We're supposed to play at Forbidden."

Shit. And to top everything else, she'd just broken up my band, too. "Oh, you're not in the band anymore," I announced in a soft voice.

Devastation lit her gaze, but she nodded respectfully. "And Sunday? You still need someone to deejay at Pick's wedding."

Damn it. I clutched my temples as a headache began. How the hell had she became so essential in just a few short weeks? I didn't have time to find Pick a new deejay and I didn't trust anyone else to work the sound system the way I trusted Sticks...aka, *her*.

"If you're still willing, Pick needs you," I managed to grit out reluctantly, wishing I could tell her to fuck off instead. But I couldn't do that to my brother, who was counting on someone to play "Baby Love" for him to dance to with Eva.

She nodded. "Of course I'll still do it."

I gave my own grateful nod before glaring and growling, "Just stay out of my way and don't fucking talk to me there. In fact, if I never see you again after Sunday, it'll be too soon."

Tears filled her eyes, but she nodded her understanding and acceptance.

Unable to stick around a second longer, I lit out of there, practically running from the building until I reached my apartment. I hissed a curse when I realized I'd forgotten to lock my place before leaving for work earlier...because I'd been too occupied with thoughts of finding Elisa.

Well, I'd found her. And I wished I hadn't.

My phone alerted me to a text message from Pick, but I couldn't answer it right now. Cursing aloud, I kicked my wall and then slapped all the things off my kitchen table, one of them being the gift bag that had once held the hand-cuffs I used with—

"Motherfucker," I roared. Then I spotted my notebook of lyrics and had to fling that across the room too. The song I'd written with her suddenly felt like one big joke.

Acid coated my tongue. I couldn't believe she'd deceived me so completely.

I sneered at the Call of Duty box on my coffee table and wanted to shred it with my bare hands. Snatching it up, I flung it across the room until it hit Mozart's cage, clanging against the metal wire.

"Shit. Sorry, Mozart," I said.

But when I checked on my pet, I frowned. Mozart wasn't in his cage. And the door to free him hung wide open. I blinked, knowing I hadn't let him out. With everything I'd been doing with Elisa these past few days, I hadn't had the time to let him run free since probably Monday.

"Mozart?" I said. Even though I knew he wouldn't be in there, I checked every inch of all his cages. Then I whirled to the bed, his favorite hidey-hole. "Mozart," I called, getting down on my hands and knees to look under the mattress. The only thing under there was a few stored nuts.

I damn near tore the place apart, but the only thing I knew for sure after an hour of searching was that my squirrel was gone.

CHAPTER 36
Remy Curran

Shattered is a mild word for what I'd felt after Asher walked out of my room. I'd been defeated before, cheated on and betrayed by a man I was going to marry, crushed when my mother lost her mind and abandoned me, left to feel like an outsider at most every family reunion I attended because I wasn't exactly like them. I was used to not getting what I wanted.

Yet somehow this felt worse, because this time I knew I deserved it. I had one hundred percent caused this, and every decision I'd made in the last month had led to this very moment. It sucked that my one stint in a band had ended this way, but what hurt the most had been watching the pained expression on Asher's face as he became increasingly aware of just how much I'd lied to him.

I don't think I'd ever hurt anyone like that before.

It killed me.

Jodi tried to console me.

Didn't help.

Then she tried her buck-up, stop-whining-and-get-back-on-that-horse approach.

That didn't work either.

I wasn't even interested in the ice cream she tried to hand-feed me.

Finally, she gave up completely and left me alone to mope in my bed, under the covers, with a handful of tissues that I went through in, like, two minutes.

I don't think anyone in life started a story, thinking they were going to come out the villain. They just knew they had a goal to conquer and they tried to reach it. I didn't even have a worthy goal, though. No one's life to save, no struggle for justice or freedom. I'd just been plain selfish, wanting to feel as if I had a place in a band. And yet, when I'd done anything and everything to reach that dream, I'd ended up trampling all over another dream I wasn't even aware was so much better...until it was too late.

At some point, Asher must've alerted Heath and Gally to the fact that we would not be playing at Forbidden the next night, and why, because the texts started pouring in around midnight.

Most were from Gally.

You're a fucking chick? What the fuck?

Way to break up the band, bitch.

Just wanted to be the next Yoko Ono, didn't you?

And the last one: *Hey, if you're hot, wanna hook up?*

The only one I received from Heath said, *THIS was why it was a bad reason to have a girl in the band.*

So I cried a little more because I'd ruined things for all the guys. At some point, I slept, but only to wake up a few hours later and return to my pity party before passing out again. My head throbbed and my eyes felt nearly swollen shut when I stumbled out of bed the next morning. Pulling my hair into a sloppy mess on the top of my head with stray dark strands dangling everywhere, I padded barefoot into the kitchen, wearing nothing but a sleep top and shorts under a quickly yanked-on half-robe.

I wasn't hungry, wasn't even really thirsty, but I was tired of being in my room, so I made myself a hot chocolate. As I was sipping it and exiting the kitchen, the door to Jodi's room opened down the hall and footsteps approached.

Expecting to see my roommate, I opened my mouth to give her a halfhearted greeting, but she wasn't the person who exited the hall. Eyes flaring wide, I yelped, "What the hell?"

Gally snickered at me, his gaze going to my bare exposed legs. "So you're the real Sticks, huh? Looks like you need to put your mask back on, sweetheart." Then he strolled out, all smug and disgusting.

His words still stung, so my hand flew self-consciously to my face, knowing I must look like hell after the night I'd had.

When Jodi's bedroom door opened again, I gritted my teeth. "I can't believe you brought that asshole here into *our* apartment last night. He's such a—*Heath*?"

As yet another member of Non-Castrato exited the hallway, my mouth dropped open. If my jaw hadn't been attached, it would've fallen so far it bounced off the floor. "Wha...how...huh?" I sputtered.

He flushed a bright crimson, but then nodded respectfully to me before hurrying toward the door and fleeing.

I gaped after him, totally not understanding.

Moments later, Jodi wandered into the front room, groaning over sore muscles and stretching as she let out a big, satisfied yawn. "Mmm...morning."

I could only stare at her as she passed by me and entered the kitchen. Turning, I followed. "Jodi?" I finally said in a low voice as I watched her brew her own steaming cup.

"Yeah?" she asked, her back to me as she worked. "You finally ready to let me cheer you up?"

"What? No. Uh...I'd rather it if you explained why both Gally *and* Heath just came strolling out of your bedroom?"

"Sure." She whirled around with a bright smile, before cringing and saying, "Oh, puta. You look like hell. You really need to shower and do something with your face."

Clenching my teeth, I muttered, "Focus, woman. Gally and Heath."

"Oh, right. Well, they kept fighting over me, so..." She shrugged. "I just taught them how to share."

The few sips of hot chocolate I'd just drunk swirled evilly in my stomach, threatening to come back up. "Eww," I said, trying not to picture the image she'd shoved into my head, and yet unable to *not* picture it.

Dumping my hot chocolate into the sink, I retreated to my room to cry some more. Not sure why seeing my roommate with two guys I didn't even want for myself spurred more tears in me, but I felt wretched and selfish enough that when Jodi stopped by to check on me a few minutes later, I was unresponsive and bitter because she hadn't halted anything in her life to be there for me, despite how she'd actually tried to do just that.

She sighed over my pathetic state and then was gone again, leaving me alone in the apartment, and I couldn't help but think how Asher wouldn't have given up on Sticks so easily if he'd been this depressed. He would've stuck around no matter what.

Which made me cry...again because I'd lost the best friend I could've ever had.

I wasn't sure how much time passed after that, but I was half out of it when someone knocked on my front door.

Thinking it might be Asher, I lurched out of bed, then almost passed out when the blood rushed so fast to my head. Taking a second to catch my bearings, I patted my face and hair, then thought *screw it* and raced to the door, flinging it open.

"Holy shit," Ten gasped, pulling back. "Is *that* what you look like as a woman?"

"Hey, give her a break," Caroline scolded, appearing from behind him. "No one could look presentable after the night she must've had. How're you doing, honey?"

I shook my head, squinting, trying to figure out why I was seeing them. Finally, I had the wherewithal to ask, "What're you two doing here?"

"Oren kind of fucked up with Asher last night too, so we're here to pow-wow with you and figure out how to get the both of you back into his good graces again."

I sniffed, wiped at my face and glanced at Ten. "So you messed up too, huh?"

He blew out a disgusted sigh before admitting, "Yep. I had to go and bring up an old issue that doesn't even bother me anymore...just because I could."

"Is that why you have a black eye?"

Nodding, he repeated, "Yep."

"Boys," Caroline muttered, taking my shoulders and getting a good look at my face. "They think hitting each other solves everything."

"Well, it usually does," Ten argued from behind her.

His wife ignored him as she clucked her tongue and said,

"First things first, we're getting you cleaned up. You won't be able to think straight until you feel human again."

"Fuck yeah." Ten rubbed his hands together greedily as he stepped inside and shut the door behind him. "My woman getting into a shower with another chick; this is going to be awesome to watch."

"You'll be staying out here," Caroline warned him with an arch of her eyebrows. "And besides, I'm sure she'll be able to wash herself." Then she turned to me and bit her lip. "Won't you?"

When I nodded, Ten mumbled a curse and called us the dirty equivalent of party poopers before plopping onto the couch and picking up the remote.

Caroline ushered me back to the bathroom and then gathered some clothes for me to change into before she started the shower and left me to finish by myself.

On autopilot, I washed, and surprisingly, I did feel a little better when I was done. I wiped a little lotion onto my face, combed out my hair and stepped from the bathroom, human once more.

The married couple looked up when I stepped into the front room. Ten's eyebrows shot up into his hairline. "Well, holy shit, what a difference a little shower makes."

"Oh, stop it." Caroline slugged him in the arm before popping to her feet and coming to me. "Do you feel better?"

I shrugged.

Cooing out her sympathy, she took my hand and led me back to the couch so I could sit between her and her man. I kind of thought I was supposed to be mad at her for the way she'd shoved me and Asher together on Tuesday night. But then...Jodi had said it right. Caroline hadn't been the one to shove his penis inside me. I could've stopped it myself at any point.

"So," she started, turning to face me as she tucked one leg under her. "We're both here to help you get Asher back. Me because I feel like pushing you two together at the restaurant the other night only made things worse, and Oren because...well—"

"Because I'll have a better chance of being forgiven for being an ass to him if he's getting some from you."

I blinked at his crude summation, but basically understood where he was coming from regardless. Then I shook my head. "No...we're not...Asher's not going to forgive me for this. I don't stand a chance in hell with him."

"Nonsense." Ten waved out a hand as if my predicament were no big deal. "Just sex him up good enough, and he'll forgive you anything."

"*Sex*," I snarled, scowling at him, "is how I got myself into this mess in the first place. If I'd just been able to keep my damn hands *off* him, I might've actually, maybe, *eventually* gotten him to forgive me." But no, I just couldn't keep my legs together, could I?

"Whatever." Ten snorted. "Sex solves everything with a guy."

"I don't know," Caroline murmured, chewing on her lip thoughtfully. "This is Asher we're talking about. Not you."

With a groan, her husband relented. "You're right. Hart's not normal." Then he flopped back deeper into the couch as if he had no more ideas.

"I know!" Caroline suddenly cried, sitting up straighter. She whirled to me and grasped my hands. "How did you draw his attention in the first place?"

I furrowed my brow, thinking about the day I'd auditioned as Sticks, but Caroline answered her own question, saying, "Your voice. When you sang on stage that first karaoke night."

I looked at her and suddenly knew exactly what she had in mind.

CHAPTER 37
Asher Hart

EVEN THOUGH THE BAND didn't play, I worked Friday night, needing something to do, not wanting to be home at my overly quiet apartment. I never found Mozart, and he never showed up at my door. When I saw a dead squirrel on the road on the way to Forbidden, I told myself that wasn't him. He'd found a nice, safe park somewhere and was living out his dream, collecting nuts and climbing trees.

I still missed the hell out of him, though.

On Saturday, I showed up to work extra early, even though it was another miserable karaoke night. At the moment, I kind of felt as if I could go about the rest of my life without ever hearing another karaoke song played ever again.

But unlucky me, about half a dozen ladies lined up first thing to sing "All About That Bass," every one of them wearing Incubus shirts, too. I hated it. It sucked even more so tonight, now that I knew who Incubus shirt girl actually was.

I was about to go out of my mind as yet another woman finished the song. It was on the tip of my tongue to tell

Quinn and Knox I was going to head into the back and check our supplies when a familiar voice spoke over the speaker system.

"So I've been watching a couple of you try to imitate my original performance."

I whipped around to see Remy—in tight blue jeans, a black snug Incubus shirt, and a guitar strapped over her shoulder with her long hair flowing down her back.

"And I must say, some of you..." She cringed and leaned closer to the mike. "Really suck."

A lot of boos and catty comebacks rolled back, but she ignored them as she smiled at the crowd as if oblivious. "If you were curious, the exact Incubus shirt I was wearing that night looked like this." She tugged at the sides of her shirt to display it. "Oh and the redhead who sang was with me... Right there." She motioned toward the stairs up to the stage where Jodi was standing.

Jodi waved and blew kisses to everyone as Remy seated herself on a stool and positioned her guitar into her lap. "Now, I'm not going to sing 'All About That Bass' tonight because...well, Asher's sick of hearing it, for one. And also, it'd just feel tacky to recreate my original show. So I'm going to play something a little different, and since this place doesn't have karaoke music for this particular song, I brought my guitar to help me out."

She patted the side of her Taylor—shit, she had a Taylor, too—and then began to strum. Perfectly.

"I didn't know your girlfriend could play the guitar *and* drums," Quinn said from beside me as he watched Remy begin to sing "Green Eyes" by Coldplay.

"She's not my girlfriend," I murmured, my voice hoarse. "But yeah, apparently she's just *full* of little surprises, isn't she?" Because I'd had no idea she could play either.

But she played amazingly well.

My gaze was glued to the stage, and I had no idea what I felt as her clear voice sang shit like *I was her sea*, but it made all the air inside my chest compress until I could barely breathe.

They were just words, I told myself, steeling myself against the sweetness of her attempt to get my attention. Lyrics of someone else's song that meant nothing to me, like she wasn't supposed to mean anything to me. I didn't even *know* her.

Still. I couldn't believe she was up there singing...for me. Trying to beg my forgiveness.

Sure, other women had been singing "All About That Bass" to me for months. But this was Remy. That made all the difference.

Except I started thinking about every confidence I'd shared with her, how I'd poured my heart out to her and she'd only lied in return. The bitterness of that deception warred against the part of me that was melting and wanted to forgive her.

I turned away as she finished the song, glad it was over— no more mental war to keep me away. But then she went and said, "Oh, no. Sorry, honey, but I'm setting up my own little filibuster of sorts. I'm staying right here and singing until the message I'm trying to deliver reaches the ears I want to hear it. I'm not leaving this stage until Asher Hart himself comes up here and *makes* me."

I whirled around to glare at her just as she shooed away the three women who were trying to take their turn next. When she turned back to the crowd, her gaze caught mine and she winked with this knowing smile, as if she knew she was getting to me.

I hated that she knew me so well, so I scowled back, setting my hands on my hips to show her I was not amused.

But she blissfully ignored me as she started in on "The Reason" by Hoobastank, where she told me she was sorry she'd hurt me and wished she could take all my pain away.

For a minute, I stared, captivated by her beauty and her voice, by the words she was telling me. Then I remembered how she'd purposely made me think she hadn't known English and I began to wonder what the hell she was doing here, trying to torture me with her presence when the chorus came up, and it finally became clear.

She really thought singing was going to just...get me back.

"Fuck," I muttered as her gaze found mine and held on. I narrowed my eyes ominously, but she just kept singing, so I whirled away, mumbling something to Quinn before I high-tailed it from behind the bar and down the back hall. Once I reached the storage room, I paced and cursed under my breath, commanding myself not to be affected.

After a couple minutes, I eased open the door to see if a

new song had started yet. I breathed easier when I realized it had, but then...I heard her voice. She was still up there, this time singing "Please Forgive Me" by Bryan Adams.

Christ. There were a lot of fucking apology songs; she might just keep her word and sing all night.

If I didn't stop this now, I might end up doing something really stupid, like forgiving her.

So I marched out into the bar, determined. When I caught sight of Pick sitting on a stool, watching her performance, I stopped by him.

"Are you going to do something or not?" I demanded.

He turned to me, eyebrows lifted in surprise. Then he shrugged. "You heard the woman. The only person getting her off that stage tonight is you."

I opened my mouth to tell him it was his damn bar; he could kick her out if he wanted to, but then he grinned. "Besides, I already gave her permission to sing the whole night if she wanted to."

"Oh, you fucker," I breathed. "No wonder you're still here so late on the night before your wedding. You knew she was going to be here and you just wanted to see me suffer, didn't you?"

Pick scowled. "No, I do not want to see you *suffer*. I wanted to watch my brother make amends with someone who's been a good friend to him this past month and made him very happy in the process. And *she* apparently has."

I wanted to argue. But I couldn't stop remembering all the good times Remy and I'd had together...as both Sticks *and* Elisa.

"She isn't—" I started to tell him she wasn't the same person who'd befriended me. *Sticks* had been my friend. Except she was supposed to be Sticks now. I wasn't sure how I felt about that. But the irritation brewing inside me kind of took over.

I marched toward the stage.

Her eyes lit up with hope when she saw me approaching. But I didn't smile back or give her anything to hang that hope on. I turned my gaze away and focused on the karaoke station. After I called up the song I wanted, I hopped on the stage, and tugged the microphone from her startled fingers.

She blinked at me, frowning slightly even as a smile lingered on her face. She thought I was going to sing something about forgiving her. But instead, Taylor Swift's "Bad Blood" came on. And I sang it directly at her.

Her mouth came open as shock flooded her features.

About the fourth time I told her we had problems and couldn't solve them, she puffed up her chest with an annoyed scowl and hurried off the stage. I watched, thinking that was that, but she only paused at the karaoke machine and picked something else from the list.

I didn't want to be, but I was curious what she'd chosen.

So when Elton John's "Sorry Seems to Be the Hardest Word," broke over Taylor's voice and Remy stole the microphone right back from me to sing the lyrics, I shook my head. Stubborn-ass woman just didn't know when to give up, did she?

So I chased her lyrics with "Better Things to Do" by Terri Clark.

For some reason, I expected more angry determination from her. I was kind of getting into the game, relishing the back and forth and impatient to hear what she'd come up with next.

But sadness crept into her gaze as she watched me sing and listened to the bitter phrases come from my mouth. Shoulders falling with defeat, she nodded her understanding and hurried off the stage. As about twenty women cheered, Remy fled. She bumped into Jodi after a few steps, then grabbed her friend's arm and hurried from the club.

Strangely disappointed even though I didn't want to forgive her, I shook my head and stepped away from the microphone, no longer in the mood to sing. Then I hopped off stage and stormed through swarms of people until I found myself back in the storage room, pacing until the door opened, and Pick slipped inside.

I ground my teeth and shook my head, in no way willing to talk about this. "Shouldn't you be home with Eva and the kids?"

"Nope." He leaned his hip against a nearby keg. "Tinker Bell wanted to be traditional so she kicked me out. Said I wasn't allowed to see her again until the wedding." He shrugged. "It seemed like a bad time to bug Mason and Reese and beg a night on their couch, so I'd planned on renting a motel room... unless you want to take your big brother in for a couple hours."

I shrugged. "Sure. My couch isn't anything to write

home about, but...whatever."

"Thank you." Pick nodded and watched me pace and re-peatedly run my hands through my hair before murmuring, "So...Remy."

"I don't want to talk about it," I snapped, glaring at him.

He only grinned. "She pulled off a pretty good disguise. I had no idea she was really a woman. And wow, she looks...really different *as* a woman. There's no reason for you to feel like an idiot and think you should've figured it out sooner. No one else caught on either."

"I didn't say I felt like an idiot," I muttered.

But Pick lifted his eyebrows so I sighed, relenting. "Fine. I feel like a fucking idiot. But I'm also pissed. She lied to me, fucking betrayed me for weeks. It's like she made a joke of everything I ever told her. I thought I was actually making a friend, and she was just playing dress-up so she could be in a goddamn band." I couldn't even go into the deception she'd played as Elisa because....I just couldn't.

Pick opened his mouth, but I was sure he was going to say something in her defense, so I kept ranting, "And now...*now* she thinks she can just stroll in here, wiggle her hips and sing a few songs, and I'll, what, just forget what she did to me? Fuck no. I'm not getting back together with her. I don't even *know* her."

Smiling slightly, Pick said, "But don't you?"

I started to tell him, no, I didn't. Except I just couldn't. Maybe I had learned a couple things about her. I'm sure the female version of her was just as competitive as Sticks had been. She was definitely musically talented, had good taste in songs, liked to tease and get people's goat about as much as I did. Hell, she might just be the perfect person...if she hadn't hurt me so bad.

"I assume she gave you a reason for doing what she did," Pick spoke up, making me blink because I'd forgotten he was there.

I sniffed and glanced away. "She gave me something."

"But you don't believe the reason she gave?"

"I don't know." I set my hands on my hips and gazed up at the ceiling, torn.

I kind of did believe her reasons for why she'd started this entire charade because honestly, why else would she have dressed up as a guy? It couldn't have been to get close to me after learning she was Incubus shirt girl, since she would've had a lot more luck getting anything from me if she'd stayed female. But still, after a while of getting to know me, why hadn't she figured out I didn't care if she was a girl in the band; I would've fought Gally and Heath to keep her on board?

Even that lack of her faith in me hurt.

A few feet away, Pick murmured, "If you love someone enough, you find you can forgive them for just about anything, because living without them is more miserable than any grudge you could hold."

I glanced at him, but that was apparently all the sage advice he had to offer. Pushing away from the keg, he patted me on the shoulder and departed the stockroom to let me stew in peace.

Fucker, I wanted to call after him. How dare he even bring the word love into this? I didn't love Remy. I didn't even *know* her. But even as I told myself that, my brain called up all the times we'd laughed and bickered over Call of Duty.

The night we'd shared corn nuts and written a song together.

The time she'd picked me up after my bike problems and how she worried about my dad, and how she'd driven me to Mason's when I hadn't been in the right frame of mind.

Making love to her two glorious nights in a row.

I did know her. And I'd liked her.

Plus I missed her.

When I returned behind the bar to actually work, I was no longer pissed, but I still wasn't sure what I was. Pick had planted a seed in my head and the damn thing was growing.

Could I forgive her?

Could I go back to being just her friend as I'd been with Sticks?

Could I be her lover again? My body stirred at that idea, but I quickly pushed those thoughts aside, because I wasn't sure of my answers. The biggest conundrum was...

Could I live without her?

When a couple approached the counter to order drinks, I didn't pay much attention to them. They murmured lovey-dovey shit to each other in Spanish, making me curl my lip with irritation, reminding me how Remy had used Spanish to keep me from figuring out how familiar her voice was as

Elisa.

But then the guy said something like, "Eres mi nena, mi chica. Te amo," and I paused, squinting at him.

Te amo?

Remy had said that to me...a lot, as Elisa. But she'd—as Sticks—told me it meant good job, while the guy who was gazing at his lady love didn't seem to be telling her she'd done a good job. Before I knew what I was doing, I moved back to them.

"Excuse me." When they both looked up, I shook my head. "Did you just say *te amo* to her?"

The man scowled. "What?"

"What does *te amo* mean?"

He stared at me as if I was insane for even asking while the woman giggled and cuddled against his side, wrapping her arms around his one arm. "It means I love you," she said.

The breath felt knocked from my lungs as I stumbled a step back, gaping at her.

I hadn't been expecting her to say that. It just...my mind was too blown to form a proper thought.

Nodding in thanks, I spun away, and I think maybe I fixed their drinks for them, but I don't really recall doing it.

The rest of that night kind of passed in a blur. I couldn't seem to concentrate on anything except the fact that *te amo* meant *I love you*.

CHAPTER 38
Asher Hart

On Sunday afternoon, I stood beside Pick and watched him marry the love of his life in the back reception room of the Forbidden Nightclub. I guess he'd first met her in this building, just as I'd learned he was my brother here, and I'd first seen Remy on stage here.

Life felt as if it had truly begun the day I'd stepped foot inside this place. I'd laughed a lot here, made lifelong friends, formed a family of sorts, and yet...at the moment, it was the last place I wanted to be.

As soon as we walked out of this room and down the hall into the main part of the bar where the reception would take place, I knew I'd see her. I was sure she was already here, setting up the sound system, making sure everything was ready to go. She was dependable like that, or at least the Sticks version of her had been.

And what do you know, as soon as the I do's were over and the wedding party moved from the ceremony to the after-party, there she was in a dark dress that hugged her curves as she brushed her hair out of her face while she bent over the soundboard.

When someone paused next to me and slugged me companionably on the back, I glanced over, shocked to find Ten staring at Remy too. He heaved in a great sigh. "Yeah, I'd probably cave and forgive that too," he said before glancing at me and arching an eyebrow, "just like you're going to forgive me for being an ass the other night. *Right*?"

I shook my head and laughed a little over his form of apology. Besides, the brightness of his black eye helped me get over it a lot. "Nothing to forgive, man," I told him. "Like you said, we're even now."

His shoulders eased, but then he nodded. "Fuck yeah. As long as you stop flirting with Caroline just to annoy me."

"Oh, hell, no. What would be the fun in that?" When I caught sight of his wife nearby, watching us, I motioned her forward so I could sling an arm around her waist and cuddle her into my side. "Hey there, beautiful. Why don't you give the best man a little sugar?"

With a grin, Caroline pressed her lips to my jaw and hugged me closer before Ten growled and pulled her away. "Okay. Enough, asshole." Then he pointed at me and scowled. "That's it, you're on my shit list again."

I laughed, glad we were really back to being friends. Then I turned and caught sight of Remy next to the stage, watching me interact with Caroline and Ten. My grin died and lungs expanded tight against my ribcage. But then someone nudged her arm, taking her attention away from me, and I had to scowl at the big guy standing at the sound system with her.

Who the fuck was he?

I wasn't jealous. Fuck no. But I might've curled my hands into fists as he shifted closer to her. Too close.

As Remy answered him, her hands moving with a flourish, I found myself wandering toward them, unable to stay away.

She didn't see me approach—her back was still to me as she rattled off shit in Spanish to the guy. But he caught sight of me, and his glancing at me over her shoulder made her turn to look as well.

She yelped when our gazes met. Pressing her hand against her heart, she lurched backward and right into the chest of the big guy, who clasped her arm to steady her. When my gaze went to his hand on her, she breathed out my name. "Asher! Uh, what're you doing over here? I was supposed to stay away from you."

I looked into her wide, worried brown eyes. When I didn't say anything but shifted my attention to the guy with his hand still on her arm, she cleared her throat and stepped away from him so she could introduce him.

"This, uh, this is my cousin Tomás. Big T. He's agreed to be my assistant tonight. You might remember him. He played the guitar at Castañeda's when you were there and I sang..." She didn't bother to finish the explanation, as if she feared the reminder would pique my temper.

I nodded to Tomás, refusing to believe it was relief ballooning in my chest as my tensed muscles relaxed. "How's it going?"

He sent me a head bob in return. "¿Qué pasa?"

Forgetting him, I turned back to Remy. "What's wrong?"

Her eyebrows shot up. "Wrong? Why do you think anything's wrong?" She darted her cousin a quick glance before she turned back to me. Then she sniffed as if my question were completely ridiculous. "We're fine. Go back to your friends and have fun." She even nudged my arm to get me to move along. "I'm sure they hate me enough already without me hogging any of your time away from them."

I resisted her nudging. "What makes you think they hate you?"

"Well..." Her brow knit with confusion. "*You* hate me, so wouldn't they hate me too, in loyalty to you? Besides, I also lied to them about who I really was. It seems only logical."

I opened my mouth to tell her I didn't hate her. But then stopped myself. *Was* I supposed to hate her after telling her I never wanted anything to do with her again, after publically rejecting her the way I had last night?

An uncomfortable feeling slithered up my spine. Uncertainty and guilt mixed with longing. As much as I wanted to hold on to my anger and hurt, I really couldn't outright hate her. Had I been too hasty to completely turn her away? Damn it, I didn't like this sensation of wanting to be closer to her and yet not trusting anything I wanted.

So I settled with telling her, "They don't hate you. If anything, they're rooting for you and think I should forgive you already."

"Really?" Her face lit with excitement as she brought her hands to her chest and glanced across the bar. "Aww...I love your friends. You know, you should listen to them. They have your best interest at heart."

I couldn't help it, I cracked a smile. But then I faltered. Damn it. I didn't want to be charmed by her. Remy had betrayed me in one of the most embarrassing, demeaning ways possible. Curling my grin into a snarl, I said, "Stop changing the subject. What's really wrong?"

She scowled back and made a sound of frustration. "Seriously, how could you tell anything was wrong?"

Because I'd seen Sticks distressed before, and Remy was showing similar behavior now. "What's wrong?" I repeated.

Her shoulders deflated as she scowled at me and reluctantly admitted, "I can't get the sound system to turn on."

My brows furrowed. "Have you tried the main power switch?"

I usually kept it on because it had a sleep mode, and I didn't recall turning it off last night after karaoke, but I didn't remember much from last night, and with my forgetfulness...anything was possible.

As I reached for the switch, Remy scowled. "Oh, gee. Why didn't I think of that idea? *Yes*, I flipped the damn power switch!"

I grinned because her response was so typical Sticks. It made me miss my friend. But my grin fell when the system didn't respond to my command.

"And the plug-in," I started, only to stop when Remy sent me a glare. "Of course you checked to make sure it was plugged in," I answered for her, checking the cord anyway. "Maybe the connection came loose at the other end or something."

I had a feeling she'd already checked the connections at the other end as well because she sighed and folded her arms over her chest as she watched me grasp the plugged-in end and follow the cord to—shit.

The cord came off in my hand, the rest of it...not there.

"Holy fuck," Remy murmured in surprise, leaping forward to see the neatly cut wire I held. "Okay, *that* I did *not* see." I looked up into her shocked eyes as she shook her head as if apologizing for missing it. Then she gasped. "Omigod, you don't think I did this, do you?"

"What?" I shook my head, not expecting that conclusion at all. "No."

Her shoulders fell with relief. "Good, because I totally didn't." Then a thought struck her because her forehead crinkled as she studied the cut cord. "You know, this is just like the fuel line to your motorcycle, cut neatly in two." Eyebrows lifting, letting me know she had another conspiracy theory brewing in her head, she pointed. "Someone is clearly out to mess with you. I still think it's your dad."

I sighed. Yes, she was definitely Sticks in there, paranoid about my old man and everything. "How is this out to get *me*?" I lifted the cord. "This was done clearly against *Pick*."

Oh, shit. Pick. He needed music at his reception, or he was going to flip out because his vision of dancing with Eva to "Baby Love" wouldn't happen. We needed music. Fast.

"But Pick is *your* brother." Remy seemed determined to argue with me. "And he's like..." She waved out a hand. "Close to you now. The worst way to hurt you would be for someone to go after the ones you loved, right? And Pick is about the only person you really love, isn't he?"

The question made me pause. I did love Pick, didn't I? And I'd loved Mozart, who was now gone, and I was more certain now than ever that I hadn't left his cage open. But were those really the only two people I loved? My gaze traveled to Remy's concerned brown eyes, and I couldn't answer.

"Not that it really matters who cut the damn cord right now," her cousin spoke up, making me blink back to reality, "Because we have other problems, like how're we going to get this party started? Is there another kind of speaker around here? I can run home and get my guitar if I need to."

I glanced at him, my mind racing. He, Remy, and I might just be able to pull out a quick band, but then Remy snapped her fingers. "The karaoke machine," she said. "It's got a small speaker on it. That'll work."

Shaking my head, I blurted out a laugh. "What? You're just going to sing karaoke all night? This reception could go on for hours." She'd wear herself out.

She shrugged, already turning away to open a nearby closet and roll out the karaoke machine. "If I have to," she answered as she plugged it in. Then she straightened and brushed her hair out of her face. "Besides, Big T can fill in when I need a break. His voice isn't half bad."

Her cousin snorted at that, but didn't argue any of her claims.

I sighed and glanced skeptically at the karaoke machine. I usually hooked it up to the sound system, but it was also designed to play on its own if it had to.

Apparently, tonight, it was going to have to.

Remy and I bent at the same time to turn it on.

"Sorry," we murmured together when we nearly bumped foreheads. Then we shifted an inch apart, but still both going in to get the machine up and running.

"Holy shit," she murmured under her breath, turning toward me slightly. "You smell really good."

I didn't want it to, but my body reacted, remembering every touch, lick, and kiss she'd ever given me. I glanced at her face, and her eyes flared as if she was in trouble for saying such a thing.

"Sorry." She lifted both hands in some kind of surrender. "It's just...it's new. You've never smelled like that before."

Lust stirred through me. I tried to bite it back, tried to cling to the fact I was mad at her, but a need unlike any I'd ever experienced with any other person roared through my blood.

I had to shake my head and blink myself back to the present, remind myself where I really was and what I was doing. And that was most definitely not Remy Curran.

"It's, uh...Eva gave it to me as the best man gift. I figured I should wear it today."

She nodded, agreeing. "Well, it's amazing. I think I just got pregnant."

I snorted out an amused sound, not meaning to smile, but smiling anyway.

She leaned in closer to me as I set up the karaoke, and suddenly I could smell her too. Something girly and not at all like Sticks's masculine shampoo.

She smelled like...Elisa.

And yep, now I had wood.

"You have to admit," she told me as my fingers fumbled over knobs. "It must be nice not having to sneeze when I get close to you now, because you know...no more need for the latex mask anymore."

I glanced at her, about a second from leaning forward and kissing the hell out of her. But the predatory gleam in my eyes must've come off more like warning to her.

"Okay, fine." She lifted her hands. "I'm backing off. Just...damn it, one more sniff before you go." She leaned in quickly, took a quick, noisy drag, and was promptly pulling away again. "And by the way, you look sexy as hell in a tux."

"Sticks," I warned, but I wasn't really mad. I was tempted to my limit.

"I'm staying away now," she argued with a small scowl. "I swear. I'm accepting the fact I bombed any chance I might've ever had with you. From here on out, I'm going to be the real, unvarnished me, and the real me would totally flirt with you while you look like that—even if I would prefer to be home in bed, bawling my eyes out right now."

I glanced at her, not sure what to think because honestly, I was as disappointed as I was relieved by her words. Crossing an X over her heart with her finger, she kept her promise and stepped back. Then she waited until I was done and had straightened until she moved back to the machine, already searching for the first song she wanted to sing.

I scanned the crowd. All my friends from the bar were present. Even Mason, Reese, and his sister Sarah had made it. Decked out in her maid of honor dress, Reese hovered close to her fiancée, rubbing his arm as if to soothe him, and Brandt Gamble sat by Sarah's wheelchair saying something that tugged a reluctant smile to the girl's lips.

Though I knew they must be suffering from the loss of Mason's mother, I hoped tonight helped cheer their spirits a little.

Gaze wandering on, I smiled at Julian and Skylar, who ran circles around the dancefloor, making balloons fly above them. Then I caught sight of Ten and Caroline hovering around Quinn and his wife Zoey, who was holding a swaddled bundle in her arms before she passed the baby off to let Caroline hold him. Noel and his wife Aspen were over by the bar, talking to Felicity and Knox. When I spotted the bride and groom near Murphy from the repair shop, I unintentionally caught Pick glancing my way.

When I nodded to him, letting him know we were taking care of things, he turned to Eva and held out a hand to her. My heart lurched in my throat, hoping he didn't think we were ready yet. I seriously did not want to mess with his vision he had of how his first dance with his new bride was supposed to take place.

But then the music started in the karaoke machine, and

fuck me if Remy wasn't playing "Baby Love," the very song Pick had told me he danced to with his new wife.

I gaped at her, stunned.

Damn it, she was amazing.

CHAPTER 39

Remy Curran

ASHER DROVE ME CRAZY by sticking around as I sang the first song. And not only did he linger, but he watched me the entire time I sang. And the way he watched me was...affectionate.

It was enough to give a poor girl ideas, make her think his will was softening toward her, like he might actually one day forgive her.

But after the brutal way he'd turned me away last night, I knew better. I'd sung my heart out to him, told him with each lyric that I loved him and was sorry for hurting him.

And how had he responded? He'd told me right back that there was too much bad blood between us and that he was better off without me.

Ouch.

Message received. Painfully.

I was never going to have another chance with him, ever.

So why the hell was he still watching me? As the song came to an end, he shifted closer, squinting as if confused. "How'd you know to sing that specific song?"

"Huh?" I frowned and glanced at the machine. "I just

remember you once mentioning that was their song."

"Oh."

He continued to watch me as if I'd done something wrong though, so I said, "Was I supposed to sing something else?"

Shaking his head, he murmured, "No. That was perfect. Thanks again for doing this for Pick."

He reached out as if to pat my arm and maybe call me a true friend as he used to do when I'd helped him with something, but then he furrowed his brow, his hand retreated, and he turned away to stroll off.

I watched him, his hands in his pockets, which lifted the back of his tux jacket and pulled his pants snug against his ass.

Damn, he looked good dressed up. It was hard to believe I'd had him naked and under me once in my life.

"You're drooling," Big T said into my ear, making me jump. "And...we still need more music."

"Shit." I spun away from Asher's backside and unconsciously wiped at my mouth as if I really had been drooling. Then I returned to the karaoke machine and started song after song.

The night progressed, alcohol flowed freely, and my cousin picked up a few songs for me so I could rest my voice. I chugged water and watched the dancing and the laughter and the comradery. But mostly I watched Asher. He fit with this crew. His coworkers continually jostled him and laughed, joking and bantering.

It was nice.

He looked happy. Which made me glad, and yet sad because I'd never get the chance to make him happy again.

When it came time for the bouquet toss, Reese and Felicity wheeled Sarah onto the floor, and they helped her catch the flowers. Afterward, all the guys shoved a stumbling Asher into the middle of the dancefloor by himself as Pick removed Eva's garter. He turned and tried to get Mason and Knox to join him, but they both shook their heads and said they were practically married, so Asher found Noel's two younger brothers, Colton and Brandt, and dragged them out there with him.

I laughed and shook my head, amazed I remembered everyone's names. But Asher had talked about them enough, describing them all perfectly when he'd thought I was a guy, that it was easy to tell who was who. I almost felt as if I knew them as well as he did.

Brandt ended up catching the garter after Asher dive-bombed out of the way. Grinning, he waved it like a flag before carrying it over to Sarah and slipping it around her head like a headband.

When I started to play the group-dance songs like The Chicken Dance, Limbo, and Cha-Cha Slide, I couldn't help but give Asher a shout out, when it came time for the Hokey Pokey.

"Hey, everyone," I called into the microphone. "The best man's going to need a little help from all the ladies with this next song because..." I placed my hand over the mike for a bit to make a face, then I removed my fingers to lean forward, confessing, "He doesn't know his left from his right very well."

He laughed and shook his head even as he flipped me off. But then he gladly accepted all the help from Reese, Eva, Felicity, Caroline, Zoey and Aspen, who hurried forward to do the Hokey Pokey with him.

Afterward, I passed the microphone to Big T so he could entertain everyone with the Méxican Hat Dance song. The best man saw me taking a break and strolled forward in that sexy male saunter only Asher Hart could perfect, shaking his head and still chuckling.

"Thanks a lot, smart-ass," he said. "I can't believe you remember me admitting that."

I sent him a small smile as I sipped my water. "I remember everything about you."

His eyes heated at my confession, and I knew he was remembering things too. Nipples hardening and my panties growing moist, I cleared my throat and tried not to get too aroused, even though I failed.

A giggling pair of drunk girls stumbled up to us, breaking into the moment. When I realized it was the bride and maid of honor, I straightened respectfully.

"Remy," Reese called, glassy-eyed and swaying into Eva as she grasped my arm. "Can you sing 'Dear Future Husband' so I can dance for Mason? I think it could really help cheer him up."

I ground my teeth at the request for a Meghan Trainor song. I'd been hoping to avoid all of her music tonight in the hopes of not irritating Asher's ire further by reminding him of "All About That Bass." But Reese had been through a lot of shit lately, burying her mother-in-law, taking on a teen-age sister-in-law. I couldn't tell her no.

Before I could nod, though, Eva said, "And I want you and Asher to sing 'Marvin Gaye' together. I heard about your antics last night and how awesome you two sounded together, so now I want to hear it myself. Plus, I want to dance with my man to that one."

Really? These guys were trying to doom me here. Not one but two Meghan Trainor songs, and one of them with Asher? He'd flip his lid.

He and I shared a reluctant glance. He didn't want to sing with me as much as I didn't want to make him but secretly *did* want to sing with him.

Before we could refuse though, Eva lifted her arm and declared, "The bride has spoken."

"Shit," Asher muttered, but turned to Eva and said, "Whatever you want, baby doll."

"Goodie." She clapped and leapt forward to slap a kiss to his cheek. "You're the best brother-in-law ever. Now play my song first."

So, after Big T finished, Asher and I queued up Meghan Trainor and Charlie Puth and got it on. It was strange, standing so close to him when he sounded so amazing, smelled so good and looked so fine as we sang about sex together, all the while knowing I'd never get to touch him again.

I found myself glancing over at him as I sang a few meaningful lyrics, only to find his gaze on me as well. We kept eye contact for the rest of the song, and there was no way I could stop my arousal from claiming me full force by the time the last words left our lips.

He breathed out a heavy breath, staring at me, before saying, "Una más."

I crinkled my eyebrows, even though my heart leapt with excitement, thrilled he wanted to sing one more with me.

"I want to do that one from the Tinker Bell movie," he said, frowning as he tried to remember the title.

"'1000 Years' with KT Tunstall and Bleu?" I said, and he nodded, snapping his fingers.

"Yes. That one." He looked it up, found it and, yowza. If

singing "Marvin Gaye" put me in a certain mood, then "1000 Years" finished me off for good. Asher and I gazed into each other's eyes as we promised each other that our love would still be around after a thousand years.

Tears glistened in my lashes as the last of the melody faded away. Then Asher took control of the microphone. "Before you start the song for Reese, I need to say a few things to everyone."

I nodded, my heart hopping into my throat, because I kind of wished he'd say something about me, how he'd forgiven me and wanted to give us another chance.

But instead, he called, "Okay, so everyone, listen up." He waved his hand to gain the crowd's attention. "Pick told me I didn't have to give a best man speech, but I've had just enough to drink that I think I'm going to anyway."

He paused, waiting for the chuckles to die down before he started again. "I came to this establishment a little over a year ago, with no band, no real family to speak of, and no true friends. But thanks to one Patrick Ryan, I've gained all three. If it wasn't for that man right there," he pointed to Pick, "I would've given up on all the dreams I ever had. My band would've died out in its garage days, I wouldn't have gotten to know all you asshole bartenders I work with and love to death...or fallen for all your lovely lady halves." He bowed toward his group of friends. "And I never would've learned a couple months ago that I had a true-life, blood-related brother out there. Pick." He fisted his hand and held it up as a kind of salute. "I am honored to be the little brother of an amazing man like you...and jealous as fuck over the gorgeous, amazing wife and kids you got. Congratulations, man."

Pick strode forward and pulled him into a huge bear hug. When he pulled away, he wiped tears from his eyes and then laughed as Eva leapt at Asher to hug him next.

Then Reese was there because she wanted to give a maid of honor speech too, but it wasn't anything as amazing as what Asher had said...in my opinion, anyway. It did give me time to compose myself, because I was so happy that Asher had found a place to belong after a childhood of being so alone. But all too soon, Reese was thrusting the microphone at me, announcing it was "Dear Future Husband" time.

I sang her song, but I didn't sing it to her. I watched Asher, and the entire time the words left my lips he watched me right back, guzzling from a bottle of Angry Orchard as he did.

After that, Quinn and Zoey approached to relieve me from my deejaying duty, saying they'd sing a few songs before they told me to go get some cake and punch and rest a bit.

I found myself alone by the refreshment table, burying my fork into a lush-looking slice of cake when suddenly the entire plate was slapped out of my hand.

"Don't!" Asher snapped, his eyes wide with fear.

Glancing down at my empty hands, not even a crumb or hint of frosting to behold, I gaped a moment before returning my attention to Mr. Slappy. "What the hell?"

"I just overheard someone talking about how there was peanut oil in the ingredients."

"Peanut...?" I started softly. Then I gulped. "Oh, shit. Thank you."

He nodded and was gone again. I gazed after him, a small smile lifting my lips. But, hell. He'd remembered my allergy and saved me.

My hero.

Caroline caught my gaze then and sent me a thumbs-up, but I rolled my eyes, letting her know she was crazy. Just because he hadn't let me kill myself didn't mean the man was ready to hook back up with me, let alone forgive me. But a small part of me hoped she might be right, anyway.

I returned to the microphone and sang a few more songs. Since Big T had to open the restaurant the next morning, he took off early, but that was fine. I was having too much fun to care that I'd be hoarse as hell tomorrow. And besides, a couple other people were willing to give me a break and try their hand at karaoke. The most surprising pair were a drunk Ten and Asher as they stumbled toward the stage, their arms wrapped around each other's shoulders before Ten announced, "We want to sing 'I Just Had Sex.'"

Then Asher pointed and laughed, "No, *he* wants to sing it. I'm just here for the backup Akon part...and to watch Noel kick his ass."

I lifted my eyebrows, then I chuckled and shook my head. "Ten? You seriously sing?"

Ten scowled as if offended. "Fuck no, but I'm drunk

enough to right now. Plus it'll really piss off my brother-in-law, so...I must!"

I laughed and had to ask, "Your brother-in-law?"

"Noel. Didn't you know he was Caroline's brother?"

"He is? No, I had no idea." My eyebrows arched as I scanned the crowd to see Caroline and Noel gathered around Brandt , Colton, Sarah, and Aspen. "Huh."

So I handed the microphone over and started the song for them.

As soon as Ten belted out the first line, covering Lonely Island's part of the duet, an outraged Noel yelled, "You motherfucker," as he marched forward.

Afraid Asher might get caught in some crossfire, I stepped in and held up my hand to stop him. Crazily enough, he didn't try to get past me, but he did stay there and glare and flip Ten off, calling him a few dirty names.

Asher bent over, laughing so hard he could barely sing his lines. But he straightened up by the end, and even as slurred as his voice was, he sounded amazing.

Watching him have such a good time was taxing, though. It was selfish of me to want to be the only one to make him smile, but I couldn't help it. I'd fallen hard for this man.

By the time the wedding reception winded down to an end, my feet were killing me and my throat was raw. But I merely stretched the kinks of out my back before beginning to put away the karaoke machine.

Only half a dozen people remained: Knox and Felicity helping clean the floor, Ten and Caroline doing the same thing, and Asher.

Stumbling my way, he waved a hand. "Hey, sexy lady. Let me help you put that up."

I laughed and waved him away. "Oh, no you don't. I've got this just fine, plastered boy. I'm surprised you're still able to stand upright."

"I know, right?" He spread out his arms and looked down at his wobbling legs. "It's like some kind of miracle."

Damn it, he was even adorable when he was drunk off his ass.

"Yo, Drummer Girl." Tearing my gaze from Asher, I scowled toward Ten, who'd wrapped his arm and suit jacket around Caroline's shoulders as he steered her toward the exit. "Hart's not fit to drive shit, so you can get him home, right?"

My eyes flared wide. Hell no, I couldn't get Asher home. He was all sweet and drunk. What if I couldn't help myself and ended up molesting him? "Can't *you* get him home?" I asked, pleading with my eyes.

But Ten only grinned. "Fuck no. I plan on giving Caroline road head as she drives *my* drunk ass home."

"Eww." Wrinkling my nose, I couldn't argue with that, and besides, it was too late anyway. He and Caroline had just escaped through the front door, leaving me here alone...with Asher.

I gazed wildly around the place, but even Knox and Felicity had disappeared too.

Shit.

"You remember where I live, right?" Asher said, drawing his finger up my arm. "Because I remember you remembering very clearly exactly where I live."

I glanced at him and knew I was doomed. No way could I let him drive like this. And no way could I tell him no if he tried something.

From the glaze of lust in his green eyes as he watched me, he was definitely going to try something, too.

Damn it. I was fucked...literally.

CHAPTER 40
Remy Curran

JUST AS I FEARED, ASHER was a very lovey-dovey, touchy-feely, horny kind of drunk.

"You looked really good tonight," he told me from the passenger seat of my car. "Did I tell you earlier how good you looked?"

"Umm..." I bit my lip to keep myself together. "No, you didn't. But thank you."

"You're welcome. It's the truth, though. You were the most beautiful woman in that entire club. Don't tell the bride, but you were even prettier than Eva. And I get to be in this car all alone with you right now. Damn, I'm a lucky bastard. Hey..." he slurred as he rolled his head against the seat so he could face me. "Guess what?"

"What?" I asked, oh so very ready to change the subject.

He sighed as he watched me. "I learned what *te amo* really meant,"

Shit! Okay, I didn't want the subject turned to that, though.

I squeezed my hands around the steering wheel and said nothing. Why had I ever said that to him? I knew it wouldn't take anything for him to ask anyone who knew Spanish to translate it for him.

"No one's ever said that to me before," he said, his voice going hoarse. "In any language."

My heart tore for him, and I suddenly realized why I'd said it, because I pretty much already knew he hadn't heard it a lot. His mother, his father, his uncle who barely raised him. None of them would've said it. And Pick was too new a brother to go spouting fluffy love crap quite yet. So I'd said it because he'd deserved to hear it.

And I'd meant it.

He was an amazing man who just needed one person to appreciate that and tell him how special he was. I knew it shouldn't have been me, but I hadn't been able to resist. Everyone needed to hear I love you at least once in his life.

"Did you mean it?" he asked.

I clenched my teeth and concentrated on driving as I pulled into the alley that led to his place. But as soon as I cut the engine, he pushed the issue again.

"Did you?"

I blew out a deep breath and quietly told him the truth. "Yes." When I glanced over at him, his eyes were glossy with alcohol but he seemed strangely lucid. "I meant it."

Air hissed from between his gritted teeth. Then he reached out and barely grazed my bare leg with his fingertips. "I want to spend the rest of the night inside you."

"Asher." I groaned and slapped my hands over my face. "Don't do this to me. You're drunk."

He shrugged. "So?"

"So, you've obviously forgotten how you feel about me. I'm you're least favorite person on the planet right now, remember? You'll regret it in the morning."

"I know exactly how I feel about you, Remy. I'm still pissed as hell over what you did, and I don't know if I'll ever forgive you, but I still want you." His hand stroked up higher on my thigh, slipping between my legs. "And I miss you."

I shuddered and closed my eyes, trying to fight off the temptation.

But he just kept talking, just kept tempting. "I've wanted you all night, under me on a bed where I could run my hands and mouth over this body." Suddenly his touch was no longer teasing and soft. He went bold and slid his fingers under my dress, finding my panties immediately. "I mean to have you, too."

"Dios," I gasped, gripping the steering wheel as he rubbed the spot that ached the most through the silk cloth of my panties.

I groaned a split second before he did.

"Jesus, and you're already wet for me." Moving past the barrier my underwear provided, he pushed a thick digit inside me.

"Asher, wait." I grasped his wrist and squeezed my legs together, trapping his hand where it was but also preventing him from pleasuring me further.

But the damn man curled his finger inside me. "Why? You want this as much as I do." Finding my G-spot, he rubbed his finger against it, over and over again.

Throwing my skull back against the headrest of my seat, I clenched my teeth against the rising pleasure. But, God. He knew just where to touch.

Cursing him openly in Spanish, I opened my legs and bucked up my hips, meeting his pleasurable assault with greedy abandon. When the euphoria struck, I realized vaguely somewhere in my head that he was getting me off with nothing but his index finger. But I was still too high on happy endorphins to really care how embarrassing that fact was.

Every muscle in my body loosened as I slumped limp in my seat, utterly drained.

"You still spout off a shitload of Spanish when you come," Asher said from beside me. He sounded curious about his claim, as if realizing a new fact. "I guess that part wasn't a lie after all."

Still panting from my orgasm, I glanced over at him from what could only be wild, dazed eyes. "You'd be amazed by all the things that happened between us that were actually true."

His gaze was intense and expression a little feral on its own. "Come inside with me, Remy."

He was no longer asking. It was a command, and heaven help me, I followed it.

Taking his hand when he reached for mine, I went with him to his door and kissed the back of his shoulder as I waited behind him to unlock all the deadbolts. When he led me inside, he stuck close on the stairs, glancing back at me when we were halfway down the flight.

"Remember when I couldn't wait to have you and took you right here?"

God, how could I forget? It was one of the reasons I was here with him again, when I knew good and well I shouldn't be. Gripping his hand harder, I warned, "Don't you dare try that tonight. You're way too drunk to manage it now."

Asher chuckled. "Don't worry. I want you on a bed for all the things I have planned."

I shuddered and clutched his hand harder.

He took me straight to the bed and paused at the footboard to turn to me and kiss me, all the while working my dress off my shoulders. As soon as he had me down to my bra and panties, he stepped back to take in the whole picture.

"Fucking breathtaking," he breathed, grasping my fingers again to help me onto the bed. After getting me comfortable on my back, my head nestled into his pillow and my body stretched out before him, he placed a staying hand on my hip. "Lie here, just like that while I feast on you." Then taking my arms, he moved them above my head until he'd placed one hand upon the other. "Pretend you're bound here."

I grinned. "What? No handcuffs?"

He shook his head, not smiling back. "I threw them out." His green eyes seared into mine. "They kept me from chasing after you."

Gulping because I hadn't meant to bring up a sore issue, I whispered, "Sorry."

He didn't answer, his gaze too intent on my chest. Reaching out, he brushed the backs of his fingers over the cups of my bra. It wasn't as intense as skin-to-skin contact, but it still made me shiver and had my nipples perking to attention. Then he removed the bra and leaned in to suck one aching tip into his mouth. I arched up, crying out and squeezing my hands together so I couldn't break his rule and bury my fingers in his hair.

But then he moved down, grasped a teeth full of my panties and tugged them down my legs. When his tongue licked up my sex, I couldn't help it. I grabbed fistfuls of all that sexy, soft hair, and I ground my hips up against him, riding his face into oblivion.

When he sat up, wiping his mouth and grinning down at me, I shuddered out a heaving, happy sigh, loving how mussed his hair was.

"I told you how much I loved the taste of pussy, didn't I? When I thought you were another guy."

I nodded, hoping he didn't realize he was making a huge mistake by being here like this with a liar like me.

But he only smiled as if amused by revealing such a thing to me. "I told you a lot of shit. Way more than I've told any other living soul on the planet."

Not sure what to say except sorry he'd misplaced his trust in me when the entire time I'd been too afraid to even reveal my gender to him, I held my breath. Because I wasn't really sorry. I'd cherished every little confidence he'd ever fed me.

His green eyes looked sad as he looked down at me and smoothed his hand over his hip. He was still fully dressed, but I could see his arousal tenting out the front of his pants. I had to admit, I'd never had a guy in a tux go down on me before. It was kind of classy.

"Is that why you came back the second night?" he asked. "Because you knew how much I hated one-night stands? You needed to make it two nights, so I wouldn't be upset?"

I shook my head. "No. I came back to tell you the truth because I hated making you live through another one-night stand. But then you kissed me, and..." I shook my head, letting him know the rest was history.

Masculine triumph entered his gaze as his lips twitched. "So my mouth has some kind of mystical, mind-controlling power over you, huh?"

"You could say that again," I didn't mean to mutter.

He laughed and slipped from the bed to take off his jacket and then unbutton his dress shirt. "You're going to have to show me how this power I have works."

Sitting up to help him with the top buttons, since he'd started at the bottom, I smoothed my hands inside the shirt, over his chest and slipped if off his shoulders. "All you really have to do is curve it up into a smile, and I'm pretty much a goner."

"Really." His lips slid into a pleased grin. "Like this?"

"Mmm hmm." I pressed my mouth to his pecs and he buried his fingers into my hair, letting me have a little fun before he pulled me back and urged me to lie down again.

Then he removed his pants, watching me the whole time. When he reached for the condom box and took out a foiled package, he held it up between two fingers and said, "Last one. Did you know I'd end up using all of them on you when you bought them for me?"

I shook my head. "I bought them, thinking you'd never use *any* on me...and hating every woman who'd get them instead."

He concentrated on rolling it into place before he stretched out above me and gazed into my eyes. "And here, you were the only one."

I shuddered out a breath, tears glistening in my eyes because I knew I was being given a gift. I didn't deserve to be here. Gently, I brushed his hair across his forehead, relishing the moment.

"Remy," he whispered.

When he pushed inside me, I gasped and arched. He clenched his teeth and kept his gaze on mine, even as his green eyes went glazed with lust. "Goddamn," he rasped. "You always take the whole thing. I've had women ask me not to thrust the whole way in because they couldn't take it. Empty, shallow fucks. But not you. Never you." He leaned down, his lips hovering over mine as he slowly moved inside me, pushing all the way in before retreating so he could plunge again.

Then he kissed me. I wrapped my legs around him and gripped his hair while our mouths mated. He put more power behind his hips, nudging me up the mattress with each mighty thrust.

"How's my mouth doing now?" he asked between pants, his breath falling on my ear as he slid his nose along my jaw. "It let you know what I really want, didn't it?" Then his teeth nipped my earlobe before he whispered, "Say it."

God, I *did* know what he wanted, but I couldn't deliver. It'd hurt too much. So I closed my eyes and clung to him tighter as he pumped his body into mine.

He spiked into me a little harder, piercing me deeper. "Damn it, Remy. Say it."

I whimpered my refusal and clenched my eyes shut before burying my face in his neck.

But Asher cupped the back of my head with a gentleness I didn't expect. "Please."

The ache in his voice was my undoing.

"Te amo," I whispered.

He groaned and arched his neck up. I watched the satisfaction cross his face as he closed his eyes and let his mouth fall open as if he were experiencing the ultimate nirvana.

Addicted to his response, I repeated, "Te amo," as I slid my fingers up his throat before leaning in to kiss his pulse. Digging my heels into the base of his back, I urged him deeper into me and I sucked on a spot directly under his ear. "Te amo más de lo que nunca he amado a otro."

He had no idea what kind of love words I spilled, but they set him off. Clutching my ass in one hand, he gripped my hair in the other. Then he kissed the shit out of me as he surged, coming with a masculine growl of release.

"Dios," I gasped before screaming, "¡Oh, Dios mío! *Asher...*"

I swear he passed out the very moment he finished, because he remained motionless on top of me, his forehead pressed to my shoulder. But then I stroked his back and he stirred.

"Don't move." He wrapped his hand around my hip even as he sat up. "I'm just going to get rid of this. Be right back." He glanced back at me as he stood. "Do you need anything?"

I checked between my legs, and winced. "Yes, please."

With a nod, he disappeared into the bathroom. I listened to the sink water run and turn off again before he returned to me and handed over a washcloth he'd wetted with warm water.

"Gracias."

I cleaned myself and he sat beside me, watching with drowsy but intent eyes. With any other guy, that probably would've weirded me out. But I don't know. With Asher, it was different. Intimate. Almost bonding. I wasn't sure how to explain it.

When I was finished, he took the washcloth from my hand and tossed it across the room toward a laundry basket full of dirty clothes.

"You'll stay the rest of the night?" he asked, turning back to me.

My resistance was already shot to hell, and I was beyond relieved that he wasn't shoving me out after he'd gotten what he wanted, so I nodded. "Sí."

"Good." He crawled back onto the mattress with me and under the covers, curling himself behind me as he wrapped an arm across my waist. "I like sleeping with you."

I closed my eyes and told myself this didn't mean he forgave me. None of the beauty that had just transpired between us meant anything. He was still drunk. He could, and probably would, regret everything in the morning. I shouldn't get my hopes up.

But as I snuggled back into him, I sighed and began to get sleepy comfortable.

Right before I dropped off, I murmured, "I love you," in English.

His arm around my waist tightened a fraction, tugging me against him just a little bit firmer.

But he never said it back. And as much as it made the raw ache in me grow, I hadn't expected him to repeat the sentiment.

CHAPTER 41
Remy Cusan

I SLEPT IN LATER THAN I intended to. But it was okay, Asher was still passed out, breathing deeply, next to me. I had plenty of time to sneak out before he woke. Except I wasted a couple seconds gazing at him with utter awe, unable to believe I'd gotten one more night with him.

He was so freaking beautiful.

I loved how his lashes rested with such tranquil serenity against his cheekbones, and his lips just barely parted to let out each even breath. His hair swept crazily across his forehead, dark locks mixing in with blonder highlighted threads, and I couldn't help myself. I reached out to sweep it gently across his forehead.

And of course, the silken locks called to me, begging for more. So I combed two fingers through a few more pieces. My gaze wandered down over his golden bare shoulders to where white sheets were tucked up under his armpits.

I liked knowing he was a side-sleeper. I was a side-sleeper, too. Maybe in some alternate reality, we could've actually side-slept *more* nights together, spooning throughout our sleep.

But in this reality, he was still pissed at me for being a fucking liar, and he'd only slept with me because he'd been drunk and horny off his ass. And I really needed to get out of here before I woke him and stirred up a whole hornets' nest of awkward.

I didn't want to know if he was pissed at me for taking advantage of him in his non-sober state last night. No, I was going to end this on a happy, beautiful note, with him sleeping peacefully and my body all deliciously sore from his recent lovemaking.

Grabbing my clothes as soon as I slid as quietly and easily from the bed as possible, I dressed in the half dark and clutched my shoes to my chest so I could tiptoe toward the stairwell.

But from behind me, a sleep-clogged voice asked, "Leaving so soon?"

I gasped and whirled around, slapping my hand over my heart. "Oh, shit. You're awake."

"Yeah," he said. His voice still raspy, he sat up and ran his hands through his hair to cup the sides of his head. The sheets fell to his waist, revealing a warm, toned chest that made my mouth water.

I wanted to return to him so bad, crawl back under the covers and cuddle into his heat, stay for the rest of my life. But...yeah.

Reality was such a bitch.

And in reality, he winced, reminding me he must be suffering from a hangover and was truly sober for the first time in hours. Sober and cognizant. Which was why I was sneaking out and should stay away from his bed and delectable body...before he kicked me out and yelled at me for being a tramp who couldn't keep her hands off him when he was vulnerable and out of his own mind.

I winced, feeling his pain. "Sorry, I wanted to be out of here before you woke." Shifting my weight from one bare foot the other, I bit my lip. "In case, you know, you regretted last night and didn't want to see me."

He stopped clutching his head and dropped his hands to his lap so he could look at me. When he said nothing, I shifted again, growing more uncomfortable than ever.

Looking up at the ceiling, I cleared my throat and asked, "So, do you? Regret it?"

He didn't answer immediately, and I couldn't handle the suspense so I shifted my gaze back to him. He wasn't reassuring me, telling me he regretted nothing, so that had to mean he did. He must wish last night between us had never happened.

The tears and devastation moved in. I hoped I could keep them at bay long enough to leave before he saw any, but I also wanted to stick around another second in case, by some miracle, he decided to...I don't know...*forgive* me, or something.

But then he went and admitted, "I'm not sure."

I blinked, wondering at first if I'd heard him right. Then I shook my head.

Had he just said *I'm not sure?*

What the hell? I scowled, suddenly no longer crushed, but just plain pissed. But he *wasn't sure?* Surely, he knew whether he regretted having sex with me or not. Hell, the only reason a nice guy like him wouldn't be reassuring me by now *had* to be because he *did* regret it.

So, why didn't he just grow a pair and tell me that already?

"You know," I muttered, glaring hard, the pain and anger bringing out my sassy. "I realize I fucked up. Bad. I lied to you for over a month. I betrayed your trust. Hurt your feelings. And tricked you in the most horrendous way imaginable. And I am *sorry* for that. I regret it like hell. That last thing I ever wanted to do was hurt *you.* If I could take that back, I would, but..." I shook my head. "I don't know if I'd do *everything* again differently a second time through. Because if I did, I would never have gotten to know you as well as I did. I never would've learned what an...amazing person you are. I...fuck, I wouldn't have fallen for you as hard as I have. And I can't regret that part. But I also can't let you *use* my feelings and guilty conscience against me again. The next time you're horny and want sex from me, it has to *mean* something. *Got it?*"

He drew in a tormented breath and ran his hand over his face as he averted his gaze. "Yeah," he mumbled. "I got it."

"I'm going to go," I said as I whirled around, but a strange empty spot above the stairwell opening caught my attention.

Frowning, I whirled back. "Where the hell is Mozart?"

His face shot up, and his expression crumbled. "He's gone."

Gasping, I staggered back a step. Clutching at my chest, I blinked at him, trying to make sense of his words. "What do you mean *gone*?" The little critter had been so full of life, and Asher had taken good care of him. He couldn't have just...*died*. Could he?

"I mean he's fucking *gone*," he snapped, scowling at me for pressing the subject. "I came home, his cage was open, and he was nowhere in the apartment."

"But..." My brow wrinkled as I shook my head. That made no sense. "He's a *squirrel*. There was no other way for him to get out of this apartment except through that doorway up there, and he couldn't have opened that himself."

"Well, then he must've gotten free when I was coming in or going out. I don't fucking know."

I sent him an I'm-not-buying-it glance. "And you don't think you would've noticed him darting out between your legs when you opened the door?"

"I told you, I don't know. I just know I came home, and he was gone."

Chewing on my lip, I turned back to study the bare stretch of wall where Mozart's cage had once hung. "I think someone else let him out."

Asher let out a tired sigh. "Impossible. No one else has been here...except you."

I turned back slowly. "It wasn't me."

With a scowl, he growled, "I know that. So, *who* are you suggesting broke into my apartment to—" When he saw the answer on my face, he groaned. "Oh, Jesus. Are you back on the conspiracy theory that my dad's out to get me?"

"It makes sense," I said defensively. And it did...to me.

"Why would he just let Mozart go instead of, I don't know, *killing* him? And why—if he did all the other things you think he did—would he bother with such stupid irritating stunts when he could come at me with something so much more lethal, like a gun?"

"Because he's a bully. Bullies chip and pick at scabs until they get to the meat of the wound underneath. They rarely come at you with an outright assault unless they know without a doubt they're bigger and stronger and can take you. You're not a seven-year-old kid any longer; he's trying to find your weaknesses. And he probably didn't outright kill Mozart because who the fuck could actually catch that wily little thing *to* kill him? Why bother even trying when it would be just as devastating for you to find him gone?"

And I could tell it was devastating for him. His green eyes went shuttered with pain as he glanced at the spot where Mozart's cage had hung. It must've really upset him if he'd already taken the whole thing down...too painful to look at.

I hugged myself, glancing at the spot as well. "I hope he's okay."

Asher sniffed and shook his head. "He's probably living it up in some nice park full of plenty of trees and nuts."

Or he was dead, I silently worried.

Glancing at me with a scowl as if he'd read my thoughts, he muttered, "Thought you were leaving because you're pissed at me."

I sighed. "You're the one who can't decide whether you regret sleeping with me or not."

His green eyes went flat with anger. "Oh, well, *excuse* me for a being a little confused. But you hurt me more than anyone has ever hurt me, and that scares the fuck out of me. No one's ever gotten that close to me with me being so completely unaware of it before. So I'm so sorry if it's taking me longer than *you'd like* to figure out if I can really trust you again."

I shrank inside myself a little, soaking in what he'd just said. I really *had* hurt him, and on top of that, I'd left him so gun-shy he wasn't sure if he could trust again. I knew exactly how that felt. When Fisher had left me hurt and deceived, he'd broken my trust and trampled all over my feelings, making it so I didn't want anything to do with any man again...until Asher had come along.

And yet here I was, doing the very same thing to the one person who'd helped me heal from a similar wound.

Feeling the full weight of my shame, I bowed my head. "You're right. I'll go."

When I turned away, he growled a curse, then called, "Remy..." But I was already rushing up the steps to escape him.

To escape myself.

But no matter how fast I ran, or where I went, I was still there, with me...the bitch who'd wounded Asher Hart.

CHAPTER 42
Asher Hart

THE URGE TO RACE AFTER Remy and drag her back into
my apartment festered. Damn it, she was probably crying
right now, and I didn't want that. I'd just wanted my head
to stop pounding and a few minutes without questions and
lifelong commitments to think clearly again.

Didn't she understand I'd never been presented with the
opportunity to love and be loved before? Not like this. It
was scary-ass shit. And to know it had all started with a lie
and broken trust...what guy in his right mind would give
that another chance?

I guess a crazy, messed-up guy who just wanted his
woman any way he could get her. Because a second later, I
flung off my sheets and grabbed the first pair of pants I
found—the dress pants from last night's wedding. Fastening
them, I raced for the steps. By the time I shoved my way
into the alley, she was gone. All I caught sight of was the
back bumper of her car as she turned out of the alley.

"Damn it!" I clutched my aching head, and shifted my
bare feet over the dirty asphalt to keep broken glass from
digging into my heels.

I was going to have to hunt her down now, and I still wasn't sure what I wanted to say. Guess I could start with confessing that I wasn't regretful about last night at all. Last night had been...awesome. But I'd been pissed that she'd tried to sneak out on me again, and I was still finding it difficult to let go of all her lies.

Pick had been right, though. I was going to have to forgive her, because I knew I didn't want to spend the rest of my life without her. Last night had opened my eyes to the fact that I did know her. She might've deceived me about a couple big things, but inside, she was still that person who'd befriended me, and I wasn't ready to lose that friend...or lover.

Blowing out a breath, I ran my hands through my hair and turned to re-enter the apartment. I needed to put more clothes on, maybe take a few painkillers and drink about a gallon of water before I chased her down. But before I could step back inside a strange, animal-like chatter from a near-by dumpster made me pause and glance over.

I expected to see a rat, so when a bedraggled-looking squirrel with hair matted so badly even its tail wasn't bushy darted out from under the dumpster, I nearly pissed myself.

"Wha...*Mozart*?"

It must've been him because he raced straight for the opened door and sprang inside, leaping down the steps to disappear into my apartment.

"Holy shit," I gasped. My pet had come home.

Emotion swamped me, and I raked a shaky hand over my face before I hurried downstairs to get him something to eat. Life on the outside must not have treated him kindly because he shook as if cold or scared. I wanted to grab him and cuddle him close, but I knew he wouldn't like that. So I rushed to my kitchen cabinets and emptied a whole bag of peanuts onto the floor. He didn't even care that I remained right there next to the pile. He rushed forward and started filling his hands before breaking one open and eating it right there.

"Poor little guy," I murmured, getting to my feet so I could get him some water. "It was tough out there, wasn't it?"

A smile lit my face as I watched him for a minute before he decided this was enough bonding, and he disappeared under the bed. Then I blew out a shaky breath and glanced around my apartment before laughing in utter relief. "Welcome home, buddy," I said aloud, but the place was still lonely enough that my voice echoed around me. It made the empty little hollow part in me pang with need.

The first person I wanted to call was Remy. Hell, she was the *only* person I wanted to call and tell.

And that told me everything, right there.

So, she'd lied. She'd had a reason and it had never been to hurt me. She'd apologized and was truly sorry. I could get over that. Because, fuck, I loved her.

Accepting that almost instantly sparked this freeing sensation inside me. Joy rippled along my skin, and I tore off my pants to take a quick shower.

I was going to get her back.

After I cleaned myself up, I dressed, pulled on my shoes, and pocketed my phone. Making sure Mozart was still content and under the bed, I straightened from the floor and headed for the door.

Remy Elisa Curran, here I came.

Ten minutes later, I pulled up to her apartment building and killed the engine of my bike as I remained seated, just...staring at her place. I'd kind of run over here without a game plan. She'd gone all epic and put herself out there, singing songs to me in front of hundreds of people to get me back, and all I knew to say to her was, "I don't regret it."

Wincing over my own lameness, I was kind of tempted to chicken out, start my Triumph and head back home. I had no experience in love. What if I freaking failed? What if giving her—*us*—a chance ended up slaying me?

And what if I was so scared of the pain that I missed out on the best thing that could've ever happened to me? Clenching my teeth, I leapt off the seat and strode to her building. I had until the second story to boost my resolve, and I spent most of that time breathing like some kind of fighter ready to hop into a ring for his first round of blows.

Things had ended up good between Pick and me. Things could end up good here, too. And strangely, it felt as if I were once again risking everything important in my life just to build a relationship with someone. But this girl was worth it.

When I reached her door, I shook my hands out at my sides before lifting one to knock. Before my knuckles could meet wood, however, the door flew open, inward, making me jump back in surprise.

I expected Remy to be there, so I blinked in confusion when *Gally* stepped into the hall. He was so busy buckling his belt together, he was almost upon me before he realized I was in his path. Pulling up short, he yanked his head up.

"Oh, hey, man." A smug, just-got-laid grin spread across his face. "Finally decide to end your dry spell? Right on!" He lifted his fist to bump with me in congratulations just as another band member—Holden—stepped from Remy's apartment behind him, tugging on his shirt.

My mouth fell open as I gaped between the two. "What...?"

But seriously...*what?*

Gally laughed while Holden turned a bright red. Finally, my bass guitarist shrugged. "What can I say? The girl can't get enough cock. She likes it best when *every* hole is filled."

Snickering, he slugged the side of his arm against mine as if sharing some kind of inside joke. But all I could taste was acid, and all I could see was a blurry mass of light.

"Don't worry, Hart," Gally's voice irritated my ears. "We got her nice and hollowed out for you. Have fun."

I didn't stop to think it through. I don't think it was possible to even *contemplate* thinking at the moment. I just wanted to hurt the idiot bastard. Make him bleed and scream and ache deep inside...the way I ached.

With a savage roar, I dove at him, shoving him against the wall. "You're dead, asshole. I can't believe you touched her. She fucking hates you."

I popped him in one eye and would've gone for the other, but Holden yanked me backward off him.

That only pissed me off more. I tried to hit him too, but he used my own tactic against me and pinned me to the wall and pressed his forearm to my throat to subdue me.

I struggled, shoving and pushing at him to get off me, but the bastard was bigger, which made me growl in frustrated rage. If I could just have the size of Knox or Quinn, or even Noel, I so would've taken him down right then.

Calling forth some inner-adrenaline booster, I heaved at him again, making him stumble backward, away from me. About to leap after him, I jarred to a halt when I heard a voice—*Remy's* voice—cry, "What the hell?"

But it wasn't coming from the direction of her apartment. Whipping my head up, I gaped at her where she stood poised and frozen at the top of the stairwell, still wearing the dress she'd been in last night and clutching a steaming Styrofoam cup to her chest. Her eyes were red and puffy from crying, but her hair was pleasantly mussed—from me having my hands in it the night before—and she was so fucking beautiful, I took a second just to catch my breath.

Behind us, the door to her apartment opened. When I glanced over and saw Jodi peek curiously into the hall, wearing nothing but a short, silky wrap that was tied loosely enough to reveal she wasn't wearing much underneath, I closed my eyes and cursed under my breath.

"What the fuck is going on out here?" the girls demanded, nearly simultaneously.

"Ask that fucker," Gally answered, and I could tell he was pointing at me, but I was still too busy bowing my head in shame and berating myself for my stupidity to actually see it. "He's the douche who attacked us for no reason as soon as we stepped into the hall."

A second's worth of silence followed, letting me know everyone was now looking at me, waiting for my explanation.

Then Remy had to go and murmur, "Asher?" as if she were actually concerned about me.

"Damn it," I hissed and lifted my face, meeting her gaze, and wincing as soon as I did. "I..." Fuck, I couldn't confess it. But her big brown eyes were so wide and worried. I blew out a breath and admitted, "I...misread the situation."

She blinked, crinkled her brow, then glanced between Gally, Holden, and Jodi before her eyes flared with surprise. Then she whirled back to me, scowling. "Are you fucking serious?"

I winced and pressed my hand to my aching head. Shit, I'd forgotten to take painkillers for my hangover. "I don't know what I was thinking," I immediately started, pushing all the guilt and apology into my expression that I could manage. "I *wasn't* thinking. Shit. They came out of there still dragging their clothes on."

Eyebrows arching, she set her hands on her hips. "So you just *assumed* they were in there visiting *me*? *Really*? Wow, that must've been a two-minute threesome since I just saw you, what, *twenty minutes ago*."

I opened my mouth to deny my kneejerk assumption, but damn...she was right.

Not knowing when to keep his mouth shut, Gally swaggered forward, licking his lips as he eyed Remy's dress. "That's actually not a bad idea. You're looking a lot better than you did a few days ago...Remy. Why don't you show Holden and me the inside of *your* bedroom now?"

When he took one more step toward her, I growled and shoved him back. "Back the fuck off."

His eyes narrowed, and I knew he would've charged, so I turned to him fully to take him on. But Remy popped between us, pushing a hand against my chest, and holding up one in Gally's direction to ward him off.

"Okay, enough," she commanded. When Gally and I both stopped, she blew out a breath, cursed something in Spanish, and muttered, "Why are guys so freaking punchy?"

I kind of liked that she'd yet to take the flat of her hand off my chest. So I said, "Because it's a hell of a lot faster stress reliever than eating ice cream or talking smack about another chick like you girls do."

She glanced at me, her brown eyes wide with so many emotions. I detected humor in there before she scowled and then shuttered it all up with grief. "So not the time to be sexist and cute," she finally muttered.

When I whispered, "Sorry," her gaze fell to her fingers spread over my heartbeat.

I watched her lashes flutter as she pressed just a touch harder against me as if trying to imprint herself inside me before pulling her hand away. What I could've told her was that she'd already imprinted herself quite solidly to my heart.

But Gally snickered. "Oh, so *you two* have turned into fuckbuddies, huh? Tell me, Hart. You try to get into her pants before or after you found out she was really a chick?"

I curled my lip into a snarl, and Remy immediately stepped up against me, stopping me from getting punchy again. Blowing out a calming breath, I narrowed my eyes and told Gally, "You need to talk about our drummer with a little more respect than that, asshole."

With a gasp, Remy whirled to face me, her hair swishing out over her shoulder as she did.

Gally scowled and shook his head, then exchanged a glance with Holden before turning back to me. "Our drummer? I thought she was out of the band. You texted, calling off the gig Friday, saying she was a chick."

I clenched my teeth, because I *had* meant for her to be out of the band when I'd texted them those messages, but now I'd changed my mind. "I was just letting you know her change of status. And we had to cancel Friday because of...other reasons."

Remy didn't correct me, thank God. She merely zipped her gaze around to the three of us, her gaze wide and eager to hear how this conversation would end.

"So, you seriously want a fucking bitch in the band?" Gally exploded incredulously, motioning toward Remy as he glared at me. "But we're named Non-Castrato because—"

"I don't care why we're named Non-Castrato. And don't call her a bitch. The fact of the matter is she's already been *in* the band for over a month. What difference does—"

"Because I don't want a damn chick in the band!" Gally roared.

Scowling at him, I curled my hands into fists. When I glanced Holden's way, he'd yet to give his input, but I could see from his expression, he would follow Gally's wishes. Bracing my legs a couple more inches apart, I made my stand. "If she doesn't stay, then I don't stay." Beside me, Remy sucked in a surprised breath, but I kept my gaze steady on the other two members. "Remy is the best damn drummer I've ever met, and I'm going to be a part of whatever band *she's* in."

Gally glared at me a second longer before hissing out a curse and throwing up his hands. "Fine. What the fuck ever. She makes any drama for us, though, and I'm out." As he stormed off, wafting off more drama with his pouty little exit than I'd ever seen Remy exude, Holden nodded his compliance once and trailed after Gally.

I watched them go, remembering what they'd just been doing—together—with Jodi, and shook my head, perplexed.

From Remy's apartment, Jodi cleared her throat. "So, um...yeah. Once again, I'm left standing here awkwardly between you two. So...I'm just going to let you talk...again." And she disappeared inside, shutting the door to leave me alone with Remy.

I glanced at her, suddenly at a loss for words. I'd come here to get her back, but then...all this had happened, so I ended up sighing and running my hands through my hair. "I'm sorry. I wasn't thinking."

Hugging herself, she nodded. "So you already said."

"My head's still all over the place this morning," I tried to explain because it didn't look like she was going to forgive me for assuming such a thing about her and our two bandmates. "I forgot to take anything for my hangover and I was preoccupied, trying to decide what to say to you. When he opened the door...I don't know. I just...I completely lost the ability to think rationally."

I'd gone into caveman mode, ready to fight for my woman.

But Remy still wouldn't look at me.

I ground my teeth. "Damn it. I'm not used to this. Women who actually know me don't just go telling me they love me."

Finally, she looked up, her brown eyes wide with surprise.

After a deep breath, I added, "It didn't seem real. It was easier to believe you didn't mean it, that you'd already moved on. Thinking you and they had...it was just an instant, knee-jerk reaction that was really stupid and—"

She reached out and set her fingers over my mouth, hushing me. When I drew in a breath, she murmured, "It's okay."

When she lowered her hand, I sucked my bottom lip in between my teeth, trying to taste her touch.

God, I was lost for this woman.

Not sure what to say next, I blurted, "Did you know your roommate was...with *both* of them?"

Remy shuddered. "Unfortunately, yes." Then she spotted her drink she'd sat down on the newel post at the top of the stairwell. Snatching it up, she took a quick sip and then eyed me warily. "Did you really just fight with them to keep me *in* the band?"

I suddenly wasn't sure what to do with my hands, so I shoved them into my pockets.

"Well..." I heaved up one shoulder self-consciously. "It's what you wanted most in the world, isn't it?"

When she didn't answer, I looked up into her face. Her eyes looked a little watery and uncertain, so I took a step closer and whispered her name.

"Damn it," she muttered, squeezing her eyes closed.

"Yes, it used to be what I wanted most in the world."

My lips quirked up with satisfaction. "*Used to be*?" I asked.

When she bit her lip and nodded, I moved in even closer. Her breathing picked up, and my body stirred with need. "So what do you want the most now?" I asked.

Her lashes fluttered open and her chest heaved.

"Just say it," I encouraged softly.

But she shook her head. "I...I can't. I fucked everything up."

My chest swelled. "You sure about that?"

Tears filled her eyes. She whispered my name and reached for my chest, only to draw her hand back to herself after she'd barely touched me.

Now it was *my* turn to shake my head. "Because as much as I tried to regret everything and stay mad at you, I can't."

She hiccupped and then quickly pressed her fingers to her lips, her wide eyes watching me as if unable to believe what she was hearing.

So I kept talking. "I think I wanted to hate you because I felt so stupid. I should've—I just...I should've been able to figure it out."

"No." Swishing her head back and forth, she clutched my arm. "I deceived you at every turn, lied and tricked you so you couldn't realize the truth. You didn't do anything wrong. It was all me. I—"

I set my fingers over her lips to hush her. "And yet it never seemed to matter if you were Sticks or Elisa, boy or girl, I still always wanted to be around you. I..." With a small, self-deprecating laugh, I looked up at the ceiling and said, "Do you know why I was able to take you home barely ten minutes after our first kiss without a single qualm of doubt, after I'd gone on and on to you more than once about wanting to get to know a woman first and actually start a relationship with her?"

Shame filled Remy's eyes. "Yes. Because it'd been too long since you—"

"Hell, no," I growled. "My libido doesn't control me that much. I could've waited longer."

She crinkled her brow, surprised...and yet confused. "Then—"

"It was because you felt so familiar." I leaned forward

and set my forehead against hers. "Like I *did* know you and you knew me; I just didn't understand at the time that there was a reason for that. But I also hooked up with Elisa without needing to really talk to her because I was already getting the companion part of a relationship I was craving...from Sticks. Your alter ego fulfilled my emotional need, so the only thing left that I wanted was the intimacy, and then you delivered that too, so really...you gave me everything I wanted most. I just couldn't figure out it was all coming from the same person."

"Damn it," she sniffed and wiped at her nose as more tears slid down her cheeks. "You're going to forgive me, aren't you?"

"Yeah, I am." I smiled and cupped her face so I could wipe the tears off her cheeks with my thumbs.

She squeezed her eyes closed and bowed her head. "But I lied to you. I—"

"Stop," I murmured softly before letting out a big sigh and rubbing my hands over her weary face. Then I watched more tears spill down her cheeks and could only shake my head.

Taking her fingers, I gently urged, "Please stop crying."

She shook her head. "I can't help it. I've cried pretty much this entire month since meeting you, and I never cry this much. How did you turn me into such a freaking watering pot?"

I shook my head. "I guess Nazareth really knew what it was talking about."

Sniffing, she frowned at me before saying, "What? That Love Hurts?"

A smile bloomed across my face. "See. You got my music joke. I love that. I love that you get *me*. How the hell could I *not* forgive you?"

"Because I totally don't deserve it," she babbled, tears still falling down her cheeks. "I was so wrong."

All I could do was shrug as I pulled her in for a hug and kissed her hair. "Who's to say I wouldn't have done the same thing in your shoes? You told me how much you'd longed to be in a band and how no one ever gave you a chance. Honestly," my lips quirked, "it was kind of ingenious how you managed it. And I was there to see how it snowballed into a bigger lie, so I *know* you didn't do anything with any malicious intent. I *know* you never meant to hurt or trick or—"

"What about Elisa?" she blurted.

I froze, still sore about that. But still...unable to regret it. "What about her?" I asked huskily.

"That had to be my biggest deception of all. I mean, you pretty much told me how to catch you. You said you liked to pursue. And I totally didn't mean to wake up the hunter in you, but I knew—"

"I thought you said you just couldn't resist me and my mystically powered mouth," I cut in, grinning until I made her blush.

"Yeah," she muttered, rolling her eyes. "That's exactly what happened, too, you way too amazing bastard, you. But you also told me you wanted to get to know a woman before taking her to bed, and I didn't let you do that. I made you go through another one-night-stand, even though I knew you hated them, and I—"

My chuckle shut her up.

"Why the hell are you laughing?" she demanded.

"Because," I shook my head, "you're so cute, trying to defend me against yourself."

"But—"

"No. Shh." I pressed my mouth to hers, and yep, it worked. Shut her right up. And tasted good too. I wanted to go deeper, kiss her more, but there was one more thing to say before I lost myself to the pleasure that was Remy Curran.

"I *don't* regret it," I promised her. "*Any* of it. Now are you going to stop trying to argue with me about this, woman? Or are you going to accept it and come home with me already so I can show you my surprise, and then make love to you for the rest of the afternoon?"

She blinked once, then twice, her brown eyes wide with hope before she murmured, "Okay, take me home with you."

CHAPTER 43
Remy Curran

I CAME AWAKE TO LIPS pressing their way up my spine.
Every few inches, teeth would nip and a tongue would lap
up the sting. Then warm palms smoothed over my flesh
from behind and swooped around to the front, cupping my
breasts.

"Mmm," I hummed my delight, keeping my eyes closed
because I was half afraid this entire afternoon of nothing
but naked time with Asher had all been a dream. Naked on
the couch, playing Call of Duty, naked in the kitchen fixing
survival snack food together, naked in bed, working our way
through a new box of condoms...just pleasantly naked.
"That feels so...good."

"Does it?" Asher's voice filled me before he leaned in and
kissed the sensitive bare spot right behind my ear. "Then
you should really stay here while I'm gone so I can pick
right back up where I left off when I get back."

My eyes flew open. "Gone? Get back?" Frowning, I rolled
around to face him, only to gasp when I found him not-
naked. In jeans and a black shirt, he looked sexy as
hell...but still. *Leaving*?

"Where're you going?"

His green gaze traveled down my body, landing on my exposed breasts as he answered, "I have to go into work. But you can stay." Then his gaze lifted to mine and uncertainty filled his features. "Will you? You, uh, you'd actually be doing me a huge favor. I'm a little worried about leaving Mozart here alone until I get his cage put up."

He'd actually wanted to re-hang the cage earlier, but I hadn't let him put clothes on, and though I'd loved the idea of naked cage-hanging, he'd balked and instead tackled me onto the bed and taken me hard and fast. I hadn't minded that option either.

I cupped his face to help appease his worry. "Of course, I'll squirrel-sit for you. I won't let anything happen to your precious."

Lips tipping up with an immediate grin, he dove in for a quick, satisfied kiss. "Thank you, but honestly, I just wanted to come home so I could find you here asleep in my bed."

"Oh, ho..." I said, rolling my eyes. "So the truth comes out. You just want to keep me trapped here like your little sex slave, huh?"

The bastard's smile only spread. "If only I'd kept the handcuffs."

I threw back my head and laughed. Wrapping my arms around him, I kept my neck arched back so he could kiss his way up my throat. Filled with a bliss that radiated out all my limbs, I sighed and murmured, "I love you so much."

The press of his lips paused at my jawline. When he said nothing, though his line here should've been, "*I love you, too,*" I lowered my chin to meet his gaze. His green eyes swirled with need.

I knew he liked hearing my declaration, and I could see that he wanted to say it back—he was just scared—so I only smiled and gently pressed my mouth to his and stroked my fingers through his hair. He'd never said the words to a woman before, and I was kind of glad he was hesitant. It let me know that when he finally did say it, it would mean more.

Until then, I was completely okay with being patient and playing sex slave until he felt comfortable enough to tell me.

With a groan, he tore his mouth away from mine but then pressed our foreheads together. "I really need to get to work."

I grinned. "Then go to work." But even as I said it, I stretched against him and made sure my knee not-so-accidently grazed the crotch of his jeans.

"Damn you, you tempting sexy naked lady." Growling, he rolled me onto my back, cupped one of my thighs so he could slip his hips between my legs, and crawled over me as he began to unzip his jeans. "We only have time for a quickie."

"Oh, goodie!" I squealed out my joy and tugged at his shirt, peeling it off him while he ripped open a condom package. But I didn't even have time to toss it across the room before he was pushing inside. "Oh!"

Gasping in surprise, I clutched his back and dug my nails into his warm skin as he thrust without mercy.

"Por Dios, you really did mean quick, didn't you? Mmm...más rápido. ¡Más duro!"

I don't know if he was finally understanding some of my Español, or if he could just tell what my body wanted, because he delivered, heaving into me, filling me with a physical joy that burst just under my skin and made me come but also a warmth in my heart that made me close my eyes and clutch him to me as he followed with his own orgasm.

"Te amo," I whispered.

He drew out a peace-filled sigh and pressed his forehead to mine. A moment of content silence followed, where we merely held each other in the aftermath. I stroked my fingers up his back and into his hair, realizing he was getting drowsy and would probably fall asleep on me in seconds, but not quite ready to wake him up and send him off to work.

But a chattering had me glancing past Asher's bare shoulder to see Mozart standing on his hind feet at the end of the bed, watching us.

I yelped out my surprise and threw the shirt I still had wadded in my hand at him. Asher stirred on top of me and sat up to glance back and see what I'd done.

"I needed to put that back on," he slurred, still half asleep.

"Well, your *squirrel* needed to stop being a pervert," I argued back, scowling. "Seriously, he was staring at your ass."

Chuckling, Asher crawled to the end of the bed so he

could retrieve his clothes and put himself back together for work. "I'm so happy you two get along."

I crossed my arms over my chest and watched him finish dressing. "There wouldn't be a problem if he'd just learn his place." Poking a finger into my chest, I called out into the room so Mozart could hear me...wherever he was. "That's *my* man's ass, squirrel. So eyes off, got it?"

"You tell him, gorgeous." Grinning, Asher crawled back to me and cupped the back of my head as he kissed me hard and fast. When he pulled back, his smile was still smugly proud. "I kind of like you laying your claim on me."

Arching an eyebrow, I eyed his neck. "Well, if you want me to mark my property..."

I sent him on his way five minutes later with a silly, dazed grin on his face and a hickey on his neck.

Giddy warmth bloomed through me as I turned to study his apartment, wondering what I was going to do for the next eight hours or so until he came back. I wasn't sure why I actually wanted to stay, but the idea of being surrounded by his things just felt...nice. One of these days, I knew I'd have to go home and we'd have to return to normal life and try to begin our relationship from there, but for tonight, I was just going to enjoy being Asher Hart's kept sex slave.

After dressing, because being naked for Mozart wasn't nearly as much fun as being naked for his owner had been, I fixed myself something to eat. Then I tried to feed the squirrel some food, but I had a feeling I was about as whipped for that damn hairball as Asher was. When he refused my fruit offer, I broke out a couple peanuts. But I made him come up and take them from my palm...which the greedy little squirrel finally did.

As I watched him enjoy a nut, I rested my arms on my knees and shook my head. "I don't know how the heck you don't break out into hives with those things. Peanuts are freaking killers."

But Mozart didn't see the harm and kept eating, happily.

With a happy sigh, I pushed to my feet, then I raided Asher's apartment until I found the cages he'd stowed away. What I thought would be a simple enough, helpful task ended up being hours of cursing and sweat and a little blood when I scraped my arm a couple times on exposed wire, but por Dios, the cages all got hung basically where he'd had them before.

When I was finished, I scratched my head, wondering how the hell Asher ever got his tree rat back into them after letting Mozart free, but then I threw up my hands and decided he could deal with that task when he got home.

So I played a little Call of Duty, but it was no longer as much fun by myself.

I missed my man.

It was late—I could probably catch a little sleep before he made it home—but I was restless for him to return. Something in me was worried that this was all a fluke and he'd never come back, or I'd never see him again... or *something*. I know, I was in his apartment, where else would he go? But the feeling persisted.

I just didn't deserve this happy of an ending.

About half an hour before Forbidden was set to close, a knock came at the top of the stairs. At first, I jumped, but then a grin lit across my face, wondering what he was playing.

I raced up the steps and eased open the door, braced for whatever kind of entrance he had planned. But there was no Asher in the dark alley. Actually, no one was in the alley.

A feeling of unease stole over me, so I began to duck back inside when I noticed the slim box on the ground in front of the doorway. When I read the handwritten words *FOR REMY* on the top, a grin stole across my face.

How the hell had he known I loved little gifts? The man must've talked to my roommate. Swooping up the box, I closed the door and hurried back down into the apartment. Once I was seated on the end of his bed, I ripped open the brown wrapping.

The box of chocolates made me laugh. No idea why. It was such a suitor-ly thing to do, something a guy wooing his lady would do, which was probably exactly what he was doing. But damn, he already had me. There was no need for him to be this sweet.

But I'm glad he was, because chocolate sounded really

good right about now. Popping the first truffle into my mouth and moaning when my teeth sank through the outer layer and into some thick gooey...mmm, *caramel*, I moaned aloud.

I downed three before I began to wonder where Asher was. Odd that he'd left me a present and then...not showed up to receive his thank you, which ooh, reminded me. I should thank him...sexily.

If only we were at my place, I could dig into the bottom of my undie drawer and find some of that lingerie I bought because it was cute but never wore.

Well, a girl would just have to make do. After stripping naked, I riffled through his shirt drawer until I found something soft and worn that I'd seen him in more than once.

When I slid it on, a little more winded than usual, I sat on the armrest of the couch to catch my breath, frowning over my sudden exhaustion. I ate another chocolate, but for some reason, that made my pulse race...or maybe it wasn't the bonbon, but I felt awfully funny all of a sudden. Pausing mid-chew on my fourth—or was this the fifth—chocolate, I blinked rapidly when the room went sideways.

"Whoa." Putting out a hand to catch myself, I shook my head.

What the hell? I tried to swallow, but the chocolate didn't want to go down. Instead, I wheezed, and then a violent pain sliced through my stomach.

Clutching my abdomen, I slipped off the couch and landed on my knees, doubling over until I was pressing my forehead against cool wood flooring. Mozart's face appeared from under the bed as if he were worried, and coming to check on me.

I tried to tell him I was okay, but it took me another second to realize I couldn't speak...because my throat was swelling.

I blinked when the squirrel went fuzzy, my eyes swelling too.

Oh, shit. Allergic reaction. A little discombobulated because one had never really come on this fast before, I fumbled for my purse, but I couldn't remember where I'd left it. I tried to look around the room, but I could barely see anything. My breathing got worse.

I rasped Mozart's name, not sure what he could do—

fetch my purse for me?

But I was glad at least he was here with me.

My lungs seized because I could no longer get oxygen, and I think I began to vomit, but I was so weak, and my skin was so cold and clammy, I just lay on Asher's floor, shivering.

The second before I lost consciousness, a tear slipped down my cheek. This was going to hit him hard. He'd lived his whole life waiting for someone to love him, and now... now I had to leave him. Not wanting that for him, I tried one last time to crawl blindly, searching for my purse with my hands alone, only to find warm, coarse fur.

Another tear trickled down my cheek, and I petted Mozart until everything went black.

CHAPTER 44
Asher Hart

I SOFTLY SANG AVICII'S "Hey Brother" under my breath as I hurried out to my bike, ready to get home and crawl under the covers with Remy. I'd rushed through clean-up at the bar, thinking about her warm and naked in my bed.

I'd just swung my leg over my seat when Mandy, one of the waitresses, called, "Hey, Asher. My battery died again. Could you jump-start my car; I have cables."

With a little internal groan, I swung back off my Triumph, and said, "Sure," just as Quinn jogged up and said, "I can help her if you want to head out."

I was tempted to take him up on his offer. But Quinn probably wanted to get home to his wife and baby just as much as I wanted to get home to Remy.

Home.

The word swirled through me and filled me with a lovely warmth. She really was my home. And I was going to finally tell her I loved her. Tonight. As soon as I helped Mandy.

"No, you go ahead, man. I got this." I waved Quinn away and helped Mandy with her car.

Once she was good to go, and I'd waited until she could

actually drive her automobile from the parking lot, I finally fired up my baby and drove to my familiar dark alley.

The lights were on at the end of the stairwell as I unlocked the door and eased it open.

Ooh, she'd waited up for me. Even better. Grinning, I jogged down the steps and swept into the apartment, ready to find her—hopefully—naked and spread out on some piece of furniture, awaiting me...like a good sex slave.

But there was no naked Remy. And there wasn't even a sleeping Remy on the bed. In fact, the bed was empty and made.

I drew in a sharp breath, not prepared for her to have just left me like that. Not sure what it meant, or what I should make of her not being here, I started more slowly into the apartment when my whacked-out squirrel came flying out from under the bed at me.

"Jesus," I yelped, dancing my feet to dodge him, not at all certain what the hell he was doing as he scurried around the base of my feet and then took off again.

"What did she feed you?" I wondered with a scowl as I watched him pick up what looked like a bonbon off the floor and disappear back under the bed with it.

But a bonbon? *What?*

I started to investigate when only a few steps closer revealed a limp human hand on my floor where it peeked out from the other side of the couch.

"Oh God...*Remy!*" I raced to her, skidding onto my knees beside the still figure.

Her face was unrecognizable, swollen with a blotchy red rash. But it had to be her; she had the purple streaks in her hair.

"Oh, Jesus. No." I scooped her into my arms and pressed her limp body to my chest, wondering what the hell had just happened. "Remy, wake up. Talk to me. What's wrong?"

I pressed my fingers to her neck and felt a flutter. I think I felt a flutter, anyway. Fuck, I wasn't sure.

"There's a pulse," I said aloud, not talking to anyone but needing to say it anyway.

That's when I spotted the empty bonbon box only a few feet away. I stared at them a moment, wondering where they'd come from, before I yanked my phone from my back pocket and dialed 911. It seemed like it took them forever to answer.

Christ, weren't emergency operators supposed to answer instantly? When a lady finally came over the line, I tried to describe everything to her as best I could.

"Yes, unconscious," I said. "She's all swollen and...yeah, there's a rash."

After a moment of listening, the woman told me, "It sounds like an allergic reaction."

I snapped my fingers. "Peanuts. She's allergic to peanuts." My gaze strayed to the chocolate box. "Oh, God. It looks like she ate...I don't know." How many had Mozart taken off with? "There's an empty box of maybe two dozen bonbons here. They must've had some kind of peanut ingredient in them."

"Lay her flat on her back," I was told, "Lift her legs and cover her with a blanket."

I nodded, ready to try anything. After I placed her gently on the floor, I snagged a pillow and blanket off my bed. She was completely unresponsive as I gently tended to her. "Are you sending an ambulance?"

"Yes, but we need to do something now. If the reaction is as severe as you're describing, it can only take fifteen minutes with her like this without any treatment before she might die."

My heart nearly stopped in my chest. Had it already been fifteen minutes? I had no clue how long she'd been like this before I'd gotten home. Christ. "Well, then how the fuck do we treat her?"

"She should have some kind of emergency rescue medication on hand if she has a known allergy. Like an EpiPen or something."

I had no idea what an EpiPen looked like, but when I caught sight of Remy's purse on the kitchen table, I dashed to it and dumped the contents all over the table. A shit ton of stuff spilled out. Pens, old receipts, a wallet, notepad, tampons, guitar pick, lip balm, a used Forbidden coaster, but...what the hell did an EpiPen even look like?

"Jesus," I gasped, afraid I was killing her even as I stood there, too stupid to know what I was looking for; my allergy to latex wasn't anywhere bad enough to merit any kind of emergency rescue medication. I was about to throw the purse across the room in frustration when I felt a hard lump inside. I took one last look and found a zippered interior pocket.

And I nearly wept with relief when the thick black letters spelling EpiPen sprang out at me from a bright yellow box inside.

"I got it!" I yelled into the phone, racing back to Remy, where Mozart was hovering only a few feet away. I tore the box away from the pen and nodded as I listened to the instructions from the emergency operator about how to inject it. As I jabbed the needle into Remy's thigh, I closed my eyes and prayed.

Please, please, please work.

I'd just found this woman. I couldn't lose her now.

One, two, three seconds passed, and then Remy wheezed. My eyes flew open just as she stirred, trying to roll onto her side. Coughing, she wheezed again.

"Remy? Baby?" I cradled her, helping her move wherever she wanted to move. "I'm here. It's going to be okay. We're getting you some help now."

Her hand caught my wrist and she squeezed hold of me, letting me know she heard me. Tears slid down my cheeks. "You're going to be just fine. Oh, God. You're okay. You're going to be okay."

I didn't have a number of anyone to call in Remy's family, so I ended up ringing Jodi, and she met me at the hospital with sadly both Holden and Gally with her.

When I told her what had gone down, she shivered and hugged herself. "Oh, God. I'm calling her family."

As she and Gally and Holden took control of one side of the waiting room, where Jodi paced and called number after number, I sat with my knees wide, my elbows resting on them so I could bury my face into my hands.

I couldn't believe I'd come so close to losing Remy, and I hadn't even really gotten her yet. As soon as she woke up, I was letting her know good and well I loved her...and she wasn't allowed to die on me.

I sent off a text to Pick.

Not sure why I did that; he was a newly married man.

He and Eva were probably off on their honeymoon now. I shouldn't have bothered him.

But he was family, and I needed someone with me. I didn't ask him to come, though, I just told him about what had happened, and oddly, I felt somewhat better after that, just having someone to talk to.

I'd been sitting there about ten minutes, hoping someone would come and let us back to see her soon, when I spotted what looked like her cousin Tomás rush into the waiting room, followed by an older version of him—probably Remy's uncle Alonso—and a little old lady, whom I figured had to be her grandmother.

They descended on Jodi, demanding answers. As Jodi updated them as best she could, Tomás translated everything to the grandmother in Spanish, who clutched her mouth and looked as if she might pass out.

"Asher's the one who found her and saved her life." Jodi motioned to me. "He knows more about it than I do."

Her family turned, and three pairs of eyes focused on me. I straightened in my chair, not ready to be their center of attention.

"Who are *you*?" the uncle asked, eyeing me with untrusting disdain.

"I, uh..." I pushed to my feet and held out a hand. "Asher Hart, sir. I'm Remy's...friend."

The older man sniffed derisively at my palm. "She has too many gringo friends. What were you doing at her apartment?"

I blinked, not expecting this line of questioning. "I, uh... Actually, she was at my place. I came home from work and found her unconscious on the floor. 911 talked me through giving her a shot from her EpiPen."

"Bien," Tomás told me, slapping the side of my arm companionably. "Gracias for helping her."

His dad scowled at him and snapped something in Spanish, which only made his son shrug and answer with a few short unaffected words. Then Remy's uncle was spinning back to me and blinking as if he wasn't sure how to receive me now.

I'm not sure what Tomás had said, but it seemed to temper the older man some.

"Do you guys know of anyone who might want to poison

her?" I asked. "Someone gave her a box of chocolates with peanuts in them. But..." I shook my head. "I don't think it was accidental."

"Even though it very likely *was* accidental," Jodi rushed to add when alarm spread across the faces of Remy's family members.

Tomás shook his head. "I don't know, amigo. No one had it out for her. Remy's likeable, you know."

I nodded. Yeah, I knew.

"Maybe her ex. That lead singer in the band. What was his name?" For a second, I thought he was referring to me. But then he snapped his finger. "Fish 'N' Dicks. That's it."

My mouth dropped open. "Braden Fisher? She dated *him*?" I glanced at Jodi, who cringed and nodded, before I turned back to Tomás, who rolled his eyes.

"I know, right? But I can't see him wanting to get at her for any reason. He was the one who cheated and—"

When his eyes went wide as if he was about to say too much, I sighed and said, "Stole the lyrics of her song. Yeah, I know."

I tried to think of anyone else who might be mad at her for any reason. The only person I could think up was me, but then I turned my thoughts to Gally and Holden...who'd just been forced to accept her into their band. But when I glanced their way, Gally lifted a bored voice and called, "So are we getting extra sex tonight for being all charitable and coming here to check on her?"

Okay, so Gally and Holden probably hadn't poisoned her. I turned away with a frustrated sigh, but someone lurking in the hallway caught my eye. I blinked, focusing on him, but he was gone before I had a good look.

Narrowing my eyes, I followed my suspicions and stepped out of the waiting room. The man was about twenty feet away, his back to me and shoulders hunched forward as if trying to conceal his identity. But I knew that walk. Damn it.

"Hey," I hollered.

He glanced back, and yep, there was my father.

Son of a bitch.

When our gazes met, he whirled away and darted around a corner.

Remy's words suddenly echoed through my head. *The worst way to hurt you would be for someone to go after the ones you loved.* And it wouldn't take a lot of investigating for someone to realize I loved her.

I took off running and skidded around the corner in hot pursuit. When I came to another corner and hurried around it, something hit me hard in the face, taking me down to my knees. It fucking hurt too. I tasted blood and immediately saw stars.

"Christ." I dove at a pair of legs in front of me and heard my dad grunt as I tackled him to the ground. His head banged against the tiled floor, and I took advantage of the moment to leap on top of him and slam my fist into his face.

He cursed and struggled under me.

"Was it you?" I demanded. "Did you give her those chocolates?"

He laughed up at me, flashing a bloody-toothed smile. "Did it get the job done, or is she still alive?"

"You fucking bastard." I hit him again.

I would've broken his nose next, but he swung something at the side of my head, knocking me off him and ringing my bell until I saw stars.

"Too bad your stupid fucking pet wasn't as easy to get rid of," he snarled as he rose above me. "What kind of pussy has a squirrel for a pet anyway? I never could beat any kind of manliness into you, could I?"

I blinked him into focus in time to see him lift his weapon above his head, and what the fuck *was* that? Looked like a metal clipboard thing he might've stolen from a doctor or nurse. Lifting my hands to protect my head, because I wasn't sure my noggin could stand another wallop, I flinched backward.

The sick malicious relish in his eyes told me how much he loved being in this position, standing over me and making me cower. I gritted my teeth, ready to dive at his legs again, but someone pushed him from behind, making him lose his grip on the clipboard. It went flying past my head as he tripped forward and landed on his knees.

"Now, now, old man. No one's allowed to play unfair with my little brother."

I gaped up at Pick, who was toeing my father onto his back on the floor so he could then press his foot to the old man's windpipe, pinning him by his throat.

"What're you doing here?" I couldn't help but gasp in

amazement.

"You called. I came." He shrugged. "It's what I do."

Climbing to my knees, I fell back onto my haunches and blew out a relieved breath.

"So you really did do all that stupid shit, like cutting the wire to my bike's fuel line and the cord to the club's sound system?"

My dad snarled at me, but couldn't really answer since my brother was kind of crushing his vocal chords at the moment.

I only shook my head. "And you thought *I* was lame. You could've really gotten to me, old man. Yet you went this stupid route. Now you're going to lose your parole and go back to prison...without all that work you put into a revenge against me paying off at all. That's sad...just sad."

"I should've let your mama finish aborting you the day I walked into the bathroom and found her all bloody," he garbled up at me, his eyes full of hate. "Neither of us had any use for you. You never amounted to anything. Your poor mother died still despising the very sight of you."

Swallowing, I turned away only to catch Pick watching me with worried eyes. Nodding to him, I rasped, "I'm done here."

He nodded just as a pair of nurses came around the corner and skidded to a stop when they saw the tattooed, pierced guy pinning an older man to the ground with a boot to his throat.

But my brother...all he did was flash the women a pleasant smile. "Hey there, ladies. Do you think you could do me a favor and call security or maybe the police? This man here just admitted to trying to kill my brother's girlfriend."

They nodded and hurried away.

I looked up at Pick. He looked back. And we both grinned. "Thanks for coming," I finally said.

CHAPTER 45
Asher Hart

I WAS SITTING ALONE in the waiting room when Pick found me again. The doctor had come and gone, letting us know Remy was better, the swelling was down and her airways cleared again. She was resting peacefully.

As her family, and Jodi, and the rest of the band filed back to check on her, I just kept sitting there, staring at the wall, trying not to think about how close I'd come to losing her, just because my own father had hated me that much.

Was there really something so wrong with me that my own blood loathed me to this extreme? Maybe becoming involved with Remy was a bad idea. I'd just nearly gotten her killed. Falling in love wasn't worth it if I could only put the woman's life in peril.

"The police just took your dad away."

I jumped, jerking upright at the sound of my brother's voice. When he approached slowly and sat beside me, I nodded. "Good. Maybe they won't release him early this time."

"That would be nice." Rubbing his hands together, he gazed around the waiting room before he turned to me. "So what're you doing in here by yourself? I thought I saw the doctor come with an update and then everyone head down the hall to see Remy."

"You did. She's going to be okay. Her family's with her now."

"But you didn't go back with them?" he asked the obvious, staring at me as if to say, *why didn't you go back?*

I shrugged.

"You forgave her, didn't you?"

I nodded.

He sighed. "Then I don't see what the issue is here."

Grinding my teeth, I grabbed the vinyl cushions under me. "He went after her because of me. She almost died tonight, Pick. She—"

"But she didn't."

His calm words earned a glare from me. "But she *could've*," I bit out. Then I fell back in my seat and clutched my head, hard. "Jesus, what the hell am I still even doing here? I should be a hundred miles away from here, so she'll at least be safe. I don't know why I'm even trying. I know shit about love and relationships. My own fucking parents couldn't even like me, let alone love me. Why did I hope—"

"Hey." Pick squeezed the back of my neck and then forced me to lean toward him and press our foreheads together. "Don't let that shit your dad said get into your head like this."

"What?" I asked, my voice going hoarse. "The abortion part? Hell, that wasn't news to me. My mother told me about how she tried to kill me plenty of times. She *hated* me. Hated that I was his son, hated that I wasn't you, the baby she always regretted leaving, hated me just because I was there. And you want to know the real kicker?" I glanced up into Pick's brown eyes. "I really loved her. I'd listen to her talk about you and your dad with such devotion and awe, and I always wanted her to talk to me that way, to look at me and just—"

"You want to know what I think," Pick cut in. "I think our mother was a disturbed young woman who never really learned the true meaning of love, and that she had no reason bringing children into this world. But here we are, anyway, and I'm so glad and honored to have found you and learned you are my brother."

My throat felt a little choked up, so I had to clear it and

glance away as Pick kept talking.

"It doesn't matter where we came from. We both rose above it and came into our own...*on* our own. And I am so damn proud of the man you've turned yourself into. There is nothing and no reason you shouldn't have a full, content life with the people you care for most in it. I love you, brother. You're a good person, and you deserve happiness." He let go of my neck to thump me on the back. "Now, go get it."

I came awake to the soft strum of a guitar. In the background, a hospital monitor beeped and air packs around my ankles hissed out a sound as they released pressure.

Turning my face to the melody of the guitar, I blinked Asher into focus as he sat to my right, playing for me. My lashes felt gritty and my throat raw, reminding me what had happened.

The chocolates, I realized. Someone had given me chocolates with some kind of peanuts hidden in them. But I wasn't too concerned about that now. I was awake, unswollen, and breathing again, so I guessed things were bien.

For the moment, I just wanted to listen to Asher play to me. The tune was unusual, reminding me a lot of "Hey There Delilah" by the Plain White T's...and yet a little different. I didn't think I'd heard it before.

And then he began to sing.

> *I wake up early with your breath*
> *falling on the pillow next to mine.*
> *Another night spent in your arms*
> *and I know this day's just fine.*
> *Yes, it is.*
>
> *'Cause there's this promise in your smile*
> *that no matter what tomorrow brings,*

I'll make it through the mile,
with you there, right by my side.

Oh...I can do anything with you there, right by my side.

Sometimes I hold back the words
that I want to say to you,
because this thing that we've started
is way too fresh and too new.

Oh...oh, oh, oh, oh. Right by my side.

But there's this promise in your smile
that no matter what tomorrow brings,
I'll make it through the mile
With you there, right by my side.

I can do anything, anything at all, when I know
You'll be there on the morrow
Standing at my side.

You've already taught me how to love,
To laugh, and listen to your heart.
Oh, baby, I can't wait to learn some more
so we'll never truly be apart.

This time it's good.

We can do anything.
Just me and you.
Right by your side.

A grin lit my face as he strummed the last of the melody, and tears filled my eyes. "That's my song."

Asher glanced up, and his green eyes warmed. "I know. Sorry, I changed the rhythm a little. It seemed like it needed a gentler tune than the one Fish 'N' Dicks's used."

"No. This one is fine. It's perfect. Hermosa. Exactly the kind of tone I had in mind when I wrote it." I shook my head in wonder. "How did you know?"

"That they were *your* lyrics?" A grin lit his face. "It wasn't too hard to figure out."

"Thank you," I whispered, touched to the bottom of my

soul. "It's perfect. You have no idea what this means to me."

He set his Taylor down and reached out to take my hand, gently running his thumb over my IV. "And you have no idea what *you* mean to *me*." He shook his head and looked pained as if it were difficult to swallow. "Because I never told you. Jesus, Remy... You can't even imagine what it was like to hold your unconscious body in my arms and realize I never got to tell you."

"Asher," I started, shaking my head. "You don't have to—"

But he shook his head, stopping me. "I want to. I want to tell you *now*. I love you too, Remy. I've fallen so fucking in love with you this past month without even realizing it, I..." He stopped talking and shook his head as if he wanted to stop again. Then he closed his eyes briefly before opening them and looking straight at me. "Te amo," he said.

Happy tears filled my eyes. But then I shook my head. "You really don't have to say that just because I almost died. You—"

"I'm not. I promise you." Lifting my hand to his mouth, he kissed my knuckles. "I was just trying to figure out how to best say it to you when I came home and found you on the floor."

I sucked in a shuddered, surprised breath. "You were?"

He nodded, then leaned forward and pressed his forehead to my arm. "Te amo. Eres mi nena, mi chica."

A grin exploded from me. "¡Dios mío! That was...said perfectly." Relieved joy spread through me as his lips crashed to mine. I opened my mouth to him and our tongues tangled. He scooted closer and I gripped his hair harder. His fingers found the side of my throat and drifted over my thrumming pulse. He didn't pull away until voices of nurses outside my room door made us jump apart.

Simultaneously, we each touched our own lips, still remembering the kiss. Then we broke out grinning together.

I shook my head, beyond amazed this was actually happening. "Who taught you how to say that?"

Laughing, he blushed a little and admitted, "Tomás might've coached me."

"Big T?" The mention of my cousin had me glancing around expectantly.

But Asher said, "He had to go. Grumbled something

about filling in a shift for you at the restaurant since your lazy ass wasn't going to work in the morning...his words."

I grinned. "Sounds like him."

"Your uncle and grandmother were here too. Along with Jodi and...Gally and Holden."

"Really?" I arched my eyebrows. "They must've thought they'd get extra good sex from Jodi if they showed up."

Asher shook his head. "You know them well." Then he wrinkled his brow. "I don't know if Non-Castrato will make it. I don't know...shit, I don't know a lot of stuff. All I know is that from here on out, I'm going to be wherever you are. And I'll probably be the happiest man alive."

"¡Oh, Dios mío!" I sobbed with overwhelming joy as a tear of happiness slid down my cheek. "You could say shit like that to me every day."

"I plan to, mi nena. I plan to." He leaned in, looking intent to kiss me again, but then he paused and winced. "But I should probably tell you first...you were kind of right about my dad."

EPILOGUE
Remy Cullan

FOUR YEARS LATER

WELL, NON-CASTRATO ENDED UP surviving. We did lose one more member of the band, but surprisingly—or maybe I should say sadly—it wasn't Gally. Heath Holden left the group right about the time Asher's dad had been sentenced for another ten years in prison, or more importantly right around the time Jodi dropped him and Billy both, and took up with some dude in a motorcycle club. Well, she said club...I called it a gang, but whatever.

Speaking of Miller Hart. Asher hadn't been the victim of any more wire-cutting pranks or the like after his dad was arrested the day he'd given me the chocolates, so we all agreed he had been behind them, after all. And yes, being right about that felt *so* good!

Anyway, my cousin Tomás was more than happy to take up with Non-Castrato when Heath dropped out, playing the lead guitar and singing backup for Asher, much to the disappointment of Tío Alonso. Big T adjusted quite well to rock music, though. He especially liked the flock of women it brought. And Asher certainly didn't help my cousin's new man-whore ways in the least because he always shooed the ladies Big T's way.

Not that I wanted him to keep any for himself. No, Asher

Hart was all mine, and only mine.

And life was good. Oh, so...good.

We were both sweaty and exhausted after our performance at the Metro—yes, I said the freaking Metro, baby—but jazzed and ready to see our friends as he tugged me into the back of the cab behind him, then right into his lap so he could wrap his arms around my waist and kiss me soundly.

I kissed him back a few seconds before pulling away to laugh and yell, "¡Dios mío! I can't believe we just played at the Metro."

Asher kissed his way down my throat. "I can't believe we have to go see my lame friends, and I can't take you straight to bed right now. You look too good in this outfit."

He slid his hand up my thigh until it disappeared inside my short jean skirt. But I caught his wrist and sent a quick glance to the cab driver, hoping he wasn't watching us.

"Now, now, Mr. Hart," I warned with a grin, batting my nose against Asher's. "Tío Alonso explicitly told us none of that until after the wedding."

Asher groaned and pressed his forehead to mine. "Your uncle is so fucking delusional. We've been dating four years now, I've put a ring on it, *and* we're living together. Does he honestly think we haven't—"

I pressed a finger against his magical lips. "If he doesn't then I'm certainly not going to be the one to clue him in otherwise. Are you?"

"Fuck no." Asher snorted right before he trailed a row of kisses down my neck. "But neither am I going to remain celibate for another month until we're properly married."

Oh, neither was I. Pressing my mouth to his ear, I whispered, "Just wait until I have you alone in our room, and I'll show you how celibate I'm not going to be either."

He groaned and grew hard against my bottom. "That's it. We're skipping this whole friend-get-together thing and heading straight to our room with a bottle of champagne and maybe some strawberries...and chocolate syrup."

Giddy about his eagerness, because I had on a surprise under my clothes that I just knew he'd enjoy ripping off, I merely tapped the tip of his nose with my finger. "But Ten and Caroline don't get to visit often since they moved to California. I want to see them and catch up."

"Fine." He thumped his head moodily back on the seat of the car and groaned. "I'll do it for Caroline. But Ten can eat shit."

I grinned, glad he and Ten still liked to bicker and needle each other from halfway across the country. But I also knew he missed his friend and was eager to see Ten again, along with the rest of the gang.

I'd been surprised at how readily they'd all accepted me after the way my relationship had started with Asher. I feared they'd be more judgmental because I'd lied and hurt their rock star. But they'd treated me the way Asher had wanted them to treat me, with warm acceptance. And now I felt as if they were my family too.

"I still can't believe Tío Alonso told us no sex until the wedding." Taking my hand, Asher began to play with my engagement ring. "He's never going to like me, is he?"

Kissing his cheek, I said, "Hey, don't worry about it. He can't stand any kind of outsider. Hell, he barely tolerates me, and I'm his niece. But Abuela loves you to pieces, so that's all that matters."

Asher looked up at me, his brow crinkling. "Remy, your uncle loves you."

I laughed and rolled my eyes, even as my chest tightened with the idea. "Only because I'm blood. He *has* to."

But my fiancé shook his head. "No, he doesn't. Just last week, he asked me for two hundred Non-Castrato fliers to pass out to customers at the restaurant. And I've heard him brag you up to others more than once."

I swallowed a huge lump in my throat. "Really?" Okay, maybe I wasn't so abhorrent to my uncle. Wow.

"Really." Asher kissed my forehead. "No one *has* to love you, family or otherwise. We all just do...because, well, we can't help it. You're amazing."

"Look at you, being all sweet," I murmured, trying to make light of his words even though they affected me deeply. I touched my mouth to his. "You must really want to get laid tonight."

"Why, yes. Yes, I do, even though every word I speak is the truth. You're impossible not to love, Remy Elisa Curran, almost Hart."

"As are you, Ashley Jean Hart."

He gasped. "Oh, you smartass. You just couldn't resist, could you?"

"No." I giggled, and he kissed me again.

When the cab stopped next to our hotel, we were breathing hard as we pulled apart. I was about to tell him, *skip the friends for a few minutes, we could have a quickie in our room first,* but after he paid our fare, he took my hand and dragged me inside, looking up Pick's hotel room number on his phone as he went.

"It's room 312," I told him as he scowled and scrolled through his messages.

Asher glanced up. "Are you sure?"

I only nodded and smiled.

Shaking his head, he cupped the nape of my neck. "See, this is why I'm marrying you. I'd be a lost mess without my organized Remy."

After another soft kiss, he groaned and pulled away. "Okay, friends first."

Remarkably, we made it to room 312 with all our clothes still on. After Asher knocked, he kissed me again. He was always frisky after a show; the rush of performing was as much an adrenaline boost to him as it was to me. And I loved it.

The door came open. "It's about time. How many freaking quickies did you two have on the way over?" We broke apart to find Eva arching her eyebrow at us as she rubbed her very pregnant belly. "If you two aren't careful, you're going to end up like this."

Asher only chuckled as he pulled her in for a hug. "What? Aren't you ready to be an aunt?"

"Probably more ready than you are, honey." She slapped a kiss to his cheek and pulled away. "Now get in here. You're missing all the fun."

"Asher and Remy are here! *Yay*!" Aspen cried as soon as we stepped into the room. She sat on the floor with a half-empty glass in hand as she leaned against Noel. Clearly drunk, she lifted her cup to us before she tipped her head back and drained it.

Reese and Caroline popped to their feet as they hurried forward to embrace us with a round of hugs. The rest of the guys waved, while both Zoey and Quinn and Felicity and Knox remained curled together in their seats, looking too cozy to get up and greet us. Felicity's arms were full with her little bundle of joy, anyway. Mason murmured something to Pick, making Pick laugh, and Ten sat in the middle of the floor with a flushed face and...what the hell? Were those *tears* in his eyes?

An also very pregnant Reese hugged me and then Asher, telling us how much she'd loved the show. Then Caroline was butting in to grab my hand and check out my engagement ring because she hadn't gotten to see it yet.

"I'm so happy for you guys." Wrapping one arm around my neck and another around Asher's, she hugged us in to her.

"Thanks, beautiful." Asher kissed her cheek before furrowing his brow and hitching his chin toward Ten. "What's up with your husband?"

"Oh, don't mind him." Caroline waved an unconcerned hand toward Ten. "He's only a little shell-shocked. Just found out he's going to be a daddy."

"¡Oh, Dios mío!" I screeched, jumping up and down. "You're pregnant? Omigod, congratulations!" I yanked her into another hug and we laughed together as we jumped in a circle.

"Isn't it great?" Reese asked, rubbing her own belly. "Our group's just turning into a regular ol' baby-making factory."

Asher hooked an arm around my waist and pressed his mouth to my ear. "And I have this sneaking suspicion we're not going to be very far behind them."

I glanced at him, but he didn't seem appalled by the idea. Instead, he wiggled his brows and smiled as if asking, *You want to?*

Holy shit, I couldn't believe this. Asher was ready to have babies...with me?

We were already grandparents. A couple months after Asher and I had bought a house with a large, fenced-in backyard where Mozart could play to his heart's content, we'd gone to the pet store and gotten him a companion, one they'd assured us was another male. But only months later, Mozart swelled up before popping out three little babies.

Guess I hadn't been the only one posing as a dude, after all.

I had no idea how Asher and I would work a human baby into our lives, being on the road so much, singing and playing for Non-Castrato. But I wasn't worried. With a man like Asher Hart by my side, I didn't fear the next day. I only looked forward to the promise of tomorrow.

THE END

ACKNOWLEDGEMENTS

Thank you to my beta/early readers: Elisa Castro, Shi Ann Crumpacker, Alaina Martinie, Lindsay Brooks, Ada Frost, Katie Anderson, Ana Kristina Rabacca, Mary Rose Bermundo, Sarah Symonds from Inked in Books, Amanda at Beta Reading Bookshelf, Jennifer at Three Chicks and Their Books, and Michelle and Pepper at AllRomance Book Reviews.

Another very big, special thank you to Eli Castro for taking so much time to go over the manuscript and translate and explain what each translation meant!

Thank you to my editor Stephanie Parent, and proofreaders Autumn at the Autumn Review and Shelley at 2 Book Lovers Reviews!

Thank you to Ada Frost for my amazing book cover this time around.

More thanks to all the supportive people who visit my social media sites and read my stories, keeping me in business, especially everyone on the Facebook Group: The Forbidden Men Lovers! Love you guys.

Thanks to my huge family, thanks to Kurt, Lydia, and the brand new Sadie (who was with me every step of the way...literally, since she was stuck inside me the entire time) for providing me with my own happily ever after, and then finally thank you to God.

I know I don't deserve so much help and support from so many people, but I cherish and appreciate it, recognizing it for the amazing gift it is, anyway. Thank you.

ABOUT LINDA KAGE

Linda grew up on a dairy farm in the Midwest as the youngest of eight children. Now she lives in Kansas with her husband, daughter, and their nine cuckoo clocks. Her life's been blessed with lots of people to learn from and love. Writing's always been a major part of her world, and she's so happy to finally share some of her stories with other romance lovers.

Please visit her at her website:

www.LindaKage.com

SPANISH-TO-ENGLISH TRANSLATIONS

A lo hecho, pecho = What was done was done.
Abuela = Grandmother
Adiós = Good bye
Agua = Water
Amigo = Friend
Ay por Dios = Oh my God
Bien = Fine/Good/Okay/Not bad
Bien hecho = Well done
Buenas noches = Good night/ Good evening
Cállate = Shut up
chica = Girl
Chinga = Fuck
Chingaderas = Pieces of shit.
Chinguen a su madre = Motherfuckers. Literally "Fuck your mother."
Cielito Lindo = Popular mariachi song, roughly translated "Sweet Lovely One"
¿Cómo te llamas? = What's your name?
Dios = God
Dios mío = My God
Disculpa = Excuse me
En serio lo siento tanto = I am so sorry.
Eres mi nena, mi chica. Te amo = You are my baby, my girl. I love you
Español = Spanish
Espera = Hold on/Wait
Gracias = Thank you
Grande = Large
Gringo = Person from the US
Hermosa = Beautiful
Hijo de puta = Son of a Bitch
Hola = Hello
Hola. Buenas noches = Hello. Good evening/Good night.
Idiota = Idiot
Increíble = Incredible
Limpia tu camisa = Clean your shirt.
Llegas tarde. = You're late.
Lo siento = I'm sorry
Locos = Crazy

Madre = Mother
Más = More
Más duro = Harder
Más rápido = Faster
Más vale tarde que nunca = Better late than never.
Mi linda nieta = My beautiful granddaughter
Mi nena = My baby
Mi padre = My father
Mierda = Shit
Nada = Nothing
No hablo inglés = I don't speak English
No puedo esperar = I can't wait.
No sé = I do not know
Nombre = Name
Pendejo = Asshole/stupid. Literally "one pubic hair."
Por Dios = My God
Por favor = Please
Prima = (Female) cousin
Pronto = Right away/hurry/soon
Puta = Whore
¿Qué pasa? = What's up?
Que Sera Sera = Whatever will be will be.
Quedarse = Stay
Quiero sentarme en tu cara. = I want to sit on your face.
señorita = Miss/unmarried woman
Sentarse = Sit
Sí = Yes
Sí, tío querido. = Yes, uncle dearest.
Solo hazlo = Just do it.
Solo un beso = Just a kiss/Just one kiss
Te amo = I love you
Te amo más de lo que nunca he amado a otro. = I love you
more than I've ever loved another.
Te extrañé = I've missed you.
Te ves triste. = You look sad.
Tengo que hacer esto = I have to do this.
Tío = Uncle
Tu casa = Your House
Uno más = One more
Ya no puedo hacer esto = I can't do this anymore.
Yo quiero = I want to/I want

Printed in Great Britain
by Amazon